**W9-DAH-565**

# HUSTLIN' BACKWARDS

By

## MIKE SANDERS

COPYRIGHT 2004 © Mike Sanders

All rights reserved. No part of this book may be reproduced in any form or by any means without the prior written consent of the publisher.

### *Author's Note...*

I would like to take this time and thank ALL of my readers who have purchased my novels throughout the years!! You are my motivation!!!

Most of you may know me as the author of the best-selling novels Thirsty 1 & 2! However, Hustlin' Backwards is my first book and it was originally written in 2001 and published in 2004 with a publishing company that is not even worth mentioning. Only a few thousand copies of this novel were printed before they filed for bankruptcy in 2006. Although this novel is over a decade old, to this day the storyline remains relevant! While I was reediting this novel I wanted to modify a few landmarks and events so it would be up to date but I decided to keep it original.

If you have already read this book, I want to say THANKS for the support!!!! Now, here it is for you to add to your collection. After you read this book, I am positive you will be looking forward to the sequel "Snitch" will be available soon.

I hope you enjoy reading my very first novel and I would love to receive any feedback you may have. I can be reached through email at *SandersMike848@gmail.com*, add me on facebook at *facebook.com/NeverThirsty704*, and follow me on twitter *@NeverThirsty704*!!

Once again, THANKS SO MUCH FOR THE SUPPORT!!!!! And be on the lookout for *SNITCH,* the sequel to *Hustlin' Backwards*! Coming SOON to ebooks!!

Much Love,
Mike Sanders

## Prologue
### *San Juan, Puerto Rico 2002*

Surrounded by darkness, I glanced over at the nightstand beside the bed and noticed 3:26 AM is illuminated on the digital clock. Lying on my back, I sighed aloud as I folded my hands beneath my head and stared toward the ceiling. *Damn, how did I end up here, like this?* I think to myself as I feel someone stir beside me and place a warm, feminine hand on my chest.

"Capone, what's wrong? Are you okay?" Consuela's sleep-filled voice breaks the silence of the night.

"Yeah, I'm cool. I'm just thinking. Go back to sleep"

"You seem worried" she says in a deep, Spanish accent.

I ignored her comments and within minutes I hear the sound of her steady breathing which confirms she's asleep. As I eased from beneath the comforter, slipping out of bed making sure not to wake her, I tiptoed my way across the plush carpet to the restroom and quietly close the door behind me. Once inside, I searched for the light switch, squinting once the room is filled with light. When my eyes finally adjusted to the brightness, I made my way to the large mirror and stared at my reflection as if I was seeing a stranger.

"Damn Dog, you fallin' off" I commented to the person staring back at me in the mirror.

I saw a 5'10, 180-pound light brown skinned complexioned brother with short, wavy hair. Observing obvious changes in my appearance, I rubbed my head and wondered how long my dreads would be if I hadn't cut them a year ago. I surveyed my arms where my "704" and "Queen City Hustla" tattoos once resided and realize how glad I was to be rid of them along with the "Fuck tha World" which was tattooed across my stomach. Taking a deep breath, I began to reminisce about the days when I used to don the Presidential Rolex, Armani and Gators before hopping in my Range or Benz, so I could floss the streets of Charlotte.

Charlotte, North Carolina is the "Queen City" to many but in reality it's a city for a King. And that king was Me!!

Well, that was exactly one year and ten pounds ago. It was still hard to believe that a chain that was so tight could all come apart with the weakening of just one link. Never in a million years would I have thought I would be here, in Puerto Rico living the life of a fugitive.

At twenty-six years old, my life is just beginning. And here I am, on the run from the Feds.

As I continued to stare into the mirror I asked myself, "How did it all go so wrong?"

# Chapter One – Da' Early Years
## Charlotte, NC – 1993

In Little Rock Apartments projects, a group of dark-brown brick, three-story buildings that doubled as living quarters for the not-so-fortunate, is where it all began for me. Little Rock was just one of many neighborhoods located on the west side of Charlotte that was labeled "ghetto". If you weren't from my projects, or affiliated with someone there, you couldn't come there. Everyone knew each other and looked out for one another to the extreme. Growing up, if I did something I wasn't supposed to do, it was open season for an ass whuppin' from not only my mother, but also anybody's mother in the neighborhood that caught me slippin'. As with any other projects or hood, the day just didn't go right unless we heard sirens or saw some drama going down. The babies were having babies at a rate so phenomenal that Social Services couldn't even keep up with them. Every first of the month was like a small Christmas celebration because ninety-five percent of the people in my hood were on welfare and we looked forward to those checks. The five percent that weren't on welfare just didn't care. *"Live for today, we will worry about tomorrow when it arrives,"* was the ghetto anthem we lived by. Life was fairly simple and we did what we had to do to make the ends meet, regardless of the consequences.

My mother, older brother and I lived in a two-bedroom hotbox, the size of a sardine can. The heat barely worked in the winter and there was no air conditioner for the summer. Our fan only blew hot air, so my mom used to put them in the window backwards so they could suck all the hot air out of the apartments. At least that's what she said, but I couldn't tell one way or the other. Hot is hot! My brother, Bernard and I shared a room so small that we bumped into one another any time we both tried to move around at the same time. I mean, it wasn't much, but to me it was what I called *home*.

The fall of '93, I was seventeen years old and didn't have a care in the world. Like so many other teens in my hood, I couldn't wait until I turned sixteen so I could quit school. And as soon as I was able to do so, I did. *What could those up tight ass crackers teach me that I couldn't learn from the streets?*

Bernard and I were like night and day. We didn't have anything in common other than the fact that we had the same mother and lived in the same house. Bernard is a year and a half older than I am and has a totally different mind-frame from me. While he's somewhat passive and naïve, I'm always the aggressor and can recognize game coming a mile away. Bernard was a homebody—never, ever got into any trouble. On the other hand, I was always in the streets and stayed into some shit. My mother raised us the best she could, but I guess you can say I was the Black Sheep.

Bernard had just graduated high school and considered himself to be lucky for getting hooked up with a job with the City. I considered him a fool for being content working his ass off for those crackers for pennies. Me? I was just laying back and going with the flow. I had a couple of partners who apparently shared similar thoughts and viewed life the same way I did. One of my boys was Jared, but we called him Junebug or June because of the shape of his head and the way his eyes bulged like a beetle's whenever he was excited. June was just a year older than me, but thought he knew more than me because of the mere twelve-month age difference. In reality, it was the other way around. He was slightly overweight and sported a bald head because he had inherited a receding hairline. June was the typical follower of the group and was very easily influenced.

My other partner was Vonell—we called him "V" for short. He was by far the closest thing I ever had to being a best-friend. V was the same age, height and weight as me, but whereas I'm light brown skinned with dreads, he was two shades darker than me with a short, neat cut. V was the only nigga I ever knew that had a temper worse than mine and I guess that's one of the reasons we've stayed so tight for so many years. We'd been partners ever since elementary school. We were so tight of friends, everybody thought we were cousins. V knew a lot of girls and has so many liking and trying to get with him, that naturally he declared himself a young pimp. The only thing that stopped him from being a young Don Juan was the fact that was just like June and I. Neither of us could talk to a girl without ending up cursing her out of getting cursed out.

Ever since I'd quit school, my mom had been on my back about getting a damn job. But work and I didn't get along, AT ALL!! To get dough, my two partners and I were doing petty stick-ups. Basically, robbing low-scale hustlers for little of nothing. Because of our capers, we had earned a reputation of being stick-up kids without a conscious. Sometimes we wore masks, sometimes we didn't. It depended on the situation or the mood we were in at the time. Luckily, we hadn't been caught by the cops or any of the dope-boys we had been laying down. If a nigga or chick had money or dope, better yet both, we were going at them ruthlessly.

For me, robbing a nigga was an adrenaline rush. I loved to see the look of fear in a person's eyes when they stared down the barrel of my pistol and wondered what I was going to do next. Most of our robbing sprees went smoothly, without any problems, but there were also times when we had to make examples out of those who tried to buck. One thing I can say about my two road-dogs is that they were just as trigger-happy as me and I respected them for their, "Shoot first-fuck the questions" attitude. When niggas on the block saw us coming, they knew to get missing unless they wanted to be left facedown with their pockets out like rabbit ears. We used to hear cats whisper, "Oh shit, here come Mike and 'nem" and watch as they scramble to leave like roaches when the lights come on. That was a feeling of pure POWER.

Late one night, June, V and I were in our hood, sitting on the stairwell of June's apartment building smoking weed and talking shit to each other while enjoying the brisk air. It wasn't warm, but it wasn't exactly cold either because winter hadn't yet arrived. The neighborhood was fairly quiet and virtually no one was outside on this night, which was unusual for our projects. I was seated on the bottom step while June and V were one or two steps higher. While June and V clowned each other, I started thinking about our last lick and a potential problem we would possibly have to handle.

Two nights earlier, we had hit our biggest lick ever thanks to Keisha, one of V's girlfriends. She had put us up on some hustlers from New Jersey that were selling dope out of her aunt's house in the Pine Valley neighborhood on the south side of Charlotte. Keisha told us to come through right after midnight because they would be sold out by then and have the most money on them at that time. So, we ran up in there a little past 1:00 AM, just as a customer was exiting the back door. Ski-masked up and waving gats, we rushed that shit like a swat team. Everything was right where Keisha said it would be—pistols under the sofa and money underneath the kitchen sink in a cereal box. We got away clean with 6-grand and two gats, which was a major sting for us at that time. We broke Keisha off and split the rest three ways. But the problem was the fact that Keisha wasn't satisfied with her share.

As I grabbed the blunt from between June's thick fingers, I interrupted their joking, "Yo, y'all remember how them niggas eyes almost popped out when we ran up in there? I thought both them niggas was gone shit on theyself, straight up."

Thinking back to the episode I was referring to, both V and June laughed. Between chuckles, June said, "Yeah, dem niggas was scared as shit."

"Y'all know I started to dump on that tall nigga for not movin' fast enough. I 'on like New York niggas anyway." V added.

"You mean Jersey" I tried to correct him.

"New York, New Jersey—same shit, ain't no difference. I should've put hot-balls in that nigga's ass." V said, sounding regretful.

"Nah, fuck them niggas. Let me tell you 'bout yo' bitch. Keisha *know* she can act. I almost laughed at her, the way she was on the floor cryin' and shit," I spoke to V as I watched him smile with pride.

June snatched the weed from V as he said, "Speakin' of yo' bitch, I ain't givin' dat hoe no mo' money. If dat trick want some mo' dough, *you* gonna be da nigga to give it to her."

"Ain't no question 'bout that, 'cause I sho' ain't givin' her ass none." I added.

"Y'all niggas need to quit trippin' 'cause y'all know I'm a handle that shit." V said looking at me and June with a nonchalant smirk.

"Oh nigga, we know" I said sarcastically, then added "But you need to handle that bitch before she opens her big-ass mouth. 'Cause you know if them niggas find out who laid 'em down, we gonna have to deal wit 'em." I explained to my ace.

"Didn't I just say I got that? That bitch ain't gone cross a nigga 'cause she'll be puttin' herself on front street. Besides, I'm fuckin' her too good for her to flip like that. 'Cause that's what I do—fuck'em, breed'em and mislead'em." V responded while simulating a doggie-style sex act, complete with his hands spanking the air like it was her ass.

I had given the blunt to June. V was watching him baby-sit it. V grew impatient and whined, "Damn. Can a nigga smoke wit 'choo? Fat muh-fucka."

Realizing he was hogging the weed, June finally passed it to V and he took a long drag, slowly letting the smoke out through his nostrils blending it in with the night air. Savoring the sweet taste of sticky green, V admired the blunt in his hand like a damn weed-connoisseur as he offered his critique of the herb, "Damn my nigga, that boy Jo-Jo got some good shit. This is fire right here."

"Yeah, dude keep dat stank. And you now what? I been thinkin' 'bout touchin' dat nigga," June said, replacing "that" with "dat" as he often does. He rose to his feet and brushed his wide ass off, ridding it of possible dirt.

"Who? Jo-Jo?" both V and I asked in unison.

"Damn right Jo-Jo. Dat nigga slangin' much weed and I know he sittin' on a few g's up in there," June replied while shaking his left leg, trying to get the blood circulating again. Because of his weight, his leg had gone to sleep from sitting in one position for such a long period of time.

At that moment, I saw June look past me and V with puzzling eyes and it caused a chain reaction. I looked back and then V looked back. I stood up and reached beneath my sweatshirt for my pistol as Ron-Ron, the neighborhood crack head appeared from the shadows.

"Ron-Ron, you better quit sneaking up on niggas like you crazy." I barked at him for startling us like that.

"My bad, lil' Al Capone," he replied sarcastically, while smiling and revealing his badly stained teeth. "I'm tryin' to get straight. Y'all holdin'?"

He was clutching a few crumpled bills in his hand. Neither one of us had any more dope so I toyed with him.

"Yeah dirty ass nigga, we holdin' P. S. and if you don't get the fuck away from here you gone get some."

Not know what "P. S." was, but judging from my tone, he decided he didn't want any.

"Aight Al Capone," he said again with sarcasm as he turned on his heels and did a foot shuffle, imitating James Brown, before shuffling off in the direction in which he had come from.

All of us laughed at him as he walked away.

"What the hell is P. S.?" June asked once Ron-Ron was gone.

I lifted my sweatshirt and pulled out my pistol and began explaining with the blunt dangling between my lips.

"I call this mutha-fucka right here 'Problem Solver.' Ain't no problem too big or too small for this bitch to handle, ya' dig?" I finished my explanation by turning the pistol over my hands, watching as the chrome sparkled whenever a small piece of light bounced off of it.

Passing the blunt to June, I tried to remember what we were talking about before Ron-Ron had interrupted us. It finally came to me as I began to contemplate what June had said about Jo-Jo. What he'd said was indeed true—Jo-Jo was serving an awful lot of wee at his spot. I thought about agreeing with June to rob him, but then I decided against it because Jo-Jo and I went back too far.

"Nah, we ain't fuckin' wit Jo-Jo. That nigga cool wit me," I told my partners, while bringing the subject back up.

June and V both looked at me at the same time before June said, "Nigga who you 'posed to be? You tryna tell a nigga who we can't jack?"

"Yeah nigga, you gettin' a lil' beside yo'self. You don't run nothing," V laughed while putting his two-cents in.

"Dat nigga Ron-Ron was right. Dis nigga think he Al Capone or somebody. Nigga you don't call no shots. V, let's start callin' dis nigga John gotti or some shit" June added.

"Nah, dis nigga name gonna be Capone from now on" He looked me in the eyes and nodded as if to stamp the name. "Gangsta ass Capone" V joked.

"What's up Al Capone?" June laughed.

They both meant it as a joke, but the name ended up sticking. Soon, the whole city would come to know me as "Capone". From that day on, Mike was dead and Capone had just been born.

### *Chapter Two – Da' Come Up*

A light snow had fallen over the city of Charlotte and the roads were a little slippery, so me and my two road dogs were stranded in a hotel room. We had originally set up a robbery for that day, but the road conditions had thrown a monkey wrench into our plans. June wanted to go ahead and carry out the plan, but me and V decided against it because transportation would be a serious problem.

Yellow Boy, our would-be mark lived in an upscale neighborhood with plenty of nosey neighbors who were on Neighborhood-Watch, or more accurately, watching the neighborhood for niggas. So getting in and out unseen in the snow would have been a tedious task.

Yellow Boy could easily pass for white because of his high-yellow complexion and "good hair." He'd been on our hit-list for weeks. Yellow Boy had made a name for himself a couple of years earlier when he had shot and killed two niggas who had allegedly kicked in his mother's door and robbed her at gun point, all for a few G's. Now that he'd made an example out of those two flunkies, many of the city's stick-up kids were hesitant about trying to jack him. Without having to fear getting jacked, he continued to slang his shit and was well paid.

Me and my boys had seen this nigga flossing and shining on many occasions, but never mentioned trying our hand. Prior to a month earlier, when he did some foul shit, I hadn't had as much as a second thought about him. But now, he'd gotten beside himself.

He and his boys had disrespected the hell out of June's mom at a local McDonald's. She was on her lunch break, trying to get a quick bite to eat before returning to work. While in line waiting to be served, she was standing behind Yellow Boy and two of his partners. Instead of ordering his meal, Yellow Boy was trying to holler at the girl at the register who was all smiles.

Continuously checking her watch, June's mom noticed that she had to be back at the job real soon. She only had an hour for lunch and this young man in front of her was wasting precious time. She tried to be cool about the situation, but her stomach was growling and her patience was wearing thin. She mustered up all of the politeness her anger would allow and with a calm voice she said, "Excuse me, but if you're not going to order—I would like to."

Yellow Boy looked back at the woman who had interrupted his mack game and spat, "Hold up old lady, you just gonna have to wait your turn." And with that said, Yellow Boy turned back to the girl at the register and resumed his conversation.

June's mother could stand it no longer, "Listen, I gotta get back to work in fifteen minutes, so I would appreciate it if you'll step aside and let me order."

When Yellow Boy heard this, he spun around and saw his partners trying to hold in their laughter. The woman was getting under Yellow's skin and his boys found it amusing. Not to be outdone and wanting to impress the young cashier, Yellow Boy smirked and said, "Oh, so that's what it is, you worried about them crackers firin' yo' ass, huh? I'll tell you what moms … here, why don't you go next door and buy you *and* your cracker-ass boss a Whopper from Burger King."

While making that statement, he dug into his front pocket and produced a wad of bills which he began peeling off a few singles, tossing them one by one into June's moms face. As other patrons looked on, Yellow and his boys laughed and continued to taunt her until she finally sauntered out in tears. Yellow Boy didn't know the woman was June's mother, neither did his boys. But Sharon, the girl behind the register knew and couldn't wait to tell June what had happened.

The next day, Sharon got in touch with June through an associate and told June everything that had gone down between Yellow Boy and his mom. June was understandably pissed and when he told me and V, we felt his pain too. So, we began to watch that nigga and eventually followed him home one night just to see where he rested his head at. Our original plan was to run up in his house when he wasn't home and rob him for everything he had, but June decided he would rather catch Yellow Boy while he was home, so we could make an example of his ass.

The perfect opportunity presented itself when Sharon called June and informed him that she would be spending the night with Yellow Boy and that he would definitely be at home all night. Just our luck, it snowed, so we postponed our plans. I believe everything happens for a reason, so I wasn't sweating it. June was consumed with his feelings about what Yellow Boy had done to his mom, so for him, this was definitely personal. But for me and V, it was business as usual. Who knows? Maybe this was God's way of preventing us from catching a body because I knew June definitely was ready to do something real stupid.

It had been two months since we had robbed the New Jersey niggas. We hadn't heard any news concerning the robbery, so I guessed Keisha had kept her mouth shut.

While enjoying the warm air circulating throughout the hotel room, I inhaled deeply on the blunt I had dangling between my lips. *Damn, Jo-Jo got some good shit.,* I ironically thought to myself as I let the smoke curl from my mouth into my nostrils before exhaling.

We'd been sitting around in the Hampton Inn on Billy Graham Parkway all evening, smoking weed and drinking beer. We started calling every girl we knew who owned a car, but nobody wanted to travel in the snow, which was understandable. So, we had a difficult time trying to find some female company. After getting rejected at least five times each, we almost said *fuck it.* On June's last attempt, he finally convinced a girl named Meka to come and hang out with us. As fate would have it, she was sitting around with two of her girlfriends, just as bored to death as we were. All three agreed to come.

We continued to get high and talk shit while we waited for Meka and her friends to arrive. I clowned June about his baldhead and in turn he and V teased me about my dreads.

"You look like a raggedy ass mop," V teased.

It was all in fun, so I laughed it off. I rose from the couch where I had been sitting, and headed to the restroom to relieve my aching bladder from all of the Heinekens I'd consumed throughout the evening. Along the way, I stopped and peered out of the window, watching the scattered snowflakes fall from the sky to create a light film on the street and grass. It wasn't too often that it snowed in Charlotte so I was taking in the wintery sight.

After taking a leak, I stood before the mirror twisting my dreads and staring at my blood shot eyes thinking, *Damn, I'm high as shit.* Hearing a knock on the outer door brought me out of my daze. Startled and paranoid, I instinctively reached beneath my large sweatshirt for my burner. When I heard the sound of female voices I relaxed. Still playing in my hair, I was in no rush to join the group because I knew how beat up June's taste in women was. These girls were probably busted and beat up from the feet up, so I took my time before exiting the restroom. Even before leaving the bathroom, I already knew one thing—one of them had a loud as mouth.

"Damn that shit loud. Won't y'all put a towel under the door or somethin'?. I smelled that shit all the way down the hall." I heard her voice say loud enough for the entire hotel to hear.

When I finally emerged from the bathroom, I stood dead in my tracks because what I saw was not at all what I expected. The surprise and approval must have been visible on my face because June was giving me one of those "I told you so" looks. The girls had taken a seat on the sofa and June and V were standing around looking like kids in a candy store, smiling like damn fools. June finally introduced me to the girls, "Meka, Kinya, Dee, dis my nigga Capone."

"Sup," I spoke with a slight rise of the head as I surveyed the three fine sisters before me.

Meka was a milk chocolate, petite cutie with a loud ass mouth. She'd been the one commenting on the weed smell when they had entered. She was dressed in bell-bottoms with a sweater that appeared to drown her small frame. Her stylish boots looked expensive, as did her leather coat. Her hair was micro-braided so tight that her forehead looked as if it were being pulled back. I wondered what she saw in June.

Dee was a thick-built red bone with her hair dyed honey blonde. She sported a sweat suit with running shoes and had on a heavy, Tommy Hilfiger jacket, which must have costed a grip. Dee flossed much jewelry around her neck, wrists and fingers. Though she was definitely fine, she had a very annoying voice, just like the old school singer Michel'le. I could see that my man V was sprung immediately.

Kinya was a pecan tan sister with shoulder-length jet-black hair and I could tell she was thick by the way her hips and thighs spread while she was seated wearing jeans and a casual-type blouse with a waist-length leather jacket. Just like Meka, Kinya also had on boots. I couldn't stop staring at her for some reason. But the thing that really turned me on was the way she walked. When she got up to get a beer and to shed her coat, she had bowlegs and she walked like she owned the room. My eyes immediately zoomed in on the ass.

A few minutes after I had joined the group, Meka and June were standing by the door kickin' it. V and Dee were seated on the bed drinking while enjoying a blunt. I had taken a seat on the sofa and Kinya had come over and sat beside me. I wasn't mad at all about who I had ended up pairing off with. In fact, I was rather satisfied.

As I was in the process of busting open a Philly Blunt, Kinya snatched it from me and filled it with weed. I just sat back, intensely watching her hands with well-manicured fingers, as she worked a miracle of rolling one of the most perfect blunts I'd ever seen. Gawkingly, I stared at her lips as they parted while she licked the bitter leaf to seal it. She'd done it in such a seductive manner, my dick started throbbing like shit because I was imagining her lips and tongue working me like she had just worked that blunt.

I smiled devilishly and commented, "You sho' act like you know what you doin'."

By the expression on her face, I could tell that she wasn't sure if I was referring to her blunt-rolling skills, or if I was hinting at how orally satisfying she could be.

We smoked like Indians while engaging in small talk. I found out she was from Gastonia, but resided in Charlotte because she was attending Johnson C. Smith University. Hypnotized, I couldn't get over the fact that she either had the most beautiful eyes or the most beautiful contacts I had ever seen. Hell, I couldn't tell the difference, I was high as a mutha-fucka.

Dee had gone into the restroom, so V joined Kinya and me on the sofa. As soon as he sat down, he snatched the blunt from Kinya and began toking. Kinya couldn't believe how disrespectful he was and looked at me for assistance. I ignored her glare and started teasing V about Dee's squeaky ass voice. I had no idea how he was going to tolerate her vocal chords all night, but to my surprise he said her voice was a turn on.

"That bitch sound like a rat, yo," I commented.

As soon as the word "bitch" escaped my lips, Kinya's eyes shot daggers in my direction.

"That's fucked up. You don't even know my girl, but she gotta be a bitch, huh? Niggas always gotta come outta they mouth with some foul shit."

With that statement, she got up off the couch and went to join Meka who was busy searching for a cd to put into the small boom box she had brought with her. June took Kinya's spot on the couch and as soon as he sat down, the cushions sort of leaned in his direction because of all of his weight.

A few minutes later, the speakers came alive with "Ain't nothing but a G' Thang Bay-a-aby."

"Ay, turn that shit down girl, you ain't at home." I snapped, yelling from across the room trying to be heard over the loud music.

Once Meka turned the volume down to a decent level, we nodded our heads in rhythm to Dr. Dre as he and Snoop spit that gangsta shit.

All of the beer I had consumed had started expanding my bladder again, so I ventured off toward the bathroom. When I reached for the knob and twisted it, it was unlocked, so I assumed it was empty. When I opened the door, my mouth dropped to the floor because the bathroom definitely wasn't empty. There sat Dee on the toilet fully clothed with stacks of money lying at her feet and she had a wad in her hand. I could tell she was in the middle of counting it by the way she had the 100's, 50's and 20's stacked. Dee was just as surprised at seeing me standing there as I was seeing her sitting there counting all of that money. Her face turned beet red and she hastily started stuffing the money back into her purse. My mind went into overdrive, so I excused myself and closed the door behind me.

When I stepped out, V must've peeped the look in my eyes because he commented, "Damn 'Pone, let me find out you done seen my bitch naked already."

I didn't respond to his comment because I was still trying to figure out where Dee had gotten all of that damn money from. I came up with only three reasons for a female to have stacks of crumpled bills like I'd just witnessed. One, she was probably a stripper, because she definitely had the body for it. Two, she could've been slangin' and getting her grind on. Or three, she was fucking with a nigga who was doing his thing and she was holding the money for him.

If she was stripping, I could leave it alone and let my mind rest. If she was grinding, she was definitely gonna feel me soon. But, if she had a man who was in the game and trusted her enough to hold that much money for him, she could be an asset to us.

I told V that I'd holler at him later to let him know what was bothering me. By my tone, he knew something important was on my mind. I encouraged V to play Dee very close and to make sure he didn't blow it with her. He couldn't figure out what I was up to, but he had seen this same thirsty look in my eyes many times in the past and knew it had to concern money, so he just went along with it.

When Dee exited the restroom, she was clinging to her purse. She walked up to me and V while eyeing me suspiciously. I kept my game face on though and casually walked off toward the bathroom. Once Dee was within arm's reach, V grabbed her and kissed her like had missed her while glancing at me. I gave him a conspiratorial wink and disappeared to take my delayed leak.

We were all enjoying each other's company—drinking and smoking like we didn't have a care in the world. The beer and blunt supply began getting low, so I asked Kinya to accompany me to the convenience store that was located directly across from the hotel. I also asked Dee and V to walk with us so I'd have a chance to rap with him. We walked in the snow carefully so not to slip and fall on the ice because that wouldn't have been a good first impression.

When we reached the store, I dug into my pocket and handed Kinya some money to pay for the purchase. Since she and Dee were the only two old enough to legally purchase alcohol, they went in while me and V waited outside. The night air was cold and the scattered snowflakes didn't make things any better, so I pulled my hoody over my head and shoved my hands deep into my pockets for warmth.

Once the girls were out of earshot, I pulled V's coat to what I had seen in the bathroom.

"Yo, I don't know what that bitch Dee is into, but she got some dough and I mean plenty of it. I walked in the bathroom on her while she was counting it. The bitch had 100's, 50's, an' shit. Fucked-me-up. You know I wanted to take that shit, right?"

V laughed at my statements as I continued.

"I don't know how she got it, all I know is she definitely got it. It might not even be hers. I know she ain't dancing 'cause I picked Kinya for that info. She might be grindin' but I doubt it, 'cause she don't look like the type, she too timid. I'm thinkin' she holdin' that shit for a nigga. Feel me?"

It took a minute for my last statement to register and when it finally did, V's eyes lit up with that all too familiar thirst.

"Yeah exactly," I said while nodding my head at the sight of his widened eyes, knowing that we were finally on the same page. "If that's the case, I know you're just like me, you wanna *see* that nigga." I stated.

"No doubt," V responded while rubbing his hands together for warmth, "You know that's how I breed'em playboy," he added, smiling.

"Nah nigga, this bitch done already been bred. We need to find out by *who*, ya' dig? You need to shake that tree a lil' bit and see what falls out," I responded.

Just then, the two girls exited the store. Kinya was carrying a case of Heineken, so I took the load off her hands. As we walked back to the hotel, V put his arm around Dee's neck holding her close as she hugged his waist. They looked as if they had known each other for years instead of having just met. Just that quickly, my man was already setting the stage. I smiled inwardly because I had a gut feeling Dee was about to fall victim to my partner's prowess.

After smoking and drinking well into the night, it was finally time to separate. June told me he'd holler at me later because he and Meka were on their way to the front desk to get another room. Fifteen minutes after June left, V was giving me dap telling me that he and Dee were going to get another room as well, which left Kinya and I alone. Everything was going smooth with me and Kinya, that is, until I accidentally let the "B" word roll off my tongue again.

We were simply having a civilized conversation until she joked about cutting my dreads. I laughed it off and casually said, "bitch, you crazy." I didn't mean anything by it. As a matter of fact, I really didn't mean to say it. "Bitch" was just as much a part of my everyday vocabulary as "he", "she" and "they." What can I say? It was a habit. I tried to apologize at the mere sight of her cocked neck, but she wasn't trying to hear it.

Kinya got offended and went on and on about how young niggas be disrespected women so much that they don't even realize they be doing it. I was too fucked up to argue and her ranting became so irritating to me that I ended up making things worse when I said, "I tried to apologize so if that ain't good enough, fuck you then."

If looks could kill, Kinya would've been up state with a murder charge. She shook her head and reached for the telephone. Since she and Meka had ridden with Dee, I assumed she was calling a cab or some other form of transportation because I knew she wanted to leave. We weren't clicking anymore. I told her I was about to take a shower and for her to turn out the light on her way out. She refused to even respond—just rolled her eyes ghetto style and continued to hold the phone to her ear.

After showering, I exited the bathroom area to find it pitch dark in the room. As I stretched, yawned and carefully tried to find my way through darkness to the bed, I attempted to convince myself that it was good that she had left. *I didn't feel like being bothered with her ass anyway,* I thought to myself before muttering aloud, "Crazy bitch."

I used my hands like a blind man to locate one of the queen size beds as I'd just semi-satisfied myself with the consolation that with June and V gone, at least I could anticipate getting some undisturbed sleep.

Before I'd even pulled the covers all the way back, a familiar voice spoke in opposition to my muttered words.

"I thought I just told you about using that word."

Kinya wasn't gone as I'd previously thought. She was sitting on the opposite side of the bed in the dark.

"I thought you was bouncin'."

"I'm too fucked up to leave. Besides, I want my apology"

"Apology?" This bitch *was* high. I had never apologized for anything that had come out of my mouth and I wasn't about to give her the benefit. But I swear I was too throwed to argue. I laid down and slid under the covers and said "Aiight, u got that".

"I guess that's your way of saying 'sorry'" she laughed. "Can I lay down?" She asked.

I wanted to say "HELL YEAH". However, I played cool and muttered "It's your world, shorty"

I heard her boots hit the floor and felt her weight on the bed as the room all of a sudden became unbearably hot. Three minutes later, the room was so quiet you could hear a mouse piss on cotton. Lying on my back with my hands folded behind my head, I stared at the ceiling in the darkness. I coolly said "So, you was really waiting for a nigga to apologize?"

I could hear her steady and rhythmically breathing as if she had dozed off just that quickly. Eventually, she shifted around and asked, "Do you want me to leave?"

I looked toward the spot in which she lay and replied, "I'on care what 'choo do shawty, it's on you."

I didn't want to give her the impression that it made any difference one way or the other, but in actuality, I didn't want this girl to go anywhere.

As Kinya slid closer to me, it seemed as if the room was an inferno now because of the heat radiating from her body. She put her hand on my chest and began to caress me, making my dick throb like shit, she whispered in my ear in a sexy voice. "Capone, have you ever been with a woman?"

Now at this point, I became confused and angry because she was implying that I was either a virgin or gay. My anger outweighed my confusion.

"Fuck you mean by that?" I barked in an angry tone as I sat up and stared at her.

"No. No. All I meant was that I know I'm older than you and you probably used to fuckin' wit' those lil chickenheads and what-not. But have you ever been wit' a *real* woman?" Kinya cleaned her comment up very well.

"I'm a let you answer that question for yo'self in about a hour or so," I seductively replied as I pulled off the cover and began to answer her question with action.

Leaning over her, I kissed her lips. I began to lick from one corner of her mouth to the other. I licked her top lip then her bottom. She tried to open her mouth for a kiss, but I told her, "No, I'm just tasting your lips."

I could tell she was enjoying it because I felt her lips form a smile. Slowly I licked and sucked on her bottom lip while her hands caressed my back. My kisses ventured their way to her ear, down to her neck, then her collarbone as she raised up and lifted her blouse over her head. She also slipped out of her jeans. She unhooked and remove her bra. After she tossed her bra aside to the other bed, I continued my foreplay, licking and kissing her chest and the tops of her breasts while squeezing and caressing her titties. I began to lick around her left nipple. When I finally took her thumbnail-sized nipple in my mouth, I sucked it like a baby with a bottle. *"Mmmmmmm."* was the only sound she made, while breathing deeply.

Her fingers combed through my dreads and rubbed my shoulders, as I gently bit on her nipples. I slid my hands from her breast down her flat stomach until I gripped her firm inner-thighs, stroking them in an up-and-down motion. As I ventured into the dip between her pecan-tan thighs, I began to feel her heat. As I caressed her pussy through her panties, she spread her thighs further apart and began rotating her hips in tune to my wandering hand. I could feel her wetness through the thin silk fabric. Kinya raised her hips in a bridge-like manner, non-verbally urging me to remove the barrier that was preventing skin-to-skin contact. I contemplated just pulling them to the side ghetto-style, but I checked myself and eased them down over her hips, past her thighs and off her ankles.

On my way back up, I kissed her calves and licked my way up her thigh until my nose felt pubic hair. As I licked and sucked the insides of her thighs, I could smell her sweet arousal. I couldn't wait to insert two fingers. As I did, her pussy clenched down on them in a vise-like grip. She was so wet and moaning so seductively, I almost came on myself just that quick. Kinya held my head in her hands and tried to guide me toward her wetness. But little did she know, her *little man in the boat* wasn't about to get rocked like that. I kissed my way back up to her stomach, all the way up to her lips. Our tongues did a dance, trying to get familiar with one another while I continued to run my fingers through her wetness. Kinya ran her hands down along my stomach and ventured south, until she reached her destination. Reaching inside my boxers, she found what she was looking for. Using both hands, she stroked and tugged on my third leg like she was holding a rope in a school-yard tug-of-war match. The tables had turned as she now had me squirming like a bitch.

Kinya rolled me over onto my back as she began to lick and caress me like I had done her, only she gave me *more*. After she removed my boxers, she kissed her way down my stomach and I could feel her tongue licking across my *"Fuck Tha World"* tat. As she licked lower she began to make love to me with her mouth. That same sensuous mouth that had mesmerized me while she was licking blunts, was now licking *me*. My toes weren't only curling, she had a nigga's toes in knots. When she had finished, I had forgotten where I was at. She brought me back to earth when she finally whispered, "Get a rubber."

Not only did I comply with her command, but I put this thug love on her ass in every position known to mankind, even a few new ones that we just made up. The whole time I was thinking about that question she'd asked earlier, *'Have you ever been with a woman?'* It repeated itself in my head with every thrust. From the way she screamed and called out my name and God's name in the same sentence, I knew her question had been answered.

After our climax, Kinya and I both passed out into an alcohol, weed and sex-induced slumber. Kinya fell asleep with a satisfied smile on her face, while I passed out with an *'I got this bitch'* grin on mine.

Later, I heard the sounds of bells far off in the distance, consistently ringing bells. I was drawn out of my sleep by the sound of the telephone.

"Yeah," I said as I reached across Kinya to answer it.

"Will you be checking out or staying over?" asked a female voice on the other end.

I glanced over at the bedside clock that displayed that it was 11:36 AM. Damn, it was checkout time already.

"Checkin' out," I reluctantly answered as I peered at Kinya's sleeping figure and memories of the night before came flashing back. My dick got hard and I suddenly changed my mind. "Wait a minute, on second thought, I'm staying over," I told the woman. "I'll be down in a minute to pay."

Thank you Sir," she replied before hanging up.

As soon as I put the phone back in its cradle, it rang again.

"Yeah."

"Sup my nigga? Yo lazy ass still in da bed ain't cha'?" June said.

"Yeah, the bitch at the front desk just called and woke a nigga up. You ain't heard from V?" I asked.

"Yeah, V and Dee sittin' right here wit' me and Meka."

"Damn, that shit sound funny. V and Dee. I hope that ain't what he caught last night," I replied as June and I laughed at my joke.

Apparently, I had awakened Kinya because she had gotten up and was on her way into the bathroom, *naked*. Now, it was one thing to *feel* someone's body in the darkness, but it is a totally different experience *seeing* it in broad daylight.

"Damn, this bitch fine." I thought to myself as I watched those bow legs and that fat ass swing with every step. June was talking, but I wasn't hearing a word he was saying. He put V on the phone and I asked if he'd found out anything concerning the conversation we'd had at the store. He assured me that I was gonna *love* what he had to tell me but I would have to wait until later.

After walking the girls to Dee's car, we all said our goodbyes with plans of hooking up in the near future. Once we got back to the room, we fired up a blunt and compared notes on the pussy.

"That bitch Dee is a cold-freak....just like me." V said with a wide ass smile on his face.

"I know you couldn't handle Meka lil ass. As skinny as she is, I know that thang deep as the abyss and wide as this room." I joked with June.

"Nigga, you betta ask dem hoes 'bout Junebug," June defensively replied while holding his crotch.

"Yo, you fuck Kinya?" V asked.

"Nah, I just happened to steal these while she was sleep," I said as I pulled Kinya's panties out of my pocket.

V and June fell out laughing.

"Yo, let me see what that pussy smell like," V said as he reached for the underwear I had in my hand.

"Nigga, watch out, wit' yo' lil freaky ass," I said as I slapped his reaching hand and put the panties back in my pocket. "Boy, you got issues."

"I just wanna know if that thang stunk," V said while laughing.

"Nigga, you think I'm a be sittin' up here with a pair of stankin' ass panties in my pocket? Hell, if she had a twang, her ass wouldn't have still been laid up in here this mornin'. Nigga you know I don't get down like you and fat boy right here," I informed, as I exhaled a cloud of Jo-Jo's herb. I looked at V and asked, "But seriously, what's really hapnin'?"

I was referring to the business he was supposed to take care of.

"Dig this, y'all gone love this shit. Yo, the bitch fuckin' wit' a balla. You called good money 'Pone. I lied and told her I'm pushing bricks an' shit and she told me that she know a few niggas that got it like *water*. I ain't say nuthin' bout what you told me you had seen her doin' last night and she didn't volunteer no info right off bat. But after I put this muscle up in her, baby girl opened up and started spillin' her guts. She fuckin' with a nigga outta Connecticut and y'all niggas know how I feel about them up north niggas. She say the nigga be sendin' her to collect money from niggas an' shit. The money you seen her wit' last night was that nigga's. Now, this is the good part right here. She say the nigga startin' to get on her nerves an' shit. She thought 'bout just takin' the nigga's money an' runnin' off and she was thinkin' 'bout havin' somebody lay the nigga down. Now, y'all know my dick go hard when she said that. That shit right up a nigga's alley. I'm tellin' y'all, this is it right here. This the lick we been waitin' on my nigga. This is our come-up," V reported.

June and I listened intently.

"Sh-i-i-t, what we waitin' on?" June asked, jumping the gun.

"Slow ya roll fat boy. V told the bitch that *he* is slanging bricks. Hell, fo' all we know, she can be tryina set *him* up. We don't know this bitch," I explained to June.

"As soon as I find out what she up to, I'm a tell her I'm a jack-boy. This might be *it* yo," V said as he reached for the blunt I was hogging.

I handed it to him and said, "It's 'bout time. Just handle yo 'bidness playboy"

V exhaled a poison cloud and said, "Y'all know my motto. Fuck'em. Breed'em an' Mis…"

"Yeah, yeah, nigga we know, mislead'em nigga, mislead'em" June said as he finished V's sentence.

Since we were on a new paper chase, the situation with Yellow Boy would have to remain on hold.

## Chapter Three – Plottin' and Schemin'

"'Pone, why yo' mama holdin' a lil' ugly-ass monkey wrapped in a blanket right here? Oh shit, nigga dat's you." June said as he burst into laughter.

He was flipping through my mom's photo album. June and I were sitting in my mom's living room watching and talking shit. June was seated on our old-fashion plastic-covered sofa wearing a sweat suit that looked like it was two sizes too small. I was seated on the matching lounge chair wearing a jeans and a North Carolina Tarheels sweater with a matching bandana, holding my dreads up. I kept shifting positions because the springs coming up through the worn out chair were hurting my ass.

"Yo', you was a ugly ass baby." June said while pointing at another one of my baby pictures.

"Nigga is you gone look at the book or is you gone narrate the mutha-fucka?" I said, getting a little frustrated.

"Mike, I *know* you ain't cussin' in my house." my mother's voice boomed from her bedroom.

"Ma, that wasn't me. That was June." I lied.

"Stop lyin'. Miss Vanessa, you know dat wasn't me." June defended himself.

"Mike, stop lying on that boy. I done told yo' lil' disrespectful ass 'bout cussin' in my house an' shit." she shot back, not practicing what she was preaching.

*Damn.* I mumbled under my breath while June was laughing.

I looked at my gold watch to check the time.

"Man it's almost eight o'clock and that nigga ain't called yet." I commented to June.

"You know dat nigga go to losin' track o' time an' some mo' shit when he get 'round dat bitch," June replied.

June and I had been sitting around all day waiting for V to come over, or to at least call. Ever since that night at the Hampton Inn, V and Donyetta (Dee), as V now called her, had been damn near inseparable. After a few conversations with her, I began to see why V was so damn attracted to her. Dee turned out to be one of the realest chicks I've ever come in contact with. She was a real Ride-Or-Die chick, down for whatever. She had more heart than a lot of so-called thugs I knew. Dee had the brains of a hustler and the body of a goddess, which made her every thug's fantasy, if only you could get past that aggravating-ass voice. Every hustler wanted her and every chick wanted to hang out with her. My man V had her nose wide-open. I could see why that Connecticut nigga had her on his team. But little did he know, she was about to switch teams at half time.

This particular day, we were waiting for V and Dee to get back from handling some business. V had finally ended up lacing Dee with the game. He told her everything, including the fact that he was a jack-boy. That shit made her panties wet. She seemed to get off on the idea that V was a robber and she decided to put V up on the cat from Connecticut. She was supposed to point out the spots where the money and the dope were being kept; the rest was up to us. So, there we were, just sitting around waiting for V to make his appearance. I was becoming impatient and began pacing the small area of our living room.

June looked up from the photo album and said, "Damn, nigga I wish you sit yo' ass down somewhere."

I looked at him and contemplated putting his fat ass out. Just as I was about to say something, the phone rang. I snatched it up.

"Yeah." I answered.

A familiar voice on the other end said, "Yeah? Boy what have I told you about answering yo' mama's phone like that?"

"My bad Gramps, I thought you were somebody else," I replied.

"Where yo' mama at?" My grandmother asked.

"She in her room, hold on a minute. M-a-a-a-a. Telephone." I yelled loud enough for the whole block to hear me. I did it purposely just to aggravate my mom and grandma, as June looked at me like I was losing my mind.

As soon as my mom picked up her phone, I hung up and sat back on the worn-out love seat glancing at my watch a second time, this time inspecting it as if it could've been broken. As I did so, I noticed some greenish, colored spots on the band and around the face.

"Damn, my shit fadin'. This some cheap ass shit," I mumbled to myself while I was daydreaming about the day I would be able to afford a better one, maybe a Rolex. Well, maybe not anytime soon, but hell, it was wishful thinking. While I was daydreaming, the phone rang again.

"Yea—I mean hello," I answered.

"Sup nigga," V spoke.

"Hold on," I said as I went out the front door and stepped into the breezeway, dragging the phone cord behind me. I closed the door and resumed our conversation, "Yeah what up son?" I joked in a New York accent.

"Don't do that. You know I hate that shit," V replied.

"So what happened?" I asked in reference to what Dee was supposed to do.

"Where June at?"

"He in the house, I just stepped outside. We been over here waiting on yo' ass all day."

"Where punk-ass Nard at?" V asked.

"Nard moved yesterday. He got his own shit, finally," I replied. I was trying to figure out why this nigga was procrastinating.

"Yo mama home?"

"Yeah she in there, why?"

"Damn," V sighed.

"Nigga is you comin' or what?" I asked. V was starting to frustrate me.

"Man, I'm baby sittin' Jay. My mama was sittin' here waiting fo' me to walk in the door so she could leave. Donyetta just dropped me off," V responded.

Jay, whose full first-name was JayQuan, was V's eight-year-old little brother who reminds you of a little Tasmanian Devil. *Bad-as-hell.* Always into some shit.

"Oh *hell nah.* You know my mama don't like his lil' bad ass." I said.

"Yeah, I know. Why don't y'all come over here then," V suggested.

"Aiight, we on our way. I'll holla."

"Aiight den…wait, wait, 'Pone?" V tried to catch me before I hung up.

"What?." I asked.

"What yo' mama cook?"

"Nigga fuck you." I responded as I hung up on him. *Greedy ass nigga always beggin'*, I thought to myself as I re-entered our apartment to get June.

The walk to V's apartment building took less than five minutes because we lived in the same neighborhood. V opened the door as we approached.

"That's fucked up you ain't bring a nigga nuthin' to eat," he complained as we entered the apartment.

I sniffed the air and responded, "Yo' mama the one always up in the kitchen experimentin' and shit. I know she done throwed somethin' together. I can smell it."

"Man, you know I'on eat no chitlins an' shit," V responded.

"Yo mama cooked chitlins?" June asked with his mouth watering and his eyes bulging.

"Yeah, hungry ass hippo, but you ain't gettin' none," V teased.

As June and I entered the living room, V went into the kitchen. JayQuan was seated on the sofa watching television. V's apartment was the same size as ours, a two-bedroom hotbox. V's mother had more furniture than we did, which made their living room look smaller than ours. V's mom had pasted diamond-shaped mirrors along the walls of the living room as well as the hallway. There were pictures of naked black people with large Afros hanging from rusty nails and the classic picture of the *Dogs Playing Poker*. I took a seat on the love seat, while June took a seat on the sofa beside JayQuan.

V came into the living room carrying a plate full of chitterlings and a bottle of hot sauce. He handed it all to June, who almost snatched the plate out of V's hand. V left and came back with a mayonnaise jar (minus the paper wrapping) full of grape Kool-Aid, that he also gave to June. Immediately, June was busy attacking the swine like he hadn't eaten in days.

JayQuan looked at June with his nose turned up and asked in a mannish-child voice, "Dang, why you all da time eatin'?"

Without looking up from the plate, June answered his question with a question, "Why you stay in grown folk biness, you lil' bad ass niglett?"

JayQuan slid off of the couch and walked toward the hallway, near his room. When he knew he was far enough away from June so that he couldn't reach him, JayQuan said, "Dat's why Vonzell say you so fat you ain't got no ding-a-ling."

He was sticking his tongue out and making faces. June fed right into Jay's childish game by saying, "Dat's why you ain't got no front teeth. Tell yo' mama to buy you some for Christmass. Yo' lil' bad ass."

"I might ain't got no front teeth, 'least I got a ding-a-ling." JayQuan said while holding his tiny crotch.

I fell on the floor laughing.

"Jay, I'm a tell mama you showin' out. Go play somewhere." V barked at his little brother in an angry tone.

"And I'm a tell mama you givin' her food to fat people," JayQuan said as he disappeared into his room.

"Damn, why lil' dude so bad?" I asked V.

"All you gotta do is ig'em, he don't want nothin' but some attention. And June dumb ass be feeding right into it every time." V replied while looking at June.

"I know one thang, if he was my lil' brother, I'll beat his lil' bad ass." June replied, while wiping some hot sauce off of his lips.

Remembering the real reason as to why we were there, I asked V, "Yo, what's up wit that lick?"

V took a seat and began to relay what he and Dee had been up to all day.

"Check this out, the nigga she fuckin' with is living in a condo on Lake Norman with some bitch. It's a quiet lil' cracker neighborhood 'bout ten minutes outside of Charlotte," V reached into his pocket and produced a folded piece of paper.

He unfolded it and read it contents, "The condos are called Alta Habor, off exit 28 up I-77. Once you enter the neighborhood, make the first left and after you pass the second speed bump, it's the first building on the right."

He tossed the paper to me and I glanced at the chicken-scratch, trying to decipher the jumbled words while he continued.

"We rode through his parking lot and Dee pointed out his condo and his car. He drives a BMW and his girl drives a new Pathfinder. She said the nigga took her up there one weekend when his girl was outta town doing a pick-up. He be sending his bitch and her friend named Bridgette to New York and Connecticut to pick up keys and bring 'em back to Charlotte. Evidently, the nigga like to run his mouth when he gets drunk, 'cause Dee said when he took her up there he had been drinking and as soon as they stepped up in his crib he started bragging about how much dope he was coppin' and how much money he was making off these 'green ass country niggas' in Charlotte."

"Green and country, huh?" I fumed while interrupting.

If there is one thing that I can't stand, it's the matter of someone thinking because they're from up north, they're slicker than everybody else. That statement alone would end up costing that nigga more that he would ever imagine. Now, I was even more enthralled at the idea of making this nigga feel us.

"How much dope this nigga gettin'?" I asked.

"Dee said the nigga told her he be gettin' anywhere from five to seven birds every rip."

When V mentioned the five to seven kilos, June's eyes almost popped out of his head. I tried to conceal my excitement, but my mouth betrayed me.

"Daaaaamn." I accidentally said out loud.

"That's exactly what I said when she told me," V said, smiling as he continued. "That ain't even the best part. She said the nigga showed her a safe in the bedroom closet with at least a hundred and fifty g's in it."

No that info had June and me all over the living room giving high-fives to each other and bumping bellies like someone had just scored a touchdown. We were making so much noise, JayQuan peeped his head around the corner to see what was going on. V was trying to calm us down.

"Shhh, damn niggas, chill so I can finish. Y'all act like a nigga done already licked. Listen, it ain't as easy as y'all think it is, 'cause this nigga ain't a complete fool. At least he's got enough sense not to keep the money and the dope in the same spot. He use that bitch Bridgette's crib for the stash spot for the dope. I met that bitch before, a while back. I didn't know she was getting down like that. Y'all know Big Tone outta North Charlotte? Well, it's his cousin. She lives in Hidden Valley. Dee showed me her house as well. Most of the time she's home alone, no kids, no dog, no friends hanging out over there. Nothing. But sometime, that Connecticut nigga's partner be over there fucking her," V finally took a breath and then continued. "Dee said the safe he showed her was mounted into the floor and *nobody* knows the combination besides him. So, if we go up in there and he ain't home, we assed out."

"How often do Bridgette 'nem be making them trips up north?" I asked V.

"Dee said they go at least every other week," V replied.

"Yo, dis it right here. Dis da lick we been waitin' on. We ain't goin' in half steppin'. If we gone touch dat nigga, we gone rape dat nigga for all dat shit, the money *and* the dope." June spoke up by saying.

I thought for a minute, then said "We gon' have to be smart wit' this shit. We gon' have to catch them bitches as soon as they get back from a trip. We can catch that nigga anytime, all we gotta do is post up and watch his crib and wait for him to show. We gon' need at least two mo' niggas wit' us so we can hit both spots around the same time, so can't nobody make no phone calls and warn each other."

"I gotta betta idea. Why don't we catch dem bitches before dey make it to the house. Me and somebody else can stick dem hoes while the other two run up on lake and holla at dat nigga. Dat way we won't need but one mo' person," June suggested what he thought was a good idea.

Again, I thought for a minute before speaking "Nah, that ain't gone work, 'cause nine times outta ten they gon' have somebody followin' 'em. We gotta catch 'em in the crib with the dope," I vetoed June's suggestion.

V had been pacing the room the whole time silently thinking.          Eventually          he          stopped.

"Fuck all that. We gon' lay and wait for the hoes to roll up and we gone fall up in there right behind they ass. We gon' make that nigga's bitch call him to come over there. When he get there, we gon' take that nigga on a gangsta ride to his crib and make him empty the safe. Me and 'Pone gon' take care of that. June, you still got that beeper that Goldie got for you?" V asked taking control.

"Yeah, I still got it," June answered in curiosity as V continued to lay out the game plan.

"Aiight, as soon as we finish cleaning out the safe, I'm a page you and put in code *'100'* to let you know that we straight, so you can gon' head and dip and meet us at a designated spot," V explained as June and I listened intently.

"If I gotta stay wit' da bitches, I'm a need somebody wit' me to watch my back and to drive da getaway car," June required, as I felt the plan was definitely coming together. "If somebody gotta watch my back and it ain't one o' y'all, I want my lil' nigga Quick in on dis."

Lil' Quick was my cousin who is two years my junior and very quick tempered, quick to curse a bitch out and quick to lay a nigga down. He had been on a few capers with us over the past year, but his specialty was stealing cars. He had been driving ever since he was twelve when he used to steal his mother's car and joyride around the neighborhood. Then he graduated to stealing everybody else's car and joyriding. He had never breathed a word about our capers, so I didn't have to worry about him saying anything. Even if something went wrong, I didn't think he would break. Quick was a young nigga with a heart of stone, though he had a baby-face that made him look younger than he really was. He was 5'10, which was tall for his age, but only weighed a buck-o-five (105 pounds) soaking wet with bricks in his pockets. Despite his small weight, he kept big ass pistols and his cold eyes held the gleam of a killer which intimidated most people, except me and my boys, whom he respected because he'd witnessed us put in major work. The more I thought about it, the better the idea sounded, so I agreed to call him.

"Aiight, but all we gon' tell him is that we want him to drive," I told my partners while rising from the chair and heading toward the kitchen.

I blew a roach off of the wall and stepped on it, hearing it squash with a slight pop sound. After shaking it free of my shoe, I dialed Quick's number. While waiting for someone to answer, I looked around V's kitchen noticing several roaches crawling on the sink, the stove and a few were scurrying around on the floor. I covered the mouthpiece and yelled to V, "Y'all need to exterminate this mutha-fucka."

Just then, my Aunty Mattie answered the phone and told me Quick wasn't home, so I told her I would call back later. I hung up and dialed another number and waited for an answer.

"Hello?"

"Sup Baby?"

"Who is this?" Kinya asked. I took the phone away from my ear and looked at it like I couldn't believe what I was hearing.

"Fuck you mean, who is this? Who you think it is?" I shot back.

"Mike, I. was. joking....Baby you know ain't nobody else callin' here for me," Kinya said using my real name, something she does to try to soften me up. "Why you ain't been callin' me back? I know yo' mama told you I been callin'."

"I been busy as shit," I lied and she knew I was lying, but she went along with it.

"Oh. Ok, I been missin' you though," she spoke sweetly.

I listened for a minute then interrupted, "Baby, listen, I'm about to make a real big move sometime soon and if everything come out like I plan, I'm gon' be straight. Baby *we* gon' be straight. I finally got a chance to come up and I'm gon' take advantage of this shot. Either I'm getting ready to get paid, or I'm gon' die tryin'. This is my time right here. If all this shit comes together, me and you gon' be on top believe that." I told her and awaited her response.

"Baby please don't do nothin' that could cause you to get into trouble, or cause you to get hurt. I don't know what I would do if somethin' happen to you. We gon' be alright like we are, you ain't gotta do nuthin dangerous. Mike, please," Kinya spoke with genuine concern.

"Baby I been takin' penitentiary and graveyard chances all my life. This ain't nothin' but anotha chapter in that book. You gotta understand somethin', real niggas do what they have to do, fake niggas only do what they can." I replied confidently.

"Baby, just remember you got somebody that care about you right here. But I see you ain't gon' change yo' mind, I just want you to be careful." Kinya pleaded.

I heard the sincerity in her words and at that moment, I knew Kinya would be the one I would share my fortune with. That is, *if* everything went as planned.

"Baby, when am I gon' see you?" Kinya asked.

"When you gon' have the house to yo' self?"

"Why I gotta have the house to myself? Nicole don't run nothin', I pay rent too," Kinya snipped.

Nicole was Kinya's roommate who was always in everybody's business. She didn't like me and I couldn't stand her ass either. Even from the first time we met, we almost had a physical altercation. Kinya had invited me over one night and when I got there, Kinya wasn't there. She had stepped out for a minute. When I rang the doorbell, it was answered by a tall, overweight, drag queen looking bitch. Apparently she had looked through the peephole and saw me standing there. The front door flew open and she stood there with one hand on her hip and a frown on her face that made her even uglier than she already was. As she looked at me like I was at the wrong apartment or something. She said, "Can I help you?"

"Is Kinya here?" I asked, trying to keep my cool.

"No." she said and slammed the door in my face.

*No this bitch didn't.* I thought to myself as my anger rose.

I knocked on the door this time instead of ringing the bell.

The door flew open a second time and she said, "Excuse you, do you seem to have a problem understanding the word 'no' or something?"

I shot back, "Nah, I ain't got no problem, you the one wit' the mutha-fuckin' problem slammin' the door all in a nigga face an' shit. You 'on know me and I don't know you, but that won't stop a nigga from puttin' a foot in yo' disrespectful ass for that foul-ass shit you just did."

"Look, Capane...Captain or whatever yo' name is... Kinya ain't here and I suggest you get the hell away from my door before I call the police on yo' nappy-headed ass," she stated in a threatening manner.

I heard a voice behind me say, "Nicole. Don't start that stupid ass shit tonight. I told you he was on his way over here. Damn, I didn't go nowhere but to the store and now I hear you talkin' 'bout callin' the police and shit. What happened?" Kinya asked as she walked up carrying a grocery bag.

"Ain't nothin'. Yo' girl just on her period or somethin'," I said to Kinya, laughing my way inside the apartment.

"Fuck you," Nicole said.

"And fuck you too, punk," I replied as I walked past her.......

Yep, that was my first and last impression of Kinya's roommate-from-hell. She had threatened to call 'those folks', so I tried to avoid that bitch at all cost.

"Fuck Nicole, wit' her man lookin' ass. You know I ain't comin' over there while she home," I replied, continuing my conversation with Kinya while watching a roach watch me like we were in a Mexican standoff or some shit.

"Uh-uh, you know you wrong for that. You ain't have to call her that," Kinya said laughing beause she knew it was true.

"Look, I'm gon' holla at you later aight. I gotta handle some biness, ok baby."

"Ok, Mike. Please be careful," Kinya's voice urged with compassion.

"Always, baby, always." I replied reassuringly.

We said our goodbyes and hung up. I made it my mission to stomp that bold ass roach before exiting the kitchen. When I re-entered the living room June and V were arguing as usual about some nonsense. After discussing the minor details of the caper such as where we would meet, who would meet me and V and how much duct tape we would need, June and I left V to babysit baby Tasmania. I went home and June went to his two-bedroom sardine can as well.

Quick had called me back the same night I had phoned him from V's. He said he couldn't wait for me to call him back because he knew my call was about getting some money. I told him we needed him to grab a car and be on stand-by. He said it was already a done deal.

Two weeks went by without us hearing a peep from Dee. We began to think she had changed her mind until one Friday evening June and I were on V's living room floor playing Nintendo with Lil' Jay when the call came in. V answered the phone when it rung.

"Yeah."

"Hey sexy. You miss me?" Dee spoke.

"Damn, I thought you had forgot a nigga," V replied.

"Nah, baby never that. I just didn't wanna be seen wit' choo before this shit jump off. Feel me?"

"Yeah, I can dig that. So what's the deal?"

"Y'all in luck. This shit can't get no sweeter," Dee said.

"Why you say that?" V asked.

"Cause, the girls went by theyself, y'all ain't gotta worry about nobody followin' em. I guess he startin' to feel comfortable," Dee reported.

"How you know?" V asked.

"Cause he told me."

"Oh, he just come outta the blue and gave you that info?"

"Nah, he tried to get me to go to Lake Norman wit' him today, so I asked him where his bitch was at. He told me that her and Bridgette left this morning and wouldn't be back 'til Sunday night. I picked him and asked if his partner Donte was going too, because one of my girls was wantin' to holla at him if he was still town. That's when he told me they went by they self," Dee explained.

V listened before asking, "So what you gon' do? You goin' up there?"

"Nah, I told him I'm on my period. You know that's the quickest way to make a nigga leave yo' ass alone," Dee laughed.

"You ain't never lied." V confirmed.

"Y'all gone be ready when they get back?" Dee asked.

"Nah, we just been sittin' round for the last two weeks waitin' on yo' ass to call for nothin'," V responded sarcastically.

"So, I'mma see you tonight?" Dee asked.

"Hell nah, you ain't bleedin' on me." V said.

"Boy you know I was lyin' when I told him that. I'on do no nasty ass shit like that. I'll leave that up to them lil' rats you be fuckin' wit," Dee retorted in an angry tone.

"You got that. You got that, damn. Hit me later, I gotta get some things together so we can handle this biness. Aiight?" V replied.

After he hung up, he came into the living room with a disappointed look on his face. Then all of a sudden he broke into a big ass smile.

"Y'all niggas ready to get paid?" V relayed to us what Dee had told him.

We were more than ready.

***

The day Bridgette and her friend were due to arrive, it rained and I mean it rained hard. It was a damn good day for a killin'.

When we arrived at Meka's crib early that Sunday morning, Dee was already there waiting. We had told Quick to meet us there around noon, so we sat around and kicked it for a while before we got down to business. I contemplated on whether or not to put a gun in Quick's hand, but knowing him he would already have one. Or two. We checked and double-checked to make sure we had everything. We had two large black duffel bags that contained four rolls of duct tape, four black ski masks, gloves and four black sweat suits. Pistols were fully loaded and we had extra rounds just in case. Quick arrived around 12:30. I heard his loud ass mouth even before I could see him. June, V and I were seated in Meka's den, when he entered the house.

"Damn, this shit tight. This yo' shit? You the one who fuck wit' Junebug, huh?" Quick was questioning Meka, but I didn't hear her answer him. Either she was nodding silently or she was ignoring him.

When Dee heard the voice, she came out of Meka's room and sat on V's lap. As Meka and Quick entered the den, Meka told Dee to follow her back to the room. Quick saw me and yelled across the room, "What up big cuz."

June looked at the hyped Quick and questioned, "Damn, young nigga why you hollerin' an' shit?"

"Sup fat boy. I'm surprised you ain't eatin' somethin'?" Quick said as he playfully rubbed June's baldhead.

Dee stuck her head back in the door and asked if anybody wanted something to drink. Nobody wanted anything so she disappeared back into Meka's room.

"D-a-a-a-m. Baby girl voice is fucked-up. She fine as shit though. V, you fuckin' that?" Quick asked.

"Nigga, what you think?" V responded.

"I think I wanna fuck her red ass. That's what I think" Quick claimed as he simulated hitting Dee from the back and spanking her ass making us all laugh.

"Nigga sit yo' lil' happy ass down so I can put you up on what's happenin'," I said to my cousin.

I told him that he was going up in the house with us. He seemed glad to know that he was going to be part of the action and not just driving. I told him his role and he listened intently.

"What kind of car you get?" June asked Quick.

"You know I 'on steal nothing but Chevy's," Quick replied, as he and June went to look out the window at the stolen car.

Meanwhile, Dee and Meka were in Meka's room gossiping. Meka was standing in front of the mirror putting on lipstick. Dee was sitting on the bed.

"Girl, that nigga 'Pone sexy as shit, ain't he?" Dee commented.

"Uh-huh. You see how he be lookin' at me?" Meka complimented herself.

"No. But I see the way he be lookin' at me though," Dee shot back with equal the amount of vanity.

"Well, I hate to bust your lil' bubble, but I heard he don't even like red-bones," Meka said.

"Well, I happen to know that he don't like females who ain't got no ass either," Dee retaliated. Meka sucked her teeth and rolled her eyes ghetto-style as Dee continued, "Kinya said, she think he stole his dick from a horse." She laughed.

Dee crossed her legs to try to soothe the sudden ache that had erupted between her thighs just from the thought. Dee's comments forced Meka to stop applying her lipstick and look at Dee in the mirror.

"She told you that?" Meka asked.

"Yeah and she say he be goin' on for so long sometimes she have to tell him to stop," Dee said as she shifted positions on the bed.

Meka felt her nipples stiffen at the mere thought that it might be true.

"What's up wit' you and June?" Dee tried to change the subject.

"He aiight, but he ain't nobody I want to wake up to every mornin'," Meka replied with a twisting hand gesture.

"You still seein' Shawn and Corey?" Dee asked.

"Yep."

"What about Travis?"

"Yep."

"And what's the nigga name who house I took you to in Firestone?" Dee asked.

"Oh, you talkin' about Candy Man." Meka volunteered.

"Why you call him Cany Man?"

"'Cause ain't nann nigga sweeter. All you gotta do is give him a lil' head every once in a while and he kick out like a slot machine," Meka explained and then added, "I got all flavors, a pretty boy, a pay master and that thug-ass-nigga sittin' out there."

"Girl, you just better be careful," Dee warned to her friend.

"I'm on top of mine. You know if they ain't payin', they ain't playin'." Meka said as she gave Dee a high-five.

Dee had told us that the girls were due to arrive between eleven and midnight. So, around eight o'clock we started getting prepared. We all changed into our sweat suits. We even had one for Quick. Everybody's fit perfectly, except for Quick's.

"Yo, these pants too long." Quick complained like we were going to the *BET Awards* or something."

"Well, roll the mutha-fuckas up. It ain't like you ass finna go to the club," V said impatient to any further whining.

"Quick, you strapped?" I asked.

"You betta believe that." Quick replied as he lifted his sweatshirt to reveal the butt of a nine-millimeter.

June, V and I stuffed our pistols in our waists, put our gloves and ski masks in our pockets and sat down to listen to Quick tell war stories. At ten o'clock we were ready to roll, so Quick took the duffel bags to the car as June and V said their goodbyes. I stressed to Meka how important it was for to be at the designated meeting spot on time because timing was everything. She said that she understood and I hoped she did.

## Chapter Four – Layin' 'Em Down

We hurried through the rain and piled into the stolen car. June and V got into the back seat and I sat up front with Quick. As we got onto I-85, the car was silent. The only sounds to be heard were the squeak of the windshield wipers and the sound of the tires on the wet concrete…..no one uttered a word. Everybody was caught up in his own thoughts and the silence felt eerie as I watched the other cars on the highway that we passed. Adrenaline was pumping and nerves were being stilled. Quick reached down to grab a half smoked blunt that was in the ashtray, but he looked at me and changed his mind. Instead, he inserted a cd and turned the volume down to a decent level so the music wouldn't blare from the speakers. After a few seconds, I heard Scarface rapping about some gangster shit. I was mentally going over the game plan and making sure we had all angles covered and nothing was left to chance. The melodic rhythm and explicit lyrics were getting me hyped and I could tell the others were feeling the same way. I looked in the rearview and saw June and V slowly nodding their heads to the rhythm of the music as if they were being hypnotized.

We got off on the Sugar Creek exit, made a right and stopped at the light that led into the Hidden Valley neighborhood. V had taken me by Bridgette's house earlier in the week so I knew exactly where the house was and how it was laid out, therefore I was giving Quick directions.

After we made the turn into the neighborhood and followed Pondella Drive to Cinderella Lane, we made a right on Cinderella and drove until we reached Snow White Lane, Bridgette's street. We slowly cruised past Bridgette's house and saw that all of the lights were out. Bridgette's house was located near a dead-end so there would practically be no traffic we would have to worry about. At Meka's house, the question was posed about what if someone came to the house before we paged June. It was understood that anyone visiting Bridgette's house while June and Quick were there would have to be duct taped. This was our payday and nothing was going to stop it. Any surprises would have to be dealt with. We had come too far to turn back..

We had it planned out so Quick and V would hop the back fence and go in first through the back door. Once they were in, June and I would enter the front door. Bridgette didn't have a dog or an alarm, so there shouldn't have been any problems.

Once we passed Bridgette's house, we turned around and cruised back up the street. There was a park located across the street from Bridgette's house, so Quick backed into the park and parked near a dumpster. Dee told us that Bridgette and her friend would be driving a white Jeep Cherokee, so that's what we were on the lookout for. Quick killed the lights and deadened the engine. From our vantage point, we could see any car coming or going and we also had a clear view of Bridgette's house.

For what seemed like an eternity, the only sounds that could be heard were the pity-pat of rain drops on the Chevy's roof and the steady breathing of four money-thirsty young niggas.

"Damn, where these bitches at?" Quick asked, sounding impatient. I checked my watch and saw that it was eleven forty-five. I was being patient. I was prepared to wait all night if I had to. Nothing was going to stop this from being my payday. About twenty minutes later, June finally spoke and said, "I gotta piss."

"Me too," Quick followed suit.

June and Quick stood outside the car in the rain pissing. Quick got back in first and as soon as June opened the door to get in, a white Cherokee with two females in it drove past and they never looked our way.

"Yo, it's them," I said to everyone and heard them shift around in the seats. We watched as the girls pulled up and parked under the covered carport which doubled as a garage. I glanced up and down the street to make sure they weren't being followed and nobody was on the street—the streets were silent. Perfect. We watched as the driver got out and covered her head with a folded newspaper to prevent her 'do' from getting wet. She had a shopping bag in one of her hands when she ran to the front door and opened it with a key. The passenger remained seated in the jeep.

"Damn, what them hoes doing'?" I asked myself aloud. After a few seconds, we saw the light above the side door in the carport pop-on, then the side door opened. The driver came out and helped the passenger with more shopping bags. Apparently they didn't have the key to the side door, so the driver went in through the front so she could let her friend in without getting wet. When they had finished unloading the bags, we sat still for a few seconds before getting out.

Once they were inside the house, I said, "Let's go get this money."

All four doors simultaneously opened and closed then we jogged through the rain toward Bridgette's house. June was carrying the duffel bags, which would soon be filled with money and dope. I paused to look up and down the street and saw that the street was still deserted. We all had on our gloves and as we approached the house, we pulled our masks over our faces to conceal our identities. V and Quick hopped the fence that led into the backyard while June and I slowly creeped inside the carport and posted-up at the side door that the girls had entered. The light above the door was still on, so we were exposed to anyone on the street. June looked at me and I read his eyes. He was concerned about the light also. I put my ear to the door and could hear conversation between the two females. I assumed they were in the kitchen or nearby. We were waiting for V and Quick to make their entrance before we made a move.

After what seemed like an eternity, but in actuality it was only a few seconds, we heard the sound of the back door being smashed. As soon as we heard it, we followed suit and kicked in the side door.

When V crashed the back door, he and Quick rolled up on the women like Desert Storm. The women screamed at the sight of these two crazy niggas dressed in all black, wearing ski masks and waving pistols. One of the women was standing near the refrigerator, the other was seated at the dining table with a shopping bag on her lap. V recognized the woman near the refrigerator as Bridgette, Big Tone's cousin. So, the other one had to be the Connecticut nigga's bitch. The woman who was seated began to entertain the thought of trying to make it through the side door which was located directly behind her, but that thought died before it could began when she witnessed that door come crashing in and two more niggas in all black rushed in, also waving pistols and yelling demands.

"Bitch shut the fuck up." Quick said as he grabbed Bridgette and pushed her toward the living room. The woman who was seated at the table was still whimpering.

"Bitch shut up, it's too late to be cryin' an shit," I said as I grabbed a fistful of her hair and shoved her into the living room also.

"Sit down and don't say shit." V said as the women sat on the couch. June began duct taping their ankles tightly, then he taped their wrists behind their backs. Quick was busy searching the house to make sure no one else was there. When June finished taping Bridgette and her friend, they were laying on their sides, sobbing with trembling lips.

"Look, ain't nobody gon' get hurt if y'all do what a nigga tell y'all to do. But I swear to God if one of y'all bitches try some slick shit, somebody gon' find both of y'all in this mutha-fucka stankin'. Ya heard me?" I said before adding, "Y'all know why a nigga up in here. Where that shit at?"

Bridgette cried, "In-my-purse."

"Yo, check them purses and them bags," I said to Quick and June.

June pulled a small wad out of one of the purses, an unexpected bonus, while Quick came up empty.

I grabbed Bridgette by her throat forcefully and screamed, "Bitch, you think a nigga playin' wit' choo?."

Her eyes closed and she finally confessed, "It's in the hall closet on the shelf."

Before she could finish her sentence I was already on my way to the hall closet. I searched each shelf, tossing out whatever was occupying the space. When I reached the top shelf, I saw a red gym bag. I took the bag off the shelf and unzipped it. Bingo. There were five individually wrapped blocks of white powder. I tore a small hole in one of the bags and tasted its contents. My tongue was immediately numb.

"Yo, I got it." I yelled back down the hall.

June and Quick were still searching the kitchen when I walked back to the living room.

"Yo, I said I got it." I told June and Quick as I held up the gym bag. I opened one of our duffel bags and put the gym bag in it. "Tape that bitch mouth and take her in the bedroom," I told V and June and made sure to watch as they taped Bridgette's mouth and lifted her in the air. Her eyes widened and she was sobbing behind the tape and I knew exactly what she was thinking. Since she was the only one being taken to the bedroom she was thinking the worst, but little did she know we only took money and dope. We didn't take pussy. That wasn't our M. O.. I simply wanted her out of the room so there wouldn't be any unnecessary noise when we made ole girl call her man.

Once June and V had dumped Bridgette on her bed, V came back into the living room while June stayed with Bridgette. I lifted the girl up into a seated position and explained to her what I wanted her to do as she started crying.

"Bitch, you wanna die don't 'choo." I yelled as I cocked my pistol back as a warning.

The girl's mind started whirling until she finally settled on the thought that no nigga was worth her life. "Okay, okay," she whimpered.

Semi-patiently I waited for her to calm her nerves enough to make the call without showing suspicion.

"Bitch, I swear I'll blow yo' brains out all over this phone if I even think you tryin' to get slick. I'on give a fuck about you, that hoe in there or yo' nigga. So try me." V said as she felt the cold steel of the pistol V was pressing into her forehead.

She relayed the telephone number to me and I tried twice to dial it, but I was finding out how difficult it was to try to dial a phone number with gloves on. After having had to hang-up in mid-dial because the glove made me misdial, I finally got it right and held the phone up to the girl's right ear as V held the gun to her left temple. Surprisingly, she held a calm conversation with her man.

"Silk, what 'choo doing?" She said to her dude. "Yeah, I'm at Bridgette's—Come get me. –I'm ready now. –We got back 'bout an hour ago. –She in the bathroom. – I'm waitin' aiight. –Ok—Bye."

As soon as I hung up the phone, she broke down crying and informed, "He on his way."

I wasn't going be burned with more of her sobbing, so I taped her mouth and lifted her off the floor. Quick and I carried her into Bridgette's room and tossed her on the bed beside her friend. June was in the closet searching for who knows what.

"Help me hog tie these hoes," I suggested to Quick.

Together we commenced to tape the girls' ankles and wrists together so they couldn't budge an inch. I told June to stay in the bedroom with the women because V, Quick and I were going to post up and wait for Silk. I snatched a pillowcase off of one of Bridgette's pillows and hurried through the house toward the side door.

I told Quick, "Cut off the light over the door and post-up right here. If somethin' go wrong, just come out blastin', dig?"

"No question." Quick replied as he clicked-off the safety on his gun so it would be ready.

V and I exited the side door and stepped into the carport. It was still raining, so I knew Silk would want to pull into the garage as opposed to parking in the driveway out in the rain. I eyed the distance between Bridgette's Jeep and the right edge of the carport and saw that he would have plenty of space to park. I also wanted him to park on the right side of the Jeep so he couldn't see the damage of the side door from where we had kicked it in.

After making sure everything was straight, V and I ducked down behind a large tool cart that was situated inside the carport, near the back and waited for our gold mine to arrive. We didn't have too wait long. It was only a few short minutes before we heard the sound of tires on wet pavement approaching the house. Carefully, we listened to the car slowing down as it neared Bridgette's drive way and headed into the carport just as we figured. We could see the headlights as the car pulled beside the Jeep and parked. The engine and the lights died at the same time. We heard the car door open and someone was talking. I could tell it was the driver because of the direction in which the voice was coming from. I was hoping this nigga was on the phone, but as soon as I entertained the thought, I heard another voice.

*Damn, this nigga got company.* I thought as I looked at V and I could tell he was thinking the same thing from the way his eyes had widened. He shrugged his shoulders as if to say, *What now?*

I didn't care if this nigga had two busloads of mutha-fuckas with him, his ass was still getting kidnapped regardless. Patiently we waited until we heard both of the car doors shut, before we simultaneously emerged from the darkness to ambush them. I took the driver, which turned out to be Silk, who fit the description Dee had given us to a tee, while V took the passenger. We were on top of them so quickly, they didn't know what had hit them. The element of surprise was our advantage. When Silk saw me with my pistol aimed at his face, he started to say something, "What the…" was the only thing he was able to get out as the passenger at least was able to complete a full sentence, "OH SHIT."

"Nigga, shut the fuck up. Don't say shit." I demanded to Silk.

Thinking we wanted some petty cash and not knowing we already had his coke, he attempted to say, "Yo, Son. The money is in the car…"

Teaching him a lesson about not following my previously stated instructions, I drew back and swung my pistol with blunt force, coming in direct contact with his mouth, breaking three teeth and smashing his gums before he could finish his sentence.

"Bitch-ass nigga, didn't I say shut the fuck up?" I repeated myself.

"A-h-h-h." He cried as he grabbed his mouth where the blow had landed. Quick came out of the house ready for some drama, but there was none. He searched both of the dudes to make sure they weren't strapped. They weren't. Dumb ass niggas.

Quick yelled for June, "Ay, fat boy, com'ere and bring some tape."

June brought two rolls of duct-tape with him into the garage. Once Silk saw Quick and June also dressed in all black and wearing ski masks, he knew his ass was in trouble. June and Quick hog-tied the passenger and taped his mouth just like the women. They dragged him to Bridgette's room and dumped him on the floor. When the passenger saw the two women lying on the bed also hog tied, it was clear to him that this was some serious shit. Bridgette seeing Donte being dropped onto her floor made her further worry about their fate, but she couldn't do anything but cry and pray. Meanwhile, V was taping Silk's wrists in front of him. He left his legs free and he didn't tape his mouth. I pulled the pillowcase from my pocket and put it over his head. He almost fainted from the fear of the unknown. His knees buckled. He didn't know what to expect from us thirsty ass niggas. I took the car keys from Silk's pockets and unlocked the driver's side of the car, opened the door, reached in and unlocked the back door. Once the door was open, V and I tossed Silk's ass onto the floor of the back seat. I tossed V the keys to Silk's BMW and we both climbed into the front. I was on the passenger side while V was behind the wheel. I reached over the seat and started tapping Silk on the forehead with the barrel of my pistol as I threatened him.

"Mutha-fucka, hear my voice and understand me when I speak. You bet'not move a muscle and yo ass bet' not breathe too loud. This ain't nothin' but a jack, but we can turn this shit into a BODY. If you open yo mutha-fuckin' mouth wit' out me askin' yo ass a question, they gon' be scrapin' yo ass off this seat for the next two weeks, ya dig?"

Silk didn't answer, so I struck him with my pistol just hard enough to break his ego. He cried out like a bitch.

"Nigga, I asked if you dig?"

Silk stuttered, "Ye-ye-yeah, I dig, I dig."

"Good. Now shut the fuck up and enjoy the ride."

V and I took off our ski masks and backed out of Bridgette's driveway in Silk's BMW.

The ride to Lake Norman was silent and uneventful. I kept nudging Silk with the gun to make sure he hadn't passed out. Once we reached Silk's exit, we drove to his neighborhood and slowly cruised through his parking lot. Since it was so late, no one was in sight. V parked and ran up to Silk's condo. After trying the first three keys on the key ring, he finally found the one that fit. We already knew this nigga didn't have an alarm but V was hesitant anyway as he opened the front door. He didn't hear a beep so he strolled through the condo to make sure it was empty. Once he was sure no one was inside, he ran back to the car to help me lift Silk form the backseat. We hurried Silk through the breezeway and pushed him inside the condo. Once we had closed the door behind us, we put back on our ski masks and pulled the now blood-stained pillowcase off Silk's head. Silk's eyes adjusted as he became aware of his surroundings. In total shock and disbelief, he couldn't believe what he was seeing. He was standing in his own living room. He blinked twice, thinking it was an illusion, but to his dismay, it was very much real.

I jarred him out of his daze, "Mutha-fucka where the money at?"

Disorientedly looking around was Silk, until I raised my pistol and threatened to swing. He lifted his taped hands in attempt to block the would-be blow and said, "Aight, aight. It's in the safe in the bedroom closet."

We already knew exactly where it was, but we didn't want to go right to the safe without him telling us, for Dee's sake.

We drug him to his bedroom and taped his ankles together. As he lay on the floor, I rummaged through the walk-in closet, throwing clothes out of the way until I found the safe.

"What's the combo?. And it betta open." I told him as I bent down to turn the knob.

I knew Silk was thinking about all of his hard earned money that was getting ready to be taken from him. But at this point I think he would rather had lost his money than his life. And he really believed if he gave up the money, we would let him live. So, he relayed the combination that no other person on this earth knew other than himself. He spoke through the drying blood and broken teeth.

"Thirty-two, twelve, twenty-three."

I turned the knob as he spit out the digits. As I hit '23', that last digit of the combo, I heard a click and the safe popped open. What I saw inside the safe was unbelievable.

\*\*\*

Meanwhile, back at Bridgette's, Quick was in the bedroom with the three duct taped victims taunting them while impatiently pacing the floor.

He yelled to June, "Damn man, they ain't beeped you yet?"

"If dey would've beeped, we wouldn't still be here, ignorant ass nigga," June yelled back.

June had gotten so comfortable that he was rummaging through Bridgette's refrigerator looking for something to make a sandwich with. After he finally found the mayo and bologna, he had as equally of a frustrating time trying to make the sandwich with gloves on, as I had trying to dial the phone.

*** 

I couldn't believe our luck as I stared at stack upon stack of money wrapped in neat bundles.

"Toss me the bag," I instructed to V, as he threw me the black duffel bag we had brought with us.

While I was busy emptying the safe, V had taped Silk's mouth and was walking around the bedroom. He saw a diamond studded Rolex and a matching bracelet on the dresser, yet another bonus. He'd shown them to me before placing them in his pocket. When I was almost done with the safe, V picked up the phone beside the bed and dialed June's pager number. He put in the code '100' all the way across the screen. He then hung up and dialed another number just in case someone would try to get slick and press redial. Silk was watching V as he hung up the phone.

As I finished putting the last stack of money in the bag I told V "Yo, I got all of it. Let's dip." I ran out of the bedroom toward the front door.

V walked over to Silk with fire in his eyes. He tauntingly stood over him and put his pistol to Silk's temple. V looked Silk in his eyes and said, "Tell my punk-ass Daddy I said 'fuck him' when you get to hell. Bitch ass nigga."

Silk looked into V's cold eyes and saw certain death. He knew he was about to die. As V's finger tightened around the trigger, Silk's life flashed before his eyes. All he could do was close his eyes and ask Allah for forgiveness...

V squeezed the trigger and watched as Silk's entire body spasmed in fear. The only thing Silk heard was the sound of a metal-to-metal 'click'. When Silk dared to re-open his eyes, V pushed the clip-release button on his gun and showed Silk that the gun had been empty.

"Bitch-ass-nigga. I should've bodied yo' punk ass." V spewed. He spat in Silk's face before he ran out of the bedroom laughing hysterically and closed Silk's front door, steppin' out into the night.

\*\*\*

June's pager was vibrating. He looked down at the screen and saw '100-100-100-100'. He yelled for Quick, "Yo, dat's dem. Let's bounce."

Quick and June ran back to the stolen Chevy unnoticed, with a duffel bag full of cocaine and a bologna sandwich.

\*\*\*

I was behind the wheel of the BMW as we headed to our rendezvous with Meka. I prayed she was already there waiting on us like we had planned.

## Chapter Five – Layin' Low

We pulled into the Econo Lodge on Sunset Road. We saw Meka standing at the pay phone. When she saw us, she hung up the phone and headed in the direction toward her car. We parked in an empty parking space and got out. I transferred the duffel bag from Silk's car to Meka's and left Silk's doors unlocked. I pocketed Silk's keys as we piled into Meka's ride. V sat up front and I took the back so I could stretch my legs out along the seat. Once we got onto the highway, I rolled down the window and casually tossed Silk's keys out into the darkness. During the ride to Meka's apartment, I couldn't help myself from continuously peeping inside the duffel bag and smiling at our new fortune.

\*\*\*

June and Quick were already inside the apartment with Dee, once we arrived. As soon as we stepped inside, Dee grabbed V and hugged and kissed him with passion. I couldn't tell if she was really happy just to see him, or if she was glad that he had finally made it back with her part of the dough. Either way she was happy.

Meka let us use her bedroom and once the girls had left the room, I closed and locked the door. We'd decided to give Quick an equal share of the money along with Dee, but the yayo was ours. June would look out for Meka. We had the two duffel bags sitting on the bed. Though we already knew that one of them contained five bricks, the big question was 'How much money was in the safe?' Everybody wanted to know, especially me.

I opened the bag with the money in it and poured its contents on the bed. It seemed as if the money wouldn't stop flowing out of the bag. As stack after stack poured out, everybody stared in amazement. June and Quick looked like starving vultures. The money was wrapped in even stacks and bound by rubber bands. 'Dope Boy' rolls as we called them. Evidently, each stack contained the same amount. Quick and I counted one of the stacks and it totaled 2-G's exactly. There were eighty stacks which meant there was $160,000 lying on the bed. Each of us took a pile and began counting, just to make sure. After about thirty minutes of counting, we all added up our totals.

"June, what you get?" I asked.

"I came up with thirty six."

"V, what about you?" I inquired his total.

"Fifty-four."

"I came up with twenty-nine, one of 'em had three G's instead of two," Quick said.

"I counted forty-two right here. June, count that money that Bridgette 'nem had in they purses," I said.

After June finished counting the extra money, he came up with $3,200. We had stung for a total of $164,200, five kilos of cocaine and a diamond Rolex with a matching bracelet. None of the others knew about the jewelry, so V and I decided to keep it and sell it later. After splitting the money five ways, each of us came out with a cash total of a little over 32-grand. None of us had ever seen that much money before, let alone possessed it.

We discussed the risks of spending it before it was safe to do so and I emphasized to Quick how important it was for him to not to do something stupid—at least not until I said it was cool. He said he agreed, but we still didn't feel comfortable with him walking around with that much loot burning his pockets. I suggested that I keep the majority of his share until everything died down. I told him I didn't want Aunt Mattie getting suspicious if she happened to find it.

Quick thought about it for a long time and then finally said, "Aight, I'ma leave you with the 30-G's, but I'ma take the rest for right now. Cuz', you know I trust you with my life, but I'm tellin' y'all, nothin' bet' not happen to my fuckin' money." he finished, while looking at V and June with threatening eyes.

Quick left the apartment in the stolen car with a little less three grand in his pocket, but he knew as long as I was responsible for his share, it was just as good as having money in the bank.

Dee was thoroughly satisfied with her share and clearly knew the repercussions and consequences she would suffer if anyone every found out that she'd help orchestrate the robbery. We didn't have to tell Dee but once. She'd already made plans to stash her share until the time was appropriate.

$128,520 was left after Dee and Quick had gotten theirs. June, V and I decided to take 5-G's each and stash the rest until the streets became quiet. Now we were faced with the dilemma of where to keep the money and the coke.

\*\*\*

Meanwhile, Silk had finally gotten the courage to move after lying still for so long. Once he was sure the jack-boys were gone, he maneuvered his body into a seated position. Since his hands were taped in front of him, he would be free in no time. His mind kept flashing back to those eyes—those cold, death-filled eyes of the robber who had put the empty gun to his head and squeezed the trigger. A million would've, should've, could've scenarios ran through his head as he reached up and slowly peeled the duct-tape off his swollen lips. His teeth were broken and the back of his head throb like shit. But he was alive and that would prove to be a drastic mistake.

*"Them niggas don't know who they fuckin' wit."* He said to himself, while fighting the pain of his puffy lips. He made it to his feet and hopped into the kitchen. After finally cutting through the duct-tape on his wrist with a steak knife, he freed his legs. Silk picked up the phone in the kitchen and dialed a number. *Please someone, please answer the phone...* He thought to himself as he waited and prayed that someone answered.

***

After what seemed like an eternity of silence, Bridgette, Donte and Tonisha heard the sound of the telephone. All three were bound and gagged, so no one could answer. Besides, they were all too terrified to move. Each one was caught up in their own thoughts. Donte was thinking about revenge, Tonisha was praying that her man Silk wasn't hurt and Bridgette was just glad to be alive. All three made promises to God they knew they wouldn't keep once they made it out of this.

***

Silk hung up after nine rings and dialed another number, waited and entered his home number at sound of the beep. After he'd hung up the kitchen phone, he went back into the bedroom and did exactly what we'd anticipated him doing. He picked up the phone beside the bed and pressed redial. The phone rang three times then a recording answered, "Thank you for calling Power 98, the hottest radio station on the air, all the lines are tied up right now…"

Silk slammed the phone in its cradle and sat on the bed staring into space.

Silk was jarred out of his daze by the sound of the phone ringing. He answered and the person on the other end asked, "Did someone page Tone?"

Silk told Big Tone what had happened at his place and at Bridgette's. He advised Tone to go by his cousin's house to check on her. Tone was furious. His main supplier had just gotten jacked and his cousin Bridgette was in danger and possibly hurt.

***

Bridgette heard the footsteps of someone entering her house, headed toward her bedroom. She prayed it wasn't the robbers coming back to finish them off. Hesitantly, she looked up and saw her cousin and two more guys with pistols standing at her bedroom door. She had never been so glad to see someone in her whole life. All she could do was cry.

***

I called Kinya from Meka's and told her that I was stopping through and since it was late, she knew something was up. She asked me what was wrong and if I was in trouble. After I assured her that I was okay and nothing was wrong, she finally calmed down. When Meka and June dropped me off at her apartment, I told June that I would call him and V the next day so we could talk. Dee and V had gone to get a room earlier from Meka's. Kinya was at the door waiting as I approached, apparently she had been looking out for Meka's car. Kinya waved bye to her friend and we entered her apartment quietly so we wouldn't awake Nicole.

Once we were inside her bedroom with the door closed, she finally spoke.

"I hope this means you're staying for a few days, Mr. Always-on-the-Go," she said with a smile referring to the black duffel bag I had in my hand.

"Baby, we gotta talk," I said to her with a serious expression on my face.

I sat her down and laced her with the game and told her 'everything', including the way I felt about her. When I finished, she had tears in her eyes.

"Baby, why you cryin'? I told you I'm finished with the stick-up game. It's my time to shine and I want you to shine with me. Ever since that day that I told you I had big plans and you told me not to do anything that would put myself in jeopardy, I knew you was fo' real, 'cause I heard it in your voice. Baby, I know you might think a nigga ain't nothing but a playa and shit, but straight up, I feel like I found the one when I found you. I ain't never told nobody these things 'cause I ain't never cared about nobody like I care about you. Baby, I'm a man o' my word. Believe it when I tell you, as long as you wit' me and as long as you stay loyal, you ain't gon' never have to want for nothing," I bared my soul as I smiled and ran my fingers through her hair.

She smiled back and replied, "Mike, you just don't know how long I been waitin' to hear you open up and say something like that. Baby, that's why I'm crying. Ever since that night at the hotel when I first met you, I knew it was more to you than just that thugged-out side that everybody else sees. That night you intrigued me to the point where I had to know more. After you made love to me that night I knew that with you was where I wanted to be. I was supposed to leave that night, but I just couldn't, your mysterious persona had me trapped."

"My per- what? Damn, why you always usin' big words on a nigga?" I joked trying to cheer up the mood.

"Boy, you know what I mean," Kinya said as she playfully hit me in the chest.

I wiped the tears off of her cheeks and kissed her.

"Look, I'ma leave this bag with you tomorrow when I dip. Put it in a safe place. My life is in this bag. *Our* life is in this bag. And I want you to look for another crib when you finish your class tomorrow. Aight?"

"Why you want me to move?" she asked.

"Cause its time for me to move outta my mama's house. And you know I can't stay here with you and Nicole. Nicole might put on some Vicky's Secrets one night and try me when you ain't here," I said laughing.

Kinya like the idea of us moving in together. She said she knew the perfect place to go.

By the end of the week Kinya had found a nice two-bedroom apartment in a quiet neighborhood called Delta Crossing on the east side of Charlotte. I gave her the money for the depositing and 3-month's rent. Nicole seemed relieved when Kinya told her she was moving. Kinya even gave her the money for a full month's rent, instead of half. I was more than ready to make the move, because I was beginning to get paranoid about leaving all of that money and dope at her old apartment. A week later, our new apartment was ready and we moved in.

### ONE WEEK LATER...

One week. One week was all it took before I broke my promise to Kinya. I had told her I was finished with the stick-up game, but there I was again, ski-masked up and dressed in the same black sweat suit I had worn when we had robbed Silk. The air reeked of blood and gunpowder. The barrel of my nickel-plated nine was still hot from the three hollow-tips I had pumped into Sharon's head and torso...

Although we were already sitting on five kilos of Peruvian Flake cocaine and more money than any one of us had ever seen, we still decided to touch Yellow Boy. This robbery wasn't even about money. It was personal—a little too personal. The original plan was to kick in the nigga's door and rob him and Sharon for whatever money and valuables they had. Then later return Sharon's things along with a thousand's dollars for her orchestrating everything. But that night something went terribly wrong.

I already knew June had intentions of pistol-whipping Yellow Boy until he looked like the Elephant Man, but June ended up taking it a step further than I expected. After relieving Yellow Boy of nine thousand dollars and a few pieces of jewelry, June started demanding to know where the dope was. We already knew there wasn't any dope in the house, at least not in the safe where the money was. When Yellow Boy adamantly stated that there were no drugs in the house, June used that as an excuse to do something very stupid.

V and I knew June was still upset about what Yellow Boy had done to his mom, but what June did next made me question his sanity.

"Oh, nigga so you tryna buck, huh?" June spat, while bending down where Yellow Boy was laying duct-taped and bleeding profusely. He had multiple lacerations on his head and face that was a result of being struck repeatedly with the butt and barrels of June's and V's pistols.

June stuck the barrel of his pistol in Yellow Boy's mouth and snatched off his mask, revealing his identity. He looked Yellow dead in the eyes and said, "Buck dis, mutha-fucka."

At this point, I knew my partner had lost it. The blast was ear splitting, as blood mixed with brain matter and pieces of Yellow Boy's skull now decorated June's shirt.

Sharon who was duct-taped next to Yellow Boy got splattered on her face and neck with the gore. Witnessing Yellow Boy's brain getting blown out made Sharon go ballistic. She wouldn't stop screaming. V and I couldn't believe June had just done that crazy shit. It caught us completely off-guard.

After a minute or two of panicking, V finally tried to get Sharon to calm down and to stop all of that damn screaming. Realizing what he's just done, June fled from the house leaving me and V with a dead body and a screaming witness to deal with. Now, we were faced with a fucked up decision. We could've offered Sharon money and threatened her not to say anything and prayed she kept her mouth shut and didn't bear witness to five-0 because that would mean an automatic death penalty for us. Or, we could get rid of her. Without as much as a second thought, I silently cursed June as I pushed V aside and let off three quick shots which ripped into Sharon's flesh with sickening thuds.

After fleeing the robbery/murder scene, we finally caught up with June who was sitting behind the wheel of the stolen Chevy we had borrowed from Quick.

Once on the highway, I looked over at June from where I was seated on the passenger side and just shook my head in disgust. The car was silent as we cruised down I-85 toward the projects where Quick was waiting with Meka's car so we could make the switch. No words were spoken even after we had changed clothes and switched cars. On the way to my new apartment, I was in the back seat while June drove and V sat silently riding shotgun. What should have been a simple jack had turned into a senseless double homicide that no one seemed to want to talk about. What was done was done and we couldn't undo it. I mean, I leaved my niggas like brothers and would go all out with them no matter what. But, I had made my mind up—that was my last stick-up. No matter how much money and dope was on the line. From then on, I would let the opportunity pass.

June wanted to keep Yellow Boy's jewelry, for God only knows what reason. But we decided to get rid of it so the evidence couldn't link us to the crime. We gave June's mom the 9-grand we took from Yellow Boy for compensation. She questioned where it came from, not really caring because she was going to accept it regardless. Of course we didn't tell her, or any other soul for that matter, of what had happened. After the night the incident took place, it was like it had never happened.

After the situation with Yellow Boy, we wound all the way down and layed as low as possible. June moved in with Meka and started playing house, while V remained at home with his mom and Jay.

World on the street was that the jack-boys who had slumped Yellow Boy were the same ones who had jacked a high-powered nigga from up north named Silk. Now Silk was out for revenge. Everybody was a suspect. Dee had been questioned and threatened by Silk and his mob, but she kept her game face on and continued to see him occasionally, so she wouldn't seem suspicious. She reported everything she heard back to V.

## Chapter Six – Barkin' up Da' Wrong Tree

"Southern Bell. How may I help you?" said the operator.

"Yes, my name is Tonisha Childs, I would like to know if I can receive a print-out of all the telephone numbers that were called from my house within the last week?"

"Ma'am, you can request that information from customer service, please hold while I transfer you."

While Tonisha was holding, Silk walked in the room.

"What they talkin' 'bout, Ma?" Silk asked while displaying his gold teeth he had just recently gotten put in to replace the ones I had broken with my pistol.

"I'm on hold" she replied, then the customer service rep picked up. Tonisha spoke back into the receiver "Hello, yes. Childs. C-H-I-L-D-S. Yes. My number is 704-836-0215," Tonisha said to the customer service assistant.

"Oh. Can you do that for me please? Well, actually all I really need is the list for one day," Tonisha explained.

"What day is that Ma'am?" asked the operator.

"Monday, the fourteenth," Tonisha replied.

"Please hold."

While Tonisha was on the phone, Silk rummaged through his closet and found the two shoeboxes he was looking for. He opened them and took out the two mini-Uzi'she had stashed there. Holding them in each hand, he pictured himself pressing them against the back of the robbers' heads and emptying the clips. Yeah, he would definitely be bringing his "twins" out of retirement very soon.

Tonisha was still on the phone with the telephone company and she had written down eight numbers. "Thank you so much," she said to the operator and hung up before relaying to Silk, "Baby, they gave me eight numbers for that day and the times the calls were placed. The first call was made at 1:03 AM, the number is 704-555-8601. The second call was made at 1:05 AM to 704-888-9734, which is the radio station and the next number is Bridgette's. So the 555 number has to be the one they dialed. Want me to dial it?"

Silk nodded and waited as Tonisha dialed the first telephone number the operator had given her.

"It's a pager, what you want me to do?" she asked.

"Put the number in," Silk replied and watched as Tonisha entered their telephone number with the code #69, hoping whoever the pager belonged to would think it was a booty call and call right back.

***

Dee and V were at June and Meka's playing spades and smoking weed.

"I got four and a maybe," June said.

"I got two. Give us seven," said Meka as she made their bid.

"I ain't got shit," Dee said looking at a sorry ass hand.

"Ain't nothin'. We'll go board this time," V concluded.

Halfway through the hand, Dee played a diamond and June cut it as he was busy checking his pager trying to place the number he just saw. The code was #69.

"Nigga, why you reniggin'? You just cut a diamond, now you gone play one?" V said to June.

The mysterious page had thrown June off his game. He was trying to figure out what female he knew with an "836" prefix.

June asked everybody at the table "Anybody know what area 836 is?"

"That's Lake Norman," Dee answered.

"Lake Norman?" June asked suspiciously.

Dee had a look of concern on her face and asked. "What's the number?"

"836-0215," June replied.

"Oh Shit. That's Silk's number." Dee exclaimed with fear in her eyes.

For the next two days, June was receiving beeps from strange numbers, so he finally decided to trash that pager and buy a new one. June was at Dial Page on East Moorehead Street getting his new pager activated. While he was there, he decided to buy two more and add them to the same account. He would do it the same way his old associated and fellow stick-up kid, Goldie had done for him a few months back.

One particular day June didn't have any ID. But he wanted a pager and he had the money to pay for it. Since Gold was already getting one, he told the saleswoman to add another to his account. All he told June was to make sure he was on time every month for the payment. That was six months earlier. Today, June left the pager company with three pagers, a new one for himself and one each for V and me. He decided he would need them when the time came to set up shop. June called everyone who had the old pager number and gave them the new one.

\*\*\*

"'Nisha, don't your cousin still work for Dial Page? I know '555' is a Dial Page number. Call her and ask her if she can find out who that pager number belongs to for me. Tell her I'll look out." Silk said.

"Aight. Matter of fact, she at work right now. Reach me the phone," Tonisha replied.

Silk handed her the phone and she dialed.

"Dial Page South Park, can I help you?" a female voice answered.

"Rhonda, hey girl. You busy?" Tonisha asked her cousin.

"Nah, chile you know ain't nothin' happenin' up here. What's up cuz?"

"Rhonda, I need a favor. Well actually, Silk need a favor, he said he'll look out."

At the mention of Silk's name, Rhonda knew she was about to get blessed for whatever favor she was about to do. She hoped and prayed that whatever it was Silk needed done, she would be able to do. Rhonda had seen a pair of boots in Nine West, two doors down from where she worked while she was on her lunch break. She would *kill* for those boots.

"What Silk need?" Rhonda asked.

"He want you to look up this number and let him know who it belongs to."

*Damn, this is easy.* Rhonda thought to herself as she logged into her computer.

"What's the number?" she asked once she was granted access.

Tonisha relayed the number and waited.

"Somebody name Johnathan Goldsmith," Rhonda said, as she looked at the screen.

"You got an address?" Tonisha asked.

"Yeah, you ready? It's 3201 Summit Avenue, Apartment six." Rhonda said as she read what was printed on her screen.

"Thank you, cousin-in-law." she heard Silk yell in the background.

"Tell him I said, 'anytime,'" Rhonda was happy to reply.

"Thanks girl. I'll be by there before you get off, aight." Tonisha said as she hung up.

Rhonda was overjoyed.

"Nine West here I come." she mutter to herself with her mind on the money Silk was going to pay her, without realizing she had just started a war.

Silk picked up the phone as soon as Tonisha hung it up. He paged Big Tone and waited for him to return the call. As soon as the phone rung, Silk snatched it up.

"Yo."

"Yeah, what up playa?" Big Tone said in a very deep voice.

"Yo, son, I got a name," Silk informed.

"Who is it?" Tone questioned with revenge on his mind.

"Some nigga named Johnathan Goldsmith."

"Somethin' told me that bitch-ass nigga Goldie had somethin' to do with this shit."

"Yo, you know who this kid is?" Silk asked in amazement.

"Yeah and this shit is right up his alley. Everybody know he a jack-boy."

"You know where this nigga hangs out at?" Silk asked.

"Yeah, he run with them niggas off West Boulevard. It ain't hard to find dem niggas," Tone replied with anger in his voice.

"Yo, money, we 'bout to set them niggas' asses ablaze. Feel me?" Silk charged.

"No doubt. Just let me know when you ready to move on them niggas," Tone expressed that he was down.

" I'mma make a few calls to my niggas up north and let 'em know I'm about to go to war. I'll hit you back, aiight."

"Bet."

Silk made another phone call, this time to Connecticut. A familiar voice answered the phone.

"Peace." said the voice on the other end.

Silk spoke, "As-Salamu Alaykum"

"Wa-Alaykum Asalaam. Who dis?" asked the voice.

"This is Najeeh," Silk told his fellow Muslim, giving his Government.

"Sup Ock? I heard about your little demise down there. You come up with anything yet?"

"Yeah, I'm about ready to handle that. Is my brother over there?" Silk asked.

"Yeah, hold on."

Silk held the phone, waiting for his older brother Rasheed to pick up.

"Peace, 'Sup Ock?" Rasheed greeted as he picked up the phone.

"Peace. What you up to?" Silk questioned.

"Ain't shit. Just spittin' some science at these fools. Man, what you goin' through down there? I told you about tryna carry them cats soft. You did exactly what I told you *not* to do. I told you I did time in N.C. And I met some 'real' dudes while I was down there. Everybody down south ain't green bruh." Rasheed told his younger brother.

"Yeah, I know. I slipped. But they 'bout to feel me though," Silk promised.

"Listen Naj, I mean Silk, or whatever you callin' yourself down there, you know we got your back. Just let me know when you ready to strike and we on our way. We lost a lot of money in that shit and I want mine back in blood." Rasheed said.

"Meet me at my crib on the lake, Friday at about noon, aight?" Silk stated.

"Bet. Me and Hasaan will be there. Who else you got?"

"Donte and my man, Big Tone. That's Bridgette's cousin. They ready to roll right now."

"Y'all got tools?" Rasheed asked.

"You know I'm strapped, money."

"Yeah? Well you wasn't strapped when you got your grill crashed," Rasheed said.

"I told you I got caught slippin'."

"Yeah, you *did* get caught slippin' and it could've been worse. Thank Allah for that"

"I'ma see y'all Friday at my crib, right?"

"No doubt."

"Peace."

"Peace."

Silk hung up the phone, smiling to himself at the thought of sweet revenge.

\*\*\*

Goldie and two of his flunkies were in Gastonia at one of his girlfriends's houses. They'd just finished robbing some niggas on Nations Ford Road at a dice game. Goldie decided it would be best if they stayed there for a couple of days. Word was out that somebody had recognized one of his boys and called the police to report the robbery. So Goldie decided to lay low. After all, the police would never find them in Gastonia. They were safe.

*** 

Big Tone and Donte had been hanging out on West Boulevard all week trying to find out the whereabouts of Goldie and his boys. A break finally came when an associate of Tone's told him about a party in Gastonia that Goldie would definitely be attending on Saturday night. Tone called Silk.

"Yeah," Silk answered.

"Sup? It's Tone."

"What up son? Y'all hear anything?"

"Yeah, word is da niggas 'sposed to be on the run," Tone said.

"Fuck that. I don't give a fuck if them bitch ass niggas run to China, I'm gone be in a bowl of rice waitin' on they ass. Them niggas can't hide from me." Silk screamed.

"Yo, calm down dog. I know where they 'sposed to be at Saturday night," Tone replied. "In Gastonia, at a party," he added.

"Picture that. Them niggas partying with my cheddar, huh?" Silk said.

"All I know is, I'm ready to put these niggas' in a wet T-shirt contest." Tone remarked.

"Aiight, listen. I want you and Donte to meet me at my tilt Friday afternoon. I want you to meet somebody."

"I'm there" said Tone as they hung up.

***

**Friday**

"As-Salamu Alaykum." Rasheed greeted his younger brother with the traditional Muslim embrace as he entered Silk's condo.

"Wa Alaykum-Salaam," Silk embraced both Rasheed and Hasaan.

Rasheed was 6'2" and built like a football player. He and Silk could pass for twins. The only difference was their complexion; Silk was a shade darker than his brother. They stood eye to eye. Hasaan was an even 6 feet, his complexion was high yellow and he had short, naturally wavy hair. At first glance, one would think he was Hispanic. Both Rasheed and Hasaan were well respected in Connecticut for their status in the Dope Game and most of all, for the fact that when someone fucked with their money or their family, their understanding was zero. And in this situation, someone had violated both.

"What's up lil' bruh? I see you still keep the crib tight," said Rasheed.

"You gotta give 'Nisha the props for that," Silk replied.

"Where she at anyway? She ain't here is she?" Hasaan asked.

"Nah, I sent her out for a lil' while"

"Da-a-a-a-a-mn son. I just noticed this shit. Smile. Yo, them shits is mad tight" Rasheed said complimenting Silk on his gold teeth.

"Word is bond, how many you got? Let me see," Hasaan said.

"I got three," Silk replied as he flashed back to that night I had crashed his grill with my pistol. He began to feel a new fury rise in his chest as he commented, "Yo, we hittin' them fools tomorrow night. They supposed to be at a party in Gastonia."

"How far is Gastonia from here?" Rasheed asked.

"It's right up the road, about ten minutes on the highway."

"Where Donte and yo' man at?"

"They'll be here soon. Do me a favor. Don't call me by my real name around Tone. He know me as Silk. I want to keep it that way. I don't know why Donte been using his real name around here. He wouldn't listen to me."

"Aiight, *Silk*," Hasaan said sarcastically.

"Yo, I meant to tell you. I be seeing Donte's baby's mother around the way. Shorty is livin' mad foul, B. She had that kid Rob from 123$^{rd}$ laid up in Donte's coupe last week," Rasheed said.

"Word?" asked Silk in amazement.

"Yeah and she was all hugged up with some other cat at the cinema the other night, like that shit was legal or somethin'. When she saw me and Theresa she tried to play it off like it wasn't nothin' major. I'm tellin' you, shorty ain't shit but a hoodrat. I don't know *what* Donte see in her. He knows you can take a rat out of the hood, but you can't take the hood out of the rat. You can't turn a hooker into a housewife." Rasheed replied.

Silk listened then said, "Da-a-a-man, shorty got life fucked up. I'll tell Te', but that's what he get for trying to wifey a fuckin' chicken." He continued while heading to the bedroom to retrieve the twins and two semi-automatic Desert Eagle 45's to show them to Rasheed and Hasaan.

All three had taken a seat in the den with the pistols lying on the coffee table along with countless rounds of ammunition. Silk and Hasaan were discussing what had happened during the robbery and discussing their revenge.

"I swear to Allah, I'm gonna tear them fools new assholes," Silk said.

"What the fuck were you thinkin' when you sent Nisha and ole girl up to see us—alone?" Hasaan wanted to know.

Silk took a deep breath and shrugged, "Man, I don't know?"

Rasheed was wrapping up a call on his cell phone and started to join the conversation when the door bell rung.

"Yo, that's Donte an' 'nem," Silk said as he got up to answer it.

"What up." Tone spoke as Silk opened the door and led him and Donte into the den.

Rasheed and Hasaan were sitting on the sofa waiting when they entered.

"Ra, Hasaan whattup yo? Damn it's been a minute, my dudes." Donte spoke to his old buddies.

"Tone, this is my brother Ra-Ra and my partner Saan," Silk introduced everyone.

"Sup. Y'all niggas aiight?" Tone spoke.

Rasheed and Hasaan looked at Silk with a look of disgust.

Silk said, "Yo, I meant to tell you, the N-word ain't in our vocabulary, no offense but some people just don't like it."

Tone looked at Silk like he was crazy.

As many times as he had heard Silk call somebody a 'nigga.' Now here he was tryin' to check somebody because his Muslim people was up in here. And these two niggas got some fuckin' nerve. They won't call a nigga a nigga, but they'll sell coke to 'em and they'll kill 'em without a second thought? Real hypocrites... Fake ass niggas.

"My bad," Tone apologized hesitantly, then he spotted the artillery on the table and took out his glock and put it on the table also.

"Now dat's what the fuck I'm talking 'bout. It's about to be some church sangin' and flower brangin' after tomorrow night." Tone said to the group.

"Word. No question," the others agreed.

Yeah, Saturday night somebody's mama was going to be grieving. That was for certain.

## Chapter Seven – Goin' To War

Around eleven o'clock p. m., LaToya's party was in full swing and everyone she knew as in attendance. Fresh from the salon and nail shop, almost every hoodrat in Gastonia had shown up. Girls attract boys, so for every one hoodrat, there were two wannabe thugs. Goldie and his two cronies, Wes and Snake were there getting their drink and smoke on. All three were dressed in baggy jeans and with Timbs and oversized hoodies.

LaToya's parents had left for the evening and would not be returning until morning. The house was very spacious, but a little too small for the crowd that had shown up. Most of the guests had extended the party into the backyard where couples had paired off and were huddled up all over the place. Music was blaring from inside the house and was pouring into the backyard. As with any other get together or house party, due to the lack of security and organization, some if not all of the guest were probably strapped. Goldie and his boys definitely were. Goldie and Wes were in the backyard spitting game to two young redbones that looked like twins.

Goldie was seated on top of a picnic table with the girl standing between his legs. Wes was standing near the corner of the house with the other girl. Both Goldie and Wes had the mentality of jack-boys, so naturally they were positioned so they could watch the crowd.

Snake was in the dim living room dancing with a girl he had just met. He kept his back close to the wall, as he continuously watched the front door. Someone had started to scuffle in the living room because one of the young men had gotten a little too drunk and had disrespected one of the girls by squeezing her ass. They guy who was with the girl had apparently chin-checked the disrespectful cat, because when Snake looked around, the guy was getting up off the floor holding his jaw. Everyone had stopped dancing and was speculating the would-be-fight, but the guy simply stood up and staggered off with two of his drunken partners. Whenever there are too many niggas in the same place at the same time, something is bound to jump off. Especially if there is alcohol available. It is inevitable.

Five minutes later, everyone was dancing and drinking like nothing had ever happened. After dancing to two songs, Snake was tired so he ventured into the backyard to join his boys, while the girl followed closely behind. He approached Goldie and the red-bone at the picnic table.

"G, what up dog. Dis shit is off the hook." Snake said to Goldie.

"You ain't smokin' on nothing'?" Goldie asked Snake.

"Nah, everybody ran out of blunts. I still got a whole sack left," Snake replied holding up a sack of weed.

"Somebody need to go to the sto'," Goldie suggested.

The girl Snake was with spoke up and said, "I got some blunts out in the car."

"And you still standing right here? Girl, what you waitin' on?" Goldie asked.

Snake told the girl he would walk to the car with her and they exited the backyard through the gate which led you around the side of the house and out into the street. Snake lifted his head in a 'what's up.' motion to Wes on his way out.

The street was lined up with parked cars of the guests and the girl had parked on the opposite side of the street, one house up from LaToya's. When Snake and the girl reached the car they got in. Snake had decided to relax a minute and roll a blunt before he rejoined the party. The party was already packed and people were still rolling up. The girl was talking while Snake was sprinkling weed and periodically watching the cars creep by searching for parking spaces. One car caught his eye. A brand new cream colored 4-door Oldsmobile with a sticker on the back bumper that read 'Hertz Rentals.' They were five deep. Three of the occupants were big as hell, Snake could tell by the way they all bunched up. One looked like a Puerto Rican or Mexican and they all looked very much out of place. As they rolled by, they kept their eyes focused on LaToya's house and they never looked Snake's way.

Snake didn't really think much of it as he continued to roll the blunt, but he watched the car until it stopped. As soon as it stopped, a girl walked up to the driver's side and talked to the driver. Snake recognized the girl as a chickenhead from Charlotte named Stephanie. When they finished talking, the driver handed her something through the open window. She put whatever it was in her pocket and quickly walked off, damn-near running. She got into a car and sped off. The rented Old's then drove all the way to the end of the street bypassing empty parking spaces and finally parked at the corner, away from all the other cars. Snake watched with suspicious eyes.

***

As they rode down LaToya's street, they saw cars packed bumper to bumper on both sides. Silk was the driver, Rasheed was seated on the passenger side, while Big Tone, Donte and Hasaan were packed in the backseat of the rented Oldsmobile Ninety-Eight. They heard the music before they even got near the house. Silk slowly cruised past LaToya's house, looking for Stephanie and then he went to the end of the street and turned around. On his way back up he spotted her and stopped. As she approached, Silk let down the window.

"What up Steph, they still here?" Silk asked.

"Yeah, Goldie and Wes in the backyard, but Snake just left with some girl. Goldie back there sittin' on a picnic table talkin' to a girl and Wes standing by the fence as you go in through the back," Stephanie reported.

"What they got on?" Silk asked, because Big Tone was the only one who knew what they looked like, the others would at least need a description of their clothes, just in case.

"Goldie got on jeans with a Tar Heels hooded sweat shirt with some brown boots. Wes got on jeans too with a Duke hoodie and some black boots."

"Good lookin' babygirl. Here you go," Silk said as he handed her three, one-hundred dollar bills. He added, "You better go ahead and jet, because it's about to get *real* up in this bitch."

He then pulled out his Uzi from under the seat and cocked it back. He didn't have to tell Stephanie twice. Before he could blink, she had dashed to her car and sped off.

Rasheed started giving orders.

"Tone, since you know what these fools look like, you, Silk and Hasaan go in through the back where they at. Me and Donte goin' in through the front just in case they try to go back in the house" He took a deep breath and added "Aiight, let's make this shit look like the 4th of July."

Silk parked the car away from the crowd and they all got out and walked down the sidewalk toward LaToya's house. Once they reached the house, Tone, Silk and Hasaan walked toward the side gate that led into the backyard. As they approached the gate, all three simultaneously pulled out their pistols and crept into the yard. Rasheed and Donte entered the front door with their hands under their shirts ready to pull. Anyone fitting the description Stephanie had given was in for a bad night.

***

Wes was beginning to become impatient and wanted some weed so bad, he could almost taste it. He was wondering what was taking Snake so long, so he decided to go look for him. He told Goldie he would be right back beause he was going to get Snake.

Wes and the girl started toward the fence and Wes spotted them before they saw him.

*That look like Big Tone. I wonder what he doing way up here?* Wes thought. Then he spotted the guns. *They must be gettin' ready to straighten somebody. Hell, I don't like these Gastonia niggas anyway, let me Tone if they need some help with these niggas.*

Wes took a few more steps in their direction and that's when it happened. Tone and the two dudes with him raised their guns and aimed them at Wes' direction. The girl screamed and turned to run. Wes had turned his head and looked behind him to see who their target was but nobody was behind him. By the time Wes had figured out that *he* was the target, it was too late.

As he started to reach for his gun, he heard rapid pops, sounding like a machine gun. The first forceful blow felt like someone had punched him in the chest and knocked all the wind out of him. The second and third hit him in the neck and right shoulder. The shoulder blow spun him around and sent him sprawling to the grass. Wes tried to move but his body wouldn't comply. His entire being felt like it was in flames. All he could think about was trying to cool the burning sensation that was completely engulfed him. He suddenly felt the soothing of a cool vibration that started at his toes and was slowly working its way up his body. Wes didn't fight the coldness of death— he embraced it.

\*\*\*

Goldie heard someone scream. He turned to see Wes standing by the gate and the girl running away from him. He also saw three men with guns aimed at his boy. Goldie heard the shots and saw the flames jump from the barrels of the guns as the men opened fire on Wes. Goldie was in a state of rage and he was firing his weapon before Wes even hit the ground. Goldie saw two of the men fall, but the other one was firing an automatic weapon at him. Goldie ran toward the house and heard more shots and more screams coming from *inside* the house. Everyone was trying to find cover.

Once the shooting had started it was like a scene out of a movie. People in the backyard were either climbing fences or trying to run back inside the house to escape the line of fire. When gunshots erupted *inside* the house, people didn't know what to do. Nowhere to run, nowhere to hide. All they could was duck and pray.

Goldie was boxed in. He kept blasting at the man with the Uzi, but he was no match. Goldie was struck with the first bullet in the stomach. The next four hit him in the upper chest area, piercing his heart. The last thing Goldie would ever see was the concrete floor of the back porch coming up and slamming him in the face.

*\*\*\**

Tone and Hasaan had been hit. Silk had heard the gunfire inside the house, but he ignored it like a man possessed. When Goldie went down, Silk walked up and stood over him. He pressed his Uzi to the back of Goldie's head and squeezed the trigger. Silk's shirt was immediately splattered with blood and parts of Goldie's brain. Goldie didn't feel a thing because he was already dead when he'd hit the ground. Silk attempted to dash for the car hoping Rasheed and Donte would be waiting, but as he jumped off the back porch he heard more gunfire behind him. All of a sudden, he felt a sharp bee-like sting on the back of his head. His legs stopped moving and his arms wouldn't move to break the fall. He fell like a rag doll. Silk's life flashed before his eyes. He saw his mother and grandmother. He saw his brother Rasheed riding his new bike for the first time. He saw his kid's mother. He saw Tonisha at home waiting to return the rental car. He saw his son and daughter smiling. He saw Connecticut. This time he wouldn't open his eyes and see a robber standing over him with an empty gun. No, this time his eyes would never open again.

*\*\*\**

Snake had seen the three dudes go toward the back of the house with guns and had also seen the other two enter the house through the front door. Snake eased his way out of the girl's car. As he cocked his pistol, he slowly and carefully approached the front door. He hoped his boys were on point because he just knew for some reason that those guys were looking for them.

*That's probably them nigga's from that dice game,* he thought as he crept into the house.

Snake didn't see Goldie or Wes anywhere in the living room, but he saw the two dudes with guns approach the kitchen. All of a sudden, he heard rapid and continuous gunfire. When he heard the shots, he couldn't tell where they were coming form until he saw Goldie run past the kitchen window firing. Snake saw the two dudes run toward the back door with their guns in their hands, so he pulled his gun from underneath his sweater and open fired on both of them from the back.

The element of surprise is a mutha-fucka. Rasheed and Donte didn't know what had hit them because it happened so fast. Donte was killed instantly as one bullet punctured the back of his skull and another pierced his kidney. Rasheed went sprawling to the floor as two bullets shattered his spine. Rasheed couldn't move any part of his body. He was instantly paralyzed and slowly drifted into a coma. He prayed silently to Allah as he slipped into a state of unconsciousness. Snake maneuvered through the screaming crowd and stepped over the two bodies as he heard a final gunshot from the back porch. What he saw when he finally made it to the back door made him dry-heave.

Goldie was lying on the back porch with half of his head missing and his chest laying open, exposing his internal organs. Snake saw one of the three dudes from earlier running from the porch with an Uzi in his hand. Snake opened fire and saw the man fall like a log. He ran out into the yard to try to find Wes amongst the bodies. He finally spotted him laying face down in the grass. He smelled like blood and Snake could tell Wes was dead because he had shit on himself. Snake ran from the house and disappeared into the night, leaving behind six dead bodies and one man paralyzed.

\*\*\*

Early one Sunday morning, I was awakened by the sound of the telephone. I reached across Kinya to answer it.

"Yeah," I said, still half-sleep.

"Yo, nigga turn the TV on and put it on Channel-9. Hurry up." V shouted through the phone.

"Nigga, I know you ain't wake me up to watch no fuckin' TV."

"Just turn the damn TV on before you miss it."

I grabbed the remote and turned on the TV. When I turned to Channel-9 there were seven pictures in small blocks with their names underneath and I immediately recognized all but two.

The reported was saying, "...*house party in Gastonia turns into a nightmare as gunfire erupts, leaving six men dead and one man critically wounded. Among the dead are seventeen-year-old Wesley Nelson from Charlotte. Nineteen-year-old Johnathan Goldsmith was also from Charlotte. Twenty-two-year-old Antonio Jackson from Charlotte. Twenty-year-old Donte Harris from Danbury Connecticut. Twenty-one-year-old Najeeh Abdul and twenty-three year old Hasaan Mumia were also from Danbury, Connecticut. Witnesses say a shoot out erupted in the backyard when three men approached a young man and opened fire. A second shoot out occurred inside of the house moments after gunfire was heard in the yard. Witnesses told officials that a man brandishing a gun opened fire on two men as they hurried through the kitchen approaching the back door. That man apparently fled the scene. Officials say they have no motives but have reason to believe that the incident is drug-related. Witnesses are still being questioned. Officials have a description, but no positive ID on the gunman who fled the scene. If you have any information concerning this crime or others, please contact Crime Stoppers at 704-34 C.R.I.M.E. In other news...*"

I sat there with my eyes glued to the TV in a fuckin' trance.

"...'Pone. 'Pone." V screamed my name through the phone.

I was definitely awake now.

"Daaaaamn. That shit went foul as a mutha-fucka yo." I said to V.

"Dee said it was gonna happen, but damn playboy, every fuckin' body got slumped." V replied.

Dee had told us a month earlier that Silk had blamed Goldie for robbing him and everybody had already assumed that Goldie was responsible for Yellow Boy's murder. Silk was planning on retaliating so we just played it cool and laid low. Nobody had the slightest idea that we were really responsible for both incidents. We were waiting for the outcome of Silk's revenge against Goldie so we could calculate our next move. We were hoping once Silk knocked Goldie off, the situations would die with him and we could set up shop without having to worry about someone trying to put a speed bump in our game. Now, we were home-free. We didn't have anyone to worry about. Everybody was dead except for Snake who was just as good as dead because he would never see daylight again once he gets caught.

"That make thangs a helluva lot easier for us. Do June know about it?" I asked.

"Yeah. He was the one who told me about it. Somebody who was up there last night told him about it early this morning. You already know who the nigga is they looking fo'."

"It's gotta be dat nigga Snake," I replied.

"Yeah, June said that Snake was the one who slumped Silk and he was the one who blazed the two niggas in the house."

"I wonder how that nigga Snake got up out that shit?" I said, more to myself than to V.

"Somebody must've been praying for that boy," V replied.

"Yeah, well he betta start prayin' for hisself now. 'Cause when dem folks catch his ass, they gone try to put him to sleep. How a nigga gone justify all them damn bodies? Ain't no-way-in-the-hell," I said.

"Betta him than me." V responded laughing.

"That nigga in I.C.U. must've been some kin to dat nigga Silk. They got the same last name." I said.

"Who-gives-a-fuck?.? Nigga you know what this shit means? It's time to set up shop, playboy." V exclaimed.

"Yeah, I know. I already don' hollered at Lil' Rick and nem in Dalton Village, they ready to get down. That nigga Bo-Bo ever get back at you?" I asked.

"Yeah, he hollered back. And he turned me on to another nigga outta VA named T-Dog who be buyin' weight too. They already know we gon' have it for the low-low. They just waitin' on us to set that shit out. June got some lil' niggas outta Rock Hill who be slangin'. They say they can't keep no coke. They be runnin' out too quick. All we gotta do is cook that shit up and set it out. It's time to get paid, baby." V said.

"I need you and June to meet me here around noon so we can talk aiight," I replied.

"Bet, we'll be there."

V and June showed up close to one o'clock. Niggas are never on time. We all sat around the coffee table and I opened the black duffel bag that six men had lost their lives for. All of us, including Quick, had over a period of time extracted money from the bag, but we all had left twenty thousand each. Now June and V were taking their share and left forty for Quick and me. V and I had taken the Rolex and the bracelet to a pawnshop a while back and found out that the watch was just as fake as the nigga we had robbed for it. What we learned that day was if it ticks, it ain't shit. And the diamonds turned out to be cubic zirconias. Talk about some funny shit. I guess that was a tit for tat on Silk's part, but it's all good because now here we were splitting his hard earned cheese.

I took out the five kilos and set them on the table. I had it all figured out. Since this shit was free, we could sell it cheaper than anybody else and we would still come out on top. I suggested we rock up three of the bricks and bag it up ounce by ounce. The average amount you could bag up off of an ounce in those days would range anywhere from $2,500 to $3,000 if you bagged it up in $20 rocks. I suggested we only bag up $2,000 out of each ounce. That way, whoever we had serving it for us would have the biggest rocks on the block. It would sell fast because it would be more for the fiend's money and it was damn good. All we would ask for was $1,500 back for every $2,000 pack we would give out, so nobody should complain.

I added the total up and saw that we would make $186,000 off of the three kilos alone. With the two remaining kilos, we wouldn't cook those. Instead, we'd sell those in powder for $1,000 an ounce, which would total 72 grand. After we'd finish with all five kilos, we would be past the quarter million-dollar mark. After all the coke is gone, we would need to figure out how much we would use to re-up and how much we would blow. I was definitely ready to blow some money. June and V agreed enthusiastically. They almost couldn't believe we would make that much money.

"Damn, my nigga. We 'bout to be quarter millionaires." June said.

"Ain't no such thang as a fuckin' quarter millionaire, ignorant ass nigga." I said to June.

"This shit finna put a nigga on the map, playboy. We been waitin' on dis shit, my nigga." V said.

"Yo, the Queen City ain't ready for us….We 'bout to do the damn thang." I exclaimed.

## Chapter Eight – On Da Grind

The next day, right after Kinya had left for class, June and V came through. They came in carrying grocery bags. V and June sat the bags on the kitchen table and started taking out the necessities. When they had finished emptying the bags, my kitchen looked like a cocaine manufacturing center. We had five extra-large boxes of baking soda; a triple-beam scale, four glass Pyrex measuring jars, hundreds of double zero-size zip-lock bags, boxes upon boxes of Glad sandwich bags, two non-stick cooking pots and countless razor blades. It was time to put in work! Since June didn't know how to cook, he was designated to weigh out the ounces as they dried.

"I ain't never cooked more than a eight ball before and that was using a test tube and a cigarette lighter. So show me how to do this shit" V said.

I looked at him and laughed.

"I learned this shit from a vet. My uncle Herm taught me this shit before he started smoking. Now look, listen and learn as Chef-Boy-R-'Pone fry ghetto chickens" I said to V and June.

I weighed out four and a half ounces of coke and dumped it into a pot of water mixed with baking soda. As the water heated we could see the coke flake up and rise to the top of the water. The object was to heat the coke until it melted and sank to the bottom of the pot. I had to be careful as not to overcook it. As soon as the coke turned into a gel I removed the pot from the heat and poured off of all the excess water, leaving only enough to cover the gel. I poured the gel into one of the Pyrex containers and slowly added cold water until the gel began to harden. I let it sit for a couple of minutes until I was sure it had rocked up. I tore the grocery bags and laid them flat on the kitchen table. When I turned the Pyrex jar upside down, the cookie fell to the table with a *thud*. I told June to let it dry before he started breaking it and weighing it out.

I turned to V and asked "You got it?"

"Uhhhh....yeah, I got it" V said, unconvincingly.

I watched V as he started out just right, but when he tried to pour the water off the gel I watched him pour about two ounces down the drain. I tried to catch him "Yoooooo! Damn nigga, you just poured 'bout fo' g's down the damn drain! You gotta be careful wit' that shit yo. And watch what you doin'!"

Well, at least he had gotten the first few steps right. After V fucked up about two more ounces he had it down to a science. We were side by side at the stove with a pot of dope and two Pyrex jars each, cooking like Martha Stewart.

After we had finished cooking up the three kilos and weighing them out we were only four ounces short, most of which V had poured down the drain. Almost *ALL* of the cocaine came back! We hardly lost any from cooking it. This was an indication that this was some GOOD shit!!!

Kinya had called when her class was over and I told her to go to Meka's for a while because I didn't want her to see what was going on in her kitchen. It took us almost the entire night to bag up the three kilos. We bagged up 104, two-thousand dollar packages in $20 rocks! The rocks were so big we had to go by bigger packaging bags because they wouldn't fit into the small ones we had bought. Needless to say, we were exhausted but the potential money kept us motivated. With every bag we stuffed we looked at it as a twenty dollar bill!

My kitchen looked like a war zone when we had finally finished. Kinya would've surely flipped if she would've come home and seen that mess. Therefore, we cleaned up as best we could. I was scrubbing the countertops and June was scraping residue off the stove and sink while V was sweeping crumbs off the floor. Once we had the kitchen spotless, V and June left and I put all the coke in the safe until the next day for distribution.

For the next few days June, V and I were busy networking. I was using Kinya's Honda for transportation and June was using Meka's car. V rode with me. On this particular day, V and I were riding with eight two-thousand dollar sacks and my first stop was Dalton Village projects. Dalton Village was located on West Boulevard, just up the street from our old neighborhood.

I pulled into a crowded parking lot where there were five young cats apparently slanging and about nine junkies begging. I parked in an empty parking spot near a dumpster and V and I got out. When three of the young hustlers recognized me and V, they hurried to leave. Before we could get five steps away from the car they had disappeared. Evidently, they must have thought we were about to lay somebody down.

V looked at me and smiled while shaking his head. "I used to like to see that fear in them niggas' eyes. I guess they think a niga still jackin'" He told me.

"Once a stick-up kid, always a syick-up kid" I responded.

As we approached, I recognized one of the dudes who didn't run. I addressed him "Black, where Lil' Rick at?" He was sitting on an electrical power box with a blunt in his hand.

"What up, 'Pone? He just walked down his aunt's house. He'll be back in a minute. Rick say y'all got that work" He replied while looking at me sideways as if he didn't believe what Rick had said was true.

"Yeah, a nigga got a lil' somethin'. Why, you tryna get down?" I questioned.

"Depends" Black answered.

"On what?" I asked.

"Depends on how much y'all tryna pay a nigga"

"How much you gettin' right now?" I asked.

"Curt an' 'nem payin' twenty off every hundred" He responded while exhaling a thick cloud of smoke.

I looked at V and gave him an '*I told you so*' *look*. I asked "How fast y'all be moving that shit?"

"Nigga you know the 'Ville is off the chain. Dis' shit be boomin'! Especially on Fridays, we can't keep no dope." Black bragged.

"Well dig this, I'mma throw you a two pack, just brang me back fifteen-hundred. How that sound?" I replied.

"It *sound* good, but is the shit straight? These fiends around here is vets. They don't smoke no bullshit and they don't buy no crumbs either" Black said as he passed the blunt to the other cat that didn't run.

"Black, we got dat butter, nigga." V said as he pulled out one of the sacks and showed it to him.

Black couldn't believe his eyes. *As big as these rocks is, they* can't *be real. These niggas tryna get me killed,* Black thought to himself as he looked at the sack.

"V, 'Pone. What up baby?" Lil' Rock said as he walked up and gave us dap.

"Sup Rick? You ready to get paid nigga?" V asked.

"No doubt. Lemme see what y'all workin' wit" Rick said.

His eyes lit up when I gave him two of the sacks.

"Damn. What's these? Half-eights?" Rick asked with his eyes the size of golf balls.

"Nah, they twenties. Each sack got two 'G's' in it. Just give us fifteen-hundred off of each one" I said.

"Man, dis shit any good?" Rick interrogated as he motioned for one of the fiends to come over.

Rick opened one of the sacks and took out one of the smaller bags inside. He opened the small Ziploc and poured the rock into his hand and broke a piece, then put half of it back into the bag. He gave the fiend the piece he had broken and told him to test it. The fiend took a glass tube with a burnt piece Brillo on one end out of his pocket and placed the rock on the end with the Brillo. He stuck the other end between his burnt lips. Once he lit the 'glass dick' with his lighter, we could hear the rock sizzle as he inhaled. The fiend held onto the smoke for dear life before exhaling.

When Rick asked the fiend if the dope was okay, the fiend couldn't talk. The coke had his jaws locked up! A sure sign that the dope was A-1! Black and Rick looked at each other like they had struck gold.

Rick finally spoke, "Yo, Leave me wit' these two, dis shit gonna go quick"

"Yeah, leave two of 'em wit' me too," Black said.

Rick told us that the other cat who was with them was his cousin Ray-Ray. Rick said that Ray-Ray was serving coke in Clanton Park, a neighborhood right up the street from the projects we were in at that moment. Rick assured me that he would be responsible for the dope we gave Ray-Ray, so we gave him two sacks also. I gave all three of them my pager number and told them to beep me when they were finished and ready for some more. V and I had already had a reputation, so I knew these cats wouldn't put no shit in the game. They definitely didn't want beef with me and my niggas!

Just to make sure we were all on the same page, I told them, "Rick, you and Black already know that me and my dog ain't 'bout no bullshit. An' we ain't got no problem straightenin' a mutha-fucka. So from this day on, y'all on our team until y'all fuck up. If y'all got a problem wit' a muh-fucka like Curt and 'nem who don't want niggas slangin' nobody shit but theirs, holla at us. Feel me?"

Knowing I was not joking, Black said, "As big as these shits is, a nigga would be crazy to fuck dis up. Fuck Curt ' and 'nem. As long as y'all keep brangin' dis shit, it's gonna get sold"

"That's what it do. Just beep me when y'all get through. And remember…fifteen. Big as them shits is, I shouldn't have no problem gettin' mine" I said and then gave them all individual codes so I could know who was calling.

We left Dalton Village and rode down the street to our old neighborhood. I took V by his house so he could pick up some clothes and I stopped by my mom's to give her some money. She told me she was going to cook on Sunday and she wanted Kinya and I to come over. My mom sure was a hell of a lot nicer since I wasn't staying at home anymore. I don't know if she missed me, or if she was just that glad to get rid of my ass. Either way, I liked her new attitude.

Once me and V left Little Rock, we rode down the street to Boulevard Homes where my cousin Fred lived. Boulevard Homes is yet another set of projects on West Boulevard. And another  spot where cats were getting coke money.

I left the last two sacks and my pager number with my cousin Fred. On the way back to my place, June paged me. I stopped at a pay phone in North Charlotte near Piedmont Courts projects, a dangerous part of town for anybody who was caught slipping, day or night. I should know because I had jacked many niggas at the same pay phone. June was calling from a number in South Carolina, so I told V to give me some quarters.

"Why you need *some* quarters and not one quarter?" V asked.

"'Cause he in South Carolina," I explained.

"Well I ain't got but one quarter," V said.

"Broke ass nigga," I said as I got out and slammed the door.

I walked across the street to the corner store to get change and while I was at the register, two dudes walked in. They both recognized me and they spoke.

"What up 'Pone?" The tall dark-skin one whose name was Freeze spoke first.

"What up Freeze. 'Sup Dave?" I replied.

Dave was short and chubby with a neck full of gold chains. I knew they were serving in Piedmont Courts and I also knew that they knew I was a jack-boy. I told Dave and Freeze I wanted to holler at them, but I needed to make a quick call first. They eyed each other suspiciously and I knew exactly what they were thinking. But on a serious note, if I wanted to rob a mutha-fucka, do you think I would tell them to wait until I finished using the phone before I laid them down?

I walked back to the phone and called June. He said that he had been in Rock Hill, South Carolina all day fronting niggas dope and lining up customers who wanted some weight. He had a sale for six ounces all together. Niggas saw how good our shit was and started putting in orders. He said ounces were selling for thirteen hundred in South Carolina and when he told them that he would give it to them for eleven, they jumped on it with the quickness. Eleven hundred was a hundred more than what we were really selling them for but hey, some niggas you just gotta tax, if you can get away with it.

I told June to get their pager numbers and put them all on hold until the next morning. He said he would meet V and I at my place in about three hours.

When I finished using the phone I saw Freeze and Dave talking to V at the car. I walked over and saw that Dave had tucked his chains inside his shirt, trying to hide them. When white people see a black person within a hundred feet of their cars, they lock their doors. When niggas see jack-boys, they tuck in their chains and take off their rings. Only one word describes it—FEAR.

V had been telling them about the coke we had and had asked if they wanted to get down. But since we didn't have any more packs on us, I could tell they didn't believe him and thought it was a set-up. I tried to erase that fear.

"Yo, listen. A nigga ain't about no bullshit. All that robbin' and shit is dead for us. We on some other shit now, a nigga tryna get on. If a nigga wanted to jack yo' ass, I would've been laid both of y'all niggas down," I said as I raised my shirt and showed them my glock. "All that gold and shit around yo' neck would've been on *my* neck by now," I continued as I pulled Dave's collar down, exposing his chains.

"Look, a nigga fo' real, dog. If y'all wanna start gettin' some real money, holla at a nigga. Here go my beeper number. Get at me," V chimed in, while giving Freeze a piece of paper with his number on it.

When I pulled off, V had a puzzling look on his face. He finally spoke and said, "It's gonna be hard to get niggas to trust us."

"No it ain't. 'Cause when muh-fuckas see us shinin', they gonna be blowin' a nigga pager up, tryna get down. Mark my word" I replied.

I relayed what June had said about the cats in Rock Hill, so we decided we would weigh-up the remaining two kilos once we got back to my place.

We stopped by Bojangles along the way. As I pulled to the drive-thru, I saw Heavy's green Mercedes parked in the lot, so I knew he had to be inside eating. Heavy was a six foot, 360-pound nigga with a complexion that was as dark as midnight. Heavy was one of the major players in the dope game in Charlotte. He always had a dimepiece with him everywhere he went and I used to wonder how a nigga as ugly as he was always kept the baddest bitches around him. I guess he paid like he weighed......heavily.

I knew we would be needing a connect once we ran out of dope and we'd definitely need someone to re-up with so I pulled away from the drive-thru and parked beside the Benz.

"Damn that shit tight." V exclaimed.

"Nigga you ain't seen nothin' yet. Wait 'till I cop my shit. I'ma knock niggas' dicks in the dirt" I professed.

"I think I'ma get me a Beemer," V said as he admired Heavy's Benz.

"Fuck a Beemer and fuck this ugly as Benz. I gotta go Big Boy style my nigga. I'm talkin' bout some head bangin' shit." I said while exiting the Honda and walking toward the entrance.

As we neared the door, a tall, thick-built red-bone with the face of a goddess was on her way out. She was draped in gold and diamonds. I had to check myself because my gat felt like it was trying to jump out of my pants on its own. I looked at V and he had that look in his eyes. Once a jack-boy, always a jack-boy. I saw Heavy come out right behind her, dressed in a designer sweat suit with gold jewelry everywhere. He looked at me and V before speaking.

"'Sup, youngstas."

"'Sup, Hev. Can we holla at you for a minute?" I asked.

"Yeah, what's up?" Hev said as he handed the lady the keys to the Benz.

Hev also knew we were stick-up kids, but he wasn't concerned. I could see the look in his eyes, telling me that we didn't faze him. Every old school hustler I ever came across had that same look in their eyes. I suggested we go inside the restaurant to talk. Once inside, V went to the counter to order while Hev and I took a seat. I got right to the point.

"Check this out, me and my peoples doin' some big thangs right now. I done hollered at a couple mo' niggas 'bout this, but they tryin' to tax a nigga like we from outta town or somethin'. How much you lettin' them 'thangs' go for?" I said to Heavy, bluffing like I had shopped around and was looking for the best price.

He looked at the serious expression on my face and said, "I ain't in no shape to throw y'all nothin' right now. I been in kinda a drought for a few days, my people ain't straight. Maybe next week I…"

I cut him off and said, "Nah, dog I ain't tryna get fronted shit. I'm talkin' 'bout straight up buyin' it."

His eyebrows shot up and he said, "Well, I usually let 'em go for twelve a piece, but like I said I ain't straight right now."

"Twelve what? What you thank I'm talkin' 'bout?" I replied.

"Oh. Damn youngsta, you doin' it like that? Dem thangs goin' for twenty-eight."

I looked at him like he was crazy."

"Twenty-eight? Damn you can't do no better than that?" I asked.

"Sometimes, it depends on how many you getting" Hev said.

"What about five?" I asked as Hev looked at me now like I was crazy.

"You mean to tell me you tryna get five bricks? Damn youngsta, I might can get 'em for you for about twenty-four apiece."

I realized that Hev wasn't doin' it like I always thought he was. He probably wasn't buyin' nothin' but one or two kilos his damn self, so I flipped the game on him.

"You said you ain't straight yet? Well look, I got a lil' somethin' left. What you tryna get?" I asked.

"What you got?"

"What you want?"

"I need about a half to last me until I get straight," he said.

I thought for a minute. *We might be able to use this nigga in the near future. After all, we do need a connect. If we help him out right now, he might return the favor later.* So I stepped up the game.

"We ain't got nothin' but one left. It ain't cooked and like you say, it's kind of a drought goin' on right now. We was gonna break it down and put it on the block, but since you need in right now we'll sell you half for fouteen. How that sound?" I said as V was sitting down with two 4-piece chicken dinners with fries and dirty rice. V had overheard me lying to Hev and decide to add to it.

"Nah, we said we wasn't sellin' that last one in weight dog," V said to me.

"We can sell him half and still chop the rest up and parlay," I responded to V.

"Nah, fuck that." V said as he got up to get our drinks.

"What you gonna do youngsta? I got my baby waitin' on me in da car," Hev said.

"I told you, fourteen and it's yours," I responded.

"Give me a number. How long it's gonna take you to be ready?" Hev asked.

"As soon as we finish eatin'," I said as I gave him my pager number.

I told him to use code 360, so I would hit him right back. He said he would page me in an hour and a half. As he was walking toward the door, V returned with the drinks.

V sat down and smiled, "You a smooth ass nigga. I gotta give it to you. We came in here lookin' for a connect and ended up with a customer. When he see how good that shit is, he gone be comin' back and he gonna turn some mo' niggas on to us," V expressed his notions.

"Fa sho', but we still need to find a connect" I cautioned his enthusiasm.

We finished eating our chicken dinners and headed to my place.

On the way upstairs to my apartment, my pager went off. I was thinking it was probably Kinya, ready for me to pick her up, but when I checked the number I noticed it was Lil' Rick. I just knew something was wrong. The day was going too good for something not to fuck up. I called the number Rick had paged me from.

"Hello," a female voice answered.

"Yeah, is Rick there?"

"Yeah, hold on."

"Yo 'Pone," Rick said as he picked up.

"Yeah, what up?" I asked curiously.

"I just wanted to let you know I'll be through wit' that in a minute. Dis shit boomin'. These junkies love that shit. When I hit you back, I'm just gonna put in my code. That's gonna let you know to come on thru. Bring three dis time, so I ain't gotta keep callin' you and shit. Black might be ready too, so bring him some mo'. Aight."

"Damn, that shit movin' like that?" I asked.

"Man, just be ready when I page you back."

"Aiight. Later," I said as I hung up.

Hev paged me about an hour later and I told him that I was ready. He suggested we meet him at a liquor store across the street from the Bojangles where we were at earlier. I set a time and he agreed to it.

V stuffed the dope in the waist of his pants and we left the house to make our first weight sale. I drove as V sat in the passenger side ready to bail if we happened to get pulled.

"What if this nigga ain't no good and he tryna set a muh-fucka up?" V asked.

"He probably thankin' the same shit as we speak," I returned as I kept shifting my eyes from the road to the rearview mirror. It was one thing to ride around with $20 sacks. But when a nigga's riding with a half a brick, he feels like everybody on the road knows and is watching him. Talk about being paranoid?

As we approached the Bojangles, I stopped at the gas station next to it. We looked around, trying to find any signs of suspicion, but we didn't see any.

I pulled up to the liquor store and saw Heavy sitting on the passenger side of a luxury van. I parked beside it and told V to hand me the dope. I stuffed the dope in my pants and said, "You got my back right? If I be gone too long, just start blastin'. I'on give a fuck who you hit just blast"

"Nigga, you know I got you" V said as he cocked his pistol.

I took a deep breath and got out. I opened the driver's door to the van and got in. Two men were sitting in the back. One of them had a pistol lying on his lap and I noticed Heavy had a pistol between his big-ass thighs. I knew exactly what time it was. At first, I thought they were about to try and jack a nigga, but then I realized *I* was the jack-boy, that's why they had their pistols out.

I tried to calm the tension, "Yo, it ain't even that type of party, playa. I'm strapped too. But it ain't even like dat."

I lifted my shirt and showed Hev my pistol.

"Let me see what you workin' wit' youngsta," Hev said, referring to the dope.

"Where da money at?" I asked.

Hev extended his hand toward the men in the back while keeping his eyes on me the whole time. One of the men placed a shoebox in Hev's outstretched hand. Hev opened it and showed me the money. I reached in my pants for the dope and heard the two men in the back shift around. Hev also shifted positions with his hand on his pistol. I smiled at their paranoia, then pulled the dope out and handed it to Hev. He inspected the package and smiled.

After tearing a small hole in the plastic he tasted it and said, "Damn, youngsta you got that 'Peruvian Flake.' I ain't seen none of dis shit in years. Hell, you need to be turnin' *me* on to *your* connect. You sho' you don't wanna sell dat other half."

"Page me later. I'll hit you back and let you know," I said while counting the dough and noticed it was two hundred dollars more than it should've been.

It was the oldest trick in the book. He'd put the extra two hundred to test my honesty. But as we all know, there is no honor amongst thieves and if you slip, I will grip.

When I finished counting the cheese, I closed the shoebox and told Hev not to forget to page me as I stepped out of the van. I got into Kinya's car and pulled off while telling V what had happened in the van, including the two hundred dollar bonus. He laughed and said, "That fat muh-fucka thought a nigga was on some bullshit, huh?"

"Yeah, until I showed him this heat and let him know it ain't a game. Muh-fucka must be crazy, thankin' I ain't comin' suited and booted," I said as we headed up the highway.

\*\*\*

"Where y'all niggas been? Y'all know how it look for a nigga to be sittin' in his car by hisself in a white neighborhood. Crackers go to gettin' all suspicious and shit," June berated as we pulled into my parking lot and got out of the car.

"We been handlin' bidness. Bama ass nigga," I responded.

"Yeah, we been servin' that shit, while you been layin' up wit' skunks," V added.

"Why yall niggas be hatin'? I can't help it if da hoes love Junebug," June bragged as he spread his arms wide and tilted his head to the sky.

When we reached the apartment, June weighed out three ounces, four halves and four quarters for the dudes in Rock Hill.

"Yo, I thought they was gon' wait 'til in the morning," V said.

"Dig this, since I gotta go back down there tonight anyway, I told them I would brang it back wit' me," June replied as he bagged up the last quarter ounce he needed.

"What you mean you gotta go back down there tonight?" V asked.

"I know y'all niggas ain't thank I'ma let dat hotel room I got go to waste. Sheeiittt. Ali, one of da niggas who gettin' one of deez OZ's introduced me to his sister. I'm fuckin' her tonight."

I joined the conversation and told June, "Meka gonna fuck you up if she find out you ridin' them hoes around in her shit. You know how them bitches do, they leave lil' shit in yo' car so yo' bitch can find it. And Meka *gonna* know anotha' bitch been in her shit. Seem like them hoes can *smell* anotha bitch."

"Fuck Meka. She startin' to get on my damn nerves anyway. I'm movin' and getting me a ride as soon as we get straight. All dat bitch want is money. *And* she got some ugly ass feet," June said as V and I laughed.

June added, "And da btich don't keep no food in da house. I see why she so skinny, da bitch don't eat. And you know da right there alone is a conflict of interest. And she wonders why I don't wanna stay at home. Bitch you ain't got no food, dat's why."

June had us in tears from laughing so hard. After June left, V called Dee and told her to meet us at Johnson C. Smith University because Kinya had called and said she was ready for me to pick her up from class.

Kinya was attended Johnson C. Smith and only had one more year before she would graduate with honors with a degree in Business Management. She wanted to open up a beauty salon once she finished school. I planned to give her that salon for her graduation present, which would also serve as a nice investment for me.

When we got to the school, Dee was already there. She and Kinya were standing next to her car talking. I pulled into an empty spot next to Dee and V got out. I stayed in the car, waiting for Kinya to get in. Dee walked over and spoke.

"What's up 'Pone? Oooh, yo' dreads gettin' long," she said as she pulled one of my locks.

Damn, she was giving me that look that she had been giving me lately. That look when you can tell a woman wants you. I turned to see if either Kinya or V had caught it, but they didn't. V had climbed behind the wheel of Dee's car and Kinya was busy telling some girl goodbye. As Dee walked off, I couldn't help but notice the jiggle of her round ass in those skin-tight jeans. Hell, it wouldn't hurt to look, I figured. And she swung her hips like she knew I was looking.

*Damn, that's the type of shit that can get a man in trouble,* I thought as I shook myself out of the hypnotic state her ass had put me in. I played it off and pretended I was trying to holler at my man.

"V, hit me later and let me know what them VA niggas gon' do," I said as I glanced at Donyetta.

She had gotten in the car and was sitting so V couldn't see her eyes. She gave me that look again. V said he would call me and they pulled off.

***

The next couple of weeks flew by and money was coming in so fast it was unbelievable. Between the VA niggas, Lil' Quick and the Rock Hill boys, the two kilos of powder sold quickly. We got rid of all but four ounces which Heavy practically begged me to sell him. I sold him the last four for a thousand a piece. He bitched but he bought it. Lil' Rick and Black were selling out so fast, I thought they were smoking the shit but they never came a dollar short. Ray-Ray had locked his block down. He was selling more than Rick and Black put combined. June was becoming 'That Nigga' in Rock Hill. His pager stayed blowing up.

My lil' cousin Quick had collected the rest of his money from the robbery and bought a quarter-kilo from us so he could keep his money flowing. My cousin Fred fucked up one of the last two packs I gave him so I had to put in the $800 that he was short. Needless to say, I cut his ass off. Family or not, business is business.

When we had finally sold out, things got hectic. We had come out with a total of $250,000—6-grand short of what I had predicted but way more than I had ever seen. Because we sold the powder at wholesale, we had to sell it a little cheaper than expected. I kept records of all the sales and everything added up perfectly. And needless to say, we had to get a bigger safe.

We had been so busy serving the coke we already had, we hadn't tried hard enough to find a connect. We had two choices. Each of us could've walked away with $84,000 each or we could've found a connect and bubbled up. Since we were in it to win it, we opted for the latter and decided to take $40,000 each and leave $132,000 to re-up with, once we found a supplier. We had to put all of our customers on hold.

*** 

Heavy told me that his people were finally straight.

"Sup youngsta?" said Hev, as he picked up his cell phone.

"Man, I can't hear you. Turn that shit down," I replied as I listened to the volume of the music slowly descend.

"Can you hear me now?"

"Yeah, what up."

"I'm just lettin' you know that my people back on. You still ain't did nothin'?" he asked.

I didn't want to seem desperate and unorganized, so I lied.

"Yeah, I did a lil' somethin' but that shit wasn't no good. I'm almost ready again. What's up?"

"Damn youngsta, you boomin' ain't ya?" Hev replied.

"What them thangs goin' fo'?" I asked, getting right to the point.

Hev thought for a minute, then said, "They want twenty-five a piece, but if you get more than four, they'll do twenty-one a piece."

"Hard or soft?" I asked.

"Soft, of course."

"Hev what that shit like? Keep it real," I asked.

"It's that butter. I meant it ain't that flake like you had a while back, but it's A-1" he answered.

Twenty-one was damn good. But I knew if he was gonna give it to me for twenty-one, he was really getting it for nineteen or less. But hey, that's how the game goes. Can't knock a hustle.

I played my cards and told Hev, "Lemme get a half so I can see what it's like. If I like it I'll get six and a half mo'. What you gone charge me for that half?"

"Damn youngsta, you don't trust Hev?" he questioned.

"Hell nah. What was that? A joke?" I replied.

"Look, I know you good for it, so what I'ma do is front you the half so you can test it. I know my shit proper, so I know without a doubt you gonna come get the rest of it. Feel me? We'll just add everything together and make it a bill forty-seven. Dig?" Hev said, sounding too eager.

"Whoa, slow ya roll big dog. If I decide to get the rest of it, you gonna be right there while I cook a ounce outta each one, dig?" I replied.

"I ain't got no problem wit that, baby boy. Just let me know where to drop the half at."

"Let me hit you right back, aiight," I said.

"Aiight, but don't take too long, this shit goin' like hot cakes," he warned.

"Yeah, but I'm pretty sho' you ain't gonna let a sale for seven birds pass yo' ass by. I ain't new to this. Just chill 'til I hit you back," I replied.

After we hung up, I paged June and V. V was the first to call back. I heard a lot of static when I answered the phone.

"Yeah."

"What up 'P'?"

"Damn, what's all the static?" I asked.

"Oh, that's this raggedy ass cell phone I just got," V replied.

"Nigga what you doin' wit a car phone and no car?" I asked laughing.

"See, that's where you wrong at" V sad as he turned the volume up on the radio as loud as it would go.

"Nigga turn that shit down." I said.

"You ain't gonna believe this" V said.

"Believe, what?"

"I went and copped that Beemer nigga." V anxiously disclosed loud enough for the whole world to hear him.

"Nigga you ain't gotta scream all in my ear. When you get it?" I inquired.

"Two days ago. 'Member when I told you I had to take care of some real important shit? That's what I was talkin' 'bout. I put it in my mama name and she ain't even trip. 'Cause she ain't have that much credit, I put almost 6-G's down on this shit. 'Pone, my shit bangin'. I'm on my way through there so you can check it out. You hollered at Fat Boy yet?"

"Nah, I'm waiting on him to call back, his ass probably down there trickin' in Rock Hill," I answered.

"That nigga went and got a 'Lac. A shawt dog" V remarked.

"Whaaat. June got him a Cadillac?" I responded.

"Yo, that shit nice too"

"No wonder I ain't seen y'all niggas in a couple a days, y'all been out flossin' an' shit wit out a nigga," I said.

"Sheeeiiit, it ain't like a nigga ain't got it like that. Know what I'm sayin'?"

That statement was definitely true.

"I feel ya my nigga. I guess I'mma have to come out the woodworks next. I'ma make y'all niggas park y'all shit." I claimed enthusiasm.

"I doubt that. You gotta come hard to top this shit." V challenged.

I briefly daydreamt about all the bitches who would be jocking me when I finally decided to shine. Then remembering the reason I had paged him I said, "I think I found some work."

"Straight up? Who?"

"Hev just called and said he was holding. I ain't gon' talk about it right now. I'll holla when you get here."

"Aiight playboy."

"Peace."

"Peace."

My other line had beeped. I answered and it was June. He was trying to talk over the noise of the radio. Evidently, he had gotten a cell phone too.

"Nigga, I can't hear you." I said yelling as he turned down the volume.

"Oh, so you out flossin' too?" I asked.

"And-you-know-dis."

"Where you at? I need to holla at you" I said.

"I'm on yo' side 'o town, me and Lonnie."

"Drop that nigga off somewhere. Don't bring that nigga over here," I directed to June.

"Lonnie is aiight," he tried to persuade.

"Fuck Lonnie. I don't want nobody to know where I stay at. Wit' all this shit sittin' up in here. Nigga is you crazy?" I said as I took the phone away from my ear and looked at it like it had a disease.

"Aiight, I'll do dat."

"Later."

"Peace."

I hung up the phone and analyzed what had taken place since that night at the Hampton Inn. I had been a seventeen-year-old petty stick up kid who was barely surviving. I was living with my mama in the projects, struggling to come up with the weed-fair. Now here I was eighteen, living in a neighborhood where the pizza delivery truck wasn't afraid to visit. Neighbors jogged every morning and walked their dogs without a care in the world. I was making so much money, it seemed unreal and I had a woman who worshiped the ground I walked on. Back in the days, I use to fantasize about being able to cop tight ass rides and sporting jewelry that females would drool over. Now this shit was about to be reality. Yeah, it was definitely my time to shine...

*Chapter Nine – Da Good Life*

V pulled up first. He did what all first-time ballers do….he called from the parking lot.

"I'm outside."

"Aiight," I said as I hung up the phone and went outside.

V was wiping the hood of his car off with a towel.

"Daaaamn. Nigga that shit hot." I confessed as I gave him dap and inspected his new car.

V had gotten a candy-apple red 525i that was only one year old and had almost no mileage. The shit was definitely off the hook. He bragged about what all he was going to have done to it. Paint this, rims that, blah, blah, blah, stereo and whatnot. While we were in the parking lot talking and admiring his car, a two door El Dorado Cadillac pulled up and June got out. The Cadillac was wine-burgundy with gold emblems and white wall tires. It wasn't brand new, but a late model. June also boasted about what he was going to have done to his ride. I must admit, I did feel left out but both of my boys shit were hot as hell. Yeah, we were definitely coming up.

***

After getting the half key from Hev, we cooked it up and let someone test it. It was workable, so we got the other six and a half. I did just as I said I would do…..I made Hev sit and watch me cook an ounce out of each key just to keep him honest. 147-G's was enough to kill a muh-fucka over.

So, there we were, right back on the grind, serving customers like a delivery service. Black, Ray-Ray and Rick were more than ready to get back on the block. We had all of our regular customers and a few new ones who had heard about us. Even Dave and Freeze had gotten on our team. We had dope all over Charlotte. We were finally getting recognized as 'Big Boys'. We were on point this time around because before we sold out completely, we decided to re-up so we could keep the money and the dope circulating.

Right after we copped the second time from Hev, I decided it was time to floss. If you got it, you might as well enjoy it. I paid my Aunt Laurie to put a car in her name for me. I gave her 2-G's, plus the money for the down payment. Both June and V had put their cars in the shop, so I did the same thing. As soon as me and Aunt Laurie drove off the lot, I went straight to Nu-Vision Autoworks and gave them specific orders. They complied with smiles because money talks.

I became good friends with the owner, a white dude named Chad, who was at my every beck and call. I also bought Kinya a new car, an Acura Legend with 17-inch chrome rims and I kept her Honda to use as my transport car.

June had left Meka and had moved into his own apartment and V had finally moved also. H moved into a condo with Dee. I told Kinya to start looking for a house because my nosey as neighbors were starting to stare.

I didn't tell June and V about the car I had bought for myself, I was going to bring it out the same day they got theirs out of the shop.....

V called the house early one Friday morning when I was just getting out of the bed.

"Yeah," I answered the phone.

"What up playboy?" V said.

"Ain't shit. What's hapnin'?"

"You know me and June gettin' our shit out today," V boasted, referring to their cars.

"Oh yeah?"

"Yeah, June wouldn't tell me what he was getting done to his, he tell you?" V asked.

"Nah, he wouldn't tell me, just like *you* ain't said shit."

"Nigga you know I had to keep that under wraps" V said.

"I can dig that," I replied.

"Wait 'til you see my shit, niggas gon' hate a muhfucka, but the hoes gon' love me." V claimed loudly.

"Why don't we go to the club tonight and floss y'all shit." I suggested.

V thought for a minute and said, "Hell yeah, let's go get some jewelry and go to the mall and shit. You got the Honda?"

"Yeah, I'mma call June and tell him we gonna scoop him. After we leave the mall, I can take y'all to get y'all shit," I suggested.

"Nah, I don't want y'all to see my ride until tonight" V said.

"Whatever nigga," I remarked.

"Come through 'bout noon. I'mma get Dee to take me to meet Bo-Bo and T-Dog in Greensboro," V said as he bagged up the last of eighteen ounces he was about to serve to the VA niggas.

"Yo, watch them State Troopers."

"No doubt."

"Holla as soon as y'all get back," I said as I got out of bed and headed toward the bathroom.

"Aiight."

"One."

We hung up. I took a piss and then I called June's crib.

"Hello," a sweet sounding female voice said.

"Let me holla at June," I replied without speaking.

As I waited for June to pick up, I clicked on the television with the remote. I was just in time to catch an interesting report on the news. The reporter was saying, *"...a fugitive that was broadcast on America's Most Wanted was apprehended last night in Memphis, Tennessee. Authorities say that nineteen-year-old Rodney Terrell was spotted only minutes after the show aired. An informant notified police which led them to this hotel,"* the reporter said as she pointed to a cheap motel behind her. She continued, *"The man is wanted in connection with a shoot out which left six people dead and one paralyzed from the neck down. He is being held in the Memphis County jail without bail and is awaiting extradition back to Gastonia where he will face multiple charges..."*

I stared at Snake's picture on the tube and felt no remorse. June was talking, "What up playa?"

"Damn, bruh you already got bitches answering yo' shit?" I said.

"Nah nigga, dat's just the flavor of da' day. You know tomorrow my taste might change," June said, as he slapped the naked girl beside him on the ass.

"I see you still trickin'," I said.

"Deese broads just love a nigga, dats all."

"Yeah, whatever 'fat boy.' Yo, you heard about Snake?" I asked while opening my closet and browsing over all of the Nike's and Timberlands I had lined up on the floor. My closet looked like a mini Foot Locker.

"Naah, what happened?" June asked, not really caring.

"They caught that nigga in Tennessee."

"What da fuck he doin' in Tennessee? Hangin' out with Elvis 'nem?" June asked, laughing and I laughed with him. Then I changed the subject.

"Yo, me and V gonna come scoop you 'bout twelve. We goin' to blow some dough. We goin' to the club tonight since y'all niggas getting y'all shit out the shop," I said.

"I'm wit dat. Nigga, when you gonna spend some o' dat money and get you a car or somethin'? Wit you tight ass." June asked as he caressed the naked body beside him.

"I 'on know yet, I'm just gonna ride wit' y'all niggas for a change," I lied.

"You remember da last time we was up in da Sugar Shack? Bitches tried to play a nigga all the way to the left 'cause all 'dem lil' soft ass niggas was out there ballin'?" June said.

"Yeah, that was then, this is now playboy. A nigga got a lil' status now, ya know. I'm gon' grudge-fuck all them hoes who wasn't tryna see a nigga back in the days. That's how I'm playin'." I told June as I finally picked out a pair of Timbs to wear.

"I'm wit' all dat, playa. I'll be ready when y'all get here" June replied as he kicked the comforter off the bed and resumed his morning sexual ritual.

After we hung up I called my man at Urban Elite, an urban clothing store located in South Charlotte. U.E. had every black designer label fresh off the press. Whatever was new, I wanted it first. Pat, the owner, was from New York so he had no problem getting the hotness. I told Pat we would be stopping by and he was more than ready for us to spend some money with him.

Since my car had been ready for two days, I called and told Chad I would be coming to get it. Over the weeks, I had spent well over ten grand with Chad, getting my car 'tricked out.' He was loving me. I had told him that I would be bringing Kinya's car in for a paint job and wood-grain, soon. "No problem. Just stop by and drop it off. We'll get right on it. Anything you need, just let me know, pal," Chad had told me.

The power of money makes mutha-fuckas kiss your ass. *I'm beginning to enjoy having my ass kissed.* I thought.

V called around 11:30 to let me know he was back. I told him to have Dee drop him off at June's, to save time. I got dressed in a pair of baggy jeans, an oversized UNC football jersey and some light brown Timbs. I pulled my dreads up and tied them into a ponytail before leaving the house. I met June and V at June's crib near South Boulevard. Dee was still there when I arrived.

"'Sup niggas." I said as I entered the apartment.

June's apartment was the typical bachelor's pad. A living room set with a wide screen TV connected to a video game. A bedroom set, no dining room set. A refrigerator full of beer and half empty pizza boxes. Not a clean towel in the whole apartment and his place had a permanent weed smell.

Dee and V were engaged in a loud game of Mortal Kombat when I arrived. June was in the bedroom talking to somebody. Apparently, it was the same broad that had answered his phone earlier that morning. She asked him if she could stay until he got back.

"Hell nah, ain't nobody stayin' up here if I ain't here," June told the girl as she came out of the bedroom and walked past everybody without even speaking. June came into the living room smoking a blunt as he spoke, "'Sup 'Pone?"

"I'm ready to bounce, that's what's up. Damn, them two so caught up in that damn game, they probably don't even know a nigga here," I said, referring to V and Donyetta.

"Nigga I heard yo' loud ass when you came in. I'm just busy spankin' Dee ass right now," V said as he vigorously tapped the buttons on the controller pad, while keeping his eyes glued to the screen.

"Boy please. I just beat you twice before we left the house," Dee said to V, before she cut the game off.

I watched as she got up off of the floor and grabbed her purse from the sofa and then led the group outside. June and I got into the Honda while V walked Dee to her car. He hugged her with his back to me, so that meant Dee was facing me. Just as I figured, she was looking over V's shoulder at me. Damn, did she just wink at me? Nah, maybe she had something in her eye. I turned to see if June had seen it, but he was busy fucking with the radio.

I glanced back in V and D's direction and she was smiling at me.

I played it off and said, "Nigga what 'choo gon' do, take ya ass back home or bring yo' ass on?"

"Fuck you," V said as he looked at me.

He slapped Dee on that fat ass and watched her get into her car and pull off. Once he got into the back seat of the Honda, I questioned him.

"Man, you in love or what?"

"Nah playboy. I'm still fuckin'em, breedin'em and misleadin'em. You know that. Me and Dee on some ole' Bonnie and Clyde type shit tho. Ain't nothin' serious," V said convincingly and I believed him.

June put one of Kinya's cds in and we listened as Scarface rapped about the dope game, something we all could definitely relate to. I told June and V about my conversation with Pat and they wanted to stop by there before we went to the mall.

*\*\*\**

"Hey y'all," Felicia spoke as we entered the store.

We all spoke back. Felicia was Pat's sister and business partner. She was a pecan tan, five foot three, brick-house. Felicia was a few years older than us but looked like a teenager in the face. Her boyfriend was an older cat that worked for UPS. He was often in the store on the weekends watching her like a protective father. I had been infatuated with her since I had first laid eyes on her. I never tried to holler at her because I never thought I was on her level. Lately, since I'd been dropping dollars on them, she had been checking me out on the sly and lightweight flirting. This day, I was determined to pull her card.

Before purchasing our gear, I pulled Felicia outside and hollered at her. She was surprised to hear me spit game at her because she didn't see it coming. I caught her off guard. Just like I figured, she bit and was hungry for more, so I asked her out. I told her to meet me at Red Lobster on Albemarle Road at nine o' clock for a drink and she agreed, but said she was bringing a girlfriend along and I had no problem with that. The more the merrier.

"Boy, you better not have us sitting out there waiting for you and you don't show up. We are really gon' fall out," she said as we re-rentered the store.

"I wouldn't do that. If I wasn't comin' I wouldn't have just told you I was. You just make sure *you* be there," I said watching her luscious ass cheeks swing side to side.

"Hell, after chasing you all this time, I should make *you* buy *me* drinks," I laughed.

"Imagine that," she said as she took some empty boxes to the back.

Pat, June and V walked over. June and V both had clothes in their hands.

"Y'all ready?" I asked.

"Yeah, as soon as we pay for everything," June replied as they walked to the register.

Felicia had come out of the back and stood behind the register. V and I had made a bet on Felicia. If she bit, V would have to pay for my clothes and vice-versa, so I told Felicia. "Ring this up with V's."

"Nigga please," V replied.

I looked at Felicia and said, "Wait in the parking lot if I ain't there before you, aiight."

"You just better show up," she said.

V looked at me and smiled as he counted out the dough for both of our purchases.

We left Urban Elite and headed to the mall. We strolled through South Park Mall blowing money like it grew on trees and attracted several jealous stares from the hating ass niggas while the females were looking with curious eyes trying to figure out who we were.

"Dat's Capone 'nem from West Boulevard—'Dem niggas DOIN' IT!" I overheard a group a girls talking about us as we walked by.

Hearing that, made me feel like I was finally getting my props. And to think, I was just beginning!

We went to the jewelry store and spent close to 20-G's on necklaces, charms, watches, bracelets and rings. Movados were in style back then, so I got one of those with a diamond bezel, a Cuban link bracelet with diamonds and two tight diamond rings while June and V went jewelry crazy! We left the jewelry store looking like rappers. The only thing left to do was to kill time until we all decided to go our separate ways.

I dropped June off first and when I got to V's place, I had to use the bathroom. When we walked in, Dee was laying on the couch on her stomach watching TV with a pair of daisy-dukes on. I stared openly at her ass cheeks spilling out of the tiny shorts. I went into the bathroom with a hard dick and and had to wait until my erection went down before I could piss.

Their bedroom was located directly across from their bathroom and when I opened the bathroom door Dee was slowly closing their bedroom door. She was topless and smiling at me. When she closed the door completely, I emerged from the bathroom. V was in the kitchen on the phone. I told him I would meet him and June at the Mini-Mart down the street from the club at 11:30 and I left their condo with Dee on my mind.

*Home-girl gone fuck around and get what she lookin' for.* I wrecklessly thought as I got into Kinya's car.

On my way home, I stopped and got a cell phone. Now my day was almost complete. When I got home Kinya told me she had found a house she thought I might like and wanted me to accompany her to see it.

The house Kinya had looked at was a three bedroom, two-bathroom palace compared to our little apartment we were currently living in. I was immediately sold! I imagined using the big back yard for cookouts and just sitting around smoking and drinking. The yard was fenced in, which was perfect and the house already had a security system, which I would definitely need.

"I want this house." I told Kinya.

"Me too baby," she replied as she strolled about. I could tell she was imagining how she would decorate it. "Write that number down and call them first thing Monday morning, I'on care about the price. I gotta have this shit." I told Kinya, as she copied the numbers of the realtor from the sign.

We left the house and went to Auto Works where Chad was standing out front waiting on me. He walked up to Kinya's car as we parked.

"Hey my man. How ya doin'?" Chad said.

"What up Chad? Look like y'all closed," I said as I looked at the vacant building with no lights on except for the neon signs.

"Yeah, I'm taking an early day. But you know I'll wait on my main man," Chad responded as he patted me on the back, smiling from ear to ear.

*I know this cracker don't think I'm about to give his ass a tip or something. I already spent over ten grand with him. Mutha-fucka done lost his mind.*

"Yeah, that's good lookin' dog, I'm glad I called when I did," I said.

"You're right, another ten minutes and you would've missed me."

"Hell, I would've just called you at home," I responded.

Chad laughed as if I was joking, but I was dead serious because I had to have my shit, I had BIG plans.

"I'll bring it around in a sec," he said as he walked toward the garage. Kinya had only seen the car once and that was when I had first taken it to Chad and his boys, so she hadn't seen the finished product. I heard Busta Rhymes thumping from my stereo as Chad cranked up the car. The bass sounded like thunder and he wasn't even in eyesight. As the bass got louder, I could hear Chad pulling around from the back of the building. Chad turned the corner and pulled right next to Kinya and me. Kinya's eyes were as wide as golf balls. Her mouth was open like she couldn't believe what she was seeing. Chad was sitting behind the wheel of a midnight black Mercedes Benz 190E. The Benz was one year old and 190's were the shit at that time. A plain 190 acquired much respect, but a tricked-out 190 boasted status.

My shit was definitely tricked! The interior was white leather with black piping along the seams. The name "Capone" was stitched in the two front headrests in black thread. Even the floor mats were white with black Mercedes' emblems embroidered. The carpet was white also. I was feeling that. The sound system was an Alpine with a remote control, with a 12-disc CD changer in the trunk. Everything that could be wood was wood, including the steering wheel. The grill had been interchanged. The Benz emblem didn't set atop the hood like everyone else's. The grill was made with an emblem in it. All chrome! It had 18-inch chrome rims with the Mercedes emblem in the center of each one. A semi-spoiler surrounded the car. I didn't want it too low to the ground.

All letters and emblems were chrome. The inside of the trunk was snow white with four 15-inch woofers and two Fosgate amps. Even the tail pipe was chrome. The windows were crystal clear and the sunroof was open letting the last little bit of sunlight gleam on the interior. Looking at the interior while the sun was shining had caused me to squint. It was just like looking at snow. Yeah, this Benz was definitely, the shit! and it was all mine! I looked at it and couldn't help but to smile.

*Wait until June and V lay their eyes on this shit. They can't fuck with it. Wait until Felicia see a nigga roll up in it...and all those bitches at the club. I can't wait...*

Kinya was the first one to say something, "Daaaaaaaamn baby, this *can't* be the same car."

"Yep," I replied, while rubbing my hands together in anticipation.

"Capone, I would kill for a ride like this. There's going to be a whole lot of envious people when they see you driving it," Chad said.

"Fuck'em, let'em envy. That's why I got it," I said smiling.

After confirming the date I would bring Kinya's car, we shook hands and parted. I told Kinya to follow me to my Aunt's house so I could park the car until later. I got my cell phone out of her car and hopped behind the wheel of my dream mobile.

On the way to my Aunt's house, everybody I passed did a double-take. Some, most of which were women, where pointing and waving as if I were a celebrity. I was definitely getting my shine on. After I parked at Aunt Laurie's, I got back in the car with Kinya.

"I saw all them bitches wavin' at you and blowin' the horn and shit," Kinya said with an attitude.

"Damn I ain't drove the car but fifteen minutes and you already trippin' and shit." I replied.

We rode in silence the rest of the way home. When we arrived, I showered and put on some old jeans, a sweatshirt and some Nike's. When Kinya was in the bathroom, I told her I was going to handle some business and I wouldn't be back until late. I knew she didn't believe me but she knew not to question me.

I drove the Honda back to my Aunt's house and changed into my new gear and put on all my jewelry. I was ready to floss! It was ten minutes after eight, so I called June and V to make sure it was still on. They both had gotten their cars and were eager to show them off. Little did they know, so was I.

I stayed at my Aunt's until almost nine o'clock . It would take me fifteen minutes to get to Red Lobster from her house. I didn't want to be on time and I also didn't want to be too late, so I hopped in my Benz and headed to my rendezvous.

When I got to Albemarle Road, it was five past nine, so I figured Felicia and her girl should already be there waiting on me. When I pulled into the restaurant's parking lot, I slowly cruised through the aisles, wanting to be seen by everybody and everybody was looking. I spotted Felicia's Nissan and slowly cruised by it like I didn't see them. I heard her blow the horn and saw her headlights blink. I backed up and pulled in the empty space beside her. While I was parking I could tell they were talking about me because her friend kept smiling and peeping at me. They got out first and then I got out. I didn't want to bump doors, you know, with the fresh paint and all. They were admiring the Benz when I got out.

"Daaaamn, who whip?" Felicia asked.

"Lemme find out you need some glasses, shorty," I replied, pointing to my name in the seat.

"This shit is bangin'." her friend replied.

"Stop drooling Tracey," Felicia told the girl in a sarcastic tone.

Red Lobster was packed as expected for a typical Friday night and the waiting list was at least forty five minutes long.

"You wanna go somewhere else?" Felicia asked.

"Hell nah. What's yo' last name?" I asked Felicia.

She looked at me with a confused look and said, "Campbell, why?"

"Just wait right here," I said as I walked off.

I went and spoke with the hostess for a minute and when I got back to Felicia and Tracey, they were wondering what was up

"What's goin' on?" Felicia asked.

As I was about to speak, we heard the hostess say, "Campbell, your table is ready."

While we were following the hostess to our table, people who had been waiting for a table before we arrived were looking at us with fire in their eyes.

*Don't hate the playa.* I thought to myself as we strolled through the crowded restaurant.

When we were seated, Felicia asked, "How you do that?"

"Money talks," I replied.

I'd given the hostess $50 to put Felicia's name at the top of the waiting list and I knew she would bite because that fifty is more than she would make all week in tips. I was really starting to realize how much power there was in the almighty dollar because when we ordered our drinks, the waitress wanted to see my I. D. and I saw the power of money work again. She brought my Vodka and cranberry to me without hesitation. We ate and drank and drank some more.

During the conversation, Felicia asked, "So, where your girl at?" she was referring to Kinya.

So I shot back, "I'on know? She probably wit' Mr. UPS."

Felicia and Tracey laughed at my sarcasm before Felicia excused herself to go to the restroom. When she got up, my eyes zoomed in on the ass. Every brother in the place glanced at her as she passed.

Tracey started talking.

"So, 'Pone, do you pay for everything you can't otherwise have?" she asked.

"If it ain't free, then it's got a price. If a muh-fucka ain't givin' it to me, if I want it I'll buy it"

"Everything in life that's worth something can be given to you absolutely free. If you play your cards right." She replied with a heavy up north accent.

Her comments left no room for misinterpretation of her statement as she put her lips on her straw in a very seductive manner and slurped her second daiquiri without breaking eye contact. For the first time that night, I took a good look at Tracey. She was about the same height as Felicia. She looked like she was mixed with either white or Indian. At first, I thought her hair was weave because it was long, but it was real. Her body was definitely giving Felicia's a run for her money. And her eyes were truly hazel. I was definitely feeling her, so I jumped out there with my next statements.

"If I play my cards right, huh? Aiight, tell a nigga what kind of hand I'm workin' wit' right now."

She put her hand on my thigh and said, "Straight flush."

"Damn, I can't lose with that." I said, laughing.

"My point exactly. 873-1198, call me. And—uh, here comes your date," she said as she took her hand off my thigh and watched Felicia walk over.

Damn, here I was with two bad ass bitches from New York. I was trying to *get* the pussy from one and the other was trying to *give* me the pussy.

*I wonder how they feel about a threesome.* I thought to myself as Felicia slid her fine ass in the booth beside me. I kept on repeating Tracey's number in my head, trying to memorize it. However, it was to no avail. All that weed smoking had finally started catching up with me. I had quickly forgotten her digits, partially because Felicia was talking.

"What club are y'all going to tonight?" she asked me.

"We 'sposed to be going to the Sugar Shack," I responded as I checked my Movado. It was a quarter to eleven, damn time was flying."

"Why y'all going to that kiddie club?" Tracey asked.

Evidently she had no idea of how young I was.

"Yeah, we going to the Vintage," Felicia stated.

The Vintage on the Boulevard was a hot spot for the twenty-one and older crowd. It was located on Independence Boulevard on the opposite side of the adjacent parking lot from the Sugar Shack. The Sugar Shack was the most popular teen nightclub in Charlotte. Every weekend, both clubs were packed to capacity.

"If I had some I. D., I would go too," I replied.

We all finished our drinks and were ready to roll. So, I paid for the check and gave the waitress a $30 tip. She was so overjoyed she told me to come back anytime.

When we got outside, Felicia hugged me so tightly, I could feel her breast being crushed against my chest. I said 'fuck it' and let my hands roam down to that basketball-sized ass of hers and she didn't protest when I squeezed her cushiony ass cheeks. She smiled and told me to drive safe as we broke our embrace. I gave Tracey a friendly hug and told her it was nice to meet her.

When they got into the car, Felicia rolled her window down and asked for my pager number. I told her aloud as she wrote it down. I told her to use code #10. We left and went our separate ways.

I pulled up to the convenience store across the street from Red Lobster to get some gas and to buy some condoms because I was definitely not going home. I sat in the car and called June's cell phone. I told June about my date with Felicia and Tracey. While we were talking, I noticed a cream colored Volvo pulling up to the gas pump opposite of where I was parked. The occupants were four sexy-ass females who were dressed to impress.

The driver was by far the most attractive one. She was short, well-built with her hair cut into a bob. And the skirt she was wearing looked as if it were painted on. I wanted to know their destination, so I told June to hold on as I caught the driver coming out of the store and stopped her before she got back into the car.

I had a conversation with the driver whose name was Pooh. She informed me that her and her girls were on their way to the Vintage. We exchanged numbers and said our goodbyes with promises of hooking up in the near future.

When she got into the car, she drove around to the pump where I was parked and said, "Capone, my stupid friends made a bet. They wanna know if you a rapper or a ball player?"

I was trying to figure out why they would think that and then reality dawned on me. I had almost forgotten about the diamonds I had on and the ride I was sitting in.

I laughed and said, "I'm a balla, baby."

Pooh's girlfriends were all smiling at me. She told me she would call me later and pulled off.

I resumed my conversation with June and told him I would meet him and V at the meeting spot at 11:30. Since it was still early, I decided to ride past TGIFridays and The Comedy Zone to kill a little time. Both spots were packed and as I cruised by people pointed and stared at me like I was on display. I was loving that shit!

At 11:30, I headed toward the meeting spot. Handy Pantry on Independence Boulevard was the club-before the club. All of the club-heads who were on their way to the Shack and the Vintage would hang out in the store's parking lot before heading to their club of choice. The parking lot was so crowded, cars were lined up waiting to enter. I was in line, about four cars down from the entrance when traffic came to a standstill. I called V.

"Yeah," he answered.

"What up?" I said.

"Man, where you at? Me and June up here at the sto' waiting. This shit crowded as fuck," V replied.

I tried to see if I could spot them from where I was at, but I couldn't.

"I'm close, the traffic fucked up," I said. Once the traffic had begun to move again, I made my way closer to the entrance. I spotted June and V sitting on their rides side-by-side in the far corner of the parking lot surrounded by girls. I still had V on the phone.

"I see y'all got a lil' fan club," I said.

"Where you at?" he asked, looking around trying to spot me.

"I'm turnin' in now," I told him.

"OH SHIT! Nigga I *know* that ain't you in that Benz. June look at that nigga." V shouted in amazement.

I hung up the phone and pulled up next to June and V's rides. It seemed as though everybody in the parking lot was watching me as I parked and got out. I gave my boys daps and listened to them praise the Benz.

"Daamn, dis nigga got his name in da seats and shit." June said to V as if V hadn't already noticed.

My niggas' rides were tight, but they knew they would have to come hard to top my shit. June's Cadillac was the tightest in Charlotte and to this day, I still haven't seen a BMW yet that could fuck with V's. Our time to shine was definitely here.

We parlayed in the parking lot for a minute, hollering at a few cuties that couldn't keep their eyes off of us and then we headed to the Sugar Shack. The damn line was so long, you would have thought they were giving away free gifts. Heads turned as we cruised through the parking lot looking for vacant spaces. After we parked and finally made it inside the club, everybody was trying to holler at us. People who knew us and people who wanted to know us. The niggas were trying to get on our team and the females were hawking us like vultures. When we finally got a peaceful moment, we stood against the wall near the dance floor. A girl with a body like a porn star and too much weave approached us.

"Hey 'Pone. Where you been hidin' at? You ain't been out here in a minute. Damn, you lookin' good." she said, while standing a little too close to me.

"Yeah, what up Tosha?" I spoke in a nonchalant tone.

"You wanna dance?" she asked.

"Bitch, you *know* you'on fuck wit me like that. I'on even know why you over here fakin' and shit. Poof, be gone" I responded as I waved her away while June and V laughed.

Tosha walked off without saying a word and I could tell her feelings were hurt.

"Why you dis dat bitch like dat?" June asked, still laughing.

"That's one of them same hoes who wouldn't look at a nigga twice back when we ain't have shit. I see a lot of 'em up in here. I'ma shine on all these skunk bitches." I replied, while nodding in rhythm to the blaring music.

For the next hour me, June and V hollered at girls we didn't know and dissed the ones we did know. The heat was becoming unbearable and as I looked around I was starting to feel like I was in school instead of a club. Everybody started looking like little kids and I started thinking about what Tracey had said about it being a 'kiddie club.' Suddenly, I felt as if I had outgrown this club and I was ready to go. At that moment, I knew I would not be coming back to the Shack again.

When we got outside, I told June and V to follow me. We drove to the opposite side of the adjacent parking lot and saw that the Vintage was just as crowded as the Shack was. We rode past the entrance and saw that the line was long as shit, but it was a much more sedated crowd. You could tell the people were more mature than the ones we had just left. This was my type of crowd.

As we searched for parking spaces, women stared and waved at us like they knew us. The majority of the fellows didn't even hate. They were giving us props. When we all parked, V and I got in the car with June. V lit a blunt as soon as his door shut.

"Oh hell nah! Ain't nobody tell y'all niggas to get white interior. Ain't no smoking in yall rides and y'all ain't gonna smoke in my shit either," June said as he opened his door and got out.

"Nigga quit trippin'," I told June.

"Do I look like I'm playin'? Y'all get y'all ass out or put dat shit out," June replied.

We got out and finished the blunt standing outside the car. We had to respect him because they damn sure wasn't going to be smoking in my shit.

"Man how we gonna get in there wit' no I. D.?" V asked.

I pulled out a hundred-dollar bill "This *is* my I. D." I told him while walking toward the entrance.

V and June followed suit as we bypassed the people standing in line and went straight to the front.

"Yo, da' line is back there playa," the dude who was working security at the door said while pointing.

"Yeah, I see that. Lemme holla at you for a minute," I said and the dude knew exactly what I wanted.

"Look, people been tryna get VIP-treatment all night. Y'all gotta wait just like everybody else. I'm just followin' orders," he explained.

I wanted to speak with the owner, so he sent someone inside to get him. Moments later, a short, heavy-set older cat with salt and pepper cornrows and gold-rimmed specs appeared.

"Can I help you?" he asked, while eyeing me suspiciously.

"Yeah you can help me, 'cause yo' man act like *he* don't want to," I replied referring to the door security and then continued.

"Look, me and my dogs tryna get up in here. I guarantee you ain't had nobody up in here who gonna spend like us. We gonna give you a bill a piece to get in and we might end up making you sell sodas after we by you outta liquor. Feel me?"

I could tell I already had him sold with the thought of making $300 off of three people just for admission. I added, "Matter of fact, won't you send somebody to set us a table up with three bottles of Dom P., three Hennesey and cokes and two Vodka and cranberries. Can you handle that?"

The owner rubbed his chin and looked us up and down. He knew we were underaged but money was on his mind. "The first time y'all start some shit, I'm kickin' y'all lil' asses, ya heard me?" He threaten while reaching for the $300.

We had to respect him. He had the upper and hand we really wanted to get in.

When we stepped up in the Vintage, it was like a totally different world form the Shack. There were so many beautiful women, wall to wall, in different flavors. Many of them stared like we were famous. I guess the reason they were staring was because the owner himself was escorting us to a table full of Champagne. When we were seated, I told the owner to start a tab for us. I sipped my Vodka and cranberry with a straw and we poured ourselves Champagne out of our individual bottles. A waitress came and introduced herself as Vicki and asked if we needed anything else. I told her to bring back some orange juice and her telephone number, which she did without a second thought. I heard a fellow at another table complain about the waitresses not paying them any attention and not bringing their drinks. Typical Playa hatin'.

Felicia and Tracey were first to approach us.

"Hey Playas. What y'all young asses doin' up in here ballin' like y'all stars and shit?" Felicia said, smiling as she put her arm around my neck and leaned up against me.

I didn't hug her back because I didn't want any of the other females who were sweating to the think she was my girl. I introduced Tracy to June and V and I could tell she wasn't interested in either one of them. We offered them a glass of Champagne, they drunk it and then went off to dance.

As soon as they left, Pooh, the girl from the gas station and her girls walked over, so we bought them drinks and kicked it with them for a while. June and V both got numbers. After they left, June waved two more females over. They came and called two more friends and their friends called another friend. Felicia and Tracey came off the dance floor and rejoined us and Pooh and her girls came back over as well. So there we were, three young street niggas in the Vintage on the Boulevard surrounded by beautiful women and we bought drinks for everybody!

The girls were competing for attention and I was loving that shit.

*Oh yeah, I'm definitely fuckin' somebody's daughter tonight.* I thought, while trying to make up my mind about who was going to get it later.

The owner stopped by the table and gave me the numbers to the club and also the number to a strip club he was opening the following week. He told me to call in advance and he would make sure to have everything set up when we arrived. We had won him over!

June and V decided to leave with two females they had just met. I was trying to hook up with an old crush I had bumped into earlier.

Celeste was someone I had wanted to fuck ever since I was in junior high and she was in high school. I went to use the bathroom on my way out and she had stopped me. We kicked it for a minute and I told her that I was going to get a room and she asked if I wanted some company. So we exchanged numbers and I told her I would page her to let her know which hotel and what room to come to. Then I left the club solo.

When I got to my car, there was a note on the window that read:

*Capone,*

*I know this letter comes as a surprise, but I just couldn't help staring at you and fantasizing about fucking your brains out. If it is meant to be, then tonight will be your lucky night. Everytime you glanced my way, my panties got wet. Drive safe, see ya in a few.*

*Sincerely,*

*Sticky panties.*

*Damn, that's gotta be Celeste.* I thought as I balled the note up and tossed it to ground. While I was getting into my car, a red Nissan Maxima crept by slowly...a little too slowly and they were three deep. I didn't think too much of it because the parking lot was so crowded and cars were constantly coming and going.

I pulled out into traffic and headed down Independence Boulevard toward the Luxbury Hotel near Matthews. I decided to get as far away from the crib as possible because I didn't want Kinya 'accidentally' seeing my car parked at a hotel.

I stopped at a convenience store once the traffic had thinned out because I needed some orange juice and a sandwich to try and feed the alcohol I had consumed. Also, I grabbed some Alka-Seltzers for the potential hangover.

When I came out of the store, I saw the same Maxima parked at a pay phone across the street. My mind said 'coincidence', but my street instinct told me differently. These niggas were up to no good.

I got in my ride and headed the opposite way from which I had come and just like I figured, the Maxima moved the same time I did. I reached beneath the seat and put my Desert Eagle .45 on my lap. As I made a right turn on Avendale Drive and cruised through to Central Avenue, the Maxima followed suit. I laughed to myself at how obvious these niggas were. I couldn't believe this shit. These niggas were trying some shit on me that I'd been doing for years! *These niggas can't be for real*, I thought. The tables were being turned on me. Instead of *me* following a nigga to his crib, *I* was now being followed!

*"These niggas 'bout to get what they lookin' for... They fuckin' wit' the right one"*, I mumbled to myself as I periodically checked my rearview mirror.

The streets were almost deserted except for a few stray cars, the Maxima and myself. I knew these fools had to be aware of the fact that I had already peeped them. However, either they were extraordinarily stupid or they were extremely bold. Either way, I was about to disrupt their intentions.

At first it was a little funny, playing cat and mouse with them. I stopped—they stopped. I turned—they turned. Then I got frustrated because they were really trying my patience. I needed to distance myself from them, so I could find a deserted back street. I wasn't trying to lose them, I just needed a little distance so I could handle my business. My opportunity came when I approached Idlewilde Road near a shopping plaza.

When I neared the plaza, I slowed at a stoplight, as it turned yellow. As soon as it turned red I sped through the intersection, barely avoiding the collision of two oncoming cars. As I approached a deserted side street, I looked in my rearview to see where the Maxima was. It was running the red light and heading in my direction. I wanted to make sure they saw me, so I slowed before making the turn. Once I made the turn, I sped down the dark street, stopped and backed into a dark spot behind the plaza. I hopped out with my pistol in my hand and ran to a nearby abandoned car that was parked in a grove right next to the street. The windows and windshield had been broken. I opened the door and climbed into the back, where the seat was missing. As I lay on the floor and waited for the Maxima my pager continuously vibrated, but pussy was the farthest thing from my mind.

***

### The Maxima

They had been trailing the black Benz ever since it had left the Vintage. They had seen the driver and his boys flossing and spending dough like it was running water up in the club. They had made up their minds to jack one of these cats tonight. They concluded that all three of the dudes had been drinking, so they would be definitely be slipping. Since his two boys had left the club with bitches, they decided to follow the one in the Benz because he was alone. They figured he would be an easier target. As they tailed the Benz to Idelwilde Road, it began to slow for a yellow light. As soon as the light turned red, the Benz took off, almost getting hit by two other cars.

"I told you that nigga seen us," the backseat passenger said to the driver as he toyed with his pistol lying on the seat beside him.

"Nigga, shut up. I got this shit," said the driver as he kept his eyes glued to the Benz and watched as it made a right turn near the shopping plaza.

As soon as the two cars that had almost hit the Benz had cleared out of the way, the driver sped through the still red traffic light. The driver made the same right turn the Benz had made on the deserted street.

"Where dat nigga go?" asked the passenger, as they neared an old broken down car that was parked on the right side of the street.

They all looked about as they cruised slowly. As soon as they passed the spot where the abandoned car was, ALL HELL BROKE LOOSE!!!!

\*\*\*

I could hear the squeak of the brakes as the Maxima slowly cruised past the abandoned car I was hiding in. When I was sure they had passed me, I slowly peeped over the dashboard. They were about two car lengths in front of me. Since there was no windshield on the care I was hiding in, I had a clear shot. I took a deep breath, aimed at the Maxima's back window and let them 'thangs' fly!! I bust off five shots in rapid succession and saw the back window shatter! I was still spitting flames as I jumped out of the abandoned car and ran back toward my Benz. The Maxima had sped off, screeching tires down the deserted street. When I reached the other side of the street, I saw them swerve and hit a streetlight! The car didn't move after the collision. All I heard was the continuous blaring of the Maxima's horn when I jumped in my ride and sped off in the opposite direction.

***

### The Maxima

They heard the sound of gunfire as soon as they got a few yards from the spot where the broken down car was! They didn't know which direction the shots were coming from, until the back window shattered. When the glass broke, the passenger in the back seat instinctively ducked to avoid being hit.

"Oh shit!!" the dude on the passenger side screamed as a hail of bullets redecorated the car. The passenger covered his head and ducked also.

When the first few shots bombarded the back window, the driver ducked and put the pedal to the metal, as he heard bullets whizzing past his head as they exited the windshield. He tried mercifully to escape the rapid gunfire, but it was to no avail! They heard what seemed like endless shots being fired from behind and they had totally forgotten about their mission. They didn't even fire back because they were afraid of being hit. The only thing on their minds was making it out of this ordeal alive!!

Once the Maxima had sped up, the two passengers thought they were home free. Too afraid to look up, they felt the car going off the road and then all of a sudden, the car smashed into something, jolting everyone forward. When the passenger finally regained his senses, he noticed that the horn was blaring. Slowly, the coward rose up and asked, "Y'all aiight?"

The dude in the back answered, "Yeah, I'm straight," as he lifted his head up and looked back for the shooter.

Fearing the driver had gotten injured in the crash, the passenger tried to shake him awake.

"Yo, RECO! RECO! RECO!" the passenger screamed the driver's name, until he noticed the gaping hole in the back of his head leaking blood like the Red Sea.

The driver had taken a headshot and was unmistakably dead!!

"Shit! Fuck! Man let's dip!" the passenger screamed to the dude in the backseat, as they both got out and ran.

## Chapter Ten – Every Man's Fantasy

I threw the empty gun on the passenger seat and my adrenaline was pumping hard as shit. I knew somebody had gotten hit. I could tell the driver was hit when I saw the car swerve and crash and I was hoping I had hit all three, but I couldn't tell.

"Bitch ass niggas" I said to myself as I slowed to normal speed.

I took all back streets on my way to the hotel. I didn't feel like going through the trouble of driving all the way back to my Aunt's to switch cars and I definitely wasn't taking this car to my apartment.

My pager was still vibrating, so I checked it and noticed a very unfamiliar number with the code #11, but I couldn't remember giving anyone that code. Thinking it was Celeste, I called back using my cell.

"Hello," a familiar voice answered.

"Somebody page 'Pone?" I asked, trying to place the voice.

"Yeah, this is sticky panties. I assume you got my note?" she said.

"Tracey? Daaamn that was you who wrote that note? How you get my…"

"Your number? I memorized it when was giving it to Felicia at the restaurant," she cut me off in mid-sentence before continuing, "Where you at? On your way home to the wife?"

"Nah, as a matter of fact, I'm on my way to get a room. Why? You tryna see a nigga?" I asked.

"Have you already forgotten what my note said?" she asked sarcastically.

"I'm goin' to the Luxbury on Independence, you know where it is?"

"No. But I'm sure I'll find it," she replied.

I didn't want her getting lost, so I gave her directions. I got her pager number and told her I would beep her and put in the room number. Before I hung up I said, "Make sure them panties still sticky when you get there."

She laughed and replied, "Oh, I'm sure they will be."

I pulled into the Luxbury parking lot ten minutes later. I got the Presidential Suite on the second floor and since it was so late the girl at the front desk gave it to me for half price.

I parked around the back and took the elevator to the second floor. The first thing I did when I got inside the room was reloaded my pistol and hid it in the drawer beside the bed. I didn't know this bitch Tracey from Adam. For all I knew, she could've been another Dee. I paged her and put in the room number and contemplated on whether or not I should call Kinya. I knew she was at home asleep by now, waiting on me so I opted to call. When she didn't answer after seven rings, I became suspicious because, asleep or not, if Kinya heard the phone she would answer it.

I paged her, put in my cell phone number and waited for her to call back. I was stepping out of the restroom when I heard my cell phone ringing. I turned on the TV so it wouldn't sound so quiet when I answered.

"Yeah."

"Hey baby." Kinya spoke.

She was wide-awake and was calling from a car, I could hear the radio.

"Damn, where you at?" I asked surprised because she wasn't home.

"I'm on my way home."

"From where and wit' who?"

"Dee's sister gettin' married tomorrow, so she had a lil' bachelorette party. I'm wit' Dee. She gettin' ready to drop me off. Hold on," Kinya said as she handed the phone to Dee.

"'Pone is Vonzell wit' you?" Dee asked.

Damn, now this was putting a nigga on front street. I didn't know what V had told Dee, so I lied, "Yeah, we handlin' some biness, but V just went to the Waffle House for us."

"Why he ain't been calling me back all night?"

"Shit, we been busy. You see I'm just now callin' Kinya." I replied.

"Tell him to call me as soon as he get back."

"Aiight."

Kinya got back on the phone.

"What time you comin' home?" she asked.

"I'on know yet, this shit takin' longer than I thought it would."

"Oh. ok, I'll see you when you get there. Love you."

"Love you too baby. Bye," I replied as I hung up.

I layed on the bed and looked up at the ceiling, replaying the events of that crazy ass night. *The streets were deserted when I dumped on those fools, so I'm pretty sure no one had seen me. I don't know if someone is dead or what. If somebody survived, will they describe my car? Will they tell the police to check the abandoned car for prints? My fingerprints weren't on the shells, so I ain't gonna worry about that. Damn, I should've made sure all three of them were resting in peace. No witness-no case!! Fuck it, I can't cry over spilled milk. I would just have to check the news in the morning, or better yet, I'mma check the Ghetto Gazette. Word on the streets is always more accurate than the news.*

While I was lost in thought, someone knocked on the door. I looked through the peephole and saw Tracey. She was alone. I let her in and closed the door behind her.

She looked around the room and commented, "You really do go out in style, don't ya."

"Girl, you betta ask somebody about me." I replied.

I noticed she had on a long coat that was tied at the waist and a pair of 'fuck me' pumps. Not wanting to waste any time, I walked to the bed and sat on the edge. She followed me and stood between my legs, staring in my eyes. She began to untie the belt on her coat and when she opened it up, she was naked except for a pair of black silk thongs. I licked my lips as I smiled with approval.

*Look at the fleas on fluffy.* I thought as I inspected her damn-near perfect body.

Tracey's body was off the hook! Her skin was flawless. She didn't have a stretch mark or blemish in sight. Her breasts were round and full. They stood at attention with dark brown nipples that were aching to be sucked. As she turned around and modeled the thongs, I couldn't help but to drool over that high yellow ass. I didn't see any hair along her bikini line, so I assumed she had shaved. I wondered if she was completely hairless.

Her thighs were thick and tight, like a dancer's. Her toes were perfectly pedicured, as they were visible in the shoes. She had a flat stomach with a belly-ring. Yeah, her body was definitely just as beautiful as her face. Tracey had a waist like a wasp and an ass like a horse. My kind of girl!

I ran my hand up her thigh until I reached her panties. I felt to see if they were sticky for real or if she was faking. My fingers felt dampness along the crotch of the fabric. She wasn't faking! I moved the fabric to the side and traced the crease between her nether lips. Tracey had begun caressing her breast and was moaning softly with her eyes closed as I strummed her like a violin. As soon as my fingers dipped between her lips, they were immediately drenched. Tracey was soaking wet and dripping down her thighs. The heat between her legs was so intense, she felt like she was on fire and she almost buckled when I touched her clit. She couldn't take it anymore. I was teasing her to the point of insanity. She pulled my sweatshirt over my head and pushed me backwards. I lay on my back as she undressed me. I kicked off my boots as she pulled my jeans and boxers down. Then she knelt between my thighs and made love to me with her mouth, like a pro. I tried to pull her head up when I was about to cum, but she kept on sucking like she was addicted. I felt that all too familiar tingling in my nut sack just as she took me all the way down her throat. I sprayed her tonsils with my seed and her stomach welcomed it as she swallowed drop after drop.

It didn't take long for her to nurse me back to life after she had drained me the first time. We were all over the room, fucking like animals. We did it on the bathroom sink, the coffee table, the couch, the love seat, standing up against the front door, on the floor and finally the bed.

We experimented as well, so I knocked on her "backdoor" and she gladly let me in. That was a first for me and I was turned out instantly! I didn't know a female could have an orgasm from that, but Tracey damn sure did and I was glad to give it to her. She was a cold FREAK!!

After our marathon sex, she lit a blunt and we smoked until our eyelids got heavy.

As we lay side-by-side, Tracey commented, "This has been a wild night."

I exhaled a cloud of smoke and said, "Only if you knew." I was thinking about the Maxima.

"I was sure you was going home to the 'significant other' when I saw you leave from the club alone," Tracey said.

"That's what you get for assumin'. An' where's yo' *significant other?*"

"Tony hadn't come in before I left. So I have no idea," Tracey replied.

"Tony gonna whup that ass when you get home," I said laughing.

"Please. I-don't-think-so. Tony and I got an understanding. We're open like that."

"Open huh?"

"That's right. Matter of fact, Tony should've been here tonight," Tracey said.

"Doing what?" I asked.

"Spectatin' or joining in, whatever. Tony been promising me a threesome for the longest. I just hadn't found the right guy…until tonight."

"Damn. Y'all some freaky muh-fuckas. Ain't no way in the hell I'ma watch another nigga fuck my bitch," I said.

Tracey laughed and sucked on the blunt.

When she exhaled she said, "You'll be surprised as to how me and Tony get down" She looked over at me and asked "So, you game or what?" she was staring at me.

"Game for fuckin' you in front of yo' nigga? Why not, but that muh-fucka bet-not get too close to a nigga. I ain't 'bout that gay shit, ya dig." I responded.

Tracey laughed so hard she had tears in her eyes. I looked at her and thought, *Damn, it wasn't that funny. What the fuck is wrong with this crazy bitch?*

"I'on know what you laughin' at, but I'm one-hundred on that" I stated.

She was calming down and wiping her eyes, still giggling.

"Boy, you ain't got a clue," she said as she leaned over and started kissing my chest.

I saw the sun peeking through the curtains and I realized we had been going at it for hours.

"I wanna see you tonight. My place." she said.

"Holla at me after you holla at Tony. I'on wanna have to act a fool. Feel me?" I said and she laughed again, this time even harder than the first time.

She peeped my seriousness and said, "Relax, everything is gonna be aiight, Tony been promising me this. You just call me back when I hit you."

"Fa sho'," I replied.

After we went another round, we showered and departed.

I must say, Tracey really gave me a good ending to a fucked up night.

After changing cars and clothes at my Aunt's house, I went home. Kinya was asleep so I laid down beside her fully clothed. My intentions were to rest for only a few minutes, but I was asleep as soon as my head touched the pillow. I was awakened four hours later by the telephone. I reached across an empty spot where Kinya once laid and answered in a tired voice.

"Yeah."

"Sup playboy."

It was V.

"'Sup," I spoke as I yawned and checked the time.

"You still in the bed?" V asked.

"I just got home a lil' while ago."

"Yeah, me too. Dee gettin' on a nigga's nerves an' shit. She said she talked to you last night. Good lookin'."

"You know how we do," I replied.

"What you end up doin' last night?" V asked.

"You mean *who* did I end up doin'?" I said as I got off the bed and searched the apartment for Kinya.

She'd left a note on the refrigerator saying she would be back soon.

"V, you ain't gonna believe this shit. Damn, I'on know where to start at," I continued with V as I told him everything that had went down the night before, starting with the note and then about the Maxima and finally about what Tracey wanted me to do.

V listened in silence until I was finished, then he said, "Damn, 'Pone. Them niggas tried you on some old simple shit like that? You ain't recognize 'em?"

"Nah, I ain't never seen 'em before," I replied.

"Wow... But you *did* hit at least one of them mutha-fuckas tho, right?"

"I hit the nigga who was drivin', fa sho"

"Good. Anybody see you?"

"Nah, I'on think so. I took on a deserted street and handled my bizness. I think I'm cool on that" I replied.

V changed the subject "Tracey on some ole' freak-type shit, huh? So what up, you gonna fuck her while her nigga watch?" V asked.

"Yeah, I'ma fuck his bitch for him. But you gonna be readin' about his ass if he on that gay shit, I'm puttin' two in his dome. Believe That!"

V laughed and said, "You know what? I saw how that bitch kept checkin' you out, when Felecia wasn't lookin'. What's up wit' Felecia? You still gon' hit that or do you think Tracey gone try to throw salt?"

"For real, I'on even care no mo'. So many hoes sweatin' a nigga now, I can pick an' choose?" I replied.

"Dig that. Oh, I meant to tell you about ole girl I left the club wit'. Baby girl is from Miami and she got a cousin who be doin' his thang. She said he lookin' for somebody in N.C. to network wit'. She 'spose to be introducing me to him when he come back to Charlotte next week. Yo, 'Pone, you know you can't get no better than having a connect from da 'bottom'." V explained.

"I know he prolly got them thangs dirt cheap," I commented.

"No Question" V agreed.

We kicked it for a little while longer before ending the conversation.

I battled with the uncomfortable feeling of a hangover, as my stomach contracted into knots. I desperately tried to dash for the bathroom and barely made it before I called 'EARL' all over the toilet seat. Unlike most people, I didn't promise God I wasn't going to get drunk anymore because I knew I would be lying.

The rest of the day was uneventful except for serving a few customers and picking up money. After serving Candy Man in Firestone, I met June at Outback Steakhouse for a bite to eat. While eating, June was telling me about what he had heard about the shooting on Idlewilde.

"Damn nigga, I didn't know dat was you. Dat was dat nigga Reco an'nem outta Earle Village in dat Max. Reco was drivin', he got slumped. Dejuan and Trap got away. Don't nobody know nuthin' yet, but you need to chill for a minute."

"Fuck that. Them bitch ass niggas shouldn't have tried me like dat," I replied as I munched on my steak.

"What'choo do wit' the gun?"

"I got rid of it this mornin', nigga. I might be crazy but I ain't no fool" I said as I yelled for the waiter.

I added, "Guess who I seen over Candy Man's house all laid up?"

"Who?"

"That bitch Meka. She looked like she getting thick too" I said.

"Da bitch might be pregnant, her lil' slut ass," June remarked.

"You still fuckin' her?"

"Fuck nah. Hoe can't stand me." June laughed.

After splitting the check and the tip we left the restaurant and headed to Urban Elite to kick it with Pat. But I was really going so I could see Felicia's fine ass.

Felicia and I kicked it while June was showing off his Caddy to Pat. I made plans to hook up with her later that night at the club. She didn't mention anything about Tracey and me, so I figured I was in the clear. After buying more gear, June and I departed our separate ways. I headed home and June headed to his new stomping ground, Rock Hill, S.C.

Kinya and I pulled up at the same time. She had a car-full of grocery bags. After lugging all of the bags upstairs, I collapsed on the couch.

"What's up wit' you? Them all-nighters takin' it's toll, huh?" she asked in a sarcastic manner.

I looked up and shot back, "Damn, you in yo' feelin's 'cause a nigga was takin' care of bidness last night?"

She was silent as she unloaded the bags.

"Look, I gotta lotta shit I gotta do later, so I'ma get some rest" I said as I headed towards the bedroom. She didn't respond.

I stretched out on the king-sized bed and let sleep consume me......

*I was fucking Tracey doggy-style while watching our reflection in the mirror. She was howling like a werewolf as I slapped her ass. I was just about to nut when all of a sudden the bedroom door came crashing in. A nigga built like the hulk, wearing a g-string and a garter belt came running towards the bed. Tracey called his name, "Tony, come to momma."*

*I reached beneath the pillow for my pistol. Iit was gone! Tracey had my dick clenched inside of her like we were two canines stuck together. I couldn't break loose as the nigga started reaching towards me and smiling with bright-red lipstick on. I started throwing blows like Tyson. No matter how hard or fast I swung, my blows were in slow motion and landed like pillows. Tracey's pussy started to cut off my circulation and it felt like my dick was being severed. She started cumming and screamed my name, "Mike.....Mike....Mike."*

*How does she know my real name? I thought.*

*She screamed it over and over... "Mike..." I felt someone shake me.*

"Mike!" Kinya said as I slowly opened my eyes.

Damn, I was dreaming.

"Why you tossin' and turnin' like that?" she asked with concern in her voice. I noticed it had gotten dark, so I checked my watch and saw that it was a little past eight.

I showered and got dressed while Kinya was brooding in silence. I told her I would be back later, as I snatched the keys to the Honda off of the dresser and pecked her on the cheek.

"Page me or call the cell if you need me before I get back, Aiight," I talking over my shoulder as I opened the front door and stepped out into the night.

Kinya sat on the bed and seethed with anger.

*That nigga think I don't know he was at the club last night. He's lucky he left the club by hisself. I ain't gone tell Dee that Tara saw V leave with some bitch, that shit will hurt that girl. Damn, Mike lied to me and Dee last night. Although he was alone when he left the club, but I wonder where he spent the night at and who with,* Kinya thought as she stared blankly at the spot where her man used to sleep every night.

While I was in the shower earlier, for some reason I couldn't get Tracey off my mind, so I decided to page her once I got onto the highway. She called right back.

"Yeah."

"Hey sexy" she spoke in that sexy voice.

I decreased the volume of the radio so I could hear.

"'Sup, *Freakier-Than-Me*?" I said laughing.

"Oh, you got jokes tonight, huh?" Tracey replied.

As I lit a blunt that was in the ashtray I asked, "What's up wit' that ménage cuatro?"

Tracey laughed and replied, "You mean ménage trios?"

"Nah, I mean what I said. I know cuatro mean four. Me, you, Tony and my pistol," I said, as I checked the rearview and saw a State Trooper behind me.

I checked the speedometer to make sure I wasn't speeding and I wasn't. I reached down and put the blunt in the ashtray. The weed had me trippin'. I could've sworn I was doing about 100, but I wasn't. Tracey was talking, but I wasn't listening. I wanted to tell her to shut the fuck up for a minute because I was having a crisis. But in actuality, I was just paranoid. I told her to hold on for a minute, as I dropped the phone to my lap and sat straight up. I was hoping the Trooper would turn off, but he didn't, he stayed behind me. All kinds of thoughts clouded my brain, some were rational and some were very irrational.

*Damn, what if they found out that I was the one who slumped Reco last night? But nah, I'm not in the Benz, though. Damn, I'm trippin'. If I get pulled, I'm holdin' court right here on I-77, fuck that. I'd rather be carried by six than judged by twelve, especially for a body.*

As I reached the West Blvd. exit, the Trooper switched lanes and zoomed past me.

*Pheew. Damn, that was close.*

I picked up the blunt which was still burning in the ashtray, took a long ass drag and held the smoke as long as I could, before exhaling. Then I resumed my conversation with Tracey. She wanted to know if I was still coming over and proceeded to give me her address. After jotting down directions to her house which was on the South side of town, I wondered if she had discussed the situation with her man.

"You holla at yo' nigga or what?" I asked.

Tracey laughed and said, "Everything is fine, Tony agreed to it. How about an hour?"

I was trying to figure out what the fuck was so funny every time I said something about her nigga. I started to have flashbacks of that crazy ass dream, but then I shook the thought and told her I was on my way.

When I reached Nations Ford Road, I turned into the Colony Acres neighborhood and searched for Tracey's address. When I found it, I inspected the house as I parked in the driveway behind two Nissan Sentra's with matching custom plates that read T-N-T. I figured it stood for Tracey and Tony, but it could've easily meant TNT dynamite because Tracey definitely had some Bomb-ass-pussy!

The house was a very spacious, two stories with a two-car garage. The front door was one of those double-door types with a brass knocker and a brass knob. The lawn was well manicured with two statues of the Sphinx lion standing erect on each side of the walkway. The porch light was on along with a light in one of the front rooms, which I figured to be the living room. I stuffed my pistol in my pants, took a knot of money out of my pocket and put it in the glove compartment. I grabbed my cell phone and exited the car.

As I approached the front door I heard the voices of two women. I listened for a minute, then I rung the bell. A Spanish looking female, wearing short shorts and a wife beater, answered the door. She was a shade or two darker than Tracey, but just as beautiful, with an ass like 'Whoa'! She and Tracey could've easily passed for sisters.

I was thinking that maybe it *is* Tracey's sister.

"Hi. You must be Tracey's friend Capone," she said.

I was checking her out and she saw it.

"Yeah, is she in?"

Tracey stepped up behind her wearing a long T-shirt and a pair of spandex tights with no shoes and her hair was hanging down her back like she had just washed it.

"Hey sexy. Come on in" Tracey said as the other girl stepped aside to let me enter.

The living room was full of expensive furniture, with brass and glass fixtures everywhere. I was thinking, *Damn, that nigga Tony must be doin' his thing.*

I was led to the couch by Tracey while her friend walked towards another room. Once I was seated, Tracey sat next to me and said, "Welcome to my humble abode"

"Yeah, this shit is tight. I like this. I'm 'bout to buy a house myself. I want my shit like this," I replied as I looked around.

I saw pictures of Tracey and her friend in frames on the coffee table next to a section of magazines. I still saw no signs of this nigga Tony.

Tracey asked, "You want somethin' to drink?"

"What' choo got?"

"Hennessy, Vodka, Rum, Corona, Tequila and....some coolers," Tracey replied.

"Damn, what y'all runnin' a liquor house or something'?" I laughed and then asked, "You got Cranberry juice?"

"Yeah, let me guess, Vodka and cranberry, right?" Tracey asked, as she twisted one of my locks playfully.

"I see you got a good memory" I replied.

Tracey yelled, "Tony bring us two Vodkas and some cranberry juice"

I was finally getting ready to meet her freaky ass nigga. I touched my pistol for reassurance, as I flashed back to that dream again. After about five minutes or so, the girl who had answered the door brought out two glasses of Vodka and a bottle of cranberry juice and sat them on the table in front of me and Tracey.

Tracey said, "Thank you baby. You're so sweet"

The girl reacted by bending down and kissing Tracey on the lips. This wasn't a sisterly kiss. This was some passionate shit! I stared at them with my mouth open wide.

Now, everything made sense! Tracey never said she had a *nigga*. She only referred to her lover as Tony. I was the one assuming the wrong shit the whole time. No wonder Tracey laughed every time I mentioned her *nigga*. Tracey and her friend saw the expression on my face and Tracey said, "I'm sorry. I didn't introduce you two. Capone this is my girl Toni with and 'I'. Toni, this is Capone, the one I told you about. The one Felicia is crazy about, but she playin' like she all hard and shit."

I spoke up and said, "Toni with a 'I' huh? Damn, girl why you ain't tell me?"

Tracey laughed and said, "'Cause you never asked. Is there a problem?"

"Hell nah! The fuck is that, a trick question or somethin'?" I shot back.

I picked up one of the glasses of Vodka and gulped it down, straight, fuck the cranberry juice. I knew I was in for the time of my life!

"Felicia get down like this too?" I asked, wondering if Felicia also like girls.

"She wants to, but she swears she never has. I can tell it won't be long because she be asking too many questions, but she knows how I roll though" Tracey answered, as she poured some cranberry juice in her glass of Vodka.

Toni walked back out of the room, swinging that fat ass in a seductive manner. I stared at her ass and imagined her and Tracey getting down. I smiled at the thought and my dick started throbbing.

Tracey peeped me staring and said, "I gotta fine bitch, huh?"

"No Question! No wonder why all the fine bitches act like they don't need a nigga. I see now, 'cause they all got bitches"

We both laughed at my comment. Toni reentered the room and sat on the love seat across from me and Tracey. She was sensuously sipping Tequila and sucking on a piece of lime. She had her legs wide open and her shorts were so tight I could see the outline of her crotch. I openly stared between her legs as I continued to burn my chest with the straight Vodka.

"What 'choo smokin' on?" Tracey asked, as she sipped her drink.

"You know I keep some sticky. But it's out in the car. I'll be right back," I said, as I got off the couch and headed out the door.

When I reentered the house neither girl was in sight, so I sat on the couch and rolled a blunt as I awaited their return.

"Capone!" Tracey yelled from upstairs.

"Yeah, what up," I answered back as I lit the blunt.

"Come 'mere, bring my drink with you," Tracey answered.

I grabbed our Vodkas and headed up the stairs. When I reached the top, Toni was standing by one of the bedroom doors with a towel wrapped around her, concealing the portion of her body form her breasts to the top of her thighs.

*This is one bad bitch,* I thought to myself as she waved for me to come closer.

As I approached her, she took the blunt from my lips and stuck it between hers. When I entered the bedroom, Tracey was laying across the king size bed on her stomach, also with a towel on. The bottom of her ass cheeks were peeking out from beneath the terrycloth. Tracey was flipping through channels with the remote when I handed her the drink she had requested. I sat beside her and playfully slapped her ass and watched her cheeks jiggle. She closed her eyes sensuously and said, "Oooo—you know what that shit do to me". So I slapped her on her ass again. Toni took a seat on the other side of Tracey and put the blunt between Tracey's lips. Toni began to caress the back of Tracey's thighs while working her way up towards her ass. Her hand disappeared beneath the towel as Tracey's eyes closed in ecstasy.

I took the blunt from Tracey and moved from the bed and into a nearby chair.

*I gotta see this shit.* I thought as I stared intently at the fiasco, which was about to unfold before me.

They both discarded the towels and began to engage in a most passionate kiss. Tongues were everywhere. I was already about to lose it, but I checked myself and calmed down. *Down boy!*

Tracey and Toni freaked each other like porn stars, pleasing one another with tongues and fingers. I had never witnessed two women making love other than on video. I must admit, there is nothing like seeing that shit up close and personal, it blew my mind! When Toni rolled over and reached inside the bedside drawer to extract a dildo, I finally spoke up.

"Yo, it ain't no need for that shit, you might as well put that shit back."

Toni smiled at me and said, "I see you over there enjoying yourself," referring to the bulge in my pants as I stood up and approached the bed.

Both Tracey and Toni undressed me while kissing spots on my body I forgot I even had. These two beautiful women had me on cloud twelve and a half. After sliding on a condom, we were a mass of arms, legs, tongues and every other body part imaginable. I fucked Tracey while she ate Toni. I fucked Toni while she ate Tracey. Then I fucked Tracey while Toni licked my balls and then they traded positions like seasoned teammates. They both gave me head at the same time, while periodically tonguing each other and sharing my cum as I ejaculated in their mouths. It went down like that for hours! By the end of the third round, all three of us were spent. We all laid in the king size bed butt-naked. I was in the middle with them on each side of me. Needless to say, I felt like the biggest pimp on earth. Only to find out later on in life, that bitches like Toni and Tracey would come a dime a dozen. But for the time being, I was on top of the world as I lay with these two women.

After smoking another blunt and showering together, we all made plans to see each other later at the club. I had also made plans to see Felicia, Pooh and Celeste at the club and I began to contemplate how I was going to maneuver without getting caught up. I didn't want to burn any bridges, so I decided I would just not show up. I opted to use the remainder of the night to handle business.

I decided to go to Dalton Village to check on Lil Rick and Black. I didn't page them because I wanted to just drop by and see how they were handling their shit.

When I turned off of West Blvd. and into the neighborhood, I saw about ten police cars and an ambulance at the library on the corner. There was the typical crowd of nosey by-standers watching whatever was going on. I pulled up in Lil Rick's parking lot and saw no one in sight. As I parked and got out, a fiend stepped out of one of the empty apartments and spoke, "Lil' Capone, what up baby. I know you holdin'. Throw a dog a bone."

I recognized him. It was Foots, one of the neighborhood vets. "Nah, Foots, I ain't doin' nothin'. I'm looking for Rick, you seen him?"

Foots looked at me like I was asking a trick question. "You talkin' bout Lil Rick?" he asked.

"Yeah, where he at?"

"Shiiit, him, Black, and Curt 'nem just had a shoot out. Dat's why everybody up there by the library. Rick got hit" Foots reported.

Before he could finish, I had taken off running towards the library. When I reached the crowd, I saw Rick being lifted into an ambulance on a stretcher. Rochelle, Black's girlfriend was standing nearby crying.

"Rochelle, what happened?" I asked, as I put my arm around her.

When she looked up and saw it was me, she put her had on my chest and sobbed.

"What happened?" I asked again as I held her at arm's length.

Still sobbing, she said "They shot him… they shot him."

"Tell me what happened and who shot him" I asked, trying to calm her down.

She got herself together long enough to talk. "Black and Rick was at the store mindin' they biness when Curt and two more niggas pulled up. Curt and Rick had some words earlier this evening and I guess Curt was still trippin'. They started arguing again and one of the niggas that was wit' Curt pulled out a gun and started shootin'. I think Black and Rick started shootin' back and Rick got shot. He made it down here to the library and collapsed. I'on think he gon' make it 'Pone." Rochelle resumed crying again.

"Where Black at?" I asked.

"He over my sister house, but don't nobody else know he at"

"Show me where she stay," I said, as I led Rochelle away from the crowd.

We walked to the Honda and drove to Clanton Park to Rochelle's sister's house. When we arrived, Black was standing outside talking to Ray-Ray beside Ray-Ray's Infiniti.

"Damn, nigga what y'all goin through?" I asked as I stepped out of the car.

"Man, them soft ass niggas tried a muh-fucka" Black said, as I approached him and Ray-Ray. Ray-Ray had tears in his eyes.

"What happened?" I asked.

Black took a deep breath and began explaining, "Curt came on the block this afternoon wit' that bullshit, talkin' bout how he gon' start takin' niggas shit if it ain't his. You know I ain't no soft nigga, so I told that nigga, 'to get some ass you gotta brang some ass'. Niggas ain't havin' that shit. Him and Rick started arguing and Rick told him his baby mama got some 'bomb head'. Curt got in his feelin's and acted like he wanted to try Rick but all of us was standing out there, strapped. He left and we didn't see him no more until we walked to the store. Him, Nitty, and Na-Na pulled out and started bussin' shots. I started bussin' back, but Rick had already got hit. I pulled Rick around the side of the store while I was still bustin' at them niggas. They pulled off and me and Rick headed down the hill towards his Aunt's house. Rick fell in the library parking lot. I tried to carry him but I couldn't. I stayed wit him and put pressure on his stomach until I heard the sirens get close enough for me to dip. I took his money, the dope he had on him and his pistol."

"Rick had a pistol and didn't wet that nigga when they rolled up? Damn dog, that's rule number one when you beefin' wit a nigga. When Curt came back wit mo niggas y'all should've known it wasn't no mo conversatin'. All the talkin' was dead." I replied in anger.

"Yeah, I know, but damn, ain't nobody thing soft ass Curt was gon' try no shit like dat," Black said.

"You think Rick gonna be alright?" I asked.

"Man, I'on know. He was bleedin' like a hog," Black replied as he sat on the curb and put his head in his hands.

"Ain't no need to cry 'bout this shit now. Y'all know what time it is! When I first started fuckin' wit y'all, I told y'all I got y'all back. Why y'all ain't beep me?" I asked, curiously.

"I been beepin' you every since I heard about it," Ray-Ray said.

I'd forgotten about turning my pager off while I was with Tracey and Toni.

"Aiight, let me holla at V and June so we can figure out the best way to handle this shit. Black, you need to chill for a minute. Ray-Ray, I know Rick is yo' cousin and I know you heated but you gotta use yo head on this. If something happen to them niggas right now, all of us gonna get the blame for it. Feel me? Just chill until I holla back at y'all. Ray-Ray go see Rick and let me know how he doin'. Tell him we gonna handle this shit" I directed as I got back into the Honda and pulled off.

## Chapter Eleven: Ninety-Five South

After Rick got shot everybody expected a quick retaliation but we were too smart for that. We let things die down for a couple of months before responding. Rick had gotten out of the hospital and was doing fine. He had to wear a shit bag for sixty days, but after those sixty days, he was as good as new. Black and Ray-Ray were working together in Clanton Park, serving caps and weight, which I fronted them.

Curt had been seen off and on in Dalton Village since the shooting and word on the street was that he only came through to drop off dope and pick up money.

Na-Na was staying in Mt. Holly with one of his girlfriends. He hadn't been seen in Charlotte since he shot Rick. He didn't think anybody knew where he was, but what he failed to understand is that money talks. For the right price, a mutha-fucka would tell God on Jesus!! I kept tabs on Na-Na and Curt so they couldn't get away and I found out that Nitty wasn't down with shooting Rick, he was just along for the ride. My information came from a reliable source so we decided to give Nitty a pass.

June and V hollered at three young cats that Quick had turned them on to. Scrappy, Shoe and Youngsta were straight up young killers! Hired hit men who were about their business. Scrappy was a tall light-skinned brother with dark freckles and shoulder-length dreads whose pistol weighed more than he did. Shoe was the oldest of the three, dark-skinned and heavy set, with cold eyes. Youngsta was the youngest and the wildest of the bunch, tall skinny and deranged.

My birth date is April 24th and June's birth date is April 22nd, so we always celebrated our birthdays together. That year, we decided to triple date to Atlanta. Kinya and I were in the Benz, V and Donyetta were in the Beema, June was in the 'Lac with a chick he had just met named Cherone. She seemed to fit right in, like we had been knowing her forever. She looked a lot like a young Halle Berry and she seemed to dig June.

On this trip, I had various reasons for being away from Charlotte. One reason was the fact that I needed a break from the beeper and cell for a couple of days. Hustling can take its toll on you, especially when you 'go hard' and I was definitely going 'hard'. But the main reason for being out of town was, while I was hanging out at Lennox Mall, frequenting The Cheesecake Factory and tossing dollars at strippers at Magic City, Club Nikki's and The Blue Flame, Scrappy and his crew had Curt and Na-Na duct-taped in the trunk of a stolen Impala, heading to the Catawba River. I was celebrating twenty years of life, while Curt and Na-Na was fighting to get twenty seconds of air as they were thrown into the river with cinder-blocks attached to their ankles. We used the term, 'cement shoes'.

June, V, our dates and myself were in V and Donyetta's room smoking spliffs and making plans for the evening when my pager went off. I checked the number and saw the digits, 187, 187, all the way across the screen. It was Scrappy's code to let me know that they had handled their business. As I puffed on the 'L', I told V and June, "Yo, that's Scrap and 'nem."

"Everythang straight?" June asked.

"One, eight to the seven, baby" I replied.

Two less niggas to worry about! We all hung out in the ATL for the next two days, shopping and clubbing.

When we returned to Charlotte, it was business as usual. Our clientele was beginning to pick-up! Because of Curt's mysterious disappearance, there was a shortage of dope on West Blvd.

The female from Miami whom V had met at the Vintage finally introduced him to her cousin. Big Trey was a 6'3," brother whose complexion was as dark as night. He was built like a silverback gorilla with the typical Miami trademark of gold teeth and dreads. V introduced me to Trey the second time he visited Charlotte. We met at the Embassy Suites where he was staying for the weekend. Trey had another dude with him along with a female who was built like one of Luke's dancers.

We all met in the hotel's lobby near the indoor waterfall and I suggested that we discuss business over a few drinks at Jock's and Jill's sports lounge which was a few blocks away. They followed me and V to the restaurant in a rental car. Once we were inside and seated, I looked at the female with an expression as if to say, 'Damn, won't you go find somethin' to do and let us men talk'. But she stayed where she was at and Trey didn't dismiss her, so I said 'fuck it'.

"My nigga, your man tell me y'all be movin' dem thangs 'round hea," Trey said, displaying a mouth full of gold teeth. He had a very deep southern accent which made 'here' sound like 'he a'.

"Yeah a lil' light sumthin'," I replied as I sipped my Vodka and cranberry.

"What y'all payin for a bird?" the girl asked.

I looked at her and wondered why she was even in the conversation.

V answered, "What y'all lettin' em go fo?"

Trey recognized game and said, "Dig dis hea, if we gone do biness we gone have to put all dis shit on da table and not try to spin each otha', my nigga. I'mma tell ya like dis hea, I got 'em for seventeen if you come and get it, but if I gotta make Red come up da road wit' it, I'm a tax you," Trey was referring to the female with him as Red.

V and I looked at each other with a knowing look. Neither one of us showed any expression but I knew he was thinking the same thing I was. I couldn't believe this shit! We never bought a kilo for less than twenty-two. Now here we were being propositioned with a price that was five grand cheaper. I was curious about how much more he would charge if we decided not to go get it, so I asked, "What it's gonna be to have it delivered?"

The female spoke up, "Twenty at the least, depending on what type of mood I'm in."

"Damn baby, that ain't bidness, that's some personal type shit. So you sayin' a nigga might get taxed twenty-two, twenty-three if you on yo' period or somethin'? Fuck that. A nigga ain't gonna be sittin 'round waitin' for yo ass to stop crampin' before we re-up." I said as everyone laughed, including Red.

I was checking her out and wondering if she was Trey's woman. She saw me looking at her and held my gaze.

Trey said, "Look hea, I'll tell y'all what. If y'all want it delivered, den da first time on me, the rest is on you. How dat sound, dog?"

I thought about it for a minute and told him that V and I had to talk to our other partner first. I already knew June would agree. I was just stalling for time so I could have Big Trey checked out before we made any kind of move. I may have been young, but I was a long way from being a fool. V and I gave Trey our pager numbers and he gave us his. Either we had just met the man who was gonna make us rich or we had just met the man who was gonna make us start World War III!!

\*\*\*

Big Trey checked out to be, 'one hundred'! It was on and poppin'!

Kinya and I finally moved into the house we'd been drooling over. We divided all of our old furniture between her sister and my brother. Everything in our house was brand new, even the dishes.

I finally talked my mom into moving out of Little Rock and into a house I'd bought for her and my Grandmother. Since Kinya was finished with school, I surprised her with her very own building which she would convert into a beauty salon and barber shop. It was dream-come-true for her. We had all the paperwork legitimate to the tee, so if anything ever happened to me, none of the property could be touched.

After the first delivery from Big Trey, I knew we were gonna have problems with his mules. Red was on some bullshit! When she arrived in Charlotte, she didn't call until two days later. When she finally called, she was so jacked up on powder she could hardly talk, so we copped our shit and refused to deal with Red again. I called Big Trey the same night I met Red with the coke and told him about his girl. I let him know that it was real bad business and made it clear that every penny of the money was there and if it came up short, it wasn't on our end. I also told him not to bother sending someone else in her place because from here on out, we would be coming to get it.

The dope we got from Trey was just as good as the shit we had robbed Silk for. Miami is known for having that good shit for the low, low! Finally we had a consistent connect.

We ran out of dope so fast, Trey was surprised I was calling back so soon. I put my order in for 10-kilos at seventeen grand each. Trey said he was ready, but I told him to give us a couple of days because I had to pick up the transport car from the shop.

The next morning I called Chad to see if the car was ready and he told me to come by later that evening. June and I stopped by the shop after collecting the last of our money from Freeze and Dave in Earl Village. Chad brought the car around front and gave me specific instructions.

"Listen, first you gotta put the radio on 88.7, then you have to let the driver's window down, half-way. Lastly, you gotta click the 'doors locked' button."

After Chad locked the doors, we heard a click inside of the floorboards in the back. Chad removed the floor mats on both sides in the back and we saw the floor open up revealing a stash spot on both sides. The empty spaces would easily accommodate up to 15-kilos.

"Damn. Dat's some ole James Bond type shit." June remarked as he stared in amazement. I smiled at Chad with approval.

"Capone you gotta do exactly what I did in order for it to work. Just remember: Radio, window, and locks, in that order. Okay," Chad said.

"Yeah, I got it. V already straightened you, right?" I inquired about his compensation.

"Yeah, he came through earlier. I appreciate the tip too. Oh, by the way, how does Kinya like her car? Is she satisfied?" Chad asked.

"Man, that girl love that car more than she love me," I replied.

The stash car was a Honda station wagon. I figured a family car wouldn't look too suspicious especially for three niggas. The stash would hold all of the dope and guns, but the best thing of all is the fact that the spots were airtight which would eliminate the possibility of dogs sniffing out the dope. We had our shit together! The only thing we disagreed about was who was going to drive the first leg of that long-ass ride. June finally took the initiative and said he would drive to Georgia, V would drive from GA to Florida and I would take us the rest of the way to the Bottom.

We loaded the car with bags of clothes to throw the police off. We made it look as if we were taking a vacation trip or visiting family. We had a $180,000 and two tech-nine's in the stash box, ready for whatever.

I called Big Trey to let him know we were leaving out early that Friday morning and he said he would be ready and waiting. I told him I would call as soon as we entered Hollywood. We left at 5 AM on Friday morning so we wouldn't get caught up in that Jacksonville 5-o'clock traffic. I'd heard it was a beast and I wasn't trying to experience it.

We hit I-95 at about 5:30 AM pumping the Poison Clan, *'Hoe, bend over and spread dem butt cheeks. Let a nigga see dem guts freak...'*. We were nodding our heads to the rhythm as J.T. Money spit that booty shake shit. I guess we were getting into the Miami groove already. I was in the back seat, V was riding shotgun and June was handling the road like a pro. June took us to the Georgia line and then V took it to Jacksonville. I slept until it was my turn to drive, only getting up whenever we stopped for food or to take a piss.

When I took the wheel, I was wide-awake. I put Luke in the CD player and drove us all the way in. I called Trey once we entered Hollywood. He was on his way to pick up his daughter from daycare.

"Trey, what up? I'm in Hollywood. Where you at?"

"I'm goin' to get my shorty from daycare. Listen, I want y'all to meet me in Lauderdale at Jumbo's. It's right off the highway. Get off on exit-73 and make a left, you'll see da restaurant on da right. I'll be in da parkin' lot in a burnt orange Legend" Trey said.

"Aiight. Later."

I entered Ft. Lauderdale minutes after our conversation. Trey was parked in front of the restaurant in a tight ass Acura Legend with a bowling ball paint job. He was talking to his daughter who was in the back seat. I parked beside him and got out of the Honda. The heat was excruciation. Damn, it was hot! Trey wanted to go inside to eat, so I told June and V to get out.

Jumbo's was a seafood spot that was known for serving the biggest shrimp in the United States. When the waitress brought the food to the table, I could see why they called this spot Jumbo's. The shrimp were big as a mutha-fucka! I had never seen shrimp that big before in my entire life. Trey ordered conch fritters and mango juice. I had never heard of Conch. I guess you are never too old to learn something.

After we ate, we followed Trey to the Marriot in Miami Lakes and got a suite for the weekend. Trey had to take his daughter home, he said he would be back in two hours and that he wanted to take us out and show us how niggas play in The Bottom. I couldn't wait to see all those thick ass females I always saw on TV.

We all showered and got dressed for the weather. I put on a pair of Maurice Malone shorts, a UNC basketball jersey with a pair of Air Force One's. June was dressed in jeans, a tee shirt and Timbs.

"Nigga, if you don't take that hot ass shit off," I said to June.

"Fuck you, I'm wearing' dis," June replied.

V was dressed in shorts and a tank top. Trey showed up with one of his partners, a dude named Tank. Tank was a short, stocky, bald-headed brother with chinky eyes. Tank was a shade or two lighter than me with a mouthful of gold teeth with diamonds. These niggas were definitely doing their thing in Miami. Trey introduced everybody, then we smoked two blunts of that Florida kryptonite. All of the weed spots in Miami had a different name for their weed. The name was stamped on the outside of the bag. We were smoking some shit called, 'Ain't No Secret' and it definitely wasn't a secret that this shit had a nigga fucked up.

When we piled into Tank's burgundy Suburban, everybody was as high as a Georgia Kite. I told Trey we wanted to see some bitches, so he took us by a few strip clubs. Our first stop was The Mint, a hole in the wall strip joint with about ten scraggly chickens shaking what little bit of ass they had. We stayed long enough to drink a beer each, then jetted without even tipping anyone. Our next stop was Bootleggers. We could at least deal with this one. I got two dances from an Amazon red-bone named Luscious. Luscious was phat as a mutha-fucka, with a tattoo of a tongue on the inside of her right thigh. I wanted to kiss it. She kept calling me 'Dread' and I was wondering if she thought I was Jamaican, but Trey told me that everyone in Miami called you that if you're rocking dreadlocks. A few more of the girls called me Dread also, so I got use to hearing it.

June and V were enjoying themselves tremendously. June spent three-hundred at Bootleggers. I was having fun too, but I wasn't having three-hundred dollar's worth. V tricked off two-hundred on one girl who that he thought liked him. We left Bootleggers after an hour or so, because I wanted to experience the world famous, Rolexx, to see if it was all everybody made it out to be.

On the way to Club Rolexx, we put another blunt in the air. I stepped up in the Rolexx, not knowing what to expect. Everyone seemed to know Big Trey and Tank, so we got VIP-treatment. Club Rolexx had at least thirty of the finest butt-naked bitches I'd ever seen. Luke and Big Ram, from the Poison Clan, were seated in the VIP-section next to us. They both knew Trey and Tank so they joined us and kicked it with us for a minute. I got about twenty lap dances from different girls. I was in a trance by all of that butt-naked ass gyrating in my face.

One particular girl named Cream held my attention. Cream was pecan-tan, short, thick and bowlegged. She had one of the prettiest asses I had ever seen, so round and smooth, not a blemish in sight. I couldn't help but to continuously rub and caress it. She had her pubic hair trimmed into the shape of a heart and she had an earring in her clit. I tricked off so much money, I lost count and V and June lost their minds.

"P, gimme two hunnit til we get back to da room," June said.

"Nigga, I ain't got *two dollars*, these hoes don' broke me." I told him.

V gave us a grand to split until we got back to the room. If I had known it was going down like that, I would've brought the whole 5-grand I had left in the station wagon because I was turned out.

Strippers had become my aphrodisiac, I couldn't wait to get back to Charlotte so I could go to 'Just Because', R.B's club he had told me about. I got Cream's number and I gave her mine. We planned to hook up before I left The Bottom, but you know how that shit goes.

We left Club Rolexx and headed up the street to Ft. Lauderdale to a joint called Club EXXtasy. The Rolexx was alright, but club EXXtasy was off-the-chain! Everywhere I looked, I didn't see nothing but 'dimes'. I had three-hundred and forty dollars left in my pocket. I ordered four Vodka and cranberry's and a Corona. We all took seats next to the stage for an up-close and personal view of all the honeys.

The first three were okay, so I threw about twenty-dollars on stage during their routines. But when the fourth girl strolled onto the stage, I almost choked on my drink. Her name was Platinum—a caramel-complected stallion with titties like Vanessa Del Rio and an ass like a donkey. Her smile was so pretty, she had me mesmerized and entranced. Tank told me he knew her and said she was good people, so I tossed her twenty-dollars and she danced over to me. Her hair was cut into a 'bob', her face was so pretty and her body was so close to being perfect, I just knew that I would find something wrong like stretch marks or scars, but I couldn't find anything wrong with this girl and that had me skeptical. *Anybody this bad had to have some flaws.* Her teeth were perfect, her feet were pretty as fuck and her eyes were the bedroom type. Anytime I'd met someone like her, they ended up being either dumb as a brick or crazy as a fuckin' schizoid.

In any case, with Platinum, I had to find out, so I motioned for her to come over once she was finished on stage. She winked in agreement and continued her routine on stage. Once she was finished, she came and stood next to me. I admired her for a minute then told her to give me a lap dance. Within seconds, she had my dick rock-hard. I tipped her fifty-dollars and her eyes lit up.

"Let's go to VIP," I said before she took my hand and led me towards the dimly-lit back of the club area where there individual booths were located.

Once inside the booth, I sat on the couch and told her to sit beside me.

"You still gonna have to pay for each song whether I dance or not, Dread," Platinum tried to explain the rules in the most seductive voice.

"Do I look like I'm worried 'bout that? Just sit down so I can holla at 'cha for a minute," I replied.

Platinum sat next to me and let out a long, deep sigh as if to be relieved to be off of her feet for a minute.

"Damn, baby girl you sound like you tired"

"I am. I been on my feet *all* night," she said.

I was checking out her body as she spoke, she was in no way uncomfortable with her nudity.

"How long you been dancing?" I asked.

"You talkin' 'bout tonight or how long I've been dancing period?"

"Period."

She thought for a second, then responded, "I been dancin' off and on for about two years. I'm tryna get straight so I can pay off all of my loans. This is just a part-time job. I only dance on weekends. My day job is at Nation's Bank on 14th Ave. You know where that's at?"

"Nah shawty, I ain't even from here. I'm just visitin' from Charlotte"

"Oh, you from North Carolina? I gotta cousin up there in Winston," she said.

"Oh yeah? You ever go up there?" I asked.

"I been a few times, I danced at Ziggy's a couple of times"

"Ziggy's? You danced at that lil' ass hole in the wall?" I asked, not really having a clue as to what I was talking about. I had never been to Winston Salem a day in my life.

"I only danced there like three times," she responded.

"So, what yo' nigga think about you dancing? I know he be trippin'. 'Cause if I was yo' nigga, ain't no way in the fuck you'll have to dance for nobody, but me. Behind closed doors," I said trying to pick her.

"I don't have no nigga. I'm doin' just fine wit' out one," Platinum claimed.

Instantly I thought about Tracey, so I said, "You ain't got no nigga? So what you got?"

I looked at her with an inquisitive expression. She read between the lines as she shot back, "Nigga Please. A bitch can't do nothin' for me"

I laughed at her sincerity.

"You ain't gotta get all hostile baby, I was just askin'. Listen, what 'choo doin' tomorrow? Don't 'choo wanna show me around?"

"Dread, I don't know you like that. I'on even know yo' name," she replied.

"Capone. And what's yours?"

"Platinum."

"I'm talkin' 'bout yo' real name. Yo' mama ain't name you Platinum," I said.

"And yo' mama ain't name you Capone either."

"Aiight. Mike. And you?"

"Candace. But that still don't mean I'm takin' you sight-seein'," she cautioned.

"Shiit, I'm already sight-seein' right now just lookin' at yo' fine ass. I said show me around, you know, the malls, restaurants and shit like that," I replied.

She was still smiling at the compliment I had given her as I continued, "Why don't you give a nigga a number so I can holla at 'cha tomorrow. I'm only in town for the weekend and I wouldn't mind seeing you somewhere other than right here before I leave, feel me?"

"Why don't I get *yo'* number," she said and right then I knew I was fighting a lost cause.

I gave her my cell number and a hundred dollars. She danced once and then I got up to leave the VIP-section and rejoined my niggas.

June said, "Nigga, I know you ain't been back there playin Captain-Save-A-Hoe"

"Nigga fuck you." I replied before guzzling down my two watered-down Vodkas.

Candace had come out of the VIP and was now dancing for a dude in a Gucci sweat suit who kept staring in our direction. I didn't think much of it until after the dance was over and he kept on staring.

"Yo, Trey you know that nigga over there?" I asked.

Trey and Tank looked in the direction in which I was looking.

"Nah, I'on know dat nigga."

"Me neither," Tank replied.

"He lookin' like he tryin to get kidnapped or something" I said as I stared back at the dude.

Eventually he looked away, but I made it a point to remember his face because my street intuition was kicking in again.

After tricking off almost all of the money we had on us, we left and headed back to our room in Miami. Tank and Trey dropped us off and we made plans to talk business the next day. All three of us were so tired, we all passed out as soon as we got inside the room. V and June had taken the two beds and I passed out on the couch in the living room.

I was awakened by a knock on the door. I reached under the couch and pulled out one of the tech-nines and flipped the safety button off.

"Who is it?" I yelled.

"Room service, senor," replied a female with a Spanish accent.

"Room service? Ain't nobody order room service," I said without opening the door.

"I did" June yelled from the bedroom.

"Well come in here an' get this shit," I said as I put the gun back under the couch and walked to the bathroom.

June let her in and paid for the food. When I exited the bathroom, June and V were gobbling down waffles and eggs.

"P, you ain't see dat Spanish bitch who brought da food up in here, huh?" June asked.

"Nah. What she workin' wit?"

"I ain't seen no Mexican or whatever she is, dat fine in my life" June replied.

"Why one of y'all ain't holla?" I asked.

"You know I'on fuck wit them third-world hoes," V said.

"I fucked around and got tongue-tied when I seen her, but believe me, I'ma see her ass again tho," June said as he lit a blunt of Ain't No Secret. He puffed and tried to pass it to V.

"Hell Nah. I ain't fuckin' wit that shit this early. My whole day'll be fucked up," V told June.

I could feel where he was coming from, so I declined also. Besides, I wanted to have a clear head, at least until the sun went down.

Trey called a few minutes past noon and informed us that he would see us early the next morning, so we could cop the coke and blend in with the morning traffic.

To my surprise, Candace called me and we set up a date, which actually turned into a triple date. Candace introduced June and V to two of her friends named Tastee and Shawn, who were sisters. We'd agreed to meet at a local mall later that evening.

Arriving at the mall a little past 3 PM, we met Candace and her two friends in the food court area, which was jam-packed. Candace was dressed in a sundress with a pair of sandals. *Damn, baby girl looked just as good dressed as she did, undressed.* I recognized Tastee from the night before. She was about 5'7," thick and milk chocolate complected. Tastee wore her hair in micro braids and sported much jewelry. Tastee's sister whose name was Shawn was an inch or two shorter than her. Also dark skinned and mad thick. Both Tastee and Shawn had on skin-tight jean shorts that showed the outline of every curve and crevice they possessed. I couldn't stop staring at the prints that were so visible at the spots where their thighs met at the 'V'.

They both looked as if they had someone's fist balled up between their legs. June and V also zoomed in on the pussy prints, there was no way to peep without being obvious. I was wondering, *How in the hell did they get into those tight-ass shorts?* I wanted to ask, but it would've been disrespectful. So I just enjoyed the view, without commenting.

Finally I spoke, "'Sup y'all. How y'all doin'?"

They all spoke back, Candace said, "Y'all ain't get lost did you?"

In fact, hell yeah we got lost because of June's stupidity. We ended-up riding through Overtown and Scott's projects which was way out of the way. But I lied. "Nah, we come right to it"

Candace and I talked, while June and V has introduced themselves and paired off with the two sisters. We all strolled through the mall occasionally stopping at stores to browse or splurge. Everyone was getting hungry so we decided to get a bite to eat. Tastee suggested we try a Jamaican restaurant that was located only a few blocks from the mall. I thought June and V were going to try and ride with me so they could argue about which girl had the fattest pussy print, but to my surprise, once we reached the parking lot, June tossed me the keys to the Honda. He and V got into Candance's Mustang with Tastee. Shawn and Candace got into the Honda with me. I pulled out of the mall's parking lot following Tastee to the restaurant. Candace commented on all of the suitcases and bags of clothes that were strewn about.

"Y'all sho' gotta lotta clothes just for one weekend. You sure y'all leavin' tomorrow?" she asked while looking at me as if maybe I had lied.

"You know what? Since I met you, I really do wish I wasn't leavin' tomorrow. But yeah, I do gotta bounce, but I'm definitely comin' back down here, believe that" I replied. As we stopped at a red light, I continued, "Damn shawty, you wearin' that dress. You know that right?"

I was looking at those pretty brown thighs.

"You might wanna watch the road instead of watchin' me," Candace replied as she nodded towards the windshield, letting me know that the light had turned green.

I was busy wondering what those thighs would feel like wrapped around my waist, as I sped up to catch Tastee.

While we were all eating some of the hottest wings on this side of the equator at the *Jerk Machine*, Candace made an interesting comment. "I'on know what you do, but I know what Tank do. If you from outta town and you down here hollin' at Tank, you doin' somethin' you ain't got no biness."

I looked at her inquisitively and asked, "Damn, is it that obvious? What's up wit Tank? Do a lotta people 'round here know how strong he is?"

"Hell yeah. If you from the Bottom and you'on know Tank and Trey, somethin' wrong" Candace professed.

I was thinking silently about what danger might arise if we weren't careful when dealing with Big Trey. I knew if people on the streets were aware of their status, then that meant the police knew too. I thought about me and my boys and how we were flossing in Charlotte. Immediately I made up my mind not to come back to Miami to cop dope from them again. I'd also planned to talk to June and V about our hangout habits. Maybe we needed to tone it down a little. From now on, Miami would only be a vacation spot for me. I was willing to wait as long as I would have to for Trey to find another mule. This would be my first and last time on the highway with coke.

After finishing our food, we all exited the *Jerk Machine* feeling ten pounds heavier. Once outside we paired off and conversed for a minute before getting into our rides.

"Yo, hit me as soon as you finish doin' what 'choo gotta do, aiight," I said to Candace as I opened the passenger door to get into the Honda.

"You just call me back when I page you," Candace replied, as she and the two sisters got into the Mustang.

I waved 'goodbye' as she pulled off. June got into the driver's seat.

"Oh-hell-nah. Nigga you know you ain't drivin'" I barked at June.

I wasn't in the mood to be getting lost again, so I switched seats with him. I pulled out into the busy Miami afternoon traffic and proceeded to follow the mental directions, at least as much as I could remember, back to the hotel. When we stopped at a red light, a candy apple red Infiniti Q45 with tinted windows pulled up beside us. The windows were so dark I couldn't see anything, not even a silhouette. When the light turned green, I drove through the intersection and noticed the Infiniti stall before pulling off. Halfway down the block, I peeped into the rearview and noticed the Infiniti was in my lane, three cars back. June and V weren't paying any attention to the Infiniti and I didn't want to seem paranoid so I didn't mention it yet. When I made a wrong turn, V asked, "Yo, where you goin'? This the wrong street."

"Yeah, I know. I'm just tryna see something," I replied while glancing in the rearview mirror.

Just like I figured, the Q-45 made the same turn.

"I might be trippin', but I think that Infiniti followin' a nigga. Don't look back.....damn June. Ignorant-ass-nigga."

June looked back, before I could finish my sentence. I saw a *One Stop* convenience store ahead. I pulled into the parking lot and parked near a pay phone. I got out and stepped into the phone booth while June turned the radio to 88.7 and rolled the driver's window half-way down. When June pressed the 'Doors Locked' button, the two floorboards beneath V's feet opened up. V reached inside the secret compartment and retrieved the twin Tech-nine's with fully loaded, thirty-round clips. He handed one to June and rested the other on his lap. It wasn't long before the Infiniti pulled into the store's parking lot. I watched as the car pulled to the entrance of the store and deaded the engine. I was standing a few feet away from where the car was parked, but I still couldn't see inside of the car because of the tint.

After a few seconds, the driver got out and I watched as the brother entered the store without as much as a glance in our direction. I stood near the phone booth until the driver came back out of the store and got back into the Infiniti. As I watched, the more familiar the guy looked.

"Damn, I done seen this nigga somewhere" I mumbled to myself as he got into his ride and pulled off.

When I was sure he was gone, I exited the phone booth and got back into the car.

"Yo, I done seen that nigga somewhere before," I said to my partners as I pulled out into traffic.

The rest of the ride back to the hotel was uneventful and the Infiniti was nowhere in sight. When I pulled into the hotel's parking lot June put his gun back inside the secret panel and closed it. My mind was reeling and I was trying to place the driver of the Infiniti's face. All of a sudden, it came to me. "That's the nigga who was starin' at a muh-fucka last night when Candace was dancin' for him," I blurted out.

"You talkin' 'bout when you came out the V.I.P.?" V asked.

"You sure that's him?" June asked.

"Yeah, I'm positive. I'on forget no face. I might've been twisted last night, but I remember that face. And y'all know I'on believe in coincidence" I replied as we exited the car.

V stuffed his gun in the waistband of his shorts and June got the other one back out of the stash and stuffed it in his jeans before we headed inside the hotel.

"'Pone, stop by the front desk and ask if they can restock the bar for us," V suggested.

Since June and V were both strapped they headed straight to the room.

When I got to the front desk, I noticed there wasn't anyone there, so I rung the service bell. A voice from the back room, presumably the office, yelled, "just a minute."

The voice sounded real familiar. Within seconds, I was face to face with one of the most beautiful women in Miami. She had long, jet-black hair. Her face was the complexion of French vanilla, with flawless skin. Her eyes were hazel-colored and bambi-shaped. Her body was off the hook! She had to be either Dominican or Puerto Rican, she definitely wasn't white nor was she black. She spoke in a deep Spanish accent.

"May I help you?"

I peeped her nametag and said, "Yeah, I hope you can help me...*Consuela.*"

"What seems to be the problem?" she asked.

I made up some off the wall story about the window in the room not opening and tried to get her to go up with me to check it out, but she didn't fall for it. She peeped game and smiled.

"If you are trying to get me to go to your room all you have to do is ask."

Now this statement caught me off guard, but I said fuck it and jumped out there.

"Aiight den, why don't you come up and chill wit' me for a while"

"No thank you, I don't get down like that," she shot me down smiling, an indication that she was enjoying controlling the conversation.

I re-grouped by introducing myself to her and leaning on the desk in 'Mack Mode' and spit game at her for another five minutes before a customer came in complaining about his bill. I stepped aside to allow her to do her job while pondering over what I had learned about her so far.

Consuela was twenty-two years old, from Puerto Rico and she had just recently come to Florida with her aunt and uncle who lived in Miami. She was single with no kids and didn't have too many friends in Miami. I was definitely feeling her. When the angry customer had finally left, I resumed my conversation.

"Yo, don't pay that jackass no mind. If he couldn't afford it, he shouldn't have stayed his ass here. It's a Motel 6 right down the street. Cheap Muh-fucka"

"I know, right?" Consuela agreed.

I leaned in close and whispered, "El Sombreo es Mofeta."

Consuela laughed so hard, she had to wipe tears from her eyes. She was laughing at my terrible Spanish because I had no idea what I had just said. I had heard the phrase somewhere before, maybe not exactly like I had spoken it, but close.

I leaned back and asked, "What?"

I wanted to know what was so hilarious.

She stopped laughing long enough to wipe her eyes and say, "You just said, 'His hat is a skunk'"

I laughed and said, "Well hell, he smelled like one"

"Tu necesitas estudiar Español, mas," Consuela said.

"It sound like you just said something 'bout some titties," I replied.

Consuela laughed and translated her phrase for me, "You need to study Spanish more"

"Oh—si, si, wee, wee, poly vous and all that there. But for real, I'm tryna get yo' number or somethin' so I can holla at you when I come back down here. What's up?" I shot for the digits.

Consuela conceded and gave me two numbers, her cell number and her home number. I gave her my cell and pager numbers and told her to call anytime and she assured me she would. I started to walk off, then I remembered the reason I had come to the front desk.

"Oh, I almost forgot. We need our bar restocked in room…"

"Four, twenty-seven. I already did it" Consuela said as she cut off my sentence.

"How you know what room I'm in?" I asked suspiciously.

"I came up this mornin' with the room service. I didn't see you but I saw two other guys. I saw the three of you leave together, so I assumed you all were together," Consuela explained.

*So, this was the fine-ass third-world bitch June and V was talking about this morning? Damn, they definitely weren't lying. I guess I beat June to the punch.*

I left the front desk and headed to the room, which smelled like a weed factory. I entered the room and frowned at the loud ass smell, which attacked my nose as soon as I opened the door. "Damn, y'all need to open a muh-fuckin' window or sumthin'. That shit loud as a bitch." I complained.

My complaints only lasted a milli-second because as soon as I closed the door I was smoking right along with them.

"'Pone, what took you so long? We thought you got lost" V joked.

"Yeah, I did get lost. Lost-in-lust." I replied as June and V looked at me inquisitively.

"Nigga what choo talkin' 'bout?" June asked, as I hit the weed and passed it to V.

"You 'member that Spanish bitch who brought up the room service this mornin'?" I asked.

"Yo, you seen that bitch?" V asked.

"Dat bitch fine as a muh-fucka. Ain't she?" June added.

"Yo, baby girl Puerto Rican and twenty-two. And guess what?" I asked. "I got the hook up." I said not waiting for them to respond as I held up the piece of paper with her digits on it as evidence before I went into the bathroom.

"Dat's fucked up!" June screamed.

"Aw, fat-boy chill out. You the one that got tongue-tied an' shit. If you scared, say you scared," V teased.

"Damn, I guess when a sucker get lucky, a playa like me don't stand a chance" June said, loud enough for me to hear.

"Fuck you callin' a sucka?" I asked from the restroom in an angry tone. "You gon' make a nigga fuck you up. That's what you gon' do, fat ass nigga." I continued.

When I exited the bathroom, June was standing at the door blocking my way.

"Oh you gonna fuck me up, huh?" June said. He was so hot, I could've fried an egg on his forehead.

I stepped up to him eye to eye and said, "Nigga I bet you better get yo' mutha-fuckin' ass out my way 'fore I *make* you get out my way."

June stood there for a minute before he finally broke the eye contact and took two slow deliberate steps backwards and mumbled, "Punk-ass nigga."

"Why you walk off like a bitch? Nigga I knew you was soft"

He walked towards me with fire in his eyes, chanting, "What's up nigga? What's up?"

V had been ignoring us, sitting quietly smoking on the blunt, but when he saw June and I about to throw blows he stepped in between us.

"Man, I'on believe this shit! Y'all niggas 'bout to scrap over some bitch don't neither one of y'all know? Y'all some simple ass niggas. That's some bitch shit" he said while looking back and forth at June and I.

I took the blunt from him, sat on the sofa and thought about what he had just said. There was some truth, but for me, it was the principle of the situation. True enough, June had gotten in his feelings about me hollering at Consuela, but I didn't get mad until he had disrespected me and called me a sucker. June had gotten very upset about nothing, so I think he was holding that shit in for a long time and was just waiting for an excuse to let it out. I wondered what type of hidden animosity that cat had for me? Was it jealousy? Who knows? One thing I can say for sure, I had just seen his true colors.

Fifteen minutes later, I was enjoying my high while watching the preview channel. I don't know how long V and I sat there watching that shit, but neither one of us changed it. June was walking around, still pouting like a bitch.

"Damn nigga, sit down some damn where." V said to June.

June ignored him and kept walking, straight out the door.

"Where that nigga goin'?" V asked while pointing at the door after it had shut behind June.

"Fuck that bitch ass nigga," I responded.

\*\*\*\*

Meanwhile, Big Will was heading down Biscayne Boulevard with the AC blasting and the radio pumping 92.1 FM. He kept shifting positions because the .40 caliber handgun in his waistband was a little uncomfortable. He couldn't wait to get home and take a shower and relax for a few hours. He had been out all night and the streets were beating him down. Finally, he turned into this driveway and parked inside the garage. Home sweet home. He exited the car, the headlights blinked and the candy-apple red Infiniti chirped, confirming activation of his alarm.

**\*\*\*\***

June stayed gone for an hour or so before returning to the room. When he came in he sat on the sofa beside me and playfully punched me in the chest.

"Damn playboy, I was trippin'. I been goin' through some shit and I was wrong to take dat shit out on you. You still my nigga or what? Besides, I just seen dat bitch again and noticed she got a big-ass head." June apologized.

We both laughed.

"You lucky you came back just now 'cause ten mo' minutes me and V was gon' pack this shit and leave yo' fat ass down here roamin' 'round Miami," I joked with June.

He had apologized, but I still knew that he had meant every word of what he had said earlier. You can forgive, but you can't forget.

Later, as we sat around kickin' it, our conversation turned to the situation with the Infiniti.

"I wonder what dat nigga was up to?" June asked.

"I'on know, but he was about to get what he was looking for," V replied, as he stroked his gun like he was rubbing a pet.

I was silently thinking about the driver, trying to make some sense out of what he was up to. The only thing I could think of was that he was a jack boy. He had seen us with Trey and Tank and knew we were from out of town. It wasn't hard to figure out why we were in Miami. All someone had to do was peep our North Carolina tag and see us hanging out with two of the biggest dope boys in Miami. The more I thought about this, the more paranoid I became.

"Yo, this my last time doin' this shit. If Trey can't find a reliable bitch to ride that shit to us, we gonna have to pay a muh-fucka to come get this shit from now on," I told June and V.

They both agreed with me.

Candace called around 9:00 and asked if we wanted some company. As bad as I wanted to say yes, I didn't. I didn't know her and her friends well enough to let them know where we were staying, so I told her I would call her back and let her know. I knew Tank was hollering at Candace's sister, so I paged Trey to get the scoop.

Trey called back within ten minutes and informed me that Candace and Tastee were good people, but Tastee's sister Shawn was treacherous.

"I heard she be settin' up licks for a lil' young nigga she fuck wit," Trey explained.

"Ay, that's good lookin' dog. You might've just saved a muh-fucka from catchin' a body down here," I told him.

"Yeah, I'll hate to see y'all get caught up on G.P. Feel me?"

"Yeah, yeah I feel that, but dig this, you 'member that nigga in Lauderdale last night who kept staring at us when Candace was dancing for him?" I asked.

"Vaguely, but I can't remember what he look like, though," Trey responded, as he tried to remember the guy's face.

"Well, we seen that nigga today at the red light and he followed us to the store. We started to wet that fool, but he just went into the store and left."

"You sure it was the same dude?" Trey asked.

"Yeah, I'm positive. He just didn't have on the same clothes. He was drivin' a red Q45."

"What kind of plates was on the car, Dade or Broward?" Trey asked.

I had peeped the tag when we were at the store because I wanted to know if he was from Lauderdale or Miami.

"Dade," I responded.

"If he from hea, I should be able to find out who it is. I'ma ask around 'bout that car and see what I can find out about this nigga. He probably ain't nobody. I ain't got him being no jack boy if he was hangin' out like that last night. That shit don't add up. He probably a dope boy on the come up, tryin to find an outta town connect. He saw y'all with me last night and then saw y'all today and peeped the Carolina tag so he probably know what y'all doin' down hea'. He probably wanted to holla at y'all on some biness but didn't know how to go about doin' it. Feel me? Listen, I wouldn't worry about him. I'mma check up on him and see if anybody know him" Trey explained.

"Aiight dog. What time you gonna be ready tomorrow?" I asked.

"We need to do it early so y'all can blend in wit' the mornin' traffic, Feel me?"

"Yeah I can dig that. So let's set it up for 'bout 6:30. Bet?"

"That'll work. I'mma come through and have y'all follow me to the spot and y'all can dip from there"

"Aiight Player, I'll holla in da mornin'," I told him.

Before he hung up he said, "Tell June dat bitch Shawn ain't nothin' but a snake, don't fuck wit' her."

"Aiight dog. I'll tell him. Be easy."

"Later."

I relayed to June what Trey had told me.

"Damn, I knew somethin' was up wit' dat bitch. She kept askin' too many questions," June said.

"You didn't tell that bitch where we stayin' at did you?" V asked June.

"Nah, but come to thank about it, she damn sho' asked," June replied.

"You gotta watch these mutha-fuckas down here. Ain't no tellin' *what* they be up to," I told June and V.

Early the next morning, Trey knocked on the door like he was the police.

"Who is it?!" June yelled from the sofa.

"It's Trey"

June opened the door and let Trey in. We were already up and packed, but Trey thought we would still be asleep.

"Damn, I thought I was gon' have to wake y'all niggas up," he said, which explained why he was knocking so damn loud.

We carried all of our clothes and other junk to the car and we were ready to roll. I went to the front desk to check out. While I was there, I left a note for Consuela.

*Consuela, my Boricua hottie:*

*By the time you get this I will be on my way home. I hate to leave, but at least I have something to look forward to when I come back. (Smile) I'm waiting to hear from you.*

*Capone*

### Chapter Twelve – Children Are Da Future

We followed Trey to a storage room in a quiet neighborhood in North Miami where he had the 10-kilos stashed. We counted out the 170-grand and stashed the 10-kilos in the secret compartment of the floorboards.

When Trey had put the last grand in his duffel bag, he locked up the storage and led us to the highway. I drove the first leg, all the way to Jacksonville, only stopping for gas, food and to use the restroom. June and V slept most of the way. I'm glad they weren't awake to see the trooper that followed us halfway through Pompano Beach. June's dumb ass would've definitely panicked. The trooper finally turned off though. I was so tired when we reached J-Ville that I pulled over at the rest area, woke-up V and quietly crawled into the back seat. I was asleep within seconds. When I woke up June was driving and we were almost in Columbia, SC. I was thinking, *Damn that was quick.*

I checked my pager which had been vibrating for quite some time. The number displayed was a 305 area code which was in Miami. I called back from my cell phone.

"Marriott, Miami Lakes. Consuela speaking. How may I direct your call?" Consuela's beautiful Spanish accent filled my ear.

"Hey Mami. You must've got my message," I said.

"Hey, I didn't think you were calling back. I paged you two hours ago."

"I just woke up. I'm tired as shit."

"I was thinkin' 'bout tellin' you off if you didn't call back" she said.

We kicked it on the phone for about 15-minutes before hanging up. I promised her that I was coming back real soon.

We rolled up in Charlotte at 8:45 PM with two 'Tech-nine' pistols and 10-kilos of Peruvian flake cocaine in the stash box. V agreed to drop us off and keep the car at his crib until the next morning. I was dropped-off first.

"Yo, call me when you get to the crib," I said to V.

"Aiight dog," he responded.

June was silent, and I didn't say anything to him either. I left my clothes, shoes and everything in the car. Fuck it. I was just glad to be home. Mission Accomplished!

Kinya wasn't home when I arrived so I decided to surprise her when she came in. She wasn't expecting me back until the following morning. Kinya got home around ten o'clock but she wasn't alone.

I was in the bedroom with the door shut, so she couldn't see me, but I could hear her.

"Girl, I'on know what I'm a do," Kinya said.

"The only thing you gotta do is tell him. I mean what is he gon' do?" the other voice said.

The other voice was undeniably Dee's.

"I'on know. I just don't wanna tell him right now" Kinya pleaded.

Now at this point, curiosity was eating my ass up. I opened the bedroom door and watched as Kinya and Dee's eyes almost popped out of their sockets.

"Damn baby, you scared the shit out of me. When you get home? I thought you wasn't comin' back 'til in the mornin'," Kinya rambled.

I ignored her question and asked, "You don't wanna tell me what?"

Kinya looked embarrassed as Dee interrupted, "Well if *you* back, then dat mean my man back. Gotta go."

She kissed Kinya on the cheek, grabbed her purse and gave Kinya one of those 'girlfriend handle yo biness', looks. Dee said goodbye and swung that fat ass out the door in a hurry.

Once Dee was gone, I repeated my question, "Tell me what?"

Kinya turned her head and tried to avoid eye contact and she looked very nervous. Curiosity was giving way to anger and she sensed it.

"Can we talk about this later?" she requested in a nervous tone.

"Hell nah, we gon' talk about this right now."

I had no idea what it was she had to tell me. Was it another nigga? Was she finally tired of my bullshit? So many thoughts ran through my head and I was starting to get a headache. Kinya finally grabbed my hand and placed it on her stomach.

"You feel anything?" she asked while staring into my eyes.

I was confused for a second. "Girl, you pregnant?" I asked stupidly.

She nodded silently. I broke into a slow smile and grabbed Kinya, pulling her close to me while planting light kisses on her forehead. I picked Kinya up and carried her to the bedroom. I gently laid her on the bed and kissed her slow and deep. I undressed us both and then commenced to kiss my way down her body, pausing at her belly while planting tiny kisses around her navel. I continued to go further until I reached the insides of her thighs. She was expecting me to linger on her thighs and then kiss my way back up, avoiding her wetness like I did every other night. But not tonight! I spread her legs and buried my head between her caramel thighs. My tongue surprised her when I licked her lower lips and then her clit. She gasped and then moaned in ecstasy as I licked and sucked every drop of juice she had to offer. After she had multiple orgasms from my oral techniques, I kissed her and let her taste what I had tasted. I then made slow, passionate love to the woman who was carrying my child.

*****

The next few weeks were business as usual, serving customers and fronting out weight. June and I barely spoke for the first four or five days after we had gotten back from Miami. V called everyday and teased Kinya about getting fat.

"Girl you betta not blow up. You know my nigga gon' dump yo' ass." V joked.

"Fuck you, don't call here no mo'," Kinya cursed him out as usual.

I sat back and laughed at them as Kinya threw me the telephone, hitting me in the chest with it.

"Tell yo' stupid ass friend he ain't funny," she said.

"Girl, you know Uncle V just kiddin'," I said.

V was laughing when I picked up the phone.

"Yo, what up" I spoke.

"Tell that girl I was just playin'," V said.

"I done told her, but you know how broads get when they pregnant. They take shit the wrong way. All sensitive an' shit"

"Yeah, I'mma leave her alone fo' she get upset fo' real," V said.

"Yeah, that's a good idea, playboy. Yo, where yo' partna at? You ain't heard from him?" I was referring to June.

"Yeah, he called this mornin' from Greensboro. Him and that broad Cherone was up there shoppin'."

"Damn, that bitch got ole' boy gone, huh?"

"Yeah, he diggin' her for real," V responded.

I thought back to the time we all had gone to Atlanta. I just shook my head and said, "Man these bitches ain't shit out here."

"You ain't never lied," V responded.

He had no idea why I had made that comment. Maybe one day I'd pull his coat, but not just yet. My other line beeped, so I told V, I would get back at him, then I clicked over. It was Trey calling to check on me because I hadn't hollered at him in a minute. We kicked it about the usual bullshit until Trey changed the subject and mentioned the Infiniti.

"Yo, I been askin' 'bout that Infiniti you told me about. The only thing I could come up wit' was a name. Some nigga name 'Big Will'. I think he a dope boy, but don't nobody know fo sho'. If he a big boy, he gotta be gettin' money up the road somewhere, 'cause don't nobody down hea know nothin' about him."

I listened to Trey and tried to make sense out of what he was saying.

"Damn, don't *nobody* know nothin' about dude?"

"Nah, he gotta be new in town. Feel me?"

That made sense, nobody would know him if he was a new face.

"Yeah, well fuck him. But what up though? You got transpo?" I asked because we were almost ready to re-up.

"Nah dog. It's kind'a hard tryna find a mutha-fucka you can trust whole-heartedly, dig?"

"I feel ya. 'Cause I'm havin' a hard time tryin to find a driver too," I replied.

"When you think y'all gon' be ready?" he asked.

"Soon"

"Aiight. Gimme a couple o' days to get back at you. I'mma come up wit' somethin'" Trey said.

"Aiight player, holla at me."

"Bet."

"Later."

Later that day, Quick called me for a half-kilo. I was proud of my lil' cousin for finally using his head and doubling his money instead of blowing it. He had stopped stealing cars and started buying them. He owned two, an Acura Legend and a Ford Explorer. I turned him on to Chad and he got both of his vehicles candy-painted and rimmed out.

I had parked the Benz for a minute. Nobody knew where it was at. I had decided to tone down the flossing for a while and the only car I drove was the Honda.

I met Quick at his new apartment in Kimberly Glen on the East side and when I arrived, he answered the door with a blunt burning between his lips.

"What up big cuz?" he greeted me with a pound.

I stepped inside the apartment and saw five more people, three young girls and two more young cats drinking beer and smoking weed. They all spoke when they saw me. They all called me by my name, but I didn't know any of them. Quick led me to his bedroom and extracted a safe from the closet. He counted out the 13-grand for the dope and gave it to me. I pulled the dope out of my underwear and gave it to him. He threw it in the safe with the rest of his money and passed me the blunt. I took it and inhaled deeply before giving him my usual word of advice.

"Yo, you need to be mo' discreet about yo' shit. Why you got all them mutha-fuckas up in here like that and you got all this money and shit in here? I done told you 'bout that shit. Nigga you gon' learn. And don't never tell me to meet you again and you got a lot of muh-fuckas around"

"Yeah cuz. I know man. I ain't gon' do it no mo'" He lied as usual.

I had heard that same response many times before and I knew he wasn't going to learn until it was too late. And I was damned if I was going to let him get me caught up because of his asininity. I hit the blunt again and left Quick with his little groupies.

Since I was on June's side of town, I decided to stop by his place. We hadn't talked much since Miami, but he was still a business partner. I didn't call first, I just showed up. When I knocked on the door, Cherone answered it. She was wearing one of June's football jerseys and no shoes. She spoke and let me in.

"Hey stranger. What wind blew you this way?" she asked.

"I was on y'all side, so I thought I'd stop by and holla. Where June at?" I asked.

"You didn't just see him? He just left. Y'all should've passed each other."

"Nah I ain't see him, where he goin'?"

"He said he had to go see somebody in Rock Hill," she replied.

I walked into the kitchen and opened June's refrigerator to get a beer. When I closed the refrigerator, I felt a soft, naked body pressed against my back and a pair of arms circled my waist. Cherone was breathing in my ear.

"Capone baby, you know how bad I want you. I been waitin' for a chance for us to finish what we started in Atlanta."

Cherone was whispering in my ear and rubbing my dick. Damn this was a bold bitch. I turned around and saw where she had discarded the jersey she was wearing. I couldn't deny it, Cherone was a sexy bitch *and* a freaky bitch. I had experienced a little bit of what she had to offer when we were all in Atlanta.

*One particular night I had the munchies and wanted someone to ride to the store with me. No one volunteered, everyone was too high and finally Cherone said she would go. As soon as I started the engine, her hand was rubbing my thigh. She was telling me how she wanted me the first time she laid eyes on me that first day. Her hand caressed higher and higher until finally she was stroking my dick. Before I could protest, not that I tried, she had my dick in her mouth. I was parked in the underground lot and it was late, so nobody else was around. Cherone deep-throated me like Linda Lovelace until I came. Needless to say, I never made it to the store. On the way back up to the room, she was constantly fondling my dick. Cherone wanted to fuck that night, but we didn't have time.*

Now here she was, standing in her man's kitchen, butt-naked and rubbing my dick. I stood there enjoying the sensation while twisting the cap off of my beer. I took a swig and leaned back against the refrigerator while she was unzipping my pants.

"You know you trippin' right? What if yo' nigga come back in here?" I said, but not really caring if he came home or not.

"He went to *Rock Hill*. He'll be gone at least an hour and a half," she replied as she sank to her knees and pulled my pants and boxers to my ankles.

She had my dick standing at attention when she took my entire length down her throat. I grabbed the back of her head and guided her up and down on my dick. I sat my beer on the sink and reached for my cell phone while she was still slobbin' on my knob. I punched in June's cell phone number and waited for him to answer.

June answered the phone as he turned down the radio.

"Yeah."

"Ungh- yeah what up, where you at?"

"Damn, a nigga ain't heard from yo' ass in a month o' Sundays. What's up?" June replied.

"Shi-it, damn girl. Yo I'm gettin' a lil' head from this broad. This shit off-da-fuckin'-hook. Yeah, lick it baby."

June was laughing and said, "Let me hear it"

I put the phone close to Cherone's mouth and let June hear his bitch slurping on my dick.

"You hear that shit?" I asked.

"Hell yeah, damn nigga you pimpin' ain't ya?"

"Damn baby, slow down. You gone make me nut," I told Cherone as she looked up at me with a wet smile.

She continued to stroke me with her hand as she stood up and raised my shirt up to my neck. She started kissing and licking on my chest while I was talking to her man.

"Yo, hit me when you get situated, aiight."

"I'm on my way to Rock Hill, I'll hit you when I get back."

"Aiight, peace."

"Later."

I hung up the phone and pulled my shirt over my head and tossed it onto the floor. Cherone led me into the living room as I tagged along while stepping out of my clothes. She grabbed a condom off of the entertainment system and opened it. She put the condom in her mouth and then took my dick in her mouth. After two or three strokes, I pulled out of her mouth and saw that her condom was on my dick, like I had put it on with my hands!

"Damn girl. How you do that shit?" I asked in amazement.

Cherone smiled and laid back on the carpet with her knees bent and legs spread. Her pussy was already wet and I hadn't even touched her yet. She was turned-on from sucking my dick while I was talking to her man on the phone and I must admit, so was I.

I fucked Cherone's brains out. When I was about to cum, I pulled out and snatched off the rubber and purposely skeeted on June's carpet. Now, let me tell you something about the game. Rule number one is never fuck with a man's money. Rule number two is never fuck with your partner's woman. I had just broken a rule and I was definitely violating. But as we all know, it's a dirty game and hey, look at all the fun I had just had. Fuck June and fuck his bitch!

I left June's crib smiling from ear to ear while Cherone was on her hands and knees scrubbing the carpet.

As the weeks passed, we were still handling business as usual. June and I had began to kick it again. He never mentioned anything about me and Cherone. They were still together and going strong. Every time I stopped by June's crib, Cherone was there acting as if nothing had ever happened. That was cool with me. But boy, if those walls could talk they would have a hell of a story to tell. Every time I went to his crib, I looked at that spot on his living room carpet that was a shade or two lighter than the rest. That spot alone could tell a cold story.

V and Dee were still kicking it in an on-and-off relationship. She still made her usual threat of leaving him, but he knew as well as I did that she wasn't going anywhere. She wasn't trying to leave my dog and she definitely wasn't going to let some other female enjoy the riches she was enjoying.

Kinya was beginning to show a little and she was becoming very self-conscious about her weight. I was staying home as much as possible for support, but I must admit she was getting on my nerves with her mood swings and crazy food cravings.

Meanwhile, we found two reliable drivers for the trips to Florida. Two young, inconspicuous college girls who were fascinated with the life we were living.

Tammy was a twenty-year-old white girl from East Charlotte who loved rebellion. She was far from being the typical Pink-toe. Tammy was a blonde-haired, green-eyed, nympho with a body like a sister's. Her appetite for thugs was insatiable!

Wanda was a nineteen-year-old, pecan-tan sister from West Palm Beach, Florida who loved living reckless.

Tammy and Wanda were roommates at UNCC when June and V had met them at a concert at Aggie Fest in Greensboro. They ended up kicking it with them for a few weeks, before finally lacing them with the game.

Tammy and Wanda agreed to do it, once they were finally convinced that the trips would be safe and they'd be generously compensated. Since Wanda was from Florida, everything seemed to fall into place. They made the trips on the weekends with the illusion of going to visit Wanda's family. Everything was going like clockwork.

Trey was thoroughly satisfied with the arrangement as well, maybe because of the fact that he was beating Tammy's back out every time they visited.

Kinya had finally gotten all of the construction and interior designing finished at the Salon and had already hired four stylists and two barbers. My mom volunteered herself for the position of receptionist. I had no problem with her wanting to be a part of the business. In fact, I liked the idea of keeping it in the family. Kinya was ready for her grand opening. She'd named the shop "Kutz by Kinya" and set the date for a Saturday. The night before she opened, I had to rush her to the hospital. She complained about cramps and spotting blood.

After examining Kinya, the doctor told me that he wanted to admit her for overnight observation. He said he didn't think it was anything serious, but he wanted to keep an eye on her, just in case. I stayed with her all night trying to convince her to relax and stop worrying. The doctor said the baby was fine and that the cramping and bleeding was a result of Kinya's stress caused by her concern about the salon. She wanted so much for it to be a success. I told her not to worry about anything but herself and the baby's health.

The next morning she was released. I told her to postpone the grand opening until the following week, but she insisted on opening as planned. I made her stay home and relax while I took care of everything. My mom and I held the grand-opening and videotaped it so that I could show it to Kinya. When I showed the tape to Kinya she cried with joy. The grand opening was a success all within itself!

Kinya was up and about in a matter of days and the shop was doing very well. My mom stayed busy answering the phone and setting up appointments while Kinya laid back and handled all of the paperwork. I tried to stay away from the shop as much as possible because a nigga could get 'caught up' in a spot where females don't do nothing but gossip all day. I would have hated for Kinya to overhear my name being mentioned in one of their conversations.

However, no matter how hard I tried to keep my name out of those bitches' mouths, they always seemed to find something to say about me. Without fail, Kinya kept fresh rumors and gossip to confront me about every night. Consequently, the shop was more of a problem that I had anticipated. My response was the same everyday, *"Fuck them jealous ass bitches."* Although, Kinya found the rumors to sometimes be amusing, I found them to be annoying because some of that shit was true.

One night when Kinya and I were relaxing on our sofa, she grabbed my hand and placed it on her protruding belly.

"You feel that?" she asked.

It was the first time I felt my baby kick.

"Damn, shorty already tryna get up outta there" I joked.

She looked at the sincere smile on my face and asked, "What 'choo want, a boy or a girl?"

I sat back and thought for a minute.

"I want a lil' girl," I answered.

Kinya looked surprised with my response.

"Now I could've sworn I kept hearing you say *My son this, my son that*," she commented.

"Yeah, in a way I do want a lil' boy. Every man wants a son for different reasons. But seriously, I wouldn't wanna bring a son into this crazy ass world. Niggas have to go through too much shit. Look at me," I responded.

"So you don't think females go through a lot?"

"Hell nah, not as much as us niggas do. Look at you. You got it made. You workin' 'cause you *want* to, not 'cause you *have* to. You got a nigga that love the shit outta yo' black ass and don't mind takin' care of you. Niggas can't just lay down like that. We gotta go out and get ours, one way or the other. If a nigga ain't got platinum vocal chords or a wicked ass jump shot, our chances of success are slimmer than a muh-fucka on crack. And you know that."

Kinya felt where I was coming from and nodded in agreement. I sat back and thought for a minute about my future and the future of my child. Damn, things were happening fast as hell! Almost a little too fast. It seemed like just yesterday, I was a child listening to my mom give me parental advice. Now here I was twenty-years-old and on the brink of becoming a parent myself. All of a sudden, the reality of all of the responsibility associated with being a father dawned on me.

Kinya peeped my silent reflection.

"What 'choo thinkin' about?"

I looked at her and admired the glow she was radiating from motherhood.

"I was just thinkin' about our baby and what kind of life it's gonna have. I swear to God I don't want my baby to have to struggle like I did" I confessed.

I arose from the sofa and went into the kitchen to get a beer and reached inside one drawers to retrieve a long neglected pack of blunts. I hadn't smoked in a couple of days so Lord knows I needed it. I sat back on the sofa beside Kinya and rolled two fat ass blunts.

Once I was finished I opened the patio door and stepped out into the night. I left the glass door opened but I closed the screen to keep the mosquitoes out. Kinya watched from inside the house as I lit one of the blunts and took a long, slow deliberate pull. I was teasing Kinya because she wasn't allowed to smoke or drink because of her pregnancy. Still without looking at her, I exhaled a thick cloud of chronic into the night air.

"Damn, this shit is good," I said, more to myself than to Kinya but she heard me.

"Mike..."

"Hell nah." I cut her off by saying.

"You 'on even know what I was getting ready to say."

"The answer is still no, whatever it is," I replied, laughing at her because I knew what she wanted, at least I thought I knew.

She sucked her teeth and rolled her eyes at me before getting off of the sofa and strolling down the hallway. I sat back in the lawn chair, kicked my feet up on the table and enjoyed the rest of my session.

When I finally decided to go back into the house, I couldn't find Kinya. I thought maybe she had stepped out for a minute. The last place I looked was in the bedroom. When I opened the door, Kinya was laying on our bed, ass-naked and masturbating.

I stood in the doorway in a daze because this was the first time I had ever seen my woman play with herself and I was getting very aroused. She opened her eyes and saw me looking at her, but she kept right on going at is as if I wasn't even there.

"Damn shorty, you need some help." I asked as I stepped closer to the bed.

Between breaths she responded, "Remember, you told me 'Hell Nah', so I think I can finish by myself. Oooooooh shit." she barely was able to get out as she was climaxing.

I could tell that she was climaxing by the way her legs started trembling and her eyes were fluttering. I felt left out and neglected like a stepchild. *Only if women knew exactly how much power is in the pussy.*

Previously, I thought Kinya wanted some of the blunt I was smoking, that's why I told her 'Hell nah.' I truly had no idea she wanted me to make love to her.

### Chapter Thirteen – Goin' Against Da' Grain

"Yo, I'm tellin' you, that bitch runnin' her fuckin' mouth, my nigga. She got too many hoes in her bizness and shit" V said as he slurped down his Hennessey.

V, June and I were at the old TGI-Friday's on Independence Blvd., sitting at the bar discussing a potential problem. We knew the bartender, so she was letting us drink without ID. V was convinced that one of the girls we were using to transport coke was getting brand new and had suddenly developed a case of diarrhea of the mouth.

"You might be right, but a nigga ain't got no choice right now but to send them hoes one mo' time. After this time, I'mma chill for a minute anyway. Y'all can still handle business, but I'mm a lay it down for a few. This shit startin' to wear my ass out. I think I'm a take Kinya on a trip somewhere for her birthday next month. She wanna go to the Bahamas or either to Puerto Rico. I'mm a call Consuela and see if she can tell me a lil' bit about 'P.R'. You know, like what city to visit? What type o' shit to look out for and shit like that?"

At the mention of Consuela's name, June's eyes twinkled. I could tell he was thinking back to what had happened in the hotel room in Miami. Although he didn't comment about Consuela, he said "You know what? Cherone been pressin' a nigga to take her somewhere like that. Shiiit, we might as well double-date dog. You know how we do"

I couldn't believe my ears. This nigga had the audacity to suggest some shit like that! The comment was so ludicrous all I could do was give him one of those, 'Nigga, Please' looks. V ignored his comment as well and continued to press the issue about Tammy.

"I told Wanda to tell that bitch to shut da fuck up but I keep hearing shit this bitch is supposedly saying. And I know mutha-fuckas ain't lyin' because some of the shit I'm hearing is true. Ever since that cracker bitch been fuckin' that nigga Trey, her head been swellin' up. I'on know who that funky trailer-park trash ass hoe thank she is, but I'll beat that bitch ass. That bitch don't know me, yo" V fumed.

"Ok. look, I'mma talk to her and try to find out where her head's at. If it seem like she on some bullshit, we gonna fire that bitch.....then you can whup that ass!" I conceded as I took the straw out of my glass and gulped down the rest of my Vodka and cranberry.

The rest of the night was pretty much typical. We drank, got drunk. Hollered at a few females, cursed a few out and then we all headed home.

A few days later, I took Tammy to her favorite restaurant so we could talk. She thought it was a date, but in actuality it was more like an interrogation. The Blue Marlin was packed with the usual lunchtime crowd, so I paid the hostess, so we could get the next available table. I hated waiting.

As Tammy and I strolled through the crowded dining area to be seated, all eyes were on us. We were attracting the heated stares and unwanted attention that interracial couples usually get. I didn't care and Tammy didn't let it bother her because she was used to it. All she dated were black men. Tammy and I ordered our meal and chatted while we were waiting for it to be brought out.

"So… what's up with the 'let's do lunch' thing?" she asked while leaning in and looking at me with that all too familiar look.

"Nah, let's not get this twisted. I just wanna talk to you 'bout somthin'" I replied.

"oh, ok. What's up?" she sat back and got comfortable.

"You tell me. I hear you been puttin' mutha-fuckas in yo' bizness and shit. Better yet, *our* bizness"

"What do you mean by that?"

"Ever since you been seein' Trey, better yet, ever since you been *fuckin'* Trey, you been loose lippin' and act like can't nobody tell you shit. Before you started fuckin' wit' dude everything was running like clockwork and you kept yo' mouth shut. So tell me what's up. You slippin' Tam and I wanna know why". I leaned a little closer to her and asked "You must feel like you 'on need us no mo'? You act like ready to quit doin' what you doin' for us? Tell me *somethin'*"

Tammy looked at me as if she had no earthly idea of what I was talking about. I saw the look of perplexity on her face and decided to make myself clear.

"Look baby girl, I'mma tell you like this; you and I both know that you know entirely too much about what me and my niggas doin'. So if you decide to keep on lettin' the dick make you slip and you end up getting '*caught up*' on some bullshit… I pray, for your sake, that you can hold your own and keep yo' mouth shut, feel me? 'Cause me and my niggas, including Trey strictly believe in Death before Dishonor. Loose lips sink ships!"

Tammy's face showed that she was finally getting the point. She nodded silently as she listened to what I had to say. After driving the point home, I noticed a look of fear in Tammy's eyes. Fear was not what I was trying to impose, but that's the way she took it. I only wanted an understanding. I tried to calm the atmosphere and ease Tammy's nerves. So I relaxed my tone "Look, I ain't threatenin' you. I'm just tryna make sure we on the same page wit dis shit, 'cause if anything happen, *all of us* gonna get fucked up! I'm just tryna make sure you see the seriousness in this shit, 'cause this game is REAL! Stop tellin' mutha-fuckas yo' bizness"

Tammy nodded silently in agreement as the waitress placed our food and drinks on the table. Obviously, Tammy had lost her appetite because she was picking over her food with her fork. I devoured my salt and pepper catfish platter like I hadn't eaten in months. We stayed only long enough to finish our meals and no more words were spoken.

On the way back to UNCC campus, we rode in silence. As I looked over at Tammy I felt at that instance that she was going to end up being a major problem in one way or another.

I told V and June about the conversation I'd had with Tammy and they were thinking the same way I was thinking. We agreed to send Tammy and Wanda on one last trip to the Bottom to cop for us, but neither one of us felt comfortable with sending them alone for that last trip. Therefore, we decided to accompany them but in a separate car of course. I called Trey and set up a date and time.

"Yo, 'sup my nigga?" Trey said through the phone.

"What up big dog? A nigga need to see you on fourteen of them thangs, ASAP," I said to my connect.

"When dem hoes tryin to pull up?" Trey asked.

"*All of us* comin' as soon as you give the word"

"Whaaaat? Y'all niggas finally comin' to holla? It's 'bout time. Look, I got a lil' somethin' right now, but I'm sure I'll be all the way straight by time y'all get hea'"

"Aiight, we leavin' out Friday evenin', so we'll holla at you Saturday mornin'. Cool?"

"Fa sho'. See ya when I see ya"

"Peace"

I informed everyone about the trip. June and V couldn't wait to get back to Florida. Tammy and Wanda were acting a little apprehensive about our coming along. Me? I had a really bad feeling about this trip. Instead of going with my instincts, I went against the grain and headed to the 'Bottom' for one last run.

When we arrived in Miami early Saturday morning, it was so hot that I could see the steam emitting from the street. The rental car I was driving was black with black interior, so the sun was beaming in and getting trapped inside the car. The AC was blasting, but it was still hot. My head was throbbing and my stomach was growling uncontrollably. I couldn't wait to eat, crawl into a bed and pass out.

We went to the hotel we'd stayed at the last time we were there, the Marriott in Miami Lakes. Tammy and Wanda stopped off in West Palm Beach at Wanda's parent's house for a routine visit and when they finally made it to Miami, they got a room at the same hotel that we were staying at. I contemplated on telling them to go to another hotel, but I didn't.

*Well, I guess it's okay if they go ahead and stay here. What would possibly go wrong in 48-hours?* I asked myself.

That evening Trey and Tank came by our room while all of us including Tammy and Wanda were sitting around smoking blunts. I opened the door when they knocked.

"Yo, what up my niggas?" I spoke as I greeted Tank and Trey with a pound.

Everybody spoke as they entered the room. Tank was wearing a Hawaiian short set with sandals. He sported gold-rimmed Cartier sunglasses and his baldhead was shining almost as much as the diamonds in his teeth. Trey wore the usual Denim short set he was accustomed to being seen in. No matter where Trey was, or what time of year it was, he would be seen wearing a denim short set with the latest style of Nike tennis shoes. He wore his dreads loose on this particular day. I'd never seen him without his hair in a ponytail and he looked like a true islander. I figured that was what mine would look like after a few more years of growth.

Tammy and Wanda beamed with bright smiles when they saw Tank and Trey. Wanda spoke first.

"Tank why you ain't been callin' me back when I beep you?" she said as she got up from her seat and approached Tank. He grabbed her by the waist.

"Baby girl, you know a nigga be busy an' shit. You know I ain't doin' it on purpose"

I looked at June and V and saw that they were just as surprised as I was.

*Damn, these bitches been double dating the whole time. That's why these hoes acted like they didn't want us to come. They wanted fuck around instead of getting straight to the business like they knew we would make them do.* I thought silently as I watched Tank and Trey run that old ass Miami game on my two mules.

After shooting the girls verbal curve balls, Trey and Tank were ready to talk business. I sent the girls out of the room so us men could talk privately.

"Damn, I ain't know you and Wanda was kickin' it like that" I told Tank.

"Yeah I been killin' her for a minute" he responded.

"No wonder why dem hoes can't think right when dey leave from down here... cause y'all niggas fuckin' em to death," June teased.

"I was wondering why that funky ass hoe won't let a nigga tag that ass no mo'. Now I see why," V said, revealing the fact that he too was once fucking Wanda. We all laughed.

I wanted to know if Trey was ready to handle business. I didn't want to stay in Miami any longer than I had to. I was already missing Kinya and her little round belly. I had been on the phone with her practically all day. I had also called Consuela as soon as we arrived to let her know I was in her neck of the woods. She sounded so delighted to hear from me, I almost thought she was pretending. We made plans to hook up as soon as her shift was over. I told her not to come up to my room. I told her I would see her when she got off. I had kept her away from the room for various reasons.

Getting down to business, I asked Trey, "So, when you gon' be all the way straight?"

"It supposed to be in the mornin'. I'll know fa' sho' later on tonight" Trey replied. "I got two right now, twelve mo' ain't gon' be no problem," he added.

I hoped he was right, but it really didn't make too much of a difference because with two-kilos, or fourteen we were still bouncing the following evening—at least I was. I refused to stay any longer than I had to because Miami was giving me some real bad vibes.

At one point, I even contemplated calling the deal off, but June and V were adamant about making this one last transaction. They wanted to go ahead and re-up so they could grind one last time before getting out of the game and laying low for at least a few months. I had made up my mind, I was DONE once we'd made this one last lick. So the decision had been made to go ahead and cop the dope as planned.

Trey and Tank kicked it with us for about an hour before leaving. They said they were going to Club EXXtasy to 'trick off a lil' change'. June and V left with them. I decided not to go because I wasn't in the mood and besides, I had other plans.

"Yo, hit me when you know somethin', I'on wanna be sittin' around in the blind . Lemme me know what's up wit the other twelve" I told Trey on his way out the door.

"Bet that" he replied.

I shut the door behind them and went straight to the telephone and pressed zero.

"Front desk," the familiar voice answered in a deep Spanish accent.

I looked at my watch and spoke into the phone, "Que' hora es, por favor?" I said, asking what time it was. I had slowly been picking up on bits and pieces of Spanish since I'd been kicking it with Consuela.

"Los ocho y cincuenta," she answered.

It was 8:50, ten more minutes before Consuela's shift was over.

"Hey sexy, it's 'bout that time ain't it?"

"Lemme find out you're learning a little Spanish" Consuela said. I could tell she was smiling.

"I'm learning from the bes, babe. You still comin' up, right?" I asked.

"You know I am. Where are your boys? I don't hear anybody"

"They just left. They gon' be…"

"Oh, never mind. I see them" Consuela cut me off by saying. Apparently my niggas were passing the front desk.

June couldn't help but to stare at her and she tried to ignore him and finish her conversation. June stared at Consuela with lustful eyes as he passed the front desk. He just couldn't take his eyes off of her. But she just kept on smiling and talking into the telephone.

"Damn, that's a fine ass bitch," Tank commented.

"Yeah she is. You know 'Pone pulled that already. That's prolly who she talkin' to. Watch this," V said as he looked at Consuela and got her attention. "Yo, tell my nigga we out and we ain't comin' back 'til in the morning"

Consuela spoke into the telephone and then answered V, "He said 'Happy Trickin'."

V laughed at the surprised looks Tank and Trey were displaying.

"Da-a-a-a-mn, 'Pone doin' big thangs," Trey commented as they all exited the hotel and June was silently seething.

I had heard V's comment and wondered how he knew Consuela was talking to me.

"They gone yet?" I asked.

"Yeah, they gone."

"Well I'm waitin' on you. I'll holla when you get up here aiight."

"Ok, give me a few minutes so I can brief the girl who's relieving me."

"Aiight baby. Peace."

"Hosta luega."

"Ast-what?" I asked.

"Never mind, I'll see you in a minute," Consuela said laughing as she hung up.

******

Big Will was watching Tank's suburban from a distance. He was sitting in a rented Ford Mustang on his cell phone when the four men exited the hotel and piled into the SUV. When the SUV left the parking lot, so did the Mustang. He followed the Suburban from a safe distance all the way to Ft. Lauderdale. When the SUV finally stopped, they were at Clubb EXXtasy, the same strip club Big Will had followed Trey and Tank to on many other occasions. He was waiting for the perfect opportunity to lay these cats down! Little did he know, opportunity would present itself sooner than he expected!

******

...Meanwhile back at the hotel, Consuela was knocking on the door to my room. I looked through the peephole to make sure she was alone. It was moreso out of habit than any other reason. When I opened the door, Consuela was standing there in her uniform, smiling like a schoolgirl.

"Hey you," I spoke as I let her in.

"Hey stranger. Damn, I almost forgot how sexy you were, Papi," Consuela said offering me a hug.

Her body felt so good, my dick started getting hard immediately. I knew she could feel it stiffening, but I pulled her closer still, just to make certain she could. She slowly pulled away, breaking our embrace while looking at the tee-pee my dick was making in my shorts.

"Are you happy to see me, or is that something that happens every time someone gives you a hug" she seductively smiled at me while still staring at my bulge.

"Baby, I told you that shit happens every time I hear your voice. Just think of how many times we talked on the phone the past two months. Girl you know I had to deal wit' a whole lotta hard-ons" I replied laughing.

Consuela was sniffing the air as she headed towards the bedroom with her overnight bag.

"It smells like a marijuana factory in here" she said as she sat on one of the double beds and opened her bag.

I ignored her comment because before it was all over, that smell was going to be a lot stronger. I was already pulling the weed out of my pocket as she spoke.

"You mind if I take a shower?" she asked, while kicking off her shoes and unbuttoning her blouse.

"Nah, I'on mind as long as I get to wash yo' back" I replied.

Consuela smiled and continued to undress in front of me without shame or inhibition. She took everything off except for her lavender bra and matching thongs. Consuela's body was something unreal! Imagine Jennifer Lopez with a tan and an ass like Serena Williams! I couldn't stop staring at her. She was beautiful and she knew it. She took another bra and thong set out of her bag and headed to the bathroom. She was talking, but I wasn't listening. I was concentrating on the jiggle of those round, bronze-colored ass cheeks as she walked.

"Did you hear me?" she paused at the bathroom door asking.

"Nah, baby I'm sorry. My mind was somewhere else. What 'choo say?"

She repeated herself, "I said, how do you plan to wash my back if you're fully dressed?"

Her invitation for me to join her in the shower needed no additional words and I wasted no time accepting the offer. I was undressed so fast you'd think my clothes were held together by Velcro instead of zippers and buttons. Consuela came out of what little bit she had left on as we both entered the shower together. Consuela stood beneath the showerhead with her back to me and let the water soak her from head to toe. I was admiring the view, my lips moving in conversation to myself. Her hair looked like silk hanging down her back and the water made her skin glow. I imagined wrapping her hair around my hand and pulling it while hitting her from the back. My dick got hard again at that mere thought! Consuela was lathering herself down with soap while I was smearing it all over her perfectly round ass. I was imitating Mr. Myagi in the movie, *Karate Kid*. I was rubbing her ass while chanting, "Wax on, wax off."

Consuela looked back over her shoulder smiling.

"Havin' fun?" she teased.

"Not yet," I responded as I pulled her backwards until my dick was resting in the small of her back. I moved her hair to the side and began to lick and kiss on the back of her neck as she tilted her head back, enjoying the sensation. I reached around and cupped a perfectly round and soapy breast in each hand and caressed them until I felt both nipples harden. Consuela moaned when I took her nipples between my fingers and gently squeezed them. Her hands were on top of mine, guiding me and showing me exactly how she wanted me to touch her. This was turning me on unbelievably because I love a woman who knows exactly what she wants and is not afraid to let it be known!

Consuela guided my hands down across her flat stomach, past her pubic hair until I reached her warm center. She spread her legs further apart as I stroked her with a little help from her hands. She guided my left hand back up to her breast and continued to stroke herself with my right hand. Consuela's hips were rotating in tune to our ministrations. Her pussy was so wet I couldn't tell if it was the water from the spraying showerhead or if it was her juices.

Consuela took my right hand away from her pussy and sucked her juices off of my fingers. She reached back and caressed my dick while rubbing up between her soapy ass cheeks, causing me to stiffen even more. My dick was doing all of the thinking because at that moment I had no thoughts whatsoever of using a condom. She rose up on her tiptoes allowing me easy access from the back while guiding me into her tight, moist pussy with one deft motion. She was so tight she felt like a virgin. She let a loud gasp escape her parted lips as I penetrated her. I stroked her inner walls with slow, deep thrusts, pulling out until only the head was still inside, then plunging back into her wetness until I was balls-deep.

We quickly found a rhythm and once we were in tune, I thrust harder and harder triggering an explosive orgasm deep within her clutching tunnel. Her scratching fingers made a squeaky noise as she attempted to clasp the wet sides of the shower. Soon our wet thighs were slapping and the sound was echoing off the walls. I reached up to grab a fistful of her hair and wrapped it around my hand just like I'd imagined. I pulled her head backwards so that I could kiss her wet lips. The harder I tugged on her tresses, the wetter her pussy got and the louder her moans became. The painful pleasure was turning her on to no end! After a while, we changed positions to facing each other, as I picked her up and her legs wrapped around my waist while her arms circled my neck. I steadied myself, so I wouldn't slip. When I entered her the second time, she was more than ready to be filled to the hilt. I began to thrust as she thrust back while I pinned her back to the wall of the shower for support, never losing our connection. Consuela was moaning and gripping the back of my head, holding a hand full of my locks while I was sucking her nipples and pounding away.

Consuela couldn't believe the sensation she was experiencing. Her entire body felt like one gigantic nerve. She'd already released two orgasms and was on the verge of having another.

"Oh-oh-yeah baby, I'm cumming Papi... I'm cumming, oh-Oh-Ohhhhh Shittttt." she tried to hold back with everything she had but her body betrayed her and the words came out of her mouth involuntarily.

I knew Consuela was enjoying herself by the way she was moaning and groaning, but when she screamed that she was cumming, she confirmed it. I couldn't restrain myself any longer as I felt that all too familiar sensation in my testicle about to erupt. With a few more strokes, I emptied what seemed like a gallon of sperm into her clenching hole. My ejaculation was so fierce, my knees got weak and I almost dropped Consuela. I let her legs go slowly so she wouldn't fall and we were finally separated as my penis came out with a wet 'plop'.

Consuela was breathless and so was I. We finally got a chance to finish bathing and I washed her back like I had promised.

********

"Where Capone at?" Candace asked Tank.

Candace was naked and glistening with sweat. Tank, June and V were seated at the bar admiring all of the naked asses gyrating. Trey was across the room talking with an associate, while sipping on a glass of Moet.

"He at the room chillin'. Oh – he told me to tell you he said what's up and for you to call him when you get off" Tank lied.

"Ay, where yo girl at?" V asked, referring to Candace's friend Tastee.

"She 'round here somewhere, you ain't seen her?" Candace replied as she looked around for her friend.

"Nah, we just got here. If you see her, tell her I said com'mere" V said.

"Aiight, let me go see if she in the back. I'll see y'all later," Candace said as she grabbed a few napkins off of the bar to dab the sweat on her forehead and walked off.

"Damn, I'on know what dat nigga 'Pone thankin' bout. He 'posed to *been* fucked dat bitch" June commented as they all watched Candace's naked ass cheeks bounce as she walked away.

Trey rejoined the group moments later and ordered another bottle of Moet. After tipping the bartender for the champagne, he spun around on the stool and had a look of perplexity on his face.

"What Dez over there talkin' bout? Everythang, everything ain't it?" Tank asked Trey.

Trey had just finished talking with his Cuban connect Orlando Hernandez aka "Dez". Trey and Dez often used the strip club for a place to talk business.

"Nah, dude talkin' 'bout it's gonna be a couple mo' days on that" Trey announced to the group.

The news was disappointing to June and V because they had already planned on copping the 14-kilos the next day and leaving.

"Damn" June sighed disappointingly.

"Look, it ain't gonna be but one or two mo' days at the latest" Trey said. "Y'all might as well hold off 'til then. 'Cause like I said, I ain't got but two on hand. But it's up to y'all and I know two ain't gonna do y'all no good" he added.

June guzzled down his glass of champagne before responding. "Fuck it, we might as well wait. I ain't got no problem wit it."

V didn't have a problem with it either, but he knew they'd have to discuss it with me. "We gonna have to holla at 'Pone and see what he wanna do" V said to Trey.

"Matter o' fact, lemme call 'em and tell 'em what the deal is" he added, as he got off of the stool and headed towards the exit with his cell phone in his hand.

I was sitting on the sofa with Consuela's head resting in my lap watching TV, stroking her still damp hair with one hand and flicking the ashes off a fat blunt into the ashtray with the other. Consuela and I had already gone two rounds, one in the shower and another in the bedroom. We were relaxing and resting up for round three when the telephone rang. I was praying it wasn't Kinya.

When I finally reluctantly answered, I was relieved to hear V's voice.

"Yo, what up nigga?" V spoke.

"Ain't shit, just laid up and poofin'," I replied.

"Who up there? That fine ass Mexican bitch?"

Mexican, Puerto Rican, it was all the same to V.

"I called to tell you that Trey ain't gonna be straight for another day or so. He wanna know what we gonna do. Me and June told him that we ain't got no problem waitin', but we had to holla at you and see what you wanna do. So what's the word playa?" V said.

I held the phone for a few seconds before responding to what V had said.

"I'on know what *y'all* gonna do, but I'm bouncin' tomorrow, with or without that shit"

My intuition was giving me some real bad vibes and I felt like packing up my shit and catching a cab to the airport. However, I went against my gut and stayed where I was at.

"Me and June might not come back to the room tonight, bruh. I'm tryna see what's up wit' that bitch Tastee. Oh yeah, Platinum asked about you" V reported.

My curiosity was piqued, so I asked, "What they talkin' bout?" I referred to Candace as 'they' to throw Consuela off because I knew she was listening.

"Tank told her you said for her to call you when she get off" V replied.

"Why that nigga do that? You know I ain't tryna holla at those people right now"

"I'on know, but he damn sho' told her that"

"Take them folks to spin city if they try to pursue, feel me?" I was talking in codes to my partner, telling him to throw Candace a curve ball if she asked about me again.

"I got you playboy. Listen, we gonna holla in the mornin' 'bout that 'work' situation" V said.

"Aiight, holla back."

V was stopped by Tastee on his way back inside the club. She was wearing a powder blue thong with rhinestones and no top. V noticed she had both of her nipples pierced and when she spoke, he saw that she had also gotten her tongue pierced since he'd last seen her.

"Hey stranger! Long time no holla at" Tastee spoke as she began to put her top on.

"You the stranger. You ain't hit a nigga back last time I beeped you." V said.

"I changed beeper numbers. You know I call you right back every time you beep me" Tastee defended.

V couldn't deny it, she was telling the truth about calling back whenever he beeped her, no matter what time of day it is. "I guess I can forgive you this time. So, what's up? You miss me?" V asked while looking her up and down. Tastee was just as fine as the first day he had met her at the mall. Her body was just as beautiful without clothes. He remembered how fat her pussy looked in those Daisy Duke shorts, so he focused his eyes between her legs and decided he wanted to see her naked. "Damn Sexy, that earring in yo' tongue turnin' a nigga on. Why don't you take a nigga to VIP?" V suggested.

"You ain't said nothing player, c'mon" Tastee replied, grabbing his hand and leading him towards the back of the club where the VIP booths were located.

********

I hung up the telephone and thought about the worthless trip I'd just made all the way to Florida. Two lousy ass kilos wasn't worth my time, *or* the risk of getting knocked off. But I knew June and V well enough to know that once they had their minds made up there was no changing them. My mind was also made up. I called Tammy and Wanda's room to let Wanda know that she'd be leaving with me the following morning and Tammy would be staying.

After I'd hung up the phone and let out a frustrating sigh, Consuela looked up at me with those sexy brown eyes. "Everything okay?" She asked out of concern.

"Yeah, I'm good. But look, I'm bouncin' tomorrow evening"

"I heard. Damn, I'm gonna miss you. When are you coming back?" She asked.

"Soon baby, real soon" I replied while stroking the side of her face.

**********

"Aye, where yo' sister at?" June asked Tastee.

V and Tastee had left the VIP and were now standing at the bar. V took a seat and Tastee eased between his legs and stood there like he was her man.

"She at home, why? You ain't tried to get at her since you was down here last time" She answered June.

"What's her number?" June asked as he pulled out his cell phone.

"She ain't got no phone" Tastee lied.

"Oh, so it's like dat, huh?" June asked.

Tastee ignored June and told V, "I'll be back"

"Aiight," V replied and then slapped her on her ass as she turned to walk away.

Tastee looked back at V and stuck her tongue out, displaying her tongue-ring while smiling. When she was out of earshot, June asked, "You holla at 'P'?"

"Yeah, that nigga trippin'" V replied.

"What he gonna do?" Trey asked out of curiosity as he chimed in.

V sipped his champagne and replied, "He said he still dippin' tomorrow, regardless"

"Oh yeah?" Tank joined in.

"So what *y'all* gonna do?" Trey asked both June and V.

"Shiiit, I'm tryin to get straight 'fo I leave" June replied.

"Yeah me too. Fuck that dumb shit. I ain't come way down here fo' nothin'" V said.

"I can dig that" Trey agreed.

It was almost three o' clock in the morning when Trey and company left Clubb EXXtasy and instead of four, they were one short. Big Will was on the phone with his boss, watching as they piled into the SUV. All three were visibly twisted and June almost fell. Big Will recognized June immediately.

"Yo, that's the same dude I saw a couple of weeks ago in the club with Trey and Tank" Will told his boss.

"What dude?"

"This dude I'm looking at leaving the club with Trey and Tank" Will replied before continuing, "And come to think of it, I saw him again the next day in a Honda. I think it was a station wagon. You know what? I just saw the same car in the hotel parking lot. I remember following them because they looked outta place and they had North Carolina plates"

"Are you sure?"

"Without a doubt." Will responded.

\*\*\*\*\*\*\*\*\*\*

V was sitting at the bar waiting for Tastee to get dressed. He'd decided to leave the club with her. Tastee had told V that she was taking him back to her place for a private show and he was totally game for that.

\*\*\*\*\*\*\*\*\*\*

Consuela and I had sex again. This time on the couch and on the living room floor. After showering again, we both crawled into bed and passed out. I woke up to the sound of Consuela's voice. "Capone, Capone" She said as I slowly opened my squinting eyes that were trying to adjust to the sunlight shining through the curtains. "Capone, baby I got to go home. Damn, I hate I gotta leave you so soon but please promise me I'm going to see you again, soon."

I saw that she was fully dressed and had her hair pulled back into a ponytail. I wondered how long she had been up.

"I promise, I promise." I said sitting up and yawning.

Consuela bent down to kiss me on the lips, as I tried to turn my head away and offer my cheek, but she chased my lips until she caught them. I guess she didn't care about the morning breath thing, but I was self-conscious.

"Promise you're gonna call before you leave AND as soon as you get home." She said with her thick accent.

"You got that" I confirmed while trying to find the clock. *Damn, it was eleven thirty already.* I got out of bed to walk Consuela to the door.

"Are you going to miss me?" She questioned.

"Baby, I miss you already and you ain't even left yet" I charmed and slapped her across her ass as she stepped out into the hallway.

"Adios, mi amor" She said.

"Yeah, I want some mo' too." I joked and then added, "I'll holla later" Consuela kissed me again then headed home.

After I got dressed, I paged June and V. V was the first to call back. He told me that he was at Tastee's and he'd probably be there for a while. He tried to convince me to stay because Trey had said he would more than likely be ready to handle business later that day. I made it clear to him that I was still leaving as soon as he or June got back to the room.

When June called back, he was at Tank's. He bragged and boasted about the way Tank was living and the size of his mini-mansion. I couldn't have cared less. In fact, I cut him off in mid-sentence and told him to come back as soon as possible so I could leave. After my conversation with June, I called Wanda to make sure she was ready.

June and Tank showed up about an hour after I had finished speaking with him. "What up dog?" Tank spoke as he entered the room with June.

"Ain't shit, just ready to dip" I said.

"Man you might as well chill for a few. I think Trey gonna get straight today" Tank encouraged.

"See, that's what I'm talkin' 'bout. He ain't sho' if it's gonna be today or not. If he was one hundred percent positive, I'd stay. But hell, you his partna and you'on even know" I stated.

Tank was listening and nodding in agreement because he definitely wasn't sure exactly when it was going to be.

June changed the subject. "Where V at? He ain't got here yet?"

"Nah, he still wit' that bitch. Ain't nothin' happenin' right now, so I guess he ain't in no rush to get here" I answered while packing the last of my belongings into my bag.

"Where Tammy at? I'on wanna have to search for dat bitch if Trey happen to come through." June stated.

"They in the room. I just hollered at them not too long ago. Matter of fact, I'mma call down there and let Wanda know I'm ready" I replied while reaching for the telephone.

"Don't tell that bitch I'm up here. I'on feel like being bothered" Tank said as I dialed the girls' room number.

"That reminds me, tell me why you told Candace to call me last night and you know I was..." I started to chastise as Wanda picked up the phone on the first ring, which abruptly cut my conversation off with Tank. I contemplated on telling her to come up to the room to get the car keys just out of spite for what Tank had told Candace the night before. Instead, I told her to meet me at the car in the next ten minutes.

June was counting the re-up money to make sure it was exactly what we had left in the stash box in the Honda.

"Yo, I'm 'bout to dip" I informed, giving June and Tank a pound. I threw my bag over my shoulder and headed towards the door.

"Holla at a nigga" Tank said while rolling a fat blunt.

"Y'all niggas be careful and tell V I said get at me" I stated while closing the door behind me. When I reached the bottom floor, I thought about Consuela and then I remembered her shift hadn't started yet. I dialed her home number using my cell phone as I headed towards the rear exit.

"Hola" A Spanish voice answered. I assumed it was her aunt.

"Hello may I speak with Consuela?" I said.

"'Old on please" She replied in broken English and then I heard her call Consuela's name and say something in Spanish.

A moment later, Consuela picked up the phone.

"Hello"

"What up, you busy?" I asked.

"No. I'm never too busy for you. Where are you?"

"I'm getting ready to leave the hotel" I replied as I reached the car. Wanda was already there waiting. I opened the trunk and tossed my bag inside. Wanda's bag was on the ground and she was giving me one of those 'I know you're gonna pick up my bag and put it in the trunk for me' looks. So, me being the gentleman I am, I left it right where it was, walked around to the passenger side and opened the door. When I got in, I reached over and unlocked the driver's door and resumed my conversation.

"Baby girl, I'm on my way to the crib. I ain't sure exactly when I'm gonna see you again, but believe me, it's definitely gonna be soon. Even if I have to send you a plane ticket to come see me. We definitely gonna hook up again. I want you to know I enjoyed myself last night and I hope you had as much fun as I did. It's gonna be even better next time and that's my word"

"Just the thought of how you picked me up and pinned me to the wall in the shower is making me wet all over again. I loved it!" Consuela replied excitedly.

"Girl, that wasn't shit. A nigga ain't even got started yet. Just wait 'til you see what I'mma do to that ass next time" I said while putting on my gold-rimmed Ray-Ban sunglasses.

Wanda had gotten under the wheel and was about to start the car when she heard my last sentence. She looked at me and smacked her lips as if to say 'Nigga Please'. I ignored her and kept talking into the phone.

"Listen, you go to work at three right? Okay, so I'm gon' call you back when you get to work, aiight....Okay then....You too....Peace." I finished my conversation.

Wanda had put on her shades and was teasing her hair while looking into the rearview mirror. I sighed aloud, hinting that I was ready to go, but she ignored me and pulled out a tube of lip gloss. She was in the process of getting ready to apply it, when I said, "Damn girl, let's go. It ain't like yo' ass goin' on a date. Hell, you could've did all that shit before you left the room"

Wanda gawked in my direction for a brief moment and then turned her head away without uttering a word. I couldn't see her eyes, but I know she wanted to say something smart.

When we got onto the highway, I laid my seat back and enjoyed the cold air of the AC blowing on my face. Wanda was on her cell phone gossiping with one of her girlfriends; something she had been doing ever since we left the hotel. She'd told me she had to stop by her parents' house in West Palm Beach to pick up something on the way. I didn't want to make any unnecessary stops, but she said it was very important, so we stopped.

I met her parents, who turned out to be cool and more down to earth than I had expected. Wanda's mother was just as fine as Wanda was and her father gave me the impression that he had once been a player. We ended up staying for a few hours, which was much longer than I had planned. Her pops and I sat by their pool drinking beer and kicking it while Wanda and her mother ended up cooking dinner.

Three o'clock had come and gone and I had forgotten to call Consuela back. After a few beers, I excused myself and went to the car to make the phone call. Consuela answered after only one ring.

"Mariott, Miami Lakes. How may I direct your call?"

"Hey baby, you busy?" I asked.

Consuela's voice started trembling and when she spoke again she was almost whispering.

"OH MY GOD!! Capone! I was just about to call you! Something just happened in the room you were in!!

### *Chapter Fourteen – Da True Gangstas*

Big Will and his partner had been watching Trey's house all morning, waiting for him to make a move. They knew Trey was desperate for some 'work' and he had a lot of people waiting to be served later that day. They really wanted to just run up in his crib and lay his ass down and get this thing over with, but they knew Trey didn't have the dope yet. Will was really getting frustrated with Trey and Tank, but this was too important to fuck up and their boss had stressed the importance of the situation to them on numerous occasions. Besides, a lick this big would earn them major respect and rank. Laying down one of the biggest dope boys in Miami would look *real* good for them, so they decided to sit and wait it out.

They prayed everything was to go as planned and nothing would go wrong, even though the situation was pretty much already cut and dried. So they just sat and waited while keeping their eyes on the prize.

A little after three o'clock in the afternoon Trey left the house alone, which was perfect because Will hated to lay people down in front of kids and other innocent individuals. They followed him to a storage company in Hialeah where Trey punched in a code at the gate to open it. He then pulled around to the back of the storage building and disappeared from sight.

---

Trey had spoken to Dez early that morning and Dez had finally told him that everything was a 'go'. The normal routine was for Dez's people to drop off the dope at an undisclosed storage unit in Hialeah and give him the code to the gate and the location of the key to the unit. Trey parked in front of storage unit number 74 and followed Dez's directions to the key hidden underneath the front bumper of a parked car near unit number 76. Trey reached under the left side of the bumper and ran his hand from one corner to the next searching for the key while observing his surroundings.

When he reached the right corner of the bumper, the key fell onto the concrete with a quiet jingle. Trey stuck the key in the lock to unit number 74 and was granted access inside of the storage bin. Once inside, he saw everything Dez said would be there. There was an old sofa, three floor model televisions, numerous bicycles and big-wheels. However, Trey was looking for one item specifically, an old dresser. He spotted it behind a few large boxes that were piled almost ceiling high. Most of them were empty, but a few of them were packed with old clothes. Once he had cleared enough of them out of the way, he opened two of the top drawers. He noticed that each drawer contained four individually wrapped kilos of cocaine. There were a total of nine drawers and each drawer contained the same amount of coke. 36-kilos weren't bad for a spur of the moment situation! It wasn't as much as he wanted, but he had to work with what he had. He stuffed 7-kilos each into two separate duffel bags, which he had found in one of the boxes. He closed the drawers, zipped up the duffel bags and was ready to leave the storage when he heard the squeak of tires creep towards his direction. Trey's adrenaline pumped so hard, his head began to throb. He reached beneath his shirt and pulled out his 9mm pistol, anticipating trouble.

**********

June, Tank and Tammy had been sitting in the room all day smoking weed and cracking jokes. Trey had called an hour and a half after I'd left and told Tank the news. He told him that Dez had come through with some work and he'd meet them at the hotel as soon as he picked it up. June paged V to tell him the news but V took forever to call back. When he finally called back, he sounded like he was half asleep.

"Yo, what up?" V said as June answered the hotel phone.

"Damn nigga, you sound like yo ass half-dead" June replied.

"Man, this girl draining the shit outta me over here"

"Well you need to be gettin' over *here*, 'cause dis thang goin' down in a few. Trey called and said he straight. Me and Tammy gonna be ready to pull up outta here as soon as you get here, aiight?" June reported.

"Aiight. Old girl went to pick up her daughter, I'll get her to bring me back as soon as she get back. Where 'P at? He leave?"

"Yeah, dat old scared ass nigga dipped 'bout two hours ago" June stated.

"Aiight playboy. I'll holla soon as old girl get back"

"Aiight, peace."

"Peace."

**********

Trey dropped the two bags and eased toward the door of the storage with his pistol in his hand. He listened as the car slowly approached and then crept past the storage unit that he was occupying. He waited for a few seconds before peeping out to see where the car had gone. Hesitantly, he looked out and saw a brown minivan parked three doors down from where he was at. He waited for someone to get out of the vehicle before he moved a muscle. After what seemed like an eternity, the driver's door opened. An elderly white man with gray hair exited the van and helped an even older white woman out of the passenger side. Trey let out a sigh of relief, stuffed his pistol back in his pants, retrieved the two bags and exited the storage. After locking the unit, he got into his ride and headed to his rendezvous at the hotel.

**********

Big Will watched the storage building from the parking lot of a car dealership across the street as the minivan entered the gate. The occupants of the van were an elderly white couple, so his attention was faltered for a minute.

"Yo, who's that?" His partner asked from the passenger side of the Mustang.

"Just some old folks" Will replied.

The information that Will was given was that Trey was to meet some people at a hotel room at the Marriott in Miami Lakes for a transaction, so Will assumed Trey would eventually head in that direction. The word was that four guys, including Trey's partner Tank and possibly two females were supposedly in the room waiting for Trey to arrive. The hotel room was the designated spot for the ambush and Big Will's patience was running thin. His boss and other associates were already posted up inside or around the hotel, waiting. As Will and his partner waited for Trey to exit the storage company, they conversed about Trey and his activities.

"I wonder how much of that shit he's getting outta there?" Big Will's partner asked.

"Hopefully all of it" Will replied, as they both continued to watch the exit.

Minutes after the minivan entered the storage company's gate, they saw Trey exiting. Will pulled out into the busy traffic and trailed Trey from a safe distance. The direction in which Trey was traveling was an indication that he was on his way to the hotel.

"Showtime baby!" Will told his partner as they followed Trey with caution.

\*\*\*\*\*\*\*\*\*\*

V was getting restless. Tastee had been gone for over two hours and he was ready to leave. June had called to inform him that they were leaving shortly because Trey was on his way over with the coke. V was about to leave a note and call a cab just as the phone rang. He contemplated on whether or not to answer the girl's phone and then he decided against it, out of respect. Then the phone rang again just as his pager went off. Tastee's code was displayed with no number, which meant that it was her calling and she wanted him to answer. V picked up the phone.

"Hello"

"Hey, I figured you wasn't gonna answer the phone, that's why I beeped you" Tastee said.

V didn't want to hear all of that, he just wanted to know why she had left him there for over two hours, knowing he had something to do. "Where the fuck you at? Didn't I tell you I gotta take care of some business an' yo ass been gone two hours. Damn, I gotta call a cab or what?" V said angrily.

"I'm so sorry. My car caught a flat tire and I just got to my momma's house. I'm on my way home now. All I gotta do is stop and get somethin' to eat 'cause my daughter ain't ate yet. Don't leave, I wanna see you before you go. You want me to bring you somethin' to eat?" Tastee tried to apologize for being late.

Although V didn't believe her, he still decided to wait because his stomach was growling like shit. "That's the least you can do for havin' a nigga sittin' here waitin' on yo' ass" V replied.

"What 'choo want? Fast food or seafood?" Tastee asked.

"Seafood. Make sure you get some fries too" V answered.

"Ok, you like shrimp and lobster?"

"Yeah, that's cool. And listen... hurry up" V stressed.

"Okay, I'm leavin' now"

"Peace" V hung up the phone and waited.

**********

Trey pulled into the hotel parking lot next to the Honda which June, V and Tammy would be driving later. He parked, retrieved the two duffel bags from the back seat and got out. He looked around and didn't see anything suspicious, so he proceeded towards the hotel's entrance.

When he passed the front desk on the way to the elevator, he saw a young black guy dressed in a navy blue T-shirt and shorts with tennis shoes at the pay phone. Trey thought the guy looked vaguely familiar, but didn't think anymore about him as he entered the elevator and pressed the number to the floor of which June's room was on. The elevator was empty and eerily silent until it reached the second floor. The elevator stopped and the doors opened, inviting a young black couple, who were both dressed in athletic short sets and carried towels around their necks. They spoke as they entered the elevator with Trey and rode to the fifth floor, the same floor Trey was going to. When they got off, they went in the opposite direction from which Trey headed. Trey could hear June talking as he approached the room. He knocked and was let in by Tammy.

"Hey baby" Tammy said, greeting him with a kiss.

"What up y'all?" Trey spoke as he entered the room, handing a duffel bag each to June and Tank.

"Where V at?" Trey asked, looking around the room.

"He 'posed to be on his way from over dat stripper bitch house" June replied as he unzipped the bag he was holding. June counted the seven kilos and smiled.

"Yo, it's seven mo' in this bag right here" Tank told June.

June handed Trey the bag with the money in it and told him, "We just counted it. All of it's there"

"You know I ain't trippin'. Y'all ain't never come up short with a nigga" Trey said.

They all sat in the living room for a while politicking and bullshiting while smoking on a blunt. June paged V again and waited for him to call back. Tank and Trey decided they should leave so they could handle some more business because they had people on hold and waiting to be served.

"Yo June, we 'bout to dip dog. Tell 'Pone to hit me when y'all get back to Carolina"

"Aiight, I'll holla at y'all niggas late." June responded as Tank and Trey headed towards the door with the bag of money. They took three steps and were stopped dead in their tracks when the door came crashing in!!!!!

*********

Big Will and his partner followed Trey to the hotel and watched as he carried the two duffel bags inside with him. They had made the call in advance, so everybody was in place and waiting. The first person to identify Trey when he entered the hotel was Smiley. Smiley was standing at the pay phone in the lobby, posing as a patron when Trey had walked past. When Trey entered the elevator, Smiley informed LaToya and Barry who were on the second floor waiting by the elevator.

When the elevator stopped on the second floor, LaToya and Barry got on with Trey posing as a couple who had been working out. They confirmed Trey's identity from the numerous photos they'd seen of him. They also noticed the two duffel bags he was carrying. They rode the elevator with Trey to the fifth floor where they got off and headed in the opposite direction from which Trey was going. The room LaToya and Barry entered was already occupied with eight other people anxiously waiting for Big Will to give the word. Ten minutes after LaToya and Barry had arrived at the room, Big Will and his partner arrived followed by Smiley. Big Will's partner, Fernando Juarez, aka Orlando 'Dez' Hernandez, carried a search warrant that had been obtained earlier that day.

Everybody in the room was putting on bullet proof vests, checking to make sure pistols were loaded and making sure badges were visible. All of the officers were wearing hats and shirts that read FBI.

After changing into uniform, Agent William Harris, aka Big Will, led his team to the room in which Trey had entered with the bags of cocaine. Agents Johnathan Smiley and Barry Constantine carried the Bata-ram which would be used to gain entry to the room. Once they reached the door, they could hear the group's voices. Agent Harris gave the silent signal for Smiley and Constantine to come to the front with the Bata-ram. Once in position, Harris silently signaled with three fingers that they would enter on the count of three. He held one finger high in the air, then another and when the third finger rose, the Bata-ram struck the door with enough blunt force to knock it off its hinges!!

June's first instinct was to reach under the sofa for the tech-nine, as Trey and Tank automatically reached for their pistols when they saw the door being smashed! They all froze when they heard someone scream, "FBI!! Search warrant!! Search warrant!! Everybody get down!! Everybody on the floor!! Now!!"

Tammy was so scared, she couldn't move. She was frozen with fear and in total shock! Once the agents had June, Trey and Tank on the floor with their hands behind their heads, Agent LaToya Brice forced Tammy to the ground. The agents found the two guns that Trey and Tank possessed along with the tech-nine that was hidden beneath the sofa. The two bags containing the cocaine were confiscated along with the bag of money which Trey had dropped. After they were searched and cuffed, they were all led to the sofa. Agent Smiley read them their Miranda rights while the other agents searched the rest of the room. Nothing else incriminating was found except for a small sack of weed on the nightstand in the bedroom which was the least of their problems.

While sitting on the sofa, everybody was trying to make sense out of what was happening. They were all in a state of disbelief, shock and outrage. Trey felt a sense of shame and anger. He had been set up! It was a set up all along! There never was 'Dez', the Cuban drug lord. He was 'Dez' the FBI agent!

Tank was mad that he had gotten himself caught up in this bullshit. Tammy was petrified at the thought of being arrested. She sat with her head down crying quietly. June was angry with himself for being so greedy and so anxious to re-up. He was mad that he hadn't also left Miami.

After thoroughly searching the room, Agents Juarez and Harris tired to talk to the four individuals on the couch.

"Ay, what's up big man?" Harris said to June, but June didn't answer. "Oh, you can't speak to a brother? You don't remember me? Yeah, you do remember me don't you? I can see it in your eyes" Harris taunted June, while standing in front of him. June's face showed no expression as Harris questioned him.

Juarez started in "Y'all know y'all done fucked up, right? Trey, Trey, look up... I know it's hard to look at the force that brought your ass to your knees. All those times we met, you talked all of that gangsta shit. 'Fuck the police this, fuck the police that. I'm holdin' court in the streets'." Juarez imitated Trey with hand motions as he continued, "What happened to all of that gangsta shit Trey? Look at you now. You ain't shit but a bitch. A bitch that's getting ready to get fucked! You been selling all that dope I been giving you? Well, I hope you've been saving up for a lawyer, because you are definitely going to need one. And look at this girl right here. Is this the white girl you been telling me all about? What's her name again? Tameka....no Tammy. Yeah that's it, Tammy. Tammy just fucked her life up, thanks to you."

Juarez was talking mad shit to Trey, then he started with Tank, "Tank, my man. You know how long we been wanting you? Too long" he answered his own question and continued, "Thank your man Trey here for getting you a reservation for a long stay in federal prison"

The other agents found Juarez's comments funny as they laughed.

June was more confused than anything else. He was trying to figure out what in the hell was going on. He recognized the Spanish agent who was doing all of the shit talking. He was the man Trey was talking to at the strip club about the coke. He also recognized one of the black agents, Big Will, the same guy who had followed them to the store the last time they were in Miami. Will seemed like he was the one in charge, giving orders and what-not to the others. June sat and wondered if this whole thing was a set-up just to trap *him*. A million questions swirled through his head. *How in the fuck did Trey not know he was dealing with the damn police? Why was Capone in such a rush to leave? Why had V taken so long to show back up? Was dis bitch Tammy down with this shit too? Damn, what da fuck is going on?* June eyed Trey and Tank suspiciously as he tried to piece together this crazy ass puzzle.

Tank and Trey were silent while the agents were celebrating their success of the operation. Apparently Trey and Tank had been under investigation for several years, but no one could seem to infiltrate their circle. Until one day Trey was introduced to Agent Juarez, posing as a Cuban drug dealer with direct connects for receiving shipments of cocaine from across the water. Trey thought he'd found his pot of gold at the end of the rainbow and things couldn't have been better for him. He had made so much money that he couldn't keep track of it all because he was serving customers from Alabama all the way up to Virginia. One man had made it all possible by supplying him with all of the cocaine he could handle. The supply was constant and seemed never-ending and Trey often wondered how one man could keep such a steady supply of A-1 quality cocaine and never seemed to run out. That man was Orlando 'Dez' Hernandez, a smooth talking Cuban with plenty of class, plenty women and plenty of money.

Over the years, Trey and Dez had developed a business relationship that proved to be very prosperous. Trey could trust Dez with secrets he wouldn't share with any other human being. Dez wouldn't dare spill one word of it. Trey had even confided in Dez about two guys in Philly who he'd to have 'taken care of' because of an unpaid debt and Trey just knew his secrets were safe. Now, here was his friend and trusted business partner wearing a FBI uniform and placing him under arrest.

**********

V was sitting at Tastee's dining table grubbing on a shrimp and lobster platter when his pager when off. He checked it and saw that it was June paging him again from the hotel, but he ignored it for the time being. He decided he'd call back as soon as he finished eating. Tastee and her daughter were also seated at the table smacking lips and sucking fingers as they enjoyed the food. Tastee saw V check his pager and asked, "You need the phone?"

"Nah, that ain't nobody but June. He probably don't want nothin'. He can wait." V replied between bites. Once V finished eating, he and Tastee's daughter Dyneesha sat on the sofa in the living room watching TV while Tastee cleaned up the kitchen. V was full and felt extremely relaxed as he laid back on the sofa and enjoyed the cool breeze of central air blowing. He had almost forgotten about June's page. Remembering, he asked Dyneesha to go and get the cordless phone for him. Dyneesha slid her small frame off of the sofa and ran down the hallway to her mother's bedroom to retrieve the phone from the charger beside the bed.

Dyneesha was a polite, very bright and cheerful 6-year-old, whose father was in prison for armed robbery. Dyneesha's father hadn't seen her in two years because Tastee had stopped taking her to see him for no apparent reason. Because of that, V didn't respect Tastee. He loved kids and hated when their mothers tried to keep them away from their fathers, no matter what the situation was. Dyneesha handed him the phone with a smile and he dialed the number to the hotel.

"Marriott, Miami Lakes, how may I direct your call?" Consuela answered.

"Room 522." V said, while flipping through channels with the remote.

"I'm sorry, but there are to be no calls placed to that room right now, sir" Consuela said.

"Why not?" V asked suspiciously.

"Those are the orders we received, sir"

"Orders from who?" V wanted to know.

"Per the FBI." Consuela told V, trying to drop him a hint without straight up telling him because she didn't know exactly who was calling. She assumed it was one of my associates, but she wasn't sure, so she tried to stay professional.

"The what!?.." V said, thinking he had heard wrong. "What the fuck!!...um, um who am I speakin' wit?" V asked.

"This is Consuela"

"Damn, girl what happened? This Capone's man, V. Can you talk?"

Consuela looked up and saw that her nosey-ass supervisor was looking all in her grill, so she told V, "I'm sorry, but that's not possible at the moment." She hinted at V.

"Aiight, aiight, look just tell me if...shit...fuck it. Aiight then." V stumbled through his sentence, then hung up and paged me.

V was in a semi state of shock. As black as he was, his face had somehow turned red. Tastee heard V cursing and yelling into the phone, so she came into the room. Tastee's intentions were to check V for using inappropriate language around her daughter, but when she saw the look on his face, she froze. V sat on the couch with the phone resting in his lap and his eyes staring blankly into space. Dyneesha was looking at him like he had turned into a monster.

Tastee hesitantly asked, "Are you okay?" as Dyneesha slid off of the couch and ran to her mother, hugging her waist.

V ignored Tastee and kept on staring at nothing, but he had an enormous amount of thoughts swirling through his head once he'd hung up the phone. *Damn that bitch said the 'FBI'! I wonder what the fuck happened. Man, I'm glad I decided to wait on this bitch instead of catching a cab on over there. I probably would've been caught up in that shit too! No, not probably, I would've been caught up in that shit to!. Shit, I wonder what the fuck going on over there? If this bitch wasn't late getting back, I would've been fucked up!! I wonder if they're looking for me and 'Pone too? Oh shit! What if they already got 'Pone? Damn, my nigga call back. Please call back.* V sat in a state of apprehension as he waited for the telephone to ring, praying that his road dog hadn't gotten hit also.

**********

"Baby, hold up... slow down and tell me what happene." I was trying to calm Consuela down so she could tell me what in the hell she was talking about.

"Okay…um, um the FBI just raided the room where your friends are. But I don't know exactly what's happening" Consuela reported in a shaky voice.

I listened in disbelief as she told me about the Feds rushing my people. "Damn!!! Shit! Goddammit….I told them stupid ass niggas something wasn't right. But nah, they ain't wanna listen to a muh-fucka. Shit!" I couldn't contain my anger.

I was sitting in the rental stomping the floor and pounding the dashboard. "Stupid-ass-niggas!!" I punched harder and harder with every word. While I was going through my temper tantrum, my pager was going off. I ignored it and tried to calm down for a minute. Consuela was quietly listening to me expel my anger. She didn't say a word.

When I had calmed down a little, I took a deep breath and said, "Listen baby, I'm sorry 'bout that … um."

"I understand" She said quietly.

"Look, I want 'choo to keep me informed on what's going on down there, aiight. I gotta make a few calls so I can try to find out exactly what's happening" I told Consuela while I checked my pager. "V?" I said aloud when I saw a Miami telephone number with V's code.

Consuela heard me and said, "Oh yeah, he just called, right before you did"

"Who? V?" I asked with curiosity.

"Yeah, I couldn't really talk to him though, 'cause my boss was all in my face" She replied.

"What he say?"

. "He wanted me to put him through to the room, but I told him I couldn't do it, per the FBI's instructions." She reported and then added, "he pretty much reacted the same way you just did."

"I can imagine…Look, I think I'mma have to come back down there to scoop my man, so I'll hit you when I get there. If you find out anything before you hear from me, get at me and keep me posted. Aiight?"

"Okay baby, be careful. And listen, I am so glad you weren't in that room."

"Shiit, how you think I feel?" I said.

"Don't forget to call me, okay?"

"I won't. Talk to you later"

I immediately dialed the number V had paged me from as soon as Consuela and I had hung up.

**\*\*\*\*\*\*\*\*\*\***

After what had seemed like hours, but in actuality was only about fifteen minutes, the phone finally rang. V snapped out of his daze and answered it on the first ring.

"Yeah"

"Boy, what is *really* happenin'?" I asked my partner.

"'P, boy I'm glad you called back. Where you at?" V asked as he got off of the couch and went out onto Tastee's front porch.

Tastee silently watched him, relieved that he had snapped out of his trance and the color had come back to his face. V closed the door behind him for privacy and Tastee could tell something was wrong.

"I'm up here in West Palm with Wanda. We over her people's house" I replied.

"Man, June 'nem done fucked up!" V exclaimed.

"Yeah, I heard already. I just got through talking to ole girl at the hotel. She said you had just called"

"Yeah, but she ain't tell a nigga nothing. What she tell you?" V asked out of concern and curiosity.

"She just said the Feds rushed the room and they ain't want no phone calls to go through. When was the last time you talked to June?" I asked.

"I hollered at him earlier. I told him Tastee wasn't home and I would be there as soon as she got back. He said Trey had called and said he was straight and he was on his way over there. Man, I'on know *what* the fuck happened." V said.

"My nigga, I knew somethin' wasn't right 'bout this shit. I swear to God something kept on telling me to bounce. Just think, whatever happened to them could've been happening to *us* right now too" I said.

"Boy, you ain't never lied 'bout that. Don't you know I started to catch a cab back to the room when June paged me the first time? Yo, I was mad 'cause ole girl was taking too long to get back, but hell, I'm about to go in there and thank her ass for that shit" V said.

"Yo, what if they looking for me and you?"

"Yeah, I thought about that too. You think a nigga need to lay low and shit?" V asked.

"Man, I'on know. But, one thing is certain and two things fo' sho', this the Feds my nigga. And if they looking for a nigga, best believe they know where to look. And Kinya ain't been blowing a nigga's pager up so I guess ain't nothing cracking up the way. Dee been paging you?" I asked.

"Nah. I mean, she hit a nigga once earlier. But nah, she ain't been blowing a nigga's shit up" V replied.

"Aiight, so what 'choo gon' do? You want me and Wanda to come get you?" I asked.

"Hell yeah! Nigga, you know I ain't tryna stay down here"

"I feel ya, my nigga. Have ole girl take you to Lauderdale. We gonna meet you at Jumbo's" I said.

"Aiight, but what if June need a bondsman or something? What if…"

"Nigga, shit ain't that easy with the Feds, this ain't no state case and shit. June gonna need more than just a bondsman. That nigga need some *prayer*" I said as I cut V off in mid-sentence.

After hanging up with V, I dialed June's home number and waited for an answer. I wanted to talk to Cherone so I could give her what little bit of information I had concerning June. After several rings, I hung up and decided to try back later. I debated on whether or not I should call June's mom, but decided against it because I didn't want to be the one to break the news to her. I sat in the rental with a feeling of numbness, trying to figure out what in the world had happened inside of that room. I went through numerous scenarios and the outcome still ended up being the same thing. I concluded that somebody had really fucked up!!

After pondering over spilled milk, I decided to call Kinya. Kinya answered in a tired voice. "Hello"

When I heard the sound of my woman's voice, my whole world seemed to brighten.

"Hey baby, how you doin'?" I spoke.

"Hey Daddy. I'm doing fine. I'm just tired. Your daughter's wearing me out and she ain't even been born yet." Kinya responded with a little more perk in her voice, "Anyway, how you doing and when you coming home?"

"I ain't doing too good right now. I'm coming home as soon as possible, like in the morning. Look, ain't nothing strange been goin' on up there have it? I mean, ain't nobody been to the house or nothing like that, right?" I asked while unplugging the phone from the charger and exiting the car.

"No, ain't nothing happened since you left. And you know ain't nobody been over here. Why, what's wrong?" Kinya asked, sensing the fact that something wasn't right.

I took a deep breath and began to explain what I had heard happened with June at the hotel. Kinya listened silently until I was finished and then she started crying before finally responding. "Oh my God… baby, thank God you wasn't there. Baby, please come home."

"I'll be there in the morning, I promise. I'm bouncing as soon as I go get V and listen, keep tryna call Cherone and tell her what happened. Tell her to be home in the morning, 'cause I'mma stop through there on my way home. I know June gonna be don' called her by then and I need to holla at her" I directed.

"Okay and you better be careful, 'cause I swear to God I don't know what I'll do if something happened to you." Kinya replied, while wiping tears from her eyes.

"Baby, get some rest and I'll see you in the morning"

"Okay, Mike. I love you." Kinya said.

"I love you more, baby. I'll holla at you later aiight?"

"Okay, bye."

I re-entered Wanda's parent's house and smelled the aroma of fried chicken radiating from the kitchen. Pops had left the pool area and was now seated in a Lay-Z-Boy watching a Miami Heat basketball game. I peeped into the kitchen to get Wanda's attention and asked if I could speak with her for a minute. She excused herself and met me in the den. When she entered the room, I was pacing the floor, looking sick. She knew right off the bat that something was wrong.

"What's up?" She asked.

"I looked at her and just shook my head before I spoke. "Shit – is – crazy. The Feds got June and Tammy 'nem" I was talking barely above a whisper because I didn't want her parents overhearing the conversation. "V barely missed it. They rushed the room we was in. Just so happen, V hadn't gotten back over there yet"

Wanda's mouth was wide open in disbelief.

"Oh my God!! Damn, what happened? Did they have the stuff?" Wanda asked with genuine concern.

"Yeah, I'm pretty sure they had it 'cause Trey was supposed to be on his way over there with it the last time V talked to June" I answered.

I stopped pacing and was now watching Wanda's reaction. She had a perplexed look on her face, as if she was scared but at the same time, I could tell she was relieved that she wasn't in that room with them.

"I'mma go back and get V. You stay here with yo' people and we'll scoop you on the way back up" I informed her of my plans. Wanda was still in a state of disbelief. She didn't know what to say.

"Yo…. Yo…Damn girl, you aiight? You better snap outta that shit. You listening to me?" I asked.

"Uh…yeah, yeah, I um, I heard you. Damn 'Pone, I just can't believe that shit." Wanda responded.

"Well believe it 'cause it's real. Look, I'ma go 'head and dip. I got V meeting me in Lauderdale. Tell your people I had to make an emergency run and I'll be back later, aiight?"

"You want me to go with you?" Wanda asked.

"Nah, stay here and have some of that chicken wrapped up for me when I get back"

"Aiight and 'Pone be careful, okay" Wanda said as I headed towards the front door.

Wanda's father stopped me on my way out. "Where you headed youngblood? You coming back ain't ya?" He asked.

"Yeah, I'm coming back. I gotta go meet my partner. He having a lil' problem wit his girl. You know how it is." I winked as I made the comment.

He nodded in agreement, letting me know that he understood where I was coming from. I left Wanda's parents house with a feeling of dread and apprehension. I was desperately in need of a fat blunt…….

As I pulled into Jumbo's parking lot, I saw V standing near a candy apple red Nissan Sentra, playing with a little girl. Pulling into an empty spot next to the Sentra, I deaded the engine and got out to greet my partner with a pound.

"Sup my nigga?" I spoke.

"I can't call it playboy. You aiight?" V responded.

"Who is this?" I asked, referring to Tastee's daughter.

"This Tastee lil' girl. Tell him your name" V told her.

"Dy-neesha" She said with a smile.

"You so pretty, how old are you?" I asked.

"Six and a half." Dyneesha said with pride.

"Yo, we can dip as soon as her mama come out. She in there hollin' at one of her partners or somebody." V said as he playfully tickled Dyneesha making her squirm with laughter.

Seeing V play with little Dyneesha made me think about my child that Kinya was carrying. That made me even more ready to get home to my woman with her little round belly.

Tastee came out of the restaurant with another girl who had on a waitress uniform. Tastee had on a pair of white spandex almost like biking shorts, a long Miami Hurricanes T-shirt and white Reebok Classic tennis shoes. Her hair was pulled back into a ponytail and she sported gold-rimmed sunglasses. After talking with her girlfriend, she approached us with that sexy-ass walk.

"Hey Capone, how you doing?" She spoke.

"Sup?" I spoke back.

V had opened the door to the passenger side of Tastee's car and let Dyneesha in. Once she was strapped in, he gave Tastee a goodbye hug and he got into the rental.

On the way back to West Palm, V and I couldn't help but try to analyze what had taken place over the course of a few hours.

"What you think went down with that shit, dog?" V asked while rolling a blunt.

"Man, don't nobody know what happened in that room but them fools who was in there and God" I replied while keeping an eye on the speedometer, making sure I wasn't speeding. The last thing needed was to get pulled over for some bullshit.

"Boy, I had big plans for that shit we was re-up'n on. Damn, 'P you know that shit gonna put a dent in a nigga pockets" V said.

"You gotta chalk that shit up as an 'L', dog. That's all in the game my nigga. I know yo' ass ain't broke tho. That lil' bit of shit shouldn't have hurt you like that. Lemme find out..." I responded while looking at my partner with curiosity.

True enough, we had just suffered a loss but that wasn't nothing but a minor speed bump. At least that's the way I looked at it. I would've rather had lost a few G's than to have lost my freedom any day!!!!

"Besides, I had a feeling that something was about to happen. I didn't know what, but I knew it was about time for something to happen, 'cause we been doing too good. We had too long of a run without something happening. An old head once told me, *'the longer you run, the more sweat you build up. And when the sweat start dripping in yo' eyes, you lose focus.'* Meaning... we lost focus V, the sweat had a nigga blind. We didn't see that shit coming. A nigga slipped... bad." I attempted to explain fate.

V was listening, as he lit up the blunt he had been rolling. The sweet smell of chronic filled the confines of the car and I closed the sunroof to keep the smoke from escaping. V took a long drag as he reclined in the passenger's seat and thought about June and the rest of the people who were in the room when it was raided.

As he stared out the window, he thought aloud, "Shiit…better them than me"

I heard him and knew exactly what he was talking about.

"Boy, that's fucked up. That's how you feel?" I said.

"What?" V asked, acting as if he had forgotten he had made the comment aloud. "Oh, you heard that? Well hell, I ain't lying and you know you feel the same damn way" He added.

I looked at my partner and thought about how fucked up it would've been if all of us had gotten slammed. At least V and I would be able to get June a good lawyer and make sure he didn't want for anything. However, If *all of us* had gotten hit, it would have been a different story. Nobody would have been left to look out for us except our girls and families.

**********

June was seated in a small chair, still handcuffed. He felt as if his wrists were being severed and his shoulders ached from being in such an awkward position for so long and he had been complaining ever since they had first arrived. Tank, Trey and Tammy were all in different rooms, presumably being interrogated as well. They were inside the ATF building next door to the Dade County Federal Courthouse being harassed by the agents who had kicked in the door at the hotel. They had tried the oldest game in the world on June. They tried *good cop, bad cop*. One agent would come in screaming and making threats and then another one would come in and pretend to calm that agent down. Then *good cop*, would pretend to be the one that's going to help June out.

June laughed at both of them and told them, "Suck my dick, bitch ass crackas. I'on know what y'all talkin' 'bout. I ain't seen no dope *or* guns. Y'all got da wrong nigga"

June was holding his own by not letting them see him sweat and he hoped the others were doing the same.

Tank and Trey were also exercising the first amendment of the dope game, '*The Code of Silence*'. Neither of them opened their mouths. The only thing they said was, *I wanna talk to my lawyer*. Both Tank and Trey had been in trouble before so they already knew the ropes. But what they failed to understand was the fact that they weren't dealing with the state and local police. They were dealing with the true gangsters of all gangsters – The Feds. Unlike the state, the Feds don't have any rules that they play by – They ARE the rules!!

The agents saw that the three guys evidently weren't gullible and easily influenced to cooperate so they preyed on the weakest link, Tammy. They knew if anybody would cooperate, it would be the female. It always is!!

The agents questioned Tammy routinely at first, trying to feel her out, then they saw the weakness and changed tactics.

"Tammy, Tammy, Tammy. You know what your three friends are saying, don't you?" Asked Agent Shoemacher.

Agent Shoemacher was an old school veteran who had eleven years of dealing with street thugs under his belt. Shoemacher was towering over Tammy, using his size and tone of voice to intimidate her as he continued to probe. "They're saying that you knew about the transaction and you know a whole lot more. Is that true?"

He was pacing the small room while keeping an eye on Tammy, watching for any tell-tale signs of nervousness. Tammy was visibly trembling and Shoemacher peeped it, so he continued to lie, "Tammy, your friends are trying to pin *all of this* on you. What do they care about you? You're nothing to them but a fucking mule. The prissy little white girl that's expendable at all cost. They don't give a fuck about you" He was almost screaming and then he lightened up "Look Tammy, let's cut all of the bullshit, okay. Let's make sure you and I are on the same page here. I'm going to tell you what the deal is. We already know that you and another girl have been coming down here getting dope from your boyfriend and transporting it back to Charlotte. And you know I know what I'm talking about. So, this is what I want from you. I want a full statement of all the illegal activities you know about concerning those three misfits and anybody else that's involved in this, including your girlfriend who has been coming down here transporting with you. Tammy, you are in a world of trouble here and you are looking at a whole lot of prison time. I'm talking major years! Hell, just the dope alone carries twenty years or more and that's not to mention the guns. Young lady, this may be your one and only chance to help yourself. Do you want to spend twenty years of your life in prison? Especially for some people who don't give a fuck about you? I'm going to give you a few minutes to think about it, okay? And remember, I'm just trying to help you here"

Shoemacher opened the door and stepped out into the hallway with a sly smile, knowing he was going to get what he wanted from Tammy.

Trey had been interrogated by the agent whom he had been dealing with over the past couple of years. Agent Juarez knew he had Trey red-handed, but Trey was still proclaiming his innocence. Trey told Juarez that he had been entrapped and wasn't going to get cased-up that easily.

Juarez was angry because Trey wasn't bowing down. He screamed at Trey "Mutha-fucka, you know what? You've got to be the craziest man on this side of the equator! I've got tapes Trey! Endless hours of conversation! You never thought about that, huh? Ninety-percent of the times we met, I was wired. Man, you are looking at no less than a life sentence!! Remember those two bodies you told me about? Well, I did a little investigating and I found out that you *weren't* lying. You know those two cases are still open? Oops my bad, I meant to say, thanks to you and your verbal confession they are pretty much on the verge of being closed." Juarez was seated at the small interrogation table across from Trey. He leaned back and took a deep breath "Trey, why don't you go ahead and do the right thing. Help yourself man. You're looking at spending the rest of your natural life behind bars and you better pray the prosecutor doesn't push for the death penalty for the murders" He was trying to persuade Trey to snitch but Trey wasn't biting.

"Death before dishonor dog! I thought me and you already had this conversation when you was 'Dez' or whoever the fuck you was 'posed to be. I told you then and I'm telling yo' ass now. My peoples didn't breed no rats! They bred a mutha-fuckin' thoroughbred! Bitch mutha-fucka! I should've numbed yo' punk ass like I did them niggas in Philly!" Trey spat.

Seeing that he was fighting a losing battle, Juarez gathered his pen, empty notepad and rose from the chair to leave. As he approached the door, he looked back at Trey one last time and stated "I hope the next man who's gonna step up and finishing raising your daughter teaches her that there's a better way to make it in life than you did" With that said, he made his exit.

Juarez's last statement struck a nerve deep within Trey's core as he jumped up, flipping the table with his thighs and screaming threats! Trey couldn't fathom the thought of another man raising his daughter! Agents had to enter the room and restrain Trey as they held him down and hog-tied him…..

Tank was sitting in the chair, hand-cuffed and dozing off. The entire afternoon had been one big ass joke to him. The whole ordeal was wearing him down and not to mention the fact that he was coming down off of the weed they had smoked earlier. Tank had also been interrogated by agents who tried to persuade him to snitch. Tank had responded with laughter, non-stop hysterical laughter. Tank told them not to even waste their time because he didn't have anything to say. All he wanted to do was get through the processing phase so he could get to a bed and go to sleep.

### Chapter Fifteen – Switching Teams

When V, Wanda and I arrived back in Charlotte, it was early Monday morning. Me and Wanda dropped V off at home and then I took Wanda back to UNCC. As she retrieved her bags from the trunk, I let my window down and told her, "Yo, try to keep that shit under wraps as much as you can. I know muh-fuckas gonna wanna know where Tammy at and shit but try not to say nothing okay?"

I opened the glove compartment and took out a leather handbag that was full of one hundred dollar bills. I counted out four grand and gave it to her. She accepted the money with a look of curiosity. She was wondering why I had paid her so much and she hadn't done any work. I answered her unasked question. "That could've easily been you in that room yesterday along with Tammy 'nem, feel me? I feel like I owe you that" I explained.

Wanda was looking at me with tears in her eyes. She reached in and hugged me, then kissed me on the cheek. "If anything, *I* owe *you*. If you hadn't made me leave with you, it would have been *me* too. Thank you" She said while throwing her bag over her shoulder.

I was thinking, *if you feel like you owe me, then offer to give me some of my damn money back.* But she didn't offer and I didn't ask. I smiled at the thought, but didn't comment. Instead, I told her, "If Tammy calls, tell her to call my cell so I can holla at her. I know she probably down there scared to death"

"Yeah, I know she is. I know *I* would be" Wanda confessed.

I told her I would call her later to check on her as I pulled off. Instead of heading straight home, I stopped by June's apartment. When I pulled into the parking lot I saw Cherone's Prelude parked next to June's Caddy. I sat in the car for a minute, trying to imagine what was going through June's head at the time. I stared at his car and wondered what was going to happen to it if he caught a whole lot of time. I was thinking about how things had been going so well for all of us up until the previous day. *"Damn, it took June almost three years to make it and all it took was a split second to take it."* I said to myself, feeling blessed because I had escaped the wrath.

When I finally decided to get out of the car, Cherone was already standing in June's doorway. It was obvious that she had been crying because her eyes were red and swollen.

"Sup baby girl, you aiight?" I spoke as I approached the door.

Cherone nodded in silence. I could tell she was still upset from hearing the news and I was wondering if she had heard it from Kinya or if June had called her yet. She led me into the living room where we both sat on the sofa.

"You heard from June yet?" I asked.

At the mere mention of his name, she broke down crying and buried her head in my chest. While she was boo-hooing, I glanced down at that light colored spot on the carpet and had flashbacks. I thought, *Hell, that day you gave a nigga the ass right here on the floor you didn't give a damn about him. Now you sittin' up here crying over him and shit. Bitches ain't shit!*

I wanted to tell her to get her fake ass off of me with all of that Hollywood acting shit but instead, I played along with her and put my arm around her like I was comforting her.

"Cherone, chill baby. Everythang gonna be aiight" I told her as I lifted her head so she could look at me.

Her face was soaking wet with tears. She took a minute to get herself together enough to speak.

"June called late last night from the jailhouse down there. He said there were three more people in the room when they kicked the door in…wait a minute…" She said as she got up and went into the kitchen.

She came back with a piece of paper and resumed talking "…I wrote down as much as I could. He sounded so bad, like he had lost the whole world. He said that him, somebody named Trey and Tank along with a girl named Tammy had gotten locked up for some drugs and guns" Cherone began reading from her notes, "He said to tell you that Trey had been under scope from day one, whatever that means. Anyway, he said one of them drives a red Q"

"Ain't that 'bout a bitch" I thought aloud.

"Yeah, this is fucked up ain't it. He said they supposed to be going for a hearing tomorrow so they can find out exactly what the charges are. He said they got the V with the box and asked a million questions about the reg… What all that mean?" Cherone asked.

"They got the car with the stash box in it and wanna know who it's registered to" I translated.

"It ain't in none of y'alls name is it?"

"Nah, it's cool" I answered.

"Oh, he also said that they wanna know who all was with him. He said to tell you to call Swartz ASAP and get him down there on the next thing smoking. Who is Swartz?"

"A lawyer who owes us a favor" I answered while thinking, *Damn, this girl is nosey.*

"When he say he gonna call back?"

"At twelve o'clock, you gonna be over here?" Cherone asked.

"Nah, but when he call you just hit me on my cell on three-way. You got the number?"

"No. Give it to me." She replied while getting up to get a pen.

I relayed my cell number to her and told her not to hesitate to call if she needed anything. She gives me a hug and held me a little too close for a little too long so I broke the embrace and headed out the door to the rental. Cherone was still standing in the doorway watching me as I pulled out of the driveway. I nodded bye and drove home to my woman.

*********

It had been two weeks since the incident had occurred in Miami and I had been talking to June every day, sometimes more than once a day. I learned that June, Trey, Tank and Tammy had all been indicted on a conspiracy case. No one was granted bond as of yet. The US Attorney had labeled Trey and Tank as '*Menaces to Society*'. June was told that he was denied bond because he was considered to be a '*flight risk*'. Meaning that they feared that once he was free he would more than likely disappear.

Tammy was told that she may be granted bond at her next hearing, which was scheduled for the following week. Now, that was something that didn't quite click. *Why was Tammy going to get a bond and nobody else was?* Granted, I knew one of the reasons was because she was white, but these were the Feds they were dealing with. The Feds don't give a fuck if you are red, white and blue. They're going to keep your ass locked up as long as legally possible. Or at least, until you sell your soul and become a whore for the Government. When you sell your soul to the devil for a promise of leniency, they have no problem putting you back on the streets. Once they finish using you to set up your best friends and sometimes even family, they feel as if they don't need you anymore. Then they throw your ass in prison with the very people you turned against. Just like a whore, after they get *fucked*, they are useless!!

Swartz had flown down to Miami twice to visit with June. Once when he was first arrested, then again at his bond hearing. Swartz and I had talked about June's case once he got back after the second visit. V and I met the Jewish lawyer on East Trade Street at his law firm on a Friday afternoon. When V and I walked into the office building a few people stared at us like we were at the wrong place. I could pretty much understand why they stared, because V and I were dressed in urban gear and Timberlands. Pants were sagging and my dreads were swinging and bouncing with every step.

When we entered Swartz's office, his secretary beamed with a bright smile and spoke.

"Hi guys. Have a seat. Mr. Swartz is on a conference call. He'll be with you in one minute" She said.

Swartz's secretary was a middle-aged, heavy-set white woman with chubby cheeks. She'd seen us on several occasions so she knew who we were. I made it a point to flirt with her every time we visited.

"Ms. Clara you looking good today, as usual. When we going out? You been dissin' me for the last six months" I teased while leaning over her desk.

"Call me in ten years, when you're of legal age" She joked.

While we were joking around, Swartz's office door opened and he waved us in.

Larry Swartz, was a thirty-something, Jewish defense attorney who stood five-six and weighed two hundred pounds. He had on trademark, gold-rimmed Fendi glasses and an Armani suit with Alligator shoes. He also sported a gold Rolex and a diamond ring that put mine to shame. He kept his face clean-shaven, which made him look younger than he really was. Candy Man had recommended Larry Swartz to us a while back when Quick had gotten into a shoot-out with some cats from North Charlotte. Apparently someone had tried to rob one of Quick's workers and the beef had escalated. No one had gotten hurt but Quick got arrested for '*shooting in an occupied dwelling*'. Eventually, Swartz got the case dismissed on a technicality and Quick walked away scott-free. Ever since, Swartz had become a friend of ours. That friendship grew to unmeasured heights one day when Swartz met us at Red Lobster in Pineville for lunch. After we ate, Swartz was on his way to his car when he was almost robbed by a guy wielding a knife. V, June and I walked out just in time to rush the dude and beat him to a pulp. They guy limped away, empty handed and since that day Swartz had been forever grateful. What good ole Larry didn't know was that I had staged the whole thing! Making him think that we had saved him from getting jacked had put him in our debt. Now we were ready to collect that debt.

"What's up guys, how's it going?" Swartz spoke once the door was closed.

His office was very spacious! It was filled with cherry wood furniture, photos and certificates hanging from every wall along with a few trophies of stuffed Elk-heads and prized fish he'd hunted. V and I both took seats on the opposite side of the large desk in which he'd taken a seat and folded his arms across his ample belly.

"You tell me what's up playboy. You the one with the plan" V responded.

Swartz opened one of his desk drawers and extracted a manila folder labeled, '*Wilson*'. It was June's file and caseload. He opened the folder and adjusted his glasses.

"Well...I'm gonna be honest fellas. Jared's case doesn't look too good. They took the drugs and the guns, along with the money to the Grand Jury in order to obtain the indictment for the Conspiracy charge. From experience, I can tell you up front that his chances for a bond are almost less than zero. From my understanding, he is adamant about going to trial which in my opinion is not a good idea. If Jared blows trial, he is facing at least thirty years as a result of him having a prior felony. The Government sentences you by using a guideline chart like this one" Swartz said, handing me and V a copy of the Federal Sentencing Guidelines before he continued. "The amount of drugs that were confiscated from the room will put him on level 34. You see it there? Yeah, right there" He said showing the line to V. "And if you follow that line straight across to category two, you will see two figures which read 192 to 293... Well, that indicates the amount of months of imprisonment Jared's facing, not including the enhancements for the firearms which will boost it up to thirty years or more. Now, let's just say, hypothetically speaking, that one of his co-defendants starts cooperating for a deal. That will pretty much seal his fate, you understand where I'm coming from? And I wouldn't doubt it if one of them aren't already talking"

Swartz had put the file on his desk and leaned his heavy frame back into his chair, eyeing me and V, awaiting a response. I understood every word he had said but V was looking as if he were lost. Even though Swartz was considered to be a friend, he was still a lawyer and I never trusted lawyers. Lawyers are the best spin artists on earth! They talk in circles and leave you dizzy as fuck if you're not on top of your game.

"But you would know if someone was talking, right?" I responded.

"Sure, as soon as a statement becomes official, meaning once someone has given a full confession, it becomes obtainable by attorneys that are involved in the case, such as myself." Swartz responded.

"And if that does happen, you gon' let us know, right?" V asked.

"Sure, all of my info is yours as well. I'll be glad to keep you posted on what's going on."

"Aiight, let me ask you something." I said while leaning back in the plush chair. "Let's say, that the Fed's wanna know about me and V. They asked June, so I know they asked the others too. What if they found out who we are? What can they do? Considering that we wasn't in the room when all that shit jumped off?"

Swartz thought for a moment, before answering, "Well, because this is a 'Conspiracy' case, they could also arrest you and charge you with the same thing. Even though you were not in that room at that particular time. You can still be charged with conspiracy for other times you engaged in criminal activities with the defendants.

Have you ever heard the phrase, 'Guilty by Association'?"

"Damn, so what you saying is because I associated with a muh-fucka I can get charged with some shit?" V asked in disbelief.

"That's how they play ball." Swartz answered.

I was silently thinking and wondering what my life would be like if I had to go to court and battle this crazy ass shit. I shook the thought and remembered who we were talking about. We were talking about Tank and Trey, two of Miami's biggest dope boys. I knew they were going to 'go hard' and hold their own. And June, as long as I'd known him, I'd never known him to open his mouth. He despised snitches just as much as I do. But then there's Tammy, Lord knows there was no telling what was going on inside her head at the time. I had a feeling that she was already helping herself or getting ready to do it. I hoped she remembered the conversation we'd had at the Blue Marlin a few weeks back because I was graveyard serious about what I had told her. In a way, I kinda hoped she would get out on bond so I could refresh her memory a little.

"Aiight, so what you think might be in June's best interest?" I asked.

"Right now, I really can't say because it's too early in the ball game. But as time goes on and I receive more info, I'll be able to suggest what I think would be best" Swartz replied.

After giving us all of the insight he could concerning June's situation, we were ready to leave. As he escorted us out into the lobby, we shook hands and parted. He again promised to keep us updated.

**********

"Hey baby, you sho lookin' good.....How long you been out here? Dey ain't make you wait long, did dey?" June asked Cherone through the phone.

They were separated by a thick, double-sided slab of glass. Cherone was in Miami to visit with June for the weekend. On Saturday, the visit was behind the glass, but Sunday June was permitted a 'special visit', which meant that they would be in the same room together, under the watchful eye of a C.O.

"I been waitin' for 'bout fifteen minutes or so, but ANYWAY... hey sexy, I miss you" Cherone said with a bright smile.

"Girl, I miss yo' ass too. You just don't know how much I been thankin' 'bout you"

"You lookin' good, I see you keepin' yo' head up baby. How they feedin' you? You getting' yo' rest? You been gettin' my letters and the pictures I been sendin'?"

"Whoa baby, slow down, *yeah* is da answer to all of yo' questions. I know I ain't been writin' back like I should, but I been working on dis case. Girl, dey tryin to lay your nigga down from *now on*. But I feel like I'ma whup dis shit though. I'm keepin' da faith, feel me?" June optimistically replied.

"I know that's right baby, just keep prayin' and everythang gonna be alright"

June smiled at her comment, before asking, "You keepin' dat thang tight fo' a nigga?"

"Baby, you know I am. I'mma hold you down while you're in here." Cherone said convincingly.

"Dat's my girl. Baby, you know tomorrow it's gonna be *on*, right? You gonna wear dat skirt I told you to wear?"

"Yep, sure am."

"No panties…" June said licking his lips as if he could already taste her flavor. "…Damn I can't wait."

"Me neither" Cherone replied with a smile.

June asked, "Where you stayin' at?"

"The Holiday Inn right down the street"

"I wish I could call you at the room tonight" June said.

"Yeah, me too. You know I'mma be layin' in there thinking about you and wishing you was there"

"Don't worry about it, I'll be able to touch dat ass tomorrow" June replied.

"Yeah, my ass and everythang else" Cherone teased.

"You betta believe it" June said with a grin and then he changed the subject. "Listen… what 'choo gonna do 'bout the crib? You made up yo' mind yet?"

"Yeah, I think I'mma go 'head and stay there and wait on you to come home. How that sound?" Cherone asked.

"I like dat. Dat sound damn good. Dat's what I want 'choo to do. I'mma call my mama an' tell her to give you some ends to help you out wit' da bills and shit, ok?" June replied.

"I'on wanna ask yo' mama for money June"

"Girl, what 'choo trippin' on? Dat's *my* money. I left it in a safe over her house, just in case somethin' like dis was to ever happen. Baby, we straight! Money ain't no thang" June boasted.

Cherone tried not to show how excited she was from what June had mentioned about the money he had stashed. She was calm on the outside, but her insides were doing cartwheels.

"Oh baby, you so sweet. That's why I love you so much" She said, sounding sincere.          June's face lit up and he replied, "Girl, I love you too"

**********

Later that evening when Cherone returned to the hotel room she was exhausted. She plopped down on the king-sized bed and kicked her shoes onto the floor. Her stomach had been growling ever since she had left the jailhouse, so she decided to call room service. While she was on hold she heard someone shuffling around in the bathroom. She ignored the sound and continued to hold the phone up to her ear with her shoulder while taking one of her earrings out. She watched as the knob on the bathroom door slowly turned. When the door opened, Cherone smiled and blew a kiss at the person standing there.

**********

The stench was unbelievable. *How can human beings possibly emit such an odor?* Tammy thought to herself as she lay on the cold, hard steel that had become her bed for the past few weeks. The thin mattress they'd given her was so worn out and dirty that she had opted to dress up the cold slab of steel instead of sleeping on the mattress. She turned to the left, then to the right trying to find a comfortable position.

No matter how hard she tried, she just couldn't adjust to living in captivity. The food was so bad it made her vomit the first time she tried to eat it. The fact that she was locked up was already bad enough, but to top it all off, they had thrown her in the worst block in the jailhouse.

All of the women who were in her block were there for federal crimes or serious state charges. At first, Tammy thought that most of the women feared water and soap because only a handful would take showers. Tammy often saw most of the women taking birdbaths in their tiny sinks in their cells and wondered why they wouldn't shower. Her cellmate was also one of the ones that would often use the sink to wash up instead of showering. Curiosity had gotten the best of Tammy, so she finally asked her cellmate what was the deal with the shower. Tammy had used the shower with no problem and couldn't figure out what the problem was.

Tammy's cellmate sat her down and explained to her why the shower was off limits to most of the women. Tammy didn't believe what her cellmate had told her until she witnessed it for herself and what she saw had sickened her.

She entered the shower area one evening and stumbled upon two women who were double-teaming a young girl who appeared to be having the time of her life. The girl looked no older than sixteen, with a fragile body, which made her look even younger. One of the older women was ramming a banana into the young girl's vagina, while the other one was sucking the girl's breasts. The two women were black and the young girl was white. The woman fucking the girl with the banana was heavyset and dark as night. Her hair was tightly braided in cornrows. The other woman was a shade lighter and much thinner than the heavyset woman. They all looked like they were performing in a porn movie because their moves were calculated and in sync.

The first one to notice Tammy's presence was the heavyset woman. When she saw Tammy, she smiled wickedly at the thought of Tammy joining in. She immediately invited Tammy to come closer.

"We ain't gon' bite 'choo honey" She told Tammy.

"Yeah and if we do, you just might like it" The other woman chimed in.

To put emphasis on the invitation, the heavyset woman extracted the banana from the girls soaking wet vagina and put the banana in her mouth.

After sucking it clean, she offered it to Tammy, "Wanna taste?"

Tammy ran from the shower area with one hand over her mouth and the other hand on her stomach, trying to choke back the vomit that was forcing its way up her throat. That was approximately three hours earlier.

As Tammy lay on her mattress of steel, she wondered why the young girl had allowed herself to be degraded that way. What Tammy had witnessed earlier had really opened her eyes and gave her a true dose of reality. She was so anxious to go back to court, she had been calling her attorney everyday trying to see if he could arrange a sooner court date. The judge had made it quite clear that she would be released on home confinement the next time she appeared in court and she would have to stay at her parent's home with a monitor attached to her ankle pending her trial date.

Evidently, the substantial assistance she had given the government was sufficient enough for them to trust her to be released. Until her parents pressured her, Tammy had been hesitant about cooperating with the agents.

"Tam, you have already disgraced this family. Don't disgrace the government also. Baby, please cooperate with them! Do the right thing! Those niggers don't give a damn about you! They don't care if you go to prison. Those black sons of bitches! I told you about hanging out with niggers!" Her father had told her.

Her mother felt equally as hostile. Tammy had a tough decision to make, so she weighed out her options. Either she could keep her mouth shut and handle the situation like a trooper while facing a massive amount of prison time, or she could sell her soul to the devil and become a snitch. She thought about the lunch conversation at the Blue Marlin and three words kept on repeating itself over and over in her head – *Death before dishonor, death before dishonor.* She also thought about how tough prison life would be. Spending numerous amounts of years behind bars would surely drive her to the point of insanity. She pondered over those thoughts with deep concentration and finally decided that prison life was *not* for her! *NO WAY – NO HO!!* She would just have to take her chances and pray that the government in which she was assisting would also protect her life.

**********

"Damn bitch, I thought yo' ass had got lost. You been gone an awful long time. I know them visits don't last *that* long."

Cherone was still holding the phone waiting for room service when the person came from the restroom cursing. She covered the mouthpiece and replied in a sarcastic tone, "Yeah, I missed you too baby"

Then room service that she was on hold with finally answered and Cherone ordered dinner for two along with a bottle of Moet.

"How our nigga doin?" Asked the person with Cherone.

Cherone hung up the phone and replied, "He doin' ok. I gotta go back down there tomorrow at nine o'clock" She said as she stood up and approached the person to whom she was talking. They had just finished showering and was wrapped in a towel.

Cherone snatched off the towel and smiled while admiring the naked body that was before her. Their lips met with burning passion and undivided familiarity as they engaged in a deep kiss. Their bodies were no strangers to each other, as they'd been lovers for years. One knew exactly what the other wanted, liked and needed in and out of bed. Cherone slowly broke the kiss while sinking to her knees to please her long-time lover. She kissed one thigh, then the other while making her way up to the treasure she had become so obsessed with over the years. When she finally opened her mouth and took Meka's clit between her lips, she heard the sound that was music to her ears. She heard Meka moaning with pleasure. Cherone loved to please Meka in every way. Without her, Cherone didn't know what she would do. She owed her life to Meka and would do anything Meka asked. Even if it meant playing a nigga like June out of his money and everything else he had.......

Cherone had been a foster child that never had a real family. Her mother had given her up at birth for adoption. She never knew her biological parents and made no attempt to find them. Throughout her childhood she was shuffled from one foster home to another, where she was molested several times by members of her adopted families before she even reached her teenaged years. The sexual abuse left many mental scars that would take years of self-therapy to heal. She never stayed with any one family for a long period of time because either she ran away or ended up getting kicked out. Therefore, she never got to make any real friends because she was constantly relocating, until she was adopted by a family in Charlotte, NC at the age of fourteen. There, she was enrolled in West Mecklenburg High School where she was immediately labeled as an outcast. The boys never hollered at her and the girls didn't want her hanging around them. At that time, there was a popular girl named Tameka Fields who was also attending West Meck. Tameka was called the *'pretty tomboy'* because of her good looks and the fact that she loved to fight.

One day, Cherone was in the bathroom washing her hands for lunch when two girls came in. Cherone saw them and immediately regretted being there. She recognized them as being two troublemakers from the Boulevard Homes Projects and sensed trouble. One of them lit a cigarette and leaned up against the door while the other one walked past Cherone and purposely bumped her.

"Oh, excuse you" Cherone snapped at the girl.

"Bitch, who you talkin' to?" The girl asked while pointing in Cherone's face.

"I'm talking to you, fo' bumpin' into me" Cherone barked back, not backing down.

While Cherone was arguing with the girl at the sink, she didn't notice the other girl come from behind until it was too late. Everything happened so fast. The only thing Cherone remembered was lying on the floor being punched and kicked. When the abuse finally stopped, she looked up and saw another girl fighting with both of the girls who had jumped her.

In too much pain to move, Cherone just lied still and prayed that the girls wouldn't finish her off. She heard the door open and then shut moments later, before feeling a concerned hand on her back. Cherone flinched, thinking that it may've been one of the assailants.

"Yo, you okay?" She heard someone ask.

Cherone didn't answer; she just continued to clutch her aching stomach where she had been kicked repeatedly.

"Cherone, Cherone, girl you want me to go get the nurse?" The voice surprised her by addressing her by name as she slowly turned her head towards the direction of the voice and saw Tameka standing there with hair disheveled and her blouse was torn.

"Damn, them hoes whupped yo' ass girl. Ain't no tellin' how bad they would've did you if I ain't have to pee." Tameka said in a joking manner.

Cherone was in too much pain to talk and in no mood for laughter. She tried to get up from the floor, but the pain was too excruciating so she fell.

"Wait a minute, let me help you" Meka said while helping Cherone to her feet. "Girl, you need to go see the nurse. Come on." Meka helped Cherone out of the restroom and down to the nurse's office.

Because it was lunchtime, the halls were virtually empty, except for a few stragglers that stared at the two girls. While getting bandaged up, Meka and Cherone talked.

"How you know my name? And, why you help me out back there?" Cherone asked while holding and ice pack on her head.

"I know everybody's name. I got it like that. And, I helped you back there because I kinda dig you. I mean, I like yo' quiet, laid back style. Besides, I'on like them Boulevard Homes bitches anyway." Meka replied while applying some antibiotic ointment to her chest where she had been scratched.

"What 'choo doin' for the rest of the day? I'on know 'bout you but I don' had enough of school for one day" Meka said.

"If you leave, where you gonna go?" Cherone asked curiously.

"I'm goin' home. My mama 'nem don't get home 'til late at night, so they won't know" Meka replied while eyeing Cherone. She saw that Cherone was considering leaving too, so she asked, "Wanna come wit' me? We can sit around and kick it an' shit...you smoke?"

"Nah, I'on smoke cigarettes. That shit stank" Cherone replied.

"Girl I'm talkin' 'bout reefer. You 'on smoke reefer?"

"Nah, I ain't never tried it befo"

They left school and went to Meka's house for the rest of the evening to hang out and get high. Smoking weed wasn't the only new thing Cherone experienced that evening. She kissed a girl for the first time also! Meka and Cherone had gotten high and ended up kissing, caressing and fondling each other on Meka's bed. When it was over, they were both surprised that it happened and blamed it on the weed.

Cherone was having mixed emotions about what had happened, but she didn't regret it because it felt damn good! She was already at Meka's mercy for saving her in the restroom and the comforting feeling that overwhelmed her when Meka held her in her arms had made her melt. Meka was no lesbian, if anything she was just curious to see what it would be like to kiss another girl. But when the kissing turned into caressing and fondling, she made no attempt to stop it.

After that day, Meka and Cherone were inseparable. Meka took Cherone under her wing and taught her everything she knew, from how to boost clothes from the mall, to how to play a nigga out of his money. Even if it meant sex. To the average person, Meka and Cherone looked like typical best friends but if one were to take a closer look, they would've seen that what the two girls shared exceeded the limitations of friendship. They hung out with all of Meka's friends and did all of the things that best friends do. They got their hair and nails done together, they shoplifted together and they had sleepovers at each other's houses on a regular basis. Instead of sitting up talking about boys until the wee hours of the morning like other teenaged girls, Meka and Cherone made love to each other.

As the years passed, they both began to mature and they both stepped up their game. They graduated from gaming schoolboys to gaming hustlers. They knew that the hustlers were where the money was at, so they sat back and preyed on them. Cherone always followed Meka's lead. Whatever Meka *said*, Cherone *did*.

One day Meka met a stick up kid who was trying to 'get on' in the game. She saw potential in him and decided to holler. Sure enough, he hit his big lick and came up just like she had expected. They moved in together and lived lovey dovey for a while until he just decided to up and leave. She had gotten use to the ballin' lifestyle and all of a sudden he wanted to move out. She didn't put up a fight, she just let him leave and planned her revenge. Meka told Cherone about the ex-boyfriend of hers who was balling out of control, so they devised a plan.

They would arrange for Cherone to meet him by 'accident' and then try to lock his ass down. The shit worked! He couldn't get enough of Cherone! Cherone had put her thing down. Meka gave Cherone tips about his likes and dislikes. She even told Cherone the secrets of how to please him sexually. When he made love to Cherone, he was excited and totally amazed that she knew exactly what he liked and how he wanted it. He couldn't believe his luck.

The whole time Cherone was with him, she was sharing everything he gave her with Meka. The two girls had no idea that the game would pay off in a major way like it was getting ready to. Soon they would both be living lavish thanks to their ultimate mark. That mark was June!

Since Cherone had June wrapped around her fingers things were going better than they had planned. June was locked up on some serious drug shit and he was looking at major time. With Meka's guidance, Cherone had played her position with perfection and June fell for it. He even told her where the stash was at and that was about to be a grave mistake!!!!

**********

Tammy finally made bail and was living with her parents in East Charlotte on Albemarle Road. Although she was confined to the house, she was still overjoyed just to be out of that hell hole. She had to stay home 24/7 and the only time she was allowed to leave was to go to work, church or school. She didn't have a job, she had to quit school and church wasn't on her agenda, so she never left the perimeter of her parents spacious home. Tammy didn't care. She was free! She had to call a probation officer in Miami once a week to check in, but other than that, she wasn't hassled. Within only two weeks of her arrest, Tammy had agreed to make a deal with the Feds. She would be granted a lighter sentence, more than likely probation in exchange for her testimony against her co-defendants. Therefore, Tammy told the US Attorney everything she knew! She even implicated me, V and Wanda! She knew she was playing Russian roulette but she was determined to get as much leniency as she could!

### *Chapter Sixteen – Guilty or Not Guilty*

"That bitch did WHAT??!!" I asked, while rising to my feet. My eyes had suddenly turned bloodshot red and my blood had begun to boil. V and I were sitting in Swartz's office listening to him tell us that our names had been implicated in a federal drug conspiracy. Swartz had paged me earlier that day and told me he wanted to see me and V at his office. I could tell something was wrong by the way his voice sounded over the phone. I was hoping and praying that it wasn't what I thought it was, but it turned out to be exactly that! Tammy was snitching and was planning to testify on June, Trey and Tank. I couldn't believe the nerve of that bitch! Even after I had talked to her about this shit, she *still* had chosen to go against the grain! *That cracker-bitch don't know who she fuckin wit'.* I thought to myself as Swartz was reading her statements.

When he had finished, I couldn't believe that she had told so much shit! She had told everything! Swartz had told us that the statements were confidential and were not supposed to be revealed until the trial because the US Attorney wanted to present Tammy as a surprise witness. However, Swartz had pulled a few strings down at the clerk's office and had obtained the documents. V was eerily silent throughout the entire visit. He looked at me once and only once. When our eyes met, we were both on one accord. No words were needed because we both knew exactly what had to be done.

**\*\*\*\*\*\*\*\*\*\***

Kinya and I were fast asleep when the phone rang early one morning. I reached over her and answered in a tired voice "Hello"

"This is a collect call from….*June*….to accept this call…"

I pressed 'one' before the recording could continue and I heard June click on.

"Yo, what up?" He spoke dryly.

"What up player?" I spoke back.

June sounded like he was down in the dumps and I knew exactly why. He had gotten the paperwork I had sent him and he had seen Tammy's statements.

"Damn dog, you up mighty early" I said as I picked up my watch from the nightstand and checked the time.

"I couldn't sleep last night. I kept havin' dreams 'bout dat funky bitch walkin' up in da courtroom handlin' her biness"

June knew if Tammy ever got the opportunity to testify it would be curtains for him.

I heard Tank in the background speaking, *"What up 'P'?"* Tank and June were in the same block but Trey was housed on a different tier.

"Tell that nigga I said, *What up?* and tell him to stay up" I told June.

He relayed my message to Tank and then said to me, "My nigga, I know dat shit gonna get handled right?"

"Nigga, I'on even know why you asked some dumb ass shit like that" I responded.

June was referring to the situation with Tammy. The decision to 'body' that bitch had been made a long time ago. I wasn't only doing it because of June, Trey and Tank. I was doing it for *everybody*, including myself. Without Tammy, the government wouldn't be able to fuck with V and me unless somebody else took Tammy's place as a stool pigeon. In the sheets, gangsters die too young and snitches live too long.....but not this one.

When Tammy signed her named to that plea bargain, she had also signed her own death certificate. I had already hollered at Scrappy and his boys, Youngsta and Shoe. They were just waiting for me to give the word. I already knew Tammy was out of jail and living with her parents on Albemarle Road but I was just waiting for the right time to send them to handle their business.

"Yo, I'on know what I'm goin' through down here, but dis shit gettin' too real" June said with stress in his voice.

I just listened and let him vent because I knew exactly why he was fucked up. Cherone had begun to act differently towards him. Her visits had become very rare and her letters had all but stopped. I knew he wanted to ask about her, but his ego wouldn't let him.

After he had gotten everything off of his chest, I finally said "Dog, don't sweat that shit. I got that, aiight?"

I sat up in the bed and thought about how things would be if the tables were turned and *I* was the one behind bars. Honestly, I felt like June wouldn't have kept it real with me if he was out and I was the one locked up. Nevertheless, I kept it *true*. If not to June, I was definitely keeping it true to the game.

"Yo, you still gettin' yo' Charlotte Observer in there?" I asked June.

"Yeah, I'm still gettin' it, why?"

"Just keep watching the obituaries"

After our conversation, I started feeling bad for my partner in crime because we had been doing dirt together for years and now he was locked up. June had never slipped when we went on capers and he had always had a nigga's back whenever we went to war. Although we had gone through a slight misunderstanding, he was still my man and I was going to do all I could to see him come up out of his predicament. Even if it meant MURDER!!

*********

Tammy was on the sofa in her pajamas watching a late night movie, enjoying her freedom. Her parents had long been asleep and no one else was in the house but Tammy kept thinking she was hearing strange noises. She eventually blew it off and blamed it on paranoia as she kept watching the movie and eating her popcorn.

Wanda had called and said that she was stopping by because she had to talk to her about some very serious shit she had heard in school. Tammy had told her to tap on the living room window instead of ringing the bell or knocking on the door because she didn't want to awaken her parents. Tammy was anxious to hear what Wanda had to tell her. Although she had snitched on Wanda, she was confident that Wanda didn't know about because her attorney had assured her that this fact wouldn't be revealed until the trial. However, she knew whatever it was that Wanda wanted to talk about had to be important because she had never come over as late as it was. She was hoping it was some juicy gossip.

Halfway through her movie, she heard a *tap-tap-tap* on the window. She pulled the curtain aside and peeped out and saw Wanda standing there, nervously looking around. *She looks worried,* Tammy thought as she waved Wanda towards the front door.

Standing at the front door, Wanda was sweating bullets! She was so nervous her throat was dry and her palms were soaking wet. Within seconds of her standing on the porch Tammy opened the door to let Wanda in, but Wanda never ventured inside. As soon as the door opened, Youngsta pushed Wanda aside and put his pistol to Tammy's forehead in one swift motion! Youngsta had been hiding beside the door while Shoe and Scrappy were behind the shrubs on each side of the steps that led to the front porch. Tammy tried to let out a scream for help but it died in her throat as Youngsta's hand covered her mouth.

Scrappy and Shoe leapt from the bushes also brandishing pistols. Neither of them wore masks to conceal their identity because there was no need. They wouldn't have to worry about anybody identifying them once this mission was complete.

Wanda fled from the house and made it back to her car that was parked on the next block in record time. The three young hit men had driven a separate car, so Wanda was free to leave. Her heart was pumping a mile a minute as she was a nervous wreck. She fumbled with the keys as she tried to start the car. When she finally got it started and pulled away from the curb, her mind started reeling and her conscience had already begun to beat her down. She couldn't believe she'd just done the unspeakable! The thought alone had brought about a temple pounding migraine that was blurring her vision. She had just set up her ex-roommate and ex-friend to be murdered!!!

Wanda tried to rationalize the situation by repeatedly telling herself. "*It was either her or me. And I'll be damned if I'm goin' out like that*"!

**Two Days Earlier......**

Wanda had met with V two days earlier at a restaurant right next to the UNCC campus. V had told her that he wanted to talk to her about something very important and that it was urgent meet him.

During their conversation at the restaurant, V had told her, "You know that trick hoe Tammy is snitchin', right?"

Wanda had no idea Tammy had flipped and was now a rat.

"She WHAT?" Wanda asked, not wanting to believe what she was hearing.

And then when V dropped the bomb on her, she almost passed out.

"Guess who else she told on??.... YOU!" He pointed at her.

Wanda was petrified and angry at the same time. To drive his point home, V produced the paperwork with Tammy's confessions that Swartz had given us. While Wanda was reading what her friend had said about her, V commented "You know how much time this shit carries? I'm talking about Fed time, Slim. This shit is real and that cracka bitch trying to get everybody a muh-fucking life sentence, including *you*"

V was reading her demeanor as she was reading the paperwork and he saw that she was visibly hurt and highly upset from the statements Tammy had given.

He continued, "You think you can do a dub? 'Cause that's the *least* you gonna get if we don't do something about this shit"

At the mention of twenty years in prison Wanda began to feel sick! V picked up on her vulnerability and preyed on it. "I'll tell ya' what.... Me and 'Pone got big plans fo' this bitch, ya dig? But we need a lil' help. *Your* help."

"What kinda help y'all need from me?" Wanda asked curiously.

"Just tell a nigga right now if you down or not" V said before divulging any details.

Wanda knew whatever it was that V wanted her to do was going to result in aiding to kill Tammy. At first, she thought about the friendship her and Tammy once shared, especially when they were roommates. Wanda had even taken Tammy with her to her parent's house in West Palm on numerous occasions. Her parents thought she was adorable. They had gone through so much together since they had known each other. They were almost like sisters. Then those thoughts gave way to reality. If Tammy was such a friend, why did she snitch on her? Why did she want to see her locked up for the rest of her life? No true friend would ever do such a thing! Wanda began to see Tammy as the enemy and decided to comply with whatever it was that V wanted from her.

"Aiight, I'm down. What I gotta do?" Wanda asked.

V knew she would cooperate once she started seeing things his way. He told Wanda what he needed from her and watched her reaction for any signs of weakness. The last thing we needed was for Wanda to break weak on us and end up getting us all caught up on some *'conspiracy to commit murder of a government witness'* type shit.

Wanda listened to the role V wanted her to play she agreed to go along with it. "Holla when y'all get ready" Wanda told V as she got up to leave. As an afterthought she added, "I ain't going to prison because of that bitch"

V was expressionless, but on the inside he was cheesing like a Cheshire cat because he knew he had her right where we wanted her. We knew if something was to happen to Tammy, only a few people would know me and my people were behind it. Wanda was one of the few who would've known. Therefore, to guarantee she wouldn't say anything, we did the only logical thing there was. We made her an accomplice!!

**********

Tammy was being duct taped by Shoe while Youngsta held her down. Her mouth was first, then her wrists and ankles. Scrappy had tip-toed his way upstairs, checking the house for occupants. Each door he opened was an unoccupied room until he got to the master bedroom. The house was pitch-black! The only light radiating was coming from the bathroom that was attached to Tammy's parents' bedroom.

When Scrappy opened the bedroom door, he saw only one figure in the bed and then he heard the sound of the toilet flushing indicating that someone was in the restroom. Each of the killers had silencers attached to their pistols to minimize noise because they didn't need any nosey neighbors hearing gunshots. Scrappy crept up to the bed and put his pistol to Tammy's father's forehead and squeezed the trigger twice. The pistol came alive with a muffled, *'thump... thump.'* The old man never had a chance to defend himself. He never woke up and he didn't feel a thing when the bullets pierced his skull and exited the back of his head!

Scrappy let out a whispered "damn", as he looked at his gloved hand and the front of his shirt that was decorated with the old man's blood and brain matter. Scrappy was so pumped now, his adrenaline was pumping and he was ready to body someone else. The old lady was taking too long to come out of the bathroom, so Scrappy walked in on her. She was on the toilet taking a shit when she looked up and saw him standing there aiming his pistol at her. She remained on the toilet in shock! She let out a scream, which only lasted a second or two before she was silenced by a hail of bullets which hit her in the upper chest area, piercing her heart. The bullets knocked her off of the toilet and sent her sprawling to the floor.

Hyped up and loving what he was doing, Scrappy walked over and stood above her while she was on the floor in a puddle of blood. He looked down at the old lady laying on the floor with her panties around her ankles and shit running down her legs. He knew she was dead, but he couldn't resist putting a slug in her head just for good measure. He left the body in the bathroom and went back to the bedroom and started ransacking it. He opened all of the drawers and tossed the contents out and then he ransacked the closet to make it look like a burglary gone bad.

Meanwhile downstairs, Tammy had heard her mother's shrill scream which had died as soon as it started. At that instance, Tammy knew exactly what had happened and it petrified her to the point at which she almost pissed on herself! While Shoe had her on the sofa face down and duct taped, Youngsta was busy ransacking the kitchen and den. Shoe started roughly, fondling Tammy's ass through her thin pajamas and then he pulled her pajama bottoms down past her hips along with her panties and took the glove off of his right hand. He fondled Tammy's genitals with turbulence while she cried behind the duct tape and squirmed uncontrollably, trying to avoid his brutal hand.

"Bitch, shut up and be still" The young killer demanded while penetrating her with one, then two fingers! Shoe was getting a kick out of watching this white girl suffer. He kept molesting Tammy with his hand until he had worked four fingers into her vagina! Still not satisfied, he went for the gusto and brutally jammed his entire hand up into her! Tammy was in so much pain, she felt as if someone was holding a flaming match to her genitals.

After violently raping Tammy with his fist, Shoe pulled his hand out and saw that she had bled on him. At the sight of blood Shoe got excited knowing that he had caused her pain. He wiped his hand on her pajamas and stood up while looking at her with a deadly smirk on his face. He replaced his glove and raised his silenced .45 automatic to Tammy's temple. Tammy's life flashed before her eyes right before she heard a slight '*thump*', then everything went black! Shoe purposely left Tammy's pajamas half way down to leave the impression that rape had taken place. After ransacking the house and taking some jewelry along with other valuable items, Scrappy kicked in the back door from the outside to impose the illusion of 'forced entry'. When their mission was complete, they all exited the house as quietly as they had entered.

**********

"This is a collect call from..." I pressed '*one*', cutting off the recording in mid-sentence.

"Yo" I answered.

"What up my nigga?" June responded sounding alive and full of energy. He had just finished reading his daily subscription of the Charlotte Observer and saw the article about Tammy and her parents. "Boy you 'bout yo biness my nigga! Believe dat! I just got the word on dat sit-chee-ayshun. Feel me?" June asked.

I knew what he was talking about but I didn't want to discuss it on the phone so I brushed him off.

"Yeah, I feel that. But leave that alone though..." I said. Knowing that sooner or later June and his co-defendants would get questioned about Tammy's murder, I asked him if he was prepared, "...Yo, you know a spark starts a flame, right?"

June was silent for a minute, trying to decode what I was saying. When he had figured out what I was asking he answered, "Fa sho. Me and Tank talked about dat already. No dub, no 'C'." Which meant *no witness, no case.*

True enough, we had eliminated a key witness in their case, but there were still several agents who would testify. The number one witness would be Juarez, the agent that had dealt with Trey on many occasions and taped most of their conversations. Their chances of beating the case were still slim even with Tammy out of the way. June was confident that he would walk. He knew the prosecutor had Trey by the balls, but they didn't really have anything to tie him in with a  drug conspiracy. He figured the worst case scenario would be him getting convicted  of *possession of a firearm by a felon* which didn't carry as near as much time as *conspiracy.*

"Yo, I'm comin' to da crib soon, my nigga. I'mma fuck dat stankin' ass bitch Cherone up soon as I touch down" June said, promisingly.

"When the last time you heard from her?" I asked.

"I ain't heard from her ass in a minute. I know she moved out the apartment but I'on know where she at. She must thank a nigga ain't never gettin' outta here" June replied angrily.

"You know that's how them hoes act when a nigga fall. They move on to the next muh-fucka" I told June. "Don't sweat that shit. You know the game don't stop 'cause a playa got knocked. *I'mma* straighten that bitch myself if I ever see her ass out anywhere"

June had his mind set on freedom and revenge when we hung up.

\*\*\*\*\*\*\*\*\*\*

Cherone had moved out of June's apartment and was living with Meka in Sandhurst Apartments. She had stopped going to visit June and her letters had dwindled to almost non-existence. The only reason she still held any contact with him was because she was waiting for him to get convicted, which she had no doubt would happen. Once she was sure he wouldn't be coming home anytime in the near future, her and Meka would execute part two of their plan…. having June's mother robbed for the stash...

\*\*\*\*\*\*\*\*\*\*

Ironically, Kinya went into labor the same day June, Tank and Trey were read their verdict…………..

Kinya gave birth to a healthy baby girl who looked just like me. She had my eyebrows, my nose and my smile. She had Kinya's complexion and was born with a head full of hair.

I was in the delivery room when Kinya gave birth. What I witnessed that day was the most miraculous event on the face of the earth! I must admit, I did get a little sick watching my woman's vagina stretch and part like the Red Sea. However, when my little bundle of joy arrived in this world I felt nothing but sheer joy! I even cut the umbilical cord on her tiny navel. Kinya was too worn out to talk. She just motioned for me to come to her. I bent down and kissed her lips, then whispered in her ear, *"Thank you ma."* Kinya cried tears of joy when the nurse brought our baby girl to us. I held her in my arms and kissed her tiny forehead while she stared up at me like she already knew me. I started talking to her as if she could understand me *"Daddy gone buy you anything you want. Little Mink coats, baby diamond necklaces, a stroller with chrome rims on it, just say the word baby girl and it's yours. I love, yes-I-do."* I chimed as I was rocking her in my arms and smiling from ear to ear while Kinya watched with tears of joy streaming down her cheeks.

We named our daughter, Mikai Simone Sanders. (Pronounced: Ma-ky-yah)

Meanwhile, in a holding cell waiting to return to the courtroom, June, Tank and Big Trey were all sitting silently. All three men were dressed to impress. They wore the latest from Armani and were dressed better than their lawyers. June and Tank's bald heads were shining like diamonds, while Trey wore his hair cut short and faded on the sides. Trey had cut his dreads before the trial had started because he wanted to give the jury the impression that he was not a hoodlum. The trial had lasted three days and it was looking promising for them. Their attorneys were on top of their shit, making a few of the agents look like monkeys on the witness stand. The only thing that was hurting them was Agent Juarez's testimony and those damn tapes. The prosecutor had played her cards smoothly and waited until the last day of trial to introduce Juarez and his evidence so his testimony  and the taped conversations would be fresh on the jurors' minds during their deliberation. It took the jury less than two hours to reach a verdict.

Trey heard the sound of the deputy's keys jingling, signaling he was near. He looked at June and Tank with a somber expression and told his partners in crime, "Well dog, this it. I'on know 'bout y'all but I'm goin' to get me some pussy when they find a nigga not guilty" He tried to joke, but the situation was a little too serious for laughter.

The deputy approached the cell and asked, "Y'all ready?"

Deep down, June wanted to yell, *'Hell nah, I ain't ready! I ain't even 'posed to be here wit' these niggas.'* But he remained cool and kept his mouth shut because after all, he was a soldier.

"Time to put 'cha game face on baby" Tank said while rising to his feet and flashing a smile that put Fort Knox to shame.

Once back inside the courtroom, they all took a seat next to their attorneys' and watched as the jury filed in, one by one. June was trying to read the expression on their faces, looking for any sign to indicate which way the decision had gone. He then sought the reassuring face of his mother and finally spotted her and Dee in the crowd. Since this was a high profile case being that Trey and Tank were two of Miami's heaviest hitters the courtroom was filled to capacity and there was still an entourage of people gathered outside in the hallway awaiting the verdict. While June was looking around, he spotted someone else and wondered why she'd even bothered to come. Cherone was sitting in the midst of the on-lookers with her fingers crossed. She held on to the edge of her seat anticipating the verdict.

The judge asked the jury if it had made its decision and the foreman answered, "Yes, your Honor, we have."

"Pass it to the bailiff, please" The judge instructed.

The bailiff retrieved the folded piece of paper from the foreman and handed it to the judge. The judge unfolded it and read the verdict silently to himself. After reading the paper he passed it back to the bailiff, who in turn handed it back to its original source, the jury foreman.

"Please read the verdict to the courtroom, Mr. Foreman" The judge instructed.

As the foreman stood and unfolded the paper which held the fate of my niggas, Swartz gave June a soothing pat on the back.

"We the jury find the defendant Albert 'Tank' Ross guilty of count 1 conspiracy to possess, distribute and deliver cocaine. We find the defendant Albert 'Tank' Ross also guilty of count 2, possession of a firearm by a convicted felon. We find the defendant Treyon Antonio Wells guilty of all counts, one..., two... and an additional count three which is murder in the first degree."

June was a nervous wreck and the once silent courtroom was now a haven for disrupt! The judge threatened to clear the courtroom if order wasn't restored immediately! June had just heard both Tank and Trey get convicted and had a feeling it was about to be a wrap for him also. He didn't even want to hear his verdict. Once order was restored, the foreman continued to read the verdict, "We the jury, find the defendant Jared DeMond Wilson Jr... guilty of counts 1 and 2 of said indictment"

June was visibly shaken as they were led out of the courtroom and back to the holding cell. June's mother was crying uncontrollably while Dee was trying to console her and at the same time wiping her own tears. Everyone in the courtroom was upset because of the verdict, some even cursed out the judge and members of the jury on their way out.

One person in the crowd was experiencing emotions of the exact opposite. Cherone  made her way through the throng of angry protestors, smiling from ear to ear.

*Chapter Seventeen – Da Game Ain't Da Same*
*Charlotte, N.C. 1999*

It had been three years since June's guilty verdict had been read and that also meant my daughter was having her third birthday. Kinya and I threw a party for Mikai and had invited all of our little cousins and all of the neighborhood kids.

Over the years, we'd become close friends with almost everyone on our block. I gave them the impression that I was the heir of a wealthy father who had died and left me with a hefty trust-fund. Thus explaining the reason I drove a convertible Lexus Coupe and my fiancé drove a brand new Range Rover.

I had both vehicles candy painted money green with 20" rims and TV's. We gave my mom the Acura and I kept the old reliable Honda. I also bought a minivan for family use. My old Movado watch was switched and upgraded to a platinum Presidential Rolex with an iced-out bezel and customized diamond band.

My closet that once held only the latest style of urban wear such as Karl Kani, Mecca and Phat Farm was now joined by Burberry, Armani, Gucci and Versace. My taste in shoes changed radically also. No longer was I to be seen in a club wearing only with Timberlands or Nikes. I now wore mostly big block Gators by Mauri whenever I stepped up in a club or party.

My hair had grown past my shoulders which gave me a more civilized look instead of that of a thug. My money was so long I still had small faces stashed! Nonetheless, my entire outlook on life had changed since the birth of my little Queen and not to mention what had happened to June.

Kinya was the perfect mother and girlfriend. When she had our daughter she changed totally. She became engrossed with motherhood and family life, even attended Tupperware parties. Now that shit tripped me out. Nevertheless, Kinya juggled the salon, which she renamed 'Miracles by Mikai' and home life with the greatest of ease. I adored her for her strength and constantly reminded her of how proud I was of her.

My woman didn't have to want for anything as long as I had breath in my body. Kinya stayed 'killin' 'em' in her everyday Prada, DNKY and Dolce & Gabbana along with a selection of full length Chinchillas and not to mention the Range. Kinya had become the envy of every female in Charlotte and she was basking in their jealousy.

My mother had decided that being a receptionist at a salon was not for her. She had to deal with too many different cocky attitudes all day, every day. She hinted about one day owning her own soul food restaurant so that she could do what she enjoyed which was cooking. That hint didn't fall upon deaf ears because within a year after leaving the salon I made her dream come true. She opened up a restaurant that catered to black folks which specialized in fried chicken, collard greens, rice, cornbread, black-eyed peas and oh-so-sweat lemon aide. She named the restaurant after the person who had taught her everything she knew, She named it after my grandmother who also helped with all of the cooking. *IRENE'S* was and still is unsurprisingly successful!

My brother Bernard got married to his high school sweetheart, Michelle who gave birth to my first nephew Jamelle, right after Kinya had given birth to Kai. Bernard's wedding was beautifully orchestrated. Although it had cost me an arm and a leg, the happiness everyone expressed made it all worth it. My mother's restaurant catered all the soul food you could eat, so everyone partied and got their grub on!

My mother had also catered the food for the party we were about to have. Kids were arriving in flocks with their parents in tow. I was sitting on the front porch wearing shorts with all white Air Force One's. My hair was hanging loosely around my shoulders and I was watching everyone from behind a pair of platinum rimmed Cartier sunglasses. I was directing everyone to the back yard with a point of the finger while enjoying the soothing taste of a cold Heineken. Many of the kids ran to me and gave me a hug, while others shied away and ran off to play. Every parent spoke as they passed the front porch and ventured into the back yard.

I was lost in thought, thinking about what had happened to June over the past three years. First, there was his conviction which devastated everyone, especially his poor mother. Then to top it off, they gave him thirty-six years!! He tried desperately to appeal but the judge denied it, citing that there were no legitimate grounds of error. After his direct appeal was denied, he filed a motion called 2255, seeking relief. He hadn't gotten a response from that motion at the time we were having my baby's party. Swartz apologized a million and three times for what happened to June but we all understood that it wasn't his fault. June was facing more time than any of us had imagined. Although his role in the conspiracy was considered minimal, he was enhanced for the guns that were retrieved from the room, thus resulting in him ending up with twenty years for the drugs and sixteen years for the guns. June was considered lucky, compared to Tank and Trey.

Tank received a life sentence for his role as lieutenant in the drug ring that he and Trey had organized! Trey was sentenced to triple life!! He received a life sentence for each of the two murders in Philly along with a life sentence for his role as kingpin in the conspiracy! All three had held strong and went out like soldiers in the midst of a war. Trey and Tank were shipped to Allenwood, United States Penitentiary, a maximum security federal prison which was located in Pennsylvania to start their bids.

June was shipped to Beckley, a Federal medium security prison located in West Virginia to start working on the thirty-six years he had been given. I was still keeping it real by sending him magazines, ass shots of strippers, pictures from events like the Bike Rally and Freaknik and kept at least a grand on his book at all times. Yeah, old boy's account stayed fat! I even sent a couple of chickenheads to visit him every week so they could take him the balloons full of weed I promised him.

June was living like a jailhouse John Gotti. '*Penitentiary Rich*', would be the correct term for it. My nigga had lost a lot in the past three years; his freedom, Cherone and his life savings! Soon after June was sentenced, someone kicked his mother's door in and robbed her at gunpoint. She was forced to open the safe that June had stashed at her house. Rumors had circulated that some niggas from out of town were responsible for the robbery. Another speculation was that Cherone's trifling ass had something to do with it.

I searched high and low for that bitch and still couldn't find her. It was as if she had vanished into thin air. Nobody really knew anything about her, so there wasn't a whole lot to go on. Dee had said that she had heard Meka and Cherone had been in cahoots in playing June like a violin for his ends but I dismissed that thought on the grounds that I didn't believe those two tricks were that bright. But who knew??

I sat on the front porch and listened to the music and the kids' laughter echoing from the backyard. My thoughts were interrupted by the sight of a candy-apple red Cadillac Escalade with tinted windows, sittin' on some big ass rims pulling into my driveway. When the truck parked, Dee got out of the driver's side and V opened the passenger side door and stuck one leg out.

Dee walked up to me and gave me a hug, then kissed me on the cheek. After all of that time, she was still giving me that '*look*.' Dee was still fine as hell and her ass held even more of a jiggle than it did when we had first met, which made her invitations even harder to resist. Between swigs of my beer, I asked "What V doin'? He on the phone?"

Dee looked back at V with half of his body hanging out of the truck and his leg was shaking.

"'Pone, you know exactly what that fool doin'" She replied while heading around back to the party.

I got up and walked over to the truck where my boy was at and heard him cursing. *"Gott dammit. OH, you done fucked up now. Brang yo' ass here... don't run from me mutha-fucka!"* V was engaged in a personal conflict with Jax from the video game, *'Tekken'*. He was viscously tapping the controller pad while focusing on one of the many TV screens he'd gotten installed. *"Big black ass nigga. I'ma beat yo' ass!"* V yelled.

I went around to the driver's side and got in. Once I put my beer down, I grabbed the other controller and put the game on pause.

"Nigga, you must be losin' yo' mind. Why you interrupting my game like that?" He said as he slowly turned his head away from the screen and looked at me.

V was dressed in a Versace shirt with a pair of beige colored casual shorts and a pair of beige Alligator sandals. He had let his hair grow out and was sporting a neat, mini afro. Every time he opened his mouth I was almost blinded by the baguette diamonds that flooded his platinum choppers. Everything about V boasted MONEY!! Yeah, me and my nigga were the last men standing and I must say, we were doing damn well for ourselves! V and Donyetta had opened a nightclub on the corner of The Plaza and Eastway Drive named 'Silk's.' Silk's was always packed to capacity every time the doors opened and I always got treated like a celebrity whenever I attended. The club's name was a twisted and sarcastic way to thank the nigga who had put us on, so to speak.

I turned the AC on high and told V to shut the door for a minute as I pulled out a blunt that was already rolled and put fire to it. I inhaled the smoke and choked.

"Da-a-a-mn playboy, that shit got you gaggin' like that? Lemme hit that shit" V said while reaching for the blunt I was still holding.

I gave it to him and watched him puff away. I reclined in the seat and stared at the roof of the truck, thinking about how far we had come in the last six years. I turned to my partner and asked, "How much yae you got left?"

"'Bout two and a half keys. Why?" V responded.

I was in deep thought about what I was about to say. I was tired of grinding.

"It's over for a nigga. I'm hangin' my gloves up on this shit. I swear to God, I'on wanna end up like June." I explained. " A nigga ain't wantin' for nothin', I mean *nothin'*. My baby girl need a daddy that's gonna be out here wit' her. I can't do nothin' for her or nobody else if a nigga get fucked up. Feel me? I got one brick left. I'mma front it to Quick so he can come back up. You know that lil' bid he just came home from left him jive fucked up. After that, it's a wrap."

V listened in silence while checking my face for any signs of doubt, but there wasn't any.        "Playboy, you ain't playin' either is you?" V asked.

"Nah, it's a done deal bruh" I responded with sincerity.

V was thinking about all of the money I was about to miss. We had just met a new connect from California who had more birds than KFC and Bo Jangle's put together! The yae was plentiful and to top it off V and I had gotten hip to the '*whip*' game. We were cooking up yae and stretching the quantity by mixing in baking soda and whipping it with a whisk or a fork until everything was evenly mixed. The baking soda added extra weight and the yae was still good afterwards. We would usually get anywhere from forty-six to fifty ounces off of each kilo. For every three kilos we cooked, we ended up with at least an extra kilo! Me and my nigga was *killing* niggas out there!!

"What part o' the game is that, playboy?" V asked.

He couldn't grasp the reality that I was finished slangin' bricks. "So what 'choo gonna do? Cook and wait tables in IRENE's or start permin' them nappy ass hoe's heads in *Mircales*?" He asked jokingly.

"Nigga fuck you. You know a nigga ain't carryin' it like that" I replied.

We talked a while about me retiring from the game, then the conversation turned to June.

"When the last time you heard from fat boy?" V asked.

I took a deep breath and said, "He ain't called in a couple o' days. The last time I hollered at him he sounded like the reality of all that time was finally kickin' in. I *know* that nigga sick. He want a nigga to come see him but you know I'on do penitentiaries. Damn, I be thinkin' about dude sometimes and it be fuckin' me up. V, we don' all been through a lot of shit in our lifetime and a lot of that shit we went through, *TOGETHER*! If you really think about it, on the real, us three was tighter than brothers. We don' did some shit that could've got a muh-fucka bodied if we didn't have each other's backs. June was a part of that shit wit' a nigga. I know me and dude went through some minor disputes and shit but through it all, the good times outweigh the bad times in my book. I even did some shit that you don't even know about, behind June's back…"

At this point, V's eyebrows were raised in curiosity, as I continued, "…I fucked that tramp bitch Cherone on his living room flo'. I even called and let him hear that bitch givin' a nigga brains, but he didn't know it was her. And make it so bad, I skeeted on his carpet, on purpose."

V was laughing hysterically with tears in his eyes.

"Nigga that shit ain't funny" I said, while trying to keep from laughing along with him.

"When that happen?" He asked.

I told him how it all started, beginning with the trip to Atlanta. When I had finished the story he shook his head slowly and said, "Boy you a coooold muh-fucka"

We sat in the truck long enough to finish the blunt then we joined the party in the back yard.

*********

I was on my way to see my cousin, Quick. He had told me that he was finished with the kilo I had given him and he wanted me to come get my money.

While driving, my phone rang. "Yo" I answered while turning down the radio.

"Hey Boo" Consuela's voice caressed my ear as she spoke.

"Damn stranger, I thought a nigga was gonna have to come down there and look fo' yo' ass. Where you been hidin' at?" I asked.

"I went home for a few days for a family emergency. My mother is sick."

"Oh, I'm sorry to hear that. Is she gon' be aiight?"

Consuela was silent for a minute, then responded, "I don't know yet, that's why I'm calling. I need to let you know that I might be going back home for a while"

"And how long is a *while*?" I asked, really wanting to know.

"I'm not sure. I may stay permanently" She replied.

"Daaamn shawty. You just gon' up an' blaze, huh? Well, when you leavin'? 'Cause I wanna see you before you bounce." I told her.

"Within the next few weeks. I need to take care of a few things here with my Auntie and my Uncle, then I'm leaving." She said.

I could tell that she was hurt by having to leave and I must admit I didn't want her to leave either.

Consuela and I had been in constant contact over the past three years and we saw each other on a regular basis. I had her flying to Charlotte so much that she had started accumulating frequent flyer's miles. I always rented a suite at the Downtown Marriott for her to stay when she was in town. I'd even taken a gamble and told her about Kinya and Mikai. At first she was understandably pissed, but after a week of receiving bouquet upon bouquet of red and white roses at work and a few words of persuasion she broke weak. Now, she was telling me that she was leaving and probably wasn't returning.

"You can always come over to visit me and I'm sure there will be times when I can come back to see you" Consuela encouraged.

"Aiight baby girl, all that's cool. But I'm still trying to see you before you leave. What's a good day for you to fly up?"

Well, I don't know just yet. But I'll let you know for sure soon okay? I miss you so much! I gotta go, but I'mm a call you back later" She said sadly.

"Aiight Ma, holla back."

"I love you 'Pone." Consuela said with compassion.

She had gotten into the habit of saying those three words every once in a while. I never told her I loved her back though. It just didn't seem right to fix my mouth to tell any woman that except for my girl, Kinya. So, I replied the same way I did every other time she said it, I said "Okay, baby. Get back at me."

"Bye Boo"

"Holla"

I was pulling into my Aunt Mattie's driveway as Consuela and I ended our conversation. Quick was sitting on the porch, smoking a Newport with no shirt on and watching me with chinky eyes. I got out and joined him on the porch.

"What's crackin'?" He spoke, exhaling a cloud of smoke.

"Ain't shit, a nigga just maintaining, ya know."

I noticed Quick's arms and chest had swollen up while he was bidding. I had seen him a few times since he had been out, but this was the first time he had peeled out of his shirt on me.

"Daaamn nigga, you diesel like a muh-fucka. I ain't know you was ripped like that. You gon' make a nigga start going to the gym an' shit" I said while comparing my arm to his.

"Nigga, you got a long way to go to catch these guns. This shit come from a lot o' hard ass work. You can't buy this shit. You gotta work for this here big cuz." Quick proudly said while making his chest muscles jump. I was glad my cousin was finally home. He had gotten knocked with a couple of ounces in his apartment one night while he was having one of his smoke sessions. A neighbor had complained about the noise and the weed smell to the police and they ended up searching the crib and found some yae, weed and money. Needless to say, everybody got arrested but Quick stood up and took responsibility for everything that was found. Everybody's cases got dismissed except for Quick's. He received a four year sentence and ended up doing almost three. Quick went in a boy and came out a young man. He had matured beyond belief in those three years that he was gone. I was proud of my little cousin. He had done his time and had handled it like a soldier. However, I couldn't resist reminding him of my little lectures and telling him, '*I Told You So*'. I had looked out for my lil' nigga while he was down and was still looking out for him now that he was home. I didn't live by the code of '*out of sight, out of mind*'. I took care of mine!!

Quick had told me one day in a phone conversation that he was starting to see who his real friends were. Not one of those lil' tricks he was fucking with made an attempt to visit him while he was down. And none of those little snotty-nosed ass niggas who used to sit around and smoke all of his weed attempted to send him a penny. At first, Quick was planning to get back at everybody who'd shit on him but then he came to the conclusion that it wasn't worth it. The only thing he was focused on now was trying to get some money and eat like everybody else. The street game was all about a dollar and that hustling shit ran in our genes.

My father and Quick's father were both hustlers back in the day. They ran shit! Unfortunately, they both ended up dying in the prison as a result of lengthy sentences at old ages. I was determined not to go out like that. I would rather go out in a hail of bullets than to die in prison. A hustler with a life sentence and no chance of ever seeing the streets might as well be a dead man, at least that's what people think. People are going to talk about you in the past tense and you will be forgotten. So what's the difference?

Quick and I kicked it for a while before I decided to head home. While I was driving, I was thinking about something he had said about June, *"Word on the circuit is, ole boy 'bout to sprang a leak. That time gettin' to that nigga. I won't be surprised if he break down an' put a nigga on front street. June ain't cut like you and V for real. He talk that gangsta shit, but I'on think that nigga built like that, for real my nigga. You know pressure will bust a pipe, so just imagine what it'll do to a weak ass nigga."*

I hoped Quick didn't know what he was talking about because rumors are what start wars and accusations bring about consequences and repercussions. I dialed V's number while I was waiting for a light to change.

"Yo" He answered.

"What's poppin'?" I spoke.

"On my way to the Teezy wit' this lil' breezy who off the heezy fo' sheezy, my neezy." V replied enthusiastically.

He was on his way to the Embassy Suites with a young girl who was nothing short of a dime.

"Dee gonna fuck both y'all up." I teased.

"Don't hate playboy, I'm just tryna get my man on, ya dig?"

I could definitely relate. I can't explain why us men cheat and sleep around and whatnot . I think it's due to some sort of chemical imbalance that fucks with our thinking process when it comes to trying to be faithful. Men are like dogs. We try to fuck everything that moves because it's an ego thing. And the fucked up part is that we always get caught! However, don't get it twisted because women do their thing as well, but the only difference is that they are more like cats because as soon as they finish their shit, they be sure to cover it up!

I told V that I had just picked up my last piece of change from Quick and he replied, "So, that's it, huh? You through wit this shit for good, huh? No more scrilla fo' rilla, huh?" He responded, imitating Juviniles song.

So I answered him with a line from Tela's song, *I'm so tired of ballin'.*

We both laughed at ourselves.

"Well while you enjoyin' yo' lil' retirement an' shit, I'ma be out here doin' me, an' doin' what I do, 'cause the shit I do, I do damn well, ya heard me" V claimed. "Without a doubt my nigaa. Do you an' get that cheese. But you actin' like a muh-fucka ain't gon' still be blingin' on these niggas. You got me fucked up! You know I still gotta shit on these lames out here with some big boy shit. I'm finna cop another whip too. I thought about coppin' a Bentley and dubbin' that shit out for next summer. I'll hurt 'em wit' some shit like that!! Nigga I'm sick wit' this blingin' shit. You know I do that shit real heavy like!! Niggas gon' have to step up they game to fuck wit me!! You know I'm *that* nigga! The game don' blessed us fo' sho'." I told my partner, then changed my tone, getting serious. I added "But the game don' changed, it just ain't the same no mo'. Niggas ain't got no cut cards, no morals and shit. You 'on know who to fuck wit' and who *not* to fuck wit'. Niggas in Charlotte got the game fucked up! Everybody and they mama snitching these days. If a nigga don't end up gettin' caught up on some bullshit, he gon' end up dead. Niggas disrepectin' the game on some ole sucker type shit. I'll hate to end up in the pen with a body, but that's exactly what's gonna happen if a nigga stay in the game wit' these bitch, busta-ass niggas out here. Just imagine if a nigga was to lose all the shit we don' worked so hard for. Now, that would be hustlin' backwards as a mutha-fucka! We too sharp for that shit V, straight up."

V listened silently. He understood exactly where I was coming from. I told V what Quick had said about June and asked if he had heard anything about it.

"Hell nah, that shit ain't true" V reacted adamantly.

I felt the same way he felt about the rumors. I didn't believe it, but at the same time, I didn't put nothing past nobody. I told V to hit me back once he was situated.

I pulled into the Exxon on Wilkinson Boulevard to gas up and grab a box of blunts. While I was pumping gas, my two-way went off. I checked it and saw a message, which read: *Long time no holla at, have you forgotten me? This is Felicia! I'm working at Foot Locker in Freedom Mall. Off at nine. Come by.*

*Surprise?* Hell yeah, it was a surprise. I hadn't seen Felicia in over two years. I was trying to figure out how she had gotten my two-way number. Only a select few were fortunate enough to get that number. I only gave that number to women. Only one dude had my two-way number and that was V. But V and I never communicated over the wire like that unless it was an emergency. 'Work' talk was a No-No.

Since I was on the west side, I made my way up to the mall to see Felicia. I was wondering what she looked like after such a long time. *Was she still fine? Had she blown up? Why was she working in Foot Locker? And, how did she get my damn number?* Ten minutes after leaving the Exxon, I was pulling up in the Mall's parking lot. After putting the money I had collected from Quick in the trunk, I stuffed my heat in my waistband and headed to Foot Locker.

I saw her as soon as I entered the store and boy oh boy Felicia was still fine as hell, even in her little referee uniform. She greeted me with a big hug and a wide smile. Her body was still just as soft as I remembered from that night at Red Lobster. While I was hugging her, I glanced around and checked the faces of the other customers, hoping I didn't see anyone I knew because the last thing I needed was for Kinya to hear some nonsense.

I didn't see any familiar faces, but one girl caught my eye. She was modeling a pair of Airmax in front of a mirror. The girl was short, about five-feet even with a body that was giving Felicia's a battle. She was wearing a pair of low cut jeans that revealed her white thong when she finally sat down. She saw me staring and flashed a slight smile in my direction. Just then, Felicia and I broke our embrace and stared each other up and down with inspecting eyes. I was the first to speak. "Daaamn Ma, you lookin' edible. How you doin'?"

"I'm fine, I'm fine. You still look like a million. Dag, you must've been right down the street when I hit you" Felicia said while still smiling from ear to ear.

I saw that the other girl was still looking in our direction and periodically watching the entrance, then she broke into a wide grin as if she had recognized someone. I was standing in front of Felicia and I didn't want to be rude and turn around to see who the girl was smiling at so I focused my attention on Felicia.

"Yo, how you get my number?" I was curious to know.

I noticed Felicia kept peeping over my shoulder and grinning. Just when I was about to turn around, someone placed their hand on my shoulder and said, "Daaamn playboy, you must got rocket fuel in that muh-fucka. You sho' didn't waste no time"

I turned around and saw V flashing a Platinum smile while holding his two-way, so I could see the message which he had sent me for Felicia.

I gave my partner a pound and said, "I thought you'd be knee deep by now" I was referring to what he had told me he was on his way to go do.

"I'm lockin' that shit in, feel me? Buy 'em a pair of Airmax and they'll fuck a nigga to death! No lie!" V said as he strolled off in the direction of where the girl who I was checking out was seated. He sat beside her and motioned for the salesman to come over.

So this was the young girl V was on his way to go smash. Damn, my nigga sure knew how to pick them.

"Now you know how I got in touch with you. It wasn't a problem was it?" Felicia asked with her hand on her hip.

"Nah, it ain't no problem. Girl you know I wanna hear from you whenever, wherever. So, what's been up? Where you been hidin' at?" I asked.

"Well, after we closed the store last year I went back home for a few months to re-group. Then I came back about four months ago and enrolled in Johnson C. Smith. I'm a full time student now and I work here part-time. I'm trying to venture into the sports circuit, nah-mean..." Felicia's Brooklyn accent was in full effect as she added, "I'm majoring in Sports Management, you know, dealin' with agents, managers and things like that"

"Damn, do yo' thang boo. I ain't mad at 'cha." I encouraged.

Our conversation was on a more mature level than it was the last time I had seen her. I found out that her brother Pat had opened a store in Brooklyn which was doing well and still expanding. She told me that her and the UPS dude had broken up right before she went back to New York. She was currently single, but dating occasionally. I also learned that she knew about me and Tracey. "Her girlfriend Toni told me all about it one night after her and Tracey fell out*."* Felicia explained, with emphasis on the word, 'All' which sounded more like 'oil' because of her accent.

"Oh, so Toni tried to throw salt, huh?" I asked smiling.

"No she wasn't hatin' on you. She was more or less just upset and trying to hurt Tracey…. and guess what?"

"What?" I asked, curiously.

Felicia smiled coyly "Well, she told me you asked if I was getting down like them. Did you ask that?"

I thought back to that night and remembered sitting on their sofa drinking Vodka when I asked Tracey about Felicia.

"Yeah, I did ask her that. Why?"

When I answered the question, Felicia looked at me with a strange expression on her face. I tried to read her expression which was a cross between embarrassment and confusion. I was getting extremely curious at this point, so I asked, "What's up? You aiight?"

"Yeah, yeah I'm straight, it's just I'm trying to figure out the best way to say this....Fuck it. Look, Tracey slept with you, so I slept wit' Toni, there, I said it." Felicia confessed about sleeping with another woman and it hadn't been easy.

She was now trying to read my expression, so I spoke. "Well hell, at least we got somethin' in common, we both fucked Toni" I laughed trying to add humor and also to show Felicia that her confession didn't change anything between us. If anything, I was digging her even more! I probed, "You like it?"

She grinned and replied, "It's aiight"

Her answer indicated that it was still going on and not just a onetime thing. So I joked, "Now we got two things in common, we both like pussy"

Felicia playfully punched me in the chest and said, "Boy, don't be sayin' that." She was looking around to make sure no one had heard me.

It was the truth and she knew it. Therefore, she couldn't get too mad at me for calling her out.

V approached us carrying three bags of tennis shoes with the girl tagging along like a groupie. "Yo, 'Pone I'm 'bout to dip playboy. Oh I ain't introduce y'all." He turned to the girl "Baby, this my nigga Capone and that's Felicia. Y'all this, uh, uh, this..." V had forgotten the girl's name, so he introduced her as 'Baby' because that was the only thing he could ever remember calling her. "...This Baby right here" The girl elbowed V and shot him an ice cold look. V played it off and said, "Girl I was just playin', tell'em yo' name."

The girl introduced herself as Robin and V made a mental note to remember the name. I shook my head and laughed at my partner while Felicia was looking like she wanted to say 'That's a damn shame'.

Felicia and I continued to kick it for about a half an hour after V left with the *'flavor of the day'*. I tried on a pair of Jordans and liked the way they fit so I bought two pair, a pair for me and a miniature size for Mikai. I knew Kinya would have something to say about it, but what the hell? Whenever I brought something home for Kai and the color wasn't pink, Kinya would say, *"Mike you tryin to make her be a boy."* Which was not true at all. I just think all kids, boys and girls look good in athletic gear so I also got shorts and tee shirts to match her shoes.

I handed Felicia three big faces as she rung up my purchase. She still in disbelief about me being a Daddy.

"I know that lil' girl spoiled rotten" She commented while putting my things into bags.

"Without a doubt, you know how I do" I replied proudly.

After paying for my things, Felicia walked me out into the hallway with her hands in her pockets, making her pants fit even tighter.

"So, what 'choo doin' tonight?" She asked, using the same line I had used on her over two years earlier when I'd finally decided to holler at her at U.E.

I smiled and replied, "Damn shawty, this like reverse déjà-vu an' shit, huh? You remember me askin' you that right before we went out?"

Felicia thought back and remembered the conversation that started the spark between us.

"Yeah, that is how you came off on me, ain't it?" She replied with a smile that could melt steel.

"I might fall up in V's spot for a minute"

"V's spot?" She asked out of curiosity.

"Yeah, Silk's." I answered out of surprise because she didn't know about the club.

"Silk's? I heard about that jump-off. It's off The Plaza right?"

"Yeah, right behind Bojangle's" I replied.

"Damn, I didn't know V owns that spot. I heard that shit be crazy just about every night" Felicia said.

"No question. That shit be off the meter" I boasted, not hiding the fact that I was proud of my partner for all of the things he had accomplished.

"I might come out there for a minute. I'm gonna call Toni and see if she wants to come out with me" Felicia informed.

At the mention of Toni's name, I had flashbacks of how freaky she was. Toni and Tracy left a very impressionable memory that was hard to shake. Since the threesome with them, I've had a few ménage trios but Toni and Tracey was my first and by far the most memorable.

Before we parted I gave Felicia my two-way number and she gave me her home and cell number. With promises of keeping in touch, I left and Felicia went back to her *9- to -5*.

Over the years, Felicia and I had both changed mentally. We were each more conscious of life and more mature. Although that mutual attraction was still evident, neither one of us volunteered to step out there and take the plunge. Lovers or friends, whichever way it ended up between us I wouldn't complain.

**********

As soon as I stepped through the door Mikai was all over me!

"Heeeyy, baaaby. How's Daddy's boo-boo doin'?" I said as I dropped the bags I was carrying and picked my Princess up and smothered her with kisses.

"Gooood" Mikai said in her sweet, angelic voice.

Kinya entered the living room wearing a Chanel bathrobe and matching slippers with her hair pinned up, indicating she was about to get into the tub. She walked over and kissed me on the lips and asked Kai if she was ready to take her bath. Kai squeezed my neck and pulled away from her mother as to say, *'Leave me alone, I'm with my Daddy.'*

I told Kinya, "Go 'head, she'll be in there in a minute"

Kinya playfully poked her finger in Kai's chest and said "Okay, okay, see how you do? Yo' Daddy come home and you wanna act funny. That's okay."

After teasing Kai, she asked about the bags and just like I figured, she riffed about the Jordans I had bought for Kai. We had our usual spat before she ventured off into the bathroom with Kai trailing behind her, looking like her 'mini-me'.

After putting the shoes and clothes away, I put the money I had collected from Quick in my safe and headed to the back patio. I closed the sliding glass door behind me and took a seat in my favorite lounge chair. I rummaged through the selection of CD's that were on the table beside me until I found what I was looking for. Once I found it, I waved my hand across the face of my  sound system and watched as the CD player slowly opened, waiting to be fed. I put the CD in and reclined in my chair, waiting for sounds to pour from the speakers. Within seconds the speakers came alive with *'Back in elementary-y, I thrived off misery. Left me alone, I grew up amongst a dying breed...'*. Tupac, the greatest rapper of all time was spitting some real shit in my ear. I lit up a blunt and let the sounds engulf me as I lost myself in thought. I thought about everything I had experienced over the years since I had quit school. I went from robbing and stealing to dealing and killing. What a helluva transition. I had paid my dues and went through the struggle of coming up in the projects just  like so many others. The only difference was the fact that I had gotten lucky. I was lucky enough to get the opportunity to escape the slums. But don't get it twisted, I loved the projects with all of my heart. It was crazy how niggas wondered why I didn't hang out in the same places I used to and why I didn't spend more time in the spot where I came from.

I had to laugh at this thought because niggas got so much animosity and envy in their hearts. They hate to see a nigga make it! Most of them smiled and grinned in my face but I knew without a doubt if they had the opportunity, they wouldn't have hesitated to take everything I possessed away from me. That's the very reason I had chosen to limit my associates and I kept my circle just as tight as virgin pussy. I'd learned that being with too many niggas will get you in a world of trouble. It's definitely true what they say: *"Niggas are just like flies, they stay in some shit."*

I thought about Kinya and Kai and how much I loved them both totally and unconditionally. I would have given my life for either one of them in a blink of an eye.

As I smoked and took a trip down memory lane, my cell phone rang. I flipped it open and answered. "Yo"

I heard, "This is a call from Federal prison…" I pressed '5' and waited for June to click on.

"Yo, playa" Tank spoke in a thick, southern drawl.

"What up my nigga? I thought you was June. Damn, a nigga ain't heard from you in a month of Sundays. What's poppin'?" I spoke back.

"Man, shit crazy up here right now. I know you heard 'bout Trey, huh?" Tank asked sadly.

I was trying to figure out what he was talking about because I hadn't heard anything about my man Trey. I was curious to find out so I asked, "What happened wit' him?"

Tank sighed deeply and then said "A nigga slumped him comin' outta the shower"

I was stunned by the news and I knew he was serious because Tank didn't play games like that. Tank continued "Man, that shit fucked me up! I was on the rec yard when it happened. When a nigga came to get me it was too late, they was takin' that nigga away on a stretcher. We just now gettin' off lock down for that shit. They said he got hit like twelve times wit' some shit that looked like a muh-fuckin' sword."

I was listening and wondered why somebody would want to body Trey, so I asked, "They find out who did it?"

"Yeah, they got the bitch PC'd up right now. You know what though? This shit crazy as fuck my nigga. You 'member them two bodies they charged Trey wit'? The niggas in Philly? Well, it was one of them nigga's cousin. They said the nigga been plannin' on doin' Trey ever since we got here. I guess he was layin' and waitin' to catch 'im by hisself an' slippin'"

I could hear the hurt and pain in his voice. The nigga he had done so much dirt with, done so much balling with and went to trial like a true soldier with was now gone.

"Damn my nigga, I still can't believe that nigga gone. Me an' that nigga ran Miami, you know that right?" Before I could answer, he continued, "Me an' Trey done been thru so much shit together. I'm talkin' 'bout from gettin' cake to fuckin' the same hoes. Man, me an' old boy don' went to war wit' plenty niggas, an' like a brother I could count on that nigga watchin' my back."

I was silently listening to my nigga vent and wondered where he was going with the conversation. Then he answered my unasked question. "Yo, I said that to say this. I should've been somewhere close by when that shit went down. I ain't have my dog's back! I slipped an' my nigga paid for that shit with his life!"

Tank was shook up and had no shame expressing his pain to me. When I finally spoke again I couldn't find the right words to say. "Damn dog...shit! Um, man, shit. I'on even know what to say. That's fucked up, yo!" I tried.

"June ain't tell you 'bout that?" Tank asked.

I thought about how long it'd been since I had heard from June realized it had been a minute. "Nah, I ain't heard from June lately." I responded while thumping ashes into the ashtray on the table in front of me.

Tank was silent for a moment, then said, "I wonder what ole boy goin' through. I wrote him an' told him about Trey an' he ain't even get back at me. Usually, that nigga would write me right back" As an afterthought Tank added, "You know they shot down his 2255 motion"

Tank was referring to the motion June had filed with the courts for a potential time cut due to discrepancies surrounding their case.

"Damn, that's fucked up. That nigga probably up there on that mountain stressin' an' shit" I told Tank. I leaned over and clicked the repeat button on the stereo and then I asked, "He got another shot at it, don't he?"

"Yeah, he still got a chance to file a 2241 but the remedy process is fucked up. There's so many procedures an' shit to go through that by the time you finish filin' all of 'em, a nigga would be done did his whole bid already. I'm still waitin' to hear somethin' about *my* appeal. I ain't layin' down on this shit my nigga. I'm tryin' a come to the crib, ya heard me? I ain't tryna spend the rest of my life in this bitch. I'm tryna leave here, but I ain't tryna get my freedom the way Trey got his though. Hell nah! I ain't goin' out like that, my nigga."

Tank was in his feelings and it was understandable because he had lost his road dog, his partner in crime and most importantly, his best friend. It takes a helluva friend to remain true to the game and be down with you enough to take this treacherous, crooked ass government head-on with no questions asked. The average nigga would've panicked and ended up copping a plea to avoid a life sentence. Even if it meant, becoming a rat! But Trey had held true to the code of the streets, Death Before Dishonor!

"Yo, you straight? You 'on need nuthin' do you?" I asked.

"Nah dog, I'm aiight" He replied.

I knew Tank well enough to know if he needed something, he wouldn't ask for it. He was a lot like me when it came to being prideful. We both hated to ask anybody for anything, so I said, "Be lookin' out for some mail from me tomorrow. I'ma send you somethin'"

I had to make sure my man's commissary was straight. Over the past two years, I knew Tank, Trey and June had spent a grip on lawyers, PI's and other legal shit to help fight their battle, so I tried to do all I could to keep them comfortable while they were down.

"Yo, that's good lookin' my nigga" Tank thanked me.

"Ain't shit. Just keep yo' mutha-fuckin' head up and get ready to come up outta there 'cause it ain't gon' be long. Somethin' gonna happen for a nigga! Somethin' gotta change dog. These muh-fuckas lockin' up too many niggas, too fast. Ya heard me?"

While I was talking, I heard the 'beep', which indicated that the call was about to end.

"Ay, look here, this phone 'bout to hang up" Tank informed me.

"Yeah, I know. An' nigga don't take so long to holla back"

"Aiight, my nigga. Peace."

"One love, big dog."

The phone hung up, disconnecting us.

I closed my phone and reclined in my lounge chair with a totally different mindset from which I had before the phone had rang. I started thinking about everything that was going on with me. I put my life under the microscope and examined it. I began to see everything for what it really was, instead of what I wanted it to be. I knew my life wasn't some shit out of a happily-ever-after fairytale. It was more like the diary of an old ass man. I had seen things over the years that would've driven the average nigga my age insane!

I thought about the turn of events that had taken place over the past twenty minutes. In a blink of an eye, my man Trey was gone! Just like that, he was gone. I thought about the beautiful little girl he had left behind and winced at the thought of being taken away from Kai forever. All of the money and power on earth isn't worth losing your life for.

I settled on the thought of me being out of the game and finally came to the conclusion that I had made the right decision. If for no other reason at all, I was doing it for Kai. I didn't want her to have to grow up answering the questions of, "Where is your Daddy?" With a response like, "He in jail", or "He got killed". Oh hell nah, not I! Fuck that!

I called V while I was finishing up my blunt and still bobbing my head to Tupac. V picked up and I told him everything that Tank had told me. As expected, he was at a loss for words. He couldn't believe Trey was gone and I felt his pain through his silence. I also told him what Tank had said in reference to June, but he showed little concern. Maybe I was overreacting and getting worried for nothing, but I was feeling a little uneasy about June.

V was still laid up with Robin, the girl he'd bought the shoes for and he was complaining about her pussy.

"She was a dead fuck" He shared before wanting to know about my conversation with Felicia, "You finally fuckin' that or what?"

"See, that's why yo' shit keep on goin' in circles when it comes to bitches. You too simple V. A bitch gonna always know how you comin' at her 'cause you too predictable. You don't leave nothin' to the imagination. You gotta keep a bitch intrigued and guessin' and not knowing what's coming next. The best bitch is an off balance bitch; a bitch that don't know what to expect from you. Never let her figure you out playboy. Bitches look at niggas like we are books. If they can read your ass in sixty-seconds, they don't want you. And once they read you, they put your ass on the shelf. Why read the same book twice?" I let my comments sink in before I added, "Nigga, stop being Horror and Science Fiction to them hoes and try being a Mystery sometimes. Bitches love that suspense shit."

V listened silently, then replied "Damn, why you clownin' a nigga like that?"

"I'm just speakin' my mind my nigga, 'cause it hurt like shit when I bite my tongue. Feel me?"

## Chapter Eighteen – Celebratin'

The spacious VIP section of Silk's was plushly furnished with leather sofas and love seats. Videos were playing on a sixty-one inch flat screen TV that occupied one corner of the room. Three coffee tables held opened bottles of Dom, Moet and Cristal. The VIP was situated on the upper deck of the club, surrounded by 2-way glass. It reminded me of a skybox at an arena, giving you a view of the entire club from the VIP section. You could see out but no one could see in, making it totally secluded for the exclusive. Everything was burgundy, including the carpet. The dim lights were no brighter than candles and the strobe light from the club was bouncing off of the glass deeming a funkadelic atmosphere.

One sofa was occupied by Lil' Rick and two groupies drinking Dom 'P' and passing a blunt back and forth. Lil' Rick, dressed in a Coogi sweater with a pair of Coogi jeans and brown Timberland boots kept on smiling, revealing his platinum grill while trying to impress the ladies who were with him. His earlobes held diamonds the size of the nail on a pinky finger. He sported a platinum link necklace with a charm that read DV which was encrusted in diamonds. His platinum Rolex almost had just as much ice as mine. Lil' Rick was one of the very few who could come to the club wearing jeans and boots. The dress code was strictly enforced at Silk's. There were times when I came to the spot dressed like a thug too, but on rare occasions.

The two love seats were occupied by Black, Ray-Ray and their dates who were just as fine as the two women Lil' Rick had with him. Black was dressed in a multi-colored Versace shirt with a pair of dark colored slacks and Kenneth Cole loafers. He was dripping ice from his jewels and his baldhead was shining just as much as his dark skin. His date was a red-bone with long, jet-black hair. She was dressed in Chanel with a matching handbag.

Ray-Ray was the coolest and most laid back of my three protégés. Ray-Ray was draped in an Armani shirt and slacks with a pair of Italian-made kicks and his date was wearing a Prada dress that was fit for a princess. Her skin was the color of peanut butter, which indicated she was mixed with something exotic.

Each of the four had their own individual bottles of Moet, sipping like rich white folks. Black, Ray-Ray and Rick all sported their platinum DV charms with pride. The DV stood for *'Dalton Village'*, the projects which had made them rich. I had been a big brother figure to my lil' niggas ever since I had given them that first package. They all stayed down with me and remained loyal throughout the years. I never shit on them once. I made sure everyone in my circle was eating lovely and they always respected me for that and loved me like a brother. They hated the fact that I was getting out of the game but they respected my decision. They knew they could still deal with V, so it wasn't like things would change monetary-wise.

I occupied the last sofa that sat in the back of the VIP, the one that was furthest from the door. I had chosen that seat for specific reasons. I was turning up a bottle of Cristal, taking it to the head. *You can take a nigga out of the streets, but you can't take the streets out of a nigga.* I was rocking an Armani sweater with Armani slacks and a pair of big block Gators with the matching belt. My locks were hanging loosely, draped around my shoulders and I was viewing the world through a pair of platinum Gucci frames with very lightly tinted lenses. My jewels put the entire VIP to rest. I was almost frostbitten from sporting so much ice.

On the table in front of me there were two more bottles of Cristal and two glasses with lipstick on them. I was sandwiched between two of the most beautiful women in the club. Felicia was seated to my right with her legs crossed, smiling at me. She was dressed in a Coogi dress with matching Gator boots, looking like a star. Toni was seated to my left staring at me with chinky eyes. She was wearing a pair of black, skintight Dolce and Gabbana jeans with a matching colored D&G sleeveless blouse and a pair of Prada boots. Her hair was in cornrows like Alicia Key's and her eyes were as red as the furniture. She was as high as a skyscraper!

Big Dre kept coming to check on us periodically to make sure everything was okay. Dre was a part of the security team that worked for V. A host of waitresses were in and out all night hoping we needed some service so they could receive a generous tip.

I'd seen V only once since I had been in the VIP area. He had left and said he'd be right back over an hour ago. I told the two women to excuse me for a minute as I stood up, still clutching the champagne bottle. I walked to the glass that overlooked the dance floor and searched the thick crowd for V. V was nowhere to be found, but I did spot Dee making her way through the crowd toward the stairs that led up to the VIP.

"Shit," I cursed under my breath. I didn't want Dee to see me with Felicia and Toni.

Then I saw one of the security guys stop her on the third step. They talked for a minute and then headed back down the steps in the opposite direction from where she'd come.

"Damn, that was close" I thought as I strolled back over to the sofa and plopped down between Toni and Felicia.

Toni had fired up a blunt and was in the middle of trying to give Felicia a shotgun right before I interrupted.

"Let a nigga show you how to do that" I told Toni while taking the blunt.

"Close your mouth, I want you to inhale the smoke through yo' nose" I ordered Felicia as she nodded in agreement.

I took a deep breath and placed the blunt between my lips backwards. I could feel the heat as I began to bow smoke out of the other end and into Felicia's nostrils. Halfway through, she turned her head, indicating that it was too much for her to handle. Toni tapped my shoulder and told me to give her a shotgun also. Toni sucked up every bit of the smoke like a true vet.

While I was smoking and drinking Cristal from the bottle, the door opened. I was hesitant about looking up because I thought it was Dee.

"'Pone, my mutha-fuckin' nigga. What's the deal baby." V screamed from the door.

I raised my bottle at him and kept on smoking.

He was still standing at the door with the door ajar when he said "Yo, somebody wanna holla at you"

I was trying to figure out who it could be and before I could ask, V stepped aside and my little cousin Quick entered the VIP dressed like a Don. Quick was dressed in a silk Gucci outfit. His hair was twisted in tiny, neat knots, beginner's dreadlocks.

I stood up and greeted my little cousin with a hug and a pound.

"I been down there straightnin' them niggas at the door. They ain't know who Quick was so I had to get out there and handle that. Quick was 'bout to flip on them niggas too. Yeah you was nigga," V said to Quick because Quick was shaking his head 'no.'

I looked around and felt a sense of power and invincibility. There I was, surrounded by the niggas I cared about like brothers! All in the same room at the same time, shining like celebrities!

The hood had definitely been lovely and had blessed a nigga beyond belief. We'd all put in work and had paid our dues and now we were reaping the benefits of our labor. The world was at our fingertips and nothing seemed unobtainable. V grabbed a bottle of Dom off Black's table and tapped on it with a key.

"Yo, yo, y'all listen up. I wanna make a toast to my nigga 'Pone. Niggas, *y'all* all know why! And to y'all females, if y'all don't know why then it ain't ya' damn biness" V toasted to my retirement.

All of us laughed and raised whatever we were drinking sky high.

"This to you, my nigga. Enjoy that shit!" V yelled as everybody drank up.

Without a doubt, I felt like I was on top of the world at the moment! My entire street family was in attendance and showing much love. As I looked around the room I suddenly felt a small sense of guilt because someone was missing.

I yelled "Yo! Ay y'all listen up! Let's make one mo' toast for my niggas who ain't here. This right here for Big Trey, rest in peace my nigga! For Tank and for my nigga June. Y'all know he should've been here wit' us"
We all drank up again to my toast.

The remainder of the night consisted of everybody getting drunk and high as me as my niggas reminisced about all of the shit we had been through over the years. While we talked about past experiences and long forgotten stick-ups, the women listened in astonishment occasionally giving an "Oooh" or "Aaah" when they heard graphic details.

Rick was saying, "On everything I love, I ain't think that nigga was gonna try a muh-fucka like that" He was telling the story about when he had gotten wet up by that bitch-ass-nigga, Na-Na.

Quick brought up the caper that had put us on the map. "Old boy looked like he was gone piss on hisself when 'Pone smacked him wit' that pistol" Quick said imitating the look Silk had on his face and everybody laughed.

Quick continued, "When 'Pone and V left wit' the nigga, me and June stayed at the crib wit' his partna and two bitches. Y'all should've seen how scared they was, but the nigga was mo' scared than the two broads was. He kept sayin', 'Please don't kill me, son. Please don't kill me.' He went out like a cold-bitch in front of them hoes. And to top it all off, that greedy ass nigga June had the nerve to go in the bitch fridge an' make a sandwich"

The whole VIP erupted in laughter, even the women found it funny.

I was buzzing from the champagne and the weed and my hormones were jumping like crazy. Once the VIP had calmed back down I resumed my position between Felicia and Toni on the sofa and began to put my bid in.

"So what's the deal, ma? Y'all gonna put a nigga on or what?"    I was talking to both of them at once and they both knew what I was getting at. Toni and Felicia looked at each other with knowing eyes. I already knew Toni was down, but Felicia looked as if she was a little uncomfortable.

"Aw shit, girl I know you ain't doin' it like that?" I asked after peeping Felicia's demeanor.

"Doin' it like what?" Felicia said.

"Lemme find out you tryna hog the pussy" I laughed.

Felicia and Toni both laughed along with me. As the conversation continued, I learned that Felicia had never participated in a threesome before. However, I was a firm believer in the old saying 'There's a first time for everything.' Toni was trying to encourage Felicia to throw caution to the wind and let her hair down for once. I saw that Felicia was giving it serious consideration but she didn't give a sure answer, so I began to get restless. I felt like Felicia was trying to get a nigga to beg for the pussy but little did she know, I wasn't pressed for the ass. I could've had any broad in the entire club, including all of the gold diggers in the VIP.

After a few long minutes, Felicia was still undecided so decided to let my nuts hang and mingle with the other chicks for a while. I got up from the sofa and glided over to where Rick was seated with two model chicks. He and Quick had paired off with the two women and were all over them. I still flirted with both of them and they flirted back just like all of the other girls in the room. Felicia and Toni saw me flirting and played it off like it wasn't bothering them so I stood across the room and raised my bottle of Cristal to them in a 'What's up' fashion. They both raised their glasses in return.

Just then, my two-way went off and I checked the message that was displayed. The message read:

*Hey Boo.*

*Missing you like crazy. Let's set up a date. Call me soon. I love you,*

*Consuela.*

So, Consuela had made up her mind and was ready to come visit for the last time. I was more than ready to see her and I loved spending time with her whenever I could get away. I put my two-way back on my hip and strolled back to the sofa where Toni and Felicia were still seated. Instead of taking a seat between the two of them like I had been doing all night, I sat on the arm of the leather sofa closest to Felicia. Without a word, I began to make a soft, feathery trail down the back of Felicia's neck with my fingers. Felicia looked at me with glassy eyes and leaned her head back, enjoying my touch. Without warning, I moved from her neck to the side of her face, then to her lips, testing here. Toni was silently watching me with a slight smirk as if she knew what I was doing. While tracing Felicia's lips with the tip of my finger, I watched as they slowly parted, inviting it inside. I stuck my finger in her mouth and felt her lips close around it as she began to suck, simulating oral sex. My dick started rising in my Armani slacks. She took my finger out of her mouth and started licking it up and down as if she were licking a lollipop. She definitely had natural talent! I looked around the dimly lit room to see if anyone was paying use any attention and noticed everybody else was in their own little worlds. Quick and Rick had the two ladies on the other sofa macked out, while Black and Ray-Ray were doing everything but fucking their dates on the two love seats.

Just as I was about to take a seat between Toni and Felicia, Dre opened the door and called my name. The music from downstairs was pouring into the room and his voice was almost drowned out by the noise so instead of using words, he signaled for me to come to the door. I was almost upset because he had interrupted me just when I was about to erase any doubt Felicia had about our threesome. While walking toward the door I was mouthing the words, "This betta be important."

Dre read my lips and pulled me out of the VIP.

"Oh believe me, it's important. Guess who in the house?"

I wasn't in the mood for guessing games and my face must've shown in because Dre answered his own question without waiting for me to respond.

"Yo' girl downstairs talking to Dee and V"

I thought I had heard him wrong and I was hoping I had misunderstood him so I said, "My *what*?"

"Kinya, nigga that's what" Dre replied.

"Kiss-my-as," I said to myself, then asked, "Where they at?"

"They was walkin' toward the office so I guess that's where they at. V sent me to get you.I guess he took her in there so she wouldn't see you comin' from up here"

That was good looking out on V's part. Dre walked in front of me as we went down the stairs.

When we almost reached the bottom, Dre advanced and told me to hold up. He was making sure the coast was clear for me. When he was sure everything was straight, he motioned for me to come on down. As soon as I reached the bottom step, I felt as if all eyes were on me. It seemed like the entire club had stopped what they were doing and was checking me out. Me being the stunner that I am, I pushed the sleeves of my shirt up a little, just enough to let the Rollie and the bracelet blind mutha-fuckas. I was still clutching my almost empty bottle of Cristal, so I turned it up and drained the bottle. I stopped Reesy, one of the waitresses and told her to bring me another bottle of Cris and to send one to the VIP with two roses.

"Who am I 'sposed to give it to?" she asked.

"Ain't but two girls up there who been drinking Cris all night, so it shouldn't be hard to figure it out. Just look fo' the bottles on the table" I told her while handing her a fifty-dollar tip. Reesy smiled and thanked me for the generous tip before heading back to the bar to fill my request. While waiting for Reesy to return, at least twenty people stopped by where I was standing and spoke as if we were old friends. Some of them I had never seen a day in my life and others I may have only seen in passing but I didn't know any of them personally.

When Reesy finally returned, she was carrying a tray with the two bottles of champagne along with the two roses. I took one of the bottles from the tray and thanked her before going to holler at my woman. I walked to V's office and noticed that the door was closed. I stood in front of the door and took a deep breath before entering. Instead of knocking, I walked right in and noticed the relief that was more than visible on V's face when he saw me.

V was seated behind his cherry wood desk smoking a Black & Mild while Kinya and Dee were standing on the opposite side of the desk with their arms folded. V's office reminded me of Swartz's because that's where V had gotten the idea to hook his up. Instead of plaques and certificates hanging from the walls, he had paintings of all the blacks that had made history. He had everyone from Harriet Tubman to Tupac and Biggie posted up. Just like the VIP, everything was burgundy which was V's favorite color.

Dee was standing next to Kinya in a form fitting spaghetti strap, cream colored dress with matching colored open toe pumps that had strings which wrapped around her leg up to her calves. Kinya was wearing an all black Prada pantsuit with matching Prada shoes and a pair of Chanel glasses. Both girls had their hair done up to perfection and they both were sporting much jewelry!

"What up y'all. Hey baby, how long you been here?" I asked.

Kinya was looking at me like she was trying to see if I had been fucking up but I played it cool and stood there like an innocent man, swigging Champagne from the bottle.

"I just got here, where you been all night?" Kinya replied.

I looked at my partner and saw him wink his right eye, letting me know which excuse to use.

"Gamblin'," I said with a straight face.

If V had winked his left eye, my excuse would've been the VIP.

"I been back there getting my wig split in the dice game. Why?"

I knew that's what V had told them and I knew Dee didn't know if I was lying or not because she never ever when to the back room where the gambling took place.

"Oh, I was just askin'," Kinya replied while coming to give me a hug and a kiss.

Damn, it was hard being a playa!!!

Kinya and I left V's office hand in hand, looking like a ghetto Donald and Irvana Trump. Since I was halfway drunk, Kinya tried to persuade me to get on the dance floor with her. She knew I would get out there and act a fool if I was totally fucked up, but I wasn't at that point yet so I steered her toward an empty table. We sat down and enjoyed the music that was blaring from the speakers and invading our souls. My man from Power 98, DJ Storm, was putting his thing down on the ones and twos. He was mixing old school with new school and he had the crowd hyped up beyond belief. When he broke it down and played Jaheim's *"Just in Case,"* the ladies lost their minds. The theme of the song was hitting home for almost everyone in the club because the majority of the crowd were hustlers and their women.

I was sitting back swigging out of the bottle I was still clutching while Kinya was in her chair singing along with the record and getting her grove on. I stopped Debbie, an overweight waitress who I knew had a secret crush on me and told her to bring Kinya a Hennessey and Coke on ice. Debbie discreetly rolled her eyes at Kinya out of jealousy, not thinking anybody had seen her, but I did and it make me laugh.

"What 'choo laughin' at? I know you ain't clownin' my singin'," Kinya asked.

I told her I was just thinking about something someone had said earlier at the dice game, just to dead the issue. She brushed it off and continued to groove to the music.

Halfway through the song, Kinya stopped grooving abruptly and looked over my shoulder with a familiar scowl. Just as I turned to see what had caught her attention, I heard a familiar voice.

"Hey Kinya, girl how you doin'? Congratulations, I heard about the baby" Felicia spoke with Toni at her side.

Both girls were visibly twisted and I prayed that wouldn't put a nigga on front street. I looked at Kinya and saw that all-too-familiar fake-ass smile as she spoke back.

"Thank you. Girl where you been hidin' at? I ain't seen you in a while" she responded.

"I went back up top for a while, you know, just layin' low" Felicia replied and then she introduced Toni.

"Y'all, this my girl Toni, Toni that's Kinya and her man Capone"

I was smiling inside at how cool they were acting and that's the very reason why I don't trust chicks to this day. They can fuck up, then turn around and act as if nothing ever happened! They are too smooth!!

Felicia looked at me with red, chinky eyes and said "Tell yo' friend who sent the champagne and roses we said thanks and we understand"

She was secretly thanking me without arousing Kinya's suspicion.

"I'm sho' it wasn't no problem, but I'll be sure to tell him" I replied between swigs of the Cristal.

Toni and Felicia were ready to leave and I wanted to leave them, but I didn't want to start World War III so I stayed grounded while the two girls said their goodbyes.

"Well, it was nice seeing y'all again. We 'bout to get outta here" Felicia said while eyeing me.

I was trying to avoid her sensuous stare, but she had me trapped.

"It was nice to meet you. Enjoy the rest of your night" Toni added.

They both turned to leave and I must say, I sure hated to see them leave but I was loving watching them walk away.

MMPH-MMPH-MMPH, I thought to myself as I watched two of the finest women in the club disappear in the crowd. Well, there goes my ménage a trois!

Shortly after Toni and Felice left, Dee and V joined us at the table and we kicked it like old times. Kinya and Dee were sipping Hennessey and Coke while secretly clowning most of the other women in the club about their hair or their clothes.

"Giiirl no-she-ain't got the nerve to have on white boots," Kinya said to Dee about a girl who was on the dance floor dropping it like it was hot.

"Oooh, look at Miss Thang wit' the bad ass weave tryna' Harlem Shake. She betta chill, fo' that shit fall out" Dee said to Kinya, then added, "Chile, you need to slang one of yo' biness cards at that heffa"

Kinya laughed at her comment. V and I was sitting there, doing what we do best. We were 'Hoe-Hunting!' While Kinya and Dee were clowning the girls, V and I were watching those same girls' asses and titties bounce and sway to the rhythm of the beat.

When the girl with the white boots on squatted in our direction, her skirt rose up and gave us a panty shot.

"That's a triflin' ass bitch," Kinya commented.

Dee didn't see it, but V and I damn sure saw it. I looked at V and he looked back at me, but no words were spoken. Me and my road dog knew each other well enough to know what the other was thinking. We both would have smashed that under different circumstances! What can I say? Niggas ain't shit!

**\*\*\*\*\*\*\*\*\*\***

Meanwhile, June was laying in his bunk staring up at the ceiling while his cellmate was rummaging around in one of the wall lockers.

"Damn, I can't find my batteries. Cellie, let me get two batteries until I go to the sto' Wednesday," Donnell said to June.

June was used to his cellie Donnell borrowing things from him. He had been doing so for the past two years that they had been cellmates.

Sometimes Donnell returned the items, sometimes he didn't. It didn't matter to June because he and Donnell had become as tight as brothers over the years. Living with someone in a confined area every day for a long period of time had caused a bond to form between the two. They became accustomed to each other's ways and habits and automatically adjusted to each other's personalities. Donnell, like June, was also from the Queen City so they could relate. They had both once balled out of control and had achieved admirable status in the dope game and both young men's names had been ringing bells in prison even before they'd arrived. Donnell had been transferred to West Virginia from the maximum security prison in Terrehaute Indiana due to a change in the point security system. He had stayed out of trouble in the maximum security prison which enabled him to be allowed to be moved from to a medium security facility. Donnell and June had met on the prison bus as they left Atlanta's holdover facility heading to the airport to be flown to Oklahoma and then to their destination, West Virginia.

They sat together on the bus and kicked it during the uncomfortable trip. They discovered that they knew a lot of the same people. They were also placed next to each other on the plane going to Oklahoma. The two men clicked instantly and had been best friends ever since. Donnell and June also had in common the fact that they were two of the very few that were *true soldiers* in West Virginia. They had taken their chances and fought the government head-on while many of the other inmates at the prison were rats. (Hot niggas, snitches, stool pigeons, or whichever word you prefer.) The only difference was the fact that June only had 36 years and Donnell had *life*.

"Oh yeah, Trick say he tryna get a cap" Donnell added. He was referring to one of the Chap Stick caps full of weed that June sold for twenty dollars each.

June finally broke his trance and looked at his cellie. "You know I'on fuck wit' dat hot ass nigga. I'on know *why* he keep sendin' muh-fuckas up here"

June had become the number one weed man on the compound, keeping a steady supply of head bangin' kush. He had graduated from swallowing balloons in the visitation room to paying an officer to bring it in for him. Everyone suspected June had a contact on the inside but no one actually knew if it was true. June had kept his mouth shut about the crooked officer and the officer respected him for that, thus keeping him abundantly supplied.

Donnell watched June as he continued to stare at the ceiling as if he were in the twilight zone. He had noticed June's indifferent attitude for the past couple of months and tried to get him to talk about whatever it was that was bothering him. When June refused to discuss his problem, Donnell respected it because many nights he had also gone through stress syndromes. With a life sentence, who wouldn't?

After Donnell left the room, June lay there in silence thinking about what had been eating away at him for the past few months. After he was sentenced he was more than certain that his appeal would be granted but to his dismay, he got denied. Soon afterwards, the courts also denied his 2255 motion which left him feeling almost hopeless.

Still staring into space, June thought, *shit, I don't want to be in this shit until I'm damn near sixty, I don't even have kids yet.* He reached under his mattress and got the letter in which Tank had written him telling him about Trey. June had reread that letter more than ten times and he still couldn't believe Trey was dead! June hadn't responded to that letter or any other letter he had received over the past month or so because he was too caught up with a personal battle he was fighting within himself. It all boiled down to the fact that June was becoming restless and plain and simple….. He wanted to go HOME!!

*********

I began to spend more time at home with Kinya and our daughter and less time in the streets. A man's home is supposed to be his castle, I thought as I sat on our king-sized bed and stared around our spacious room. Kinya had decorated our entire house alone and our bedroom was by far the most elegant room in the house. Above the bed was a life size portrait of our little family, which was painting by some expensive ass artist. All of our furniture was made from cherry wood, including our bed frame and head board. At the foot of the bed sat a large cherry wood chest that doubled as storage for the television. With the click of a button on the universal remote, a fifty inch flat screen arose from the chest, which also contained a DVD player. Each of the large windows in the room was covered by Venetian blinds, which were partly open allowing the moonlight to shine through.

I walked over and opened the door that allowed access to our large walk in closet and inspected myself in the full-length mirror that was attached to the door. I saw a stranger staring back at me, someone whom looked every bit of thirty years old. I saw myself aging right before my eyes. Living the fast life and constantly chasing street dreams will add unwanted years to any person's life. I rubbed underneath my eyes where there was slight puffiness from lack on rest.

Just then, Kai came running into the room and ended up tripping over her own feet, sending herself sprawling to the floor. Her little accident startled me, causing me to rush to her aid. I picked her up and made sure she wasn't injured.

"Dag girl, you aiight?" I asked her while holding her in my arms.

"Yeees" she answered while holding her knee.

"What I tell you 'bout runnin' like that. You gonna mess around and get hurt one day" I said while rubbing her tiny knew where she had slightly bumped it when she'd hit the carpet.

I kissed her knee and told her to be careful next time. I played with my daughter for the remainder of the night and enjoyed the feeling of contentment which she brought into my life.

### *Chapter Nineteen – From Sugar to Shit*

On a Friday afternoon, Swartz had paged me and told me he needed to see me. V and I arrived at his office late that evening just before the building closed for the weekend. We had no idea what to expect on this visit. I was thinking that maybe Swartz had found a loophole in my man's case and was about to bring him back to court. V was thinking more along the lines of it being a money issue. We made a bet to see which one of us had guess right, but neither one of use was prepared for what we had heard that day!

When we entered his lobby, the secretary wasn't there so we walked straight into his office without being invited. He was seated behind his large desk dressed like a mobster. As usual, he was on the telephone obviously engaged in a deep conversation. Swartz acknowledged me and V with a nod of his head and hand gestured that we take a seat. We sat silently and patiently, awaiting him to end the conversation that had him totally and undeniably engrossed.

Once he hung up the phone he greeted us and shook both of our hands very business-like which was unusual for him. After the formal hello, Swartz paced the floor while beating around the bush without getting straight to the point. After about five minutes of small talk he dropped the bomb on us!

"Listen fellas, I don't know how to say this… Well, I guess the best thing to do is to come right out with it."

Swartz was acting very nervous and I knew something was definitely wrong. He took a deep breath before continuing. "Your names were implemented in a Federal investigation AGAIN. This time, the investigation has already begun because of the extent of the information that was given and the source in which it's coming from"

V and I couldn't believe our ears! We were sitting there dumbfounded and bewildered with no clue as to where all of this shit was coming from. Mentally, I'd started trying to narrow down the possibilities of who could've been the traitor. One thing for sure was the fact that whoever it was had evidently given up some credible information because Swartz had said the investigation had already begun.

My circle was very limited and I always kept it airtight, at least *I* thought so. *If the feds were investigating, then what exactly did that mean? Were we about to get indicted? How much time would we have before it all took place?* My mind reeled with a trillion questions and I knew my partner V was fucked up by the sudden news also. V was just sitting there silently and trying to make some sense out of what Swartz was saying. *How could this be?*

Swartz took a seat behind the desk, pulled out a file from one of his drawers and handed it to V. The file was in a large manila envelope two inches thick with no label on it. V opened the file and the title page read: *WEST BOULEVARD HUSTLERS*

"Who the hell is the West Boulevard Hustlas?" I asked Swartz.

"Keep reading" Swartz responded.

V and I read the next page and V almost dropped the file! There were names mentioned that only a select few people knew we were connected to in any way. The names ranged from me and V, all the way down to Scrappy, Candy Man and the cats in VA, Bo-Bo and T-Dog. I read about the robberies and transactions which had taken place in the past along with places and dates. We also read about the home invasion, kidnap and robbery of Silk and his people! I even read about murders in which we were responsible for including Tammy, her parents, Yellow Boy, Sharon, and Curt and Na-Na! To add fuel to the fire, I read about Reco's murder. When I saw that statement, I knew without a shadow of a doubt who the snitch was. I told V to turn to the last page so I could confirm my suspicion and there it was at the bottom of the page! Signed next to US Attorney, Gracie Shehard's name was none other than Jared Wilson, Jr!! My man June had gone sour and switched teams on us! V and I were speechless and Swartz knew that we were both highly upset and shocked by the news. I was feeling hurt *and* betrayed beyond description. However, my hurt outweighed my anger by unmeasured amounts!

As we sat there totally spellbound and in silence, we all had tons of unasked questions.

Swartz was the first to speak. "Guys…what in the hell happened between you all for him to just up and flip like this?"

I looked at V and he had tears in his eyes. He wanted to cry because he never saw it coming. Not in a billion years did he think June would bow down and let the adversary rape him of his dignity, but boy was he wrong!

We asked Swartz every question we could think of concerning the unnerving turn of events which had just taken place. The most important question of all was asked by V. "What can we expect?"

Swartz had a look of disparity on his face when he answered.

"Nine times outta ten with information such as this and looking at the fact that the source was directly involved in much of the activity mentioned, coupled with the fact that your names were already mentioned previously in a preceding case, I can say with certainty that you *will* be indicted.

So, according to Swartz, many of the people who June had named were *possibly* going to be indicted. Nonetheless, V, Wanda and I were *undoubtedly* at the top of the list! Swartz had also mention the fact that V and I were facing a mandatory life sentence and whichever one of us was said to be the Organizer-Kingpin could be facing the death penalty! Out of all probability, Swartz said he was sure that the title of kingpin would be pegged to me! Because of the fact that out of the three of us that were destined to be indicted, I was the only one that had actually committed a murder! I didn't stand a chance from the statements alone!

Swartz said he could predict at least a ten-count federal indictment with charges ranging from racketeering and murder, to murder-for-hire. Swartz also informed us that he had no idea that June had flipped until he had received the statements from the prosecutor's office. He advised me and V to hire an attorney because according to him, we were definitely going to need some sort of representation. His representing us would have been a conflict of interested with June's case so we couldn't hire him.

After discussing the extent of our sure fate, V and I were ready to leave.

"Look, I don't know what to say…I just want you two to know that I had no influence whatsoever in Jared's decision to become an informant"

We listened and assured him that we understood whose fault it was for us being in the predicament we were in. We left Swartz's office knowing that we were about to be indicted because of a weak ass link in our chain that had popped under pressure. We knew at that moment that our time as free men was limited!!!

**********

It was time for me to get all of my affairs in order just in case I was caught off guard by the government's watchdogs. I double-checked to make sure that *Miracle's* and *Irene's* wouldn't be touched if I was caught. I deposited loot into Kinya's account every week so that she and Kai wouldn't want for anything. I also stashed money in a duplex that I had my Uncle rent for me. I sold all of my jewelry and the Lexus along with the Honda and kept only the van and the Range Rover. Kinya and I had a very long talk about my situation and she cried for weeks. I laced her with the game and made sure she understood how much I loved her and my daughter and no matter what happened to me or where I ended up, I would still be there with them in spirit and also in their hearts.

As much time as possible was spent with my family. Even Bernard and I had become like real brothers instead of strangers. I started back copping bricks from my man in Cali and was grinding hard because if I was going out, I was going out a very rich nigga!! I'd only seen V when it was time to re-up because he was on the grind also. It had been three months since Swartz had given us the heads up on the upcoming indictment, so we had gotten a pretty good head start on things.

Wanda had disappeared shortly after I broke the news to her and it was like she had vanished into thin air. NOBODY knew her whereabouts!

I had gotten two brand new identification cards with my picture and different names, different addresses and birth dates just in case. Swartz had told us that we probably had at least six months before any arrest warrants were issued, so me and V took advantage of it and got paid!!

**********

"Yes maam, but what's taking so long?" June asked timidly.

He was on the phone with the US Attorney, inquiring about the indictment in which she had promised him was coming. June had gone before the Grand Jury and testified on *everybody* he knew and was awaiting indictments to be issued for our arrests. Once all of us were arrested, he would then have to wait for us to be convicted before he would be eligible for a Rule-35, also known as a time cut.

After the prosecutor listened to June's pathetic pleading, she answered him. "Mr. Wilson, these things take time but I assure you after all of this is over you will not be disappointed. I know you want to go home and I'm doing all I can to get you there but you must be patient. I really appreciate your help. You did a tremendous job"

The US Attorney had flown to West Virginia to see June six months prior to this conversation and asked for his help with any information he had about our clique. June had refused to talk to her that day  but after stressing out severely, he bowed down and called her a month later and set up a date in which she could come back to see him. Since the visit to the Grand Jury, June had stayed in constant contact with Ms. Shehard. Now the only thing June could do was wait.

### *Chapter Twenty – Game Over*

The Adam's Mark Hotel in downtown Charlotte was packed with partygoers on this Sunday night. Club CJ's was off the chain and in full swing. Everybody was dressed to impress and had their whips shining like glass. I stood on the balcony of the suite I was in and looked out over the crowded parking lot at all of the stress-free, happy-go-lucky patrons exiting their cars and heading for the club. My mind was on the fucked-up predicament I had gotten myself into. The situation was so fucked-up that I couldn't even stay focused. I leaned over the balcony rail and sulked in silence. I was still in denial about being under investigation, but I knew it was true because Candy Man had told me that some agents had pulled him over one day and questioned him about me. They'd said he was speeding, but actually that was only a smoke screen so they could question him. He said they had asked him about our association but Candy Man had denied knowing me, at least that's what he told me.

V had also experienced a similar situation. One night when he was at Silk's, two agents one white and one black, cornered him near the bar and toyed with his intelligence. They spoke very frankly about his illegal activities and his association with me and many others. Obviously, V was very shaken up because he had called me on the cell phone that only he and Kinya had the number to as soon as they left. He was so spooked that he'd spooked me too.

As I stared out at the cars entering and exiting the parking lot, a lone tear fell from my right eye. I was thinking about Mikai and how much I was going to miss my princess. I never would have imagined I would be forced to leave my baby girl FOREVER. My heart burned with pain and my soul felt as if it were drowning in tears of despair at that thought. Mikai was the center of my existence and the only reason I had been able to maintain my sanity. Because of her I had quit doing the only think I knew how to do which was *hustling*. So here I was about to leave behind the only person in the world that could make me melt with a simple smile.

I knew Kinya would be straight and wouldn't have to want for anything as long as she took my advice and spent the quarter-mill I had given her with caution. Mikai would be well taken care of for a while and they would live comfortably as long as Kinya was responsible and kept Miracle's fully operational.

My mother had no idea why I had dropped off a briefcase full of money at Irene's one busy evening. I didn't answer her questions, I just gave her and my grandmother a kiss and a big hug and made sure they knew how much I loved them and left. That was the last time I'd see them. All of the money I had stashed in my duplex was now with me in the closet of the suite I was in along with a pair of clippers and an Armani suit with a pair of Prada loafers.

I continued to stare at the vehicles that continued to crowd the parking lot and my eyes widened when I saw my old Lexus enter! It still had the same rims but someone had gotten it painted.

"That nigga ain't got a clue" I said to myself while thinking about how the driver would more than likely end up if he was a hustler. I silently hoped he wouldn't end up like me with a federal indictment on the horizon and facing the electric chair.

Glancing at my watch, I noticed how time was zooming by. I had less than two hours before I would leave the Queen City forever! After stepping back inside the spacious suite, I sat on the edge of the large bed and let out a deep sigh.

"Yo, it's about that time shawty. You wanna cut this shit for me or you want me to do it" I said while pulling on my dreads.

"Baby I know how hard this is for you. I wish we could turn back the hands of time and get you out of this mess. I am so sorry" Consuela said while looking up at me with sympathetic eyes. She sat up on the bed and kissed me deeply. I broke the embrace, got up from the bed and headed for the closet.

"Yo, don't even trip like that Boo. I knew what time it was when I got into this shit. This ain't nothin' but another part o' the game Ma. I'm a real nigga and I'ma do what real niggas do, ya heard me?"

I took the two suitcases out of the closet and sat them on the bed. I opened the one that contained my clothes and the clippers. I walked over to the mirror on the wall and plugged in the clippers, getting ready to chop off my long locks which had taken years to grow. Consuela was still sitting on the bed.

"What's in this other suitcase?" she asked in her thick Spanish accent.

"Open it and see" I replied while grabbing a handful of my hair and trimming the first set of dreads, watching them fall to the floor.

I hated cutting my hair but I had to do what I had to do, so I continued to chop it off.

I heard Consuela gasp and say, "OH-MY-GOD!" I turned to see her staring wide-eyed and open-mouthed at the big faces that filled the capacity of the suitcase that she had opened. I smiled at her surprise and turned back to the mirror to complete the task at hand.

"Is this all yours?" she asked curiously.

"Nah, it ain't all mine. It's *ours*"

Consuela couldn't believe her eyes *or* her ears. She had never seen so much money in her life.

After letting Consuela cut off the remainder of the dreads on the back of my head, we got into the shower and had wild sex. Consuela was a wild bitch when it came to sex. It was as if she couldn't get enough. It was like a thirst to her that couldn't be quenched. The girl was insatiable!
We got dressed and sat on the large bed waiting for the front desk to ring the room to let us know that our taxi had arrived. I was wearing the suit that I had brought with me and I also wore a pair of platinum frame specs that gave me a more sophisticated look. I was listening to Consuela tell me about Puerto Rico and her family. I was taking it all in for obvious reasons.

"My brother Paco is darker than you are and his nickname is 'Sunburnt'" Consuela said with a giggle. She told me all about Paco and her parents.

Her brother sounded as if he might be the coolest of her family members and I wanted to meet him. We had one-way tickets to Puerto Rico and we would be flying under assumed names. We both had fake ID's. I had told Consuela to acquire a false driver's license a week earlier and to fly to Charlotte one Friday. We had been in the hotel since Friday night and now we were about to leave for good.

During the drive to the airport, I watched the passing landscape and realized that I was already home sick. I told the driver to take the long way and made him drive all the way down West Boulevard from the intersection of South Tryon and where Bojangles was located, to the top of Jackson Park, just beyond the Billy Graham Parkway. I looked at the Wilmore neighborhood and remembered when June, V and I had run up in a few houses there and laid niggas down. When we passed Dalton Village, I thought about my little niggas Rick, Black and Ray-Ray and hoped they wouldn't get caught up in this shit that June had started. As we passed Little Rock, I had a million memories flood my mind. I thought back to the times when June, V and I would play Hide-and-Go-Get-It with the neighborhood girls and wondered why ALL of the ugly girls would hide in the obvious places so they could easily be found. I thought about when June and V used to meet me at my house every evening after school and plot on what devilment we were going to do once we got older. We used to pretend to all be cousins and everybody believed it because we were so tight. No one started trouble with us because they knew if they fought one, they would have to fight all three. We had grown up in the slums and had made it out on a wing and a prayer. I trusted June and V with my life and would do anything for my boys. I truly loved them like they were my brothers.

"Baby, is that your old neighborhood you talked about so much?" Consuela asked while rubbing my head lightly.

Her hand felt funny on my nearly baldhead, but I enjoyed the new sensation.

"How'd you know?"

"I read the sign and besides I saw the way your eyes twinkled when we passed it"

I told her that I was just reminiscing about the way things used to be before we got trapped in the game.

The rest of the ride was silent and I was thinking about how addictive the dope game was. It was just like being on crack. Many think that once they get into the game they can just stop whenever they get ready, but that is far from reality. I thought I could stop after my first hundred thousand, but then I wanted two, then three. I was trapped! At that instant I realized not only was in the game but the game was also in *me* and it controlled my life undeniably.

Our flight was due for departure at 1:45 am. We arrived at Douglas International a little past 12:30 with over an hour to spare. I was a little apprehensive at the counter where our bags were checked because the personnel lady looked like an asshole and I just knew she was going to fuck with our bags. She lifted the two suitcases full of clothes off the counter first and then she tried to lift the bag which contained the money. She tried to snatch it off the counter like she had done the others, but it was too heavy and wouldn't budge.

"My God, what's in here, a body?" she tried to joke.

I was thinking, *damn, this bitch is gonna open this shit.* My entire life savings was inside that bag! If something was to happen to it I would be right back at square one. My palms started sweating and my temples throbbed uncontrollably when she called for help! "Harold come out here for a minute, will ya?" she said to one of her co-workers.

I saw a middle aged white man come from the back office and approached the counter where we stood.

"Can you take this suitcase down for me? It's awfully heavy" the woman at the counter asked.

Harold struggled with the bag and finally had it on the floor beside the other bags. Harold eyed me and Consuela and suspiciously stepped toward the counter as if he were about to say something. Just as his mouth opened someone in another line was raising their voice at a personnel officer and she screamed for her supervisor.

"Harold. Come here please!" the lady yelled.

Harold looked at me one last time and walked off in the direction in which the confrontation was taking place. Consuela looked at me with knowing eyes and held her breath, praying silently just like I was doing. The woman who was checking our bags chatted about her first visit to Puerto Rico while stapling tags on our bags. She even tagged the suitcase with the money in it. Once she was finished she gave me the stubs and with the help of another woman behind the counter, she lifted the bags onto the conveyor belt. I watched as my livelihood disappeared through the small tunnel......

Consuela and I boarded the plane and sat in our first class seats as Mr. and Mrs. Ruiz, heading to Puerto Rico. The plane ride was smooth and quiet. I started drinking as soon as the stewardess opened up shop and didn't stop until they quit serving. Needless to say, when we landed in San Juan I was fucked up!

## Epilogue
### San Juan, Puerto Rico 2002

I was staring at the spot on my stomach where the "Fuck the World" tattoo once was and I noticed some slight discoloration. The doctor who Paco had introduced me to had removed the tat for twelve hundred dollars. He had advised me that I would probably see some light spots, which would disappear over time with the use of cocoa butter. I couldn't complain because it was worth it and I definitely didn't need anything that could connect me to my past identity. Ever since I'd been in P.R. Consuela's family and friends had been treating me like a King. I didn't know if it was the money I had or if I was the fact that Consuela was happier than she had ever been in her life but I was welcomed with open arms.

After reminiscing about the good old days, I reached inside one of the drawers underneath our large sink and re-read the post card I had received in the mail earlier that morning. It read:

*What up Playboy.*

*Long time no holla at. Just dropping a few lines to let you know that a nigga still fuckin'em, breedin'em and misleadin'em! Stay up my nigga!*

*Peace.*

The card wasn't signed but I knew who it was from. It was from V letting me know that he had made it out also. I had no idea what was going on back in the States and I didn't know how V knew my whereabouts but he knew I was with Consuela last time he heard from me. So I guessed he'd put two and two together. The postcard was from Montego Bay, Jamaica. Now I knew where my partner was and I knew he was safe!

Clicking off the bright light in the restroom, I ripped up the postcard and flushed it down the toilet. The bedroom was pitch dark when I re-entered, but I knew my way to the bed without bumping into anything. Consuela's light, steady breathing let me know that she was still in La La Land so I was careful not to wake her as I eased back onto my side of the bed. Staring back up at the ceiling in darkness, I couldn't help but to think about my princess and her mother. I hadn't seen or heard from them since the day Consuela and I had left Charlotte. I knew without a doubt that they are well taken care of but I missed them tremendously! I couldn't contact them in any kind of way because I was certain that they were under surveillance and extreme scrutiny.

The day before Consuela and I had disappeared my house and V's house were both raided at the same time. ATF agents were everywhere! Kinya had called me crying hysterically after they had left and told me that the agents said I needed to contact them. *THAT HAD TO BE A JOKE*!!

I trashed all of my pagers, my cell phone, my original identification and everything that could've linked me to me true identity and then I fled the vicinity. That had been over a year ago and I hadn't looked back since.

I knew June wouldn't be able to get a time cut unless the fed's caught either me or V. I didn't know about V, but I was looking forward to seeing June do *every day* of those thirty-six years!! Sure, I probably could've had someone on the inside fuck him up but I would've much rather have had the satisfaction of doing it myself. Because of June, I had to abandon the only thing that was ever stable in my world, my baby girl Mikai. Mikai was the missing piece to my puzzling life and when she was born, I was finally complete. Without my Princess in my life, I wouldn't ever be whole again! For that reason I wouldn't be able to rest until June's good snitchin', bitch-ass was laid to rest.

I want to see him suffer first by expiring many calendars in the prison system and then when he is finally released, I will have my day!!! It doesn't matter if it's three years from now or thirty years from now, I'm willing to wait as long as I have to in order to savor the taste of sweet revenge!!

Maybe one day when all of this shit dies down I will slip back into the States on the incognito tip to secretly visit my Princess. I often have dreams of going back to get her and bringing her to PR with me, but right now that's all they are...dreams. But who knows what the future has in store for us? For now, I'm just parlayin' and enjoying my wealth and my freedom with all of these fine-ass Boricuas over here in sunny Puerto Rico.......

**GAME OVER**

### Backwards Hustlers

Lil Quick, Black, Ray-Ray and Lil' Rick took over the drug trade in West Charlotte and became a force to be reckoned with. Their empire exceeded any standards previously set by preceding hustlers. After controlling the dope game in much of the Queen City for nearly three years, they were all indicted along with twenty-two others for conspiracy. Black fled jurisdiction but the others were caught slipping. The least amount of time to be issued out amongst the twenty-five remaining co-defendants was nineteen years which Candy Man and six others received for their cooperation and testimonies. Ray-Ray, Rick and Lil' Quick all received life....

Dee and Kinya became business partners in several establishments including an after school child care facility in which both Mikai and Vonzell Jr. attended. Dee had given birth seven and a half months after V had disappeared. V Jr. never got to see his father and Dee never got a chance to let V know he had a son....

Cherone was sent to prison for twenty-five years for first-degree murder as a result of stabbing Meka to death. Shortly after having June's mother robbed, Meka fled with both her and Cherone's share of the dough. Cherone tracked Meka down to a hotel in St. Louis and gutted her lover to death after a heated argument......

Scrappy, Shoe and Youngsta were apprehended and convicted of multiple charges stemming from a murder in Brooklyn NY, for a contract killing of two Dominicans who were found slain execution-style in the Park Slope area. While fleeing the scene, a nosey neighbor saw Shoe accidentally drop his pistol while hurrying into the getaway car. She jotted down the tag number and called the police to report a man dressed in all black carrying a handgun. When attempting to pull the car over, the police became the target of spitting lead! After what became Brooklyn's bloodiest and longest high-speed chase, the three men hit men were wounded and arrested. Three officers lost their lives that day and Shoe, Youngsta and Scrappy all received the death penalty!!!!

June is still serving time in Beckley, West Virginia, living the life of a rat as he continues to await his time cut.........

# AFTERTHOUGHT

"Fast money equals slow time!!!"

If I had a dime for every time one of my loved ones told me this, I would be a Billionaire three times over. O.K—O.K. Maybe I'm exaggerating a little. Nevertheless, I did hear it quite often. If I had taken heed to this warning I wouldn't have sat in federal prison, marinating in a  lost population of men for 11 years! However, sometimes it takes something as drastic as being thrown into prison for a lengthy stay to open one's eyes and make them realize there is no future for a Hustler.

Contrary to belief, there is a no *RIGHT* way to Hustle. Many are disillusioned and are attempting to keep the game on life-support when in all actuality the game is already dead. Respect, Loyalty and Honor are no longer in existence in the streets. The street decree, "Death before Dishonor" has long been replaced with, "Why do ten when I can snitch on a friend?"

If someone chooses to engage in this paper chase, they must be willing to accept all aspects of the game. There are always two sides to every coin. When the inevitable happens to a Hustler he must be willing to accept his fate with his head held high. Trade in those Armani suits and Italian made shoes for prison khakis and steel-toes at the drop of a hat because there is no negotiation for freedom!

*Hustlin' Backwards* was originally written in 2001 and is purely a work of fiction, which depicts true-to-life situations. Each and every character was derived from my imagination, however I am sure many readers can related to at least one. Every city throughout the globe has its *V's* and *Capones* has and extremely too many *Junes*! As you can see, the life of a Hustler isn't for everybody, especially the weak-hearted. The dope game is like one large desert which is full of mirages and illusions. Nothing or no one are ever what they seem to be. Just because a person doesn't sport a tail doesn't mean he or she isn't a *rat*. They can be your cousins, road-dogs, girlfriends or even your brothers!! You can never tell until it is too late! Stop reading this for a moment and take a look around you....Who knows? Maybe there is a June standing or lying next to you right now.

It doesn't matter which angle you choose to view the game from, it all pans out the same—Hustlin' is Dead!!! For every two steps you take forward in the game, Hustlin's gravitational force pulls you back three! No matter how far ahead of the game you think you, trust me......you are still HUSTLIN' BACKWARDS!!!! – **M. S.**

CPSIA information can be obtained
at www.ICGtesting.com
Printed in the USA
LVOW03s1055080517
533702LV00004B/702/P

9 781535 290159